HOW I GOT HIM
BACK

—— or ——
under the cold moon's shine

HOW I GOT HIM
BACK

or
under the cold moon's shine

VALERIE SAYERS

Northwestern University Press

Evanston, Illinois

Northwestern University Press
www.nupress.northwestern.edu

Printed in the United States of America

10 9 8 7 6 5 4 3 2 1

This story is a work of fiction. Names, characters, places, and incidents either are the product of
the author's imagination or are used fictitiously. Any resemblance to actual events or locales or
persons, living or dead, is entirely coincidental.

Interior book design by Carol A. Malcolm
Cover design by Marianne Jankowski

Library of Congress Cataloging-in-Publication Data

Sayers, Valerie.
    How I got him back : a novel / Valerie Sayers.
      p. cm.
    Originally published: New York : Doubleday, 1989.
    ISBN 978-0-8101-2725-8 (pbk. : alk. paper)
    I. Title.
PS3569.A94H69 2013
813.54—dc23

                           2013010666

∞ The paper used in this publication meets the minimum requirements of the American National Standard for Information Sciences—Permanence of Paper for Printed Library Materials,
ANSI Z39.48-1992.

For my mother

And Another I will have for my wife
Then what have I to do with thee

For thou art Melancholy Pale
And on thy head is the cold Moons shine
But she is ruddy and bright as day
And the sun beams dazzle from her eyne

—BLAKE

The heart has its reasons of which reason knows nothing.

—PASCAL

CONTENTS

I

II

III

IV

V

VI

HOW I GOT HIM
BACK

or
under the cold moon's shine

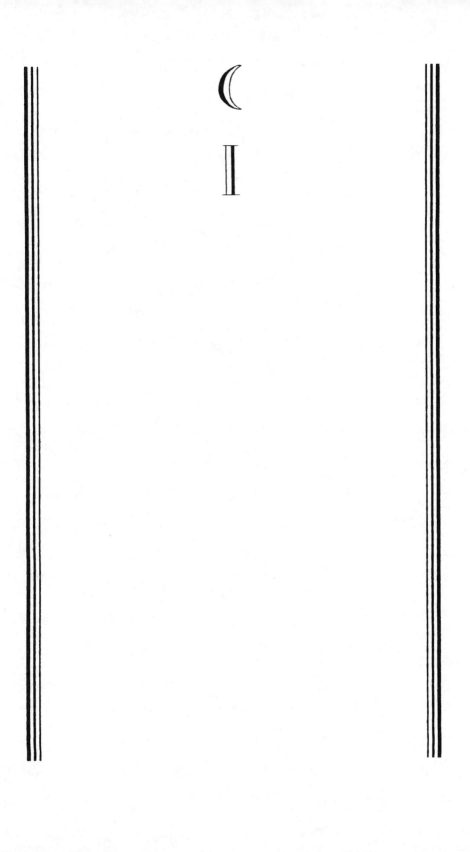

I

1

Every Cent He's Got

"HE WAITED UNTIL THE KIDS WERE IN BED one night, and then he said: 'Becky, I'm leaving you. I'm in love with another woman and I'm moving in with her.' And Becky says not but one night before they were walking by the creek together, watching the stars in the heavens and holding hands in the cold. So when he said he was leaving her, she ran into the downstairs bathroom and upchucked. It was that much of a shock. She just threw up."

"Mercy. Poor Becky."

"Poor Becky! Poor children. To have your daddy run out on you for a redheaded divorcee."

"How's Becky getting by?"

"Oh, he's bringing by *money*. The *money's* no problem. It's the living in total humiliation that's the problem."

"Has she got herself a good lawyer?"

"There's no lawyer a-tall. Becky's not going to give him that divorce."

"She's *not?*"

The three ladies of Our Lady of Perpetual Help Altar Guild considered the repercussions of this contentiousness silently. It was a dry

Saturday afternoon in January. They were doing an all-rose motif, and even though they had told Father Berkeley at least three times that the heat would have to go down for roses, it was still blasting away, and the petals were showing the first limp signs of fading. By Sunday morning the heat, like a worm, would work its way through the flowers until the petals were edged with black.

"It's not but fifty-five outside. He could turn the heat *off*. I don't know why he can't remember to turn it down at least."

"He can't remember but half the sermon. Why should he remember to turn the heat down?"

They giggled guiltily: Father Berkeley had been in a steady decline for a year, at least.

"And why Elsie Cooney's got to have *red* roses I don't know. I told her, I says Mary is such a light blue that we ought to have the pink there. Pink would do much nicer for the Blessed Mother."

The trio of flower arrangers stood in front of the plaster statue of Mary, fussing over the single vase that stood at her feet. None of them trusted the others' judgment, so they moved about the church as one, cutting stems and pulling fern and baby's breath out of a Winn Dixie bag. They gazed up now at Mary, slight and pale and sad, a slender girl draped in milky blue and perched atop a globe. Her face was a woman's face, full of resignation, but her long white fingers reached out imploringly to the Altar Guild. Often they whispered in her presence. She had crushed Satan's head beneath her delicate foot, yes—but still his long plump snake's body, full of life, curled gleefully around the globe.

"I *guess* that'll do. Pink would be so pretty there."

The three ladies shifted their vases and brown grocery bags and tissues of roses, and genuflected before they moved on to the statue of Christ, whose beard was full and manly. The ladies did not feel the need to whisper under Christ: *his* gaze was direct and open.

"What if he gets nasty?"

"Father Berkeley? He wouldn't get nasty over the heat."

"No, no, no. What if Jack Perdue gets nasty to Becky and says all right, no divorce, no money."

"She can make him pay. She doesn't have to give him a divorce. She's a Catholic!"

☾

"Sugar lamb, we are living in the 1980s. What good does that do her? Meanwhile Jack's living in sin on Lady's Island. Having all the fun."

"That's right. Jack and his honey, shacked up." The three of them giggled together again. Ten years before, they would not have breathed the words *shacked up*. Twenty years before, they would not have known an adulterous man—not in the parish. The giggles subsided, replaced by silence: reverent, fearful silence.

"I hope she sticks him for every cent he's got. I can't believe it. I can't believe it of Jack Perdue. Communion Sunday after Sunday. Walking in with his wife and those four children. I can't believe it."

"Well, you *better* believe it, May. That's the way of the world. And for every one that falls, another one takes his place. You know that Mary Faith Rapple?"

"The one with the crazy kid?"

"I see her letting the little boy play sometimes in the graveyard. I wouldn't be a bit surprised if she asked for lessons soon."

"What's that got to do with Jack Perdue?"

"She's the one taking his place."

"She's not looking to take Jack Perdue's place. She's looking to take Mrs. Stephen Dugan's place. She's hanging around the church because of Stephen Dugan."

"They're just friends. Stephen and Mary Faith."

"Oh, sure. And Jack Perdue's just living with a friend on Lady's Island."

"You suppose the whole world is living in sin?"

"You better believe it."

"I'm just like Becky Perdue. I'm in a state of shock."

They genuflected in unison and distraction, and moved together to the altar, where they looked out on a tiny church, a white clapboard church whose pews could barely squeeze in two hundred bodies. Our Lady of Perpetual Help was a Catholic church in a Protestant town, and caught between two centuries: the wood-relief Stations of the Cross had been hung in the early modest days, but now they stood between modern stained-glass windows in rectangular strips of blue and green and yellow. The Altar Guild had never liked the new windows.

The ladies surveyed the proportions of the church with dissatisfaction. A little Baldwin organ hunkered, ill at ease, in a rear platformed recess; up front, the banks of flickering votive lights, in deep blue and red glass holders, looked as if they belonged in some dark cavernous church in Boston or New York, not in Due East, South Carolina. Even the altar the ladies attended to—this modern, angular teak structure that looked to them like a *dining* room table, or somebody's dresser—was a replacement for the old altar behind it, now unused and unnoticed, the Last Supper ornately and melodramatically carved into its face.

The parish would be abandoning this tiny church soon, as soon as there was enough money in the building fund; Due East was growing too fast for such a quaint little building. The church was too small: too small for the religious revival, too small for all the resorts that had sprung up on the islands. Too small for the ladies of the Altar Guild, whose ambitions in flower arranging stretched far beyond single vases of roses.

"What on earth is Becky going to do?"

"She says she's going to get him back."

"I wouldn't let him back for a million bucks. I'd find me a retired admiral and build a swimming pool that would make Jack Perdue bright green with envy. I'd make him get down on his knees and beg me for a little dip in my new swimming pool."

"Well, that's not for Becky. She says she's going to get him back, and I wouldn't be a bit surprised if she did."

The ladies resumed their flower arranging in agitation, and started— Lordhavemercy—when the heating quit with a long shudder. The light was fading already, fading with the roses, and Father Berkeley would be in soon for the five o'clock mass.

"That's right. That's the spirit. She's going to get him back? Good for her."

☾

☾
2

The Holy Terror

MARY FAITH RAPPLE ALWAYS HELD BACK A proud smile when she described her son: "Jesse," she would say, "is a Holy Terror." Jesse Rapple was four and a half years old, and the other children in the playground cowered, bemused and bewildered, as he claimed his territory.

Mary Faith and Jesse were down at the waterfront park, taking in the noonday sun. They were on a schedule: weekdays, Mary Faith cleaned the whole house by ten o'clock and then collapsed with a book while she sent Jesse out in the yard. At eleven she made peanut butter sandwiches and packed them up, and at eleven-thirty they began a dawdling walk to the park, while Mary Faith tried to brace herself for the scrapes Jesse would get into. "Now don't you go bullying those little prisses in the pink dresses," she told Jesse, knowing all the while that nothing she said would stop Jesse from bullying the little prisses in the pink dresses. She had enrolled him in nursery school at the beginning of the year, but after two days the teacher had called her in to suggest that Jesse might need another year at home. To mature. Mary Faith told Jesse that the teacher was a warthog, anyway. "A old *wrinkly* warthog," Jesse said.

Now all of Jesse's mornings were free, and Mary Faith considered it her moral duty to find him other children to play with. Every day it didn't rain she took her son by the hand, a hand that wriggled out of hers halfway down the street, and walked him downtown with dread and pride. Jesse skipped past tabby mansions and squat frame houses with equal disregard. His hollers echoed and bounced through the narrow streets of the Point, where they lived with Mary Faith's father: the bigger and older the house they were passing, the more hair-raising the carom. The marsh behind them did its best to soak up Jesse's tremolos, but anyone on the Point still possessed of the sense of hearing knew when Jesse Rapple was passing through.

Now, safely arrived at the waterfront downtown, Mary Faith sat on a low bench and peered out from behind her book at her dark-haired boy. His sharp narrow face was already covered with grime, and he marched around the playground with a raised stick, threatening the other children.

"Follow me!" he bellowed. "Follow the leader. Join forces to defeat the cruel Emperor!"

The other children—a dozen of them, half black, half white—did not have grimy faces. They were Marines' children, mostly, their fathers drill instructors with a day off, their clothes color-coordinated striped outfits, their white sneakers clean. None of the other children played while Jesse paraded: they watched him with blank faces, their short haircuts mocking his wild curls. Jesse made his rounds of the playground three times, trying for recruits, but no one followed him. Finally he poked a bigger girl in the ribs with his stick.

"Follow me!" he cried.

The girl's father, a hairless Marine, vaulted into the sand and grabbed Jesse by the collar. Mary Faith slid the book back up past her nose and wondered if she could possibly saunter over to watch the bridge open for a shrimp boat, pretending that she'd seen nothing. "You bully!" she heard Jesse screech. "You jarhead!" She made herself put the paperback down on the bench. Her little boy—eyes streaming, nose running, high melodrama in his caterwauling—was running toward her.

She took Jesse in her arms and rested her face on his wet cheek so the Marine would not see her expression. She wanted to cry herself. The other children made tunnels in the sand and swung from the ropes and slid down the slide. Her son made scenes. What would she do next year, if they wanted to kick him out of the kindergarten at Due East Elementary? Where could she send him? She could picture Jesse at age seven, at age twelve, at age eighteen, sitting beside her in the waterfront playground, trying to learn how to behave around other human beings. She stuck her tongue out at the Marine's broad back: Jesse was the only one in the whole playground with any life. Jesse stuck his tongue out, too.

"Let's go home," whispered Jesse. "Let's just go home and lie in the dark."

Mary Faith hugged him tighter. "Why'd you say that, Jess?" she whispered back. He hadn't taken a nap in two years. What on earth possessed him to say *that*, about the dark? It didn't seem possible that he could remember how many afternoons she had lain beside him on her mother's bed, when he was a baby. It didn't seem possible that he could remember the cool numbing quietness of that dark room.

"Let's just go home and lie in the dark," he said again, patiently.

Mary Faith hugged Jesse tighter still. She had been six weeks past her sixteenth birthday when her son was born. He was nine pounds at birth, nine pounds of squalling, signifying—she was sure—a despair as deep as her own. For the first two years of Jesse's life she had felt herself almost dizzy, a misty haze of baby spit-up and diaper pail solution clouding her vision of the world outside her father's house. For two years she did not venture far past the Point with her baby, though once she had loved riding down the beach road, past the tomato and cucumber fields, past the packing sheds. Once she had loved crossing the low bridges rising up over clotted marsh grass. But for two years after Jesse was born she'd stayed close to her father and her baby in the modest old house, fighting her weariness and her dizziness: for two years she had managed to cook three meals a day and keep house for her father. For two years she managed to clothe her son and stroke his cheek and read to him from her high school Latin text: *"Tempus edax rerum,"* she read. "Time sure is devouring *us*, Jess."

And for two years she had gone to lie in the dark, and she had felt her soul sinking into that old, soft mattress she brought Jesse to every afternoon for his nap. She'd felt herself growing moldy in the dark. Sometimes when her little boy fell asleep she would put her face down into her dead mother's pillow and try to imagine what it would have been like if Jesse's father had not taken thirty Quaaludes in back of the Breeze Theatre before his son was born. Sometimes she would put her face down in her mother's pillow and try to imagine what it would have been like if *she* took thirty Quaaludes.

☾

"Let's go home," Jesse whispered again.

"No, no, Jesse," she said. "Let's stay a little minute in the sunshine."

"Is STEPHEN coming?"

This time Mary Faith laughed. *"I* don't know," she said. "Sometimes he eats lunch down here."

Jesse smirked and Mary Faith blushed: she was utterly transparent to her son. He was four and a half years old, and already he knew how to conduct his part of the affair. He knew that they were supposed to run into Stephen; he knew that Mary Faith would quit her reading and take his hand; he knew that they would walk together with Stephen down the tabby esplanade and talk about the bright January sun. He was four and a half years old, and he knew that his mother spent her mornings walking arm in arm with a married man.

"There he is, Momma," Jesse squealed, and began to tremble with excitement. "There's Stephen coming up the walk."

Mary Faith turned her head so that Stephen would think she was staring out at the bay instead of waiting for him. She didn't want to watch his loping walk: the thinner he got, the more his pants slipped down below his waist. The day was so warm that he went without a jacket, and Mary Faith knew before he came close that the white shirt would have a spot on it somewhere—an ink spot, a coffee spill. His shoes were unpolished, his beard unkempt; but the way his sandy hair receded was touching, somehow: the way he combed it back, absentmindedly. He arched his eyebrows over his glasses with an air of authority. Sometimes he could even make Jesse mind her.

"Stephen!" Jesse yelled, and ran down the walk. "Stephen, Stephen, Stephen!"

Mary Faith kept her place on the bench, holding back, and watched the two of them walk toward her hand in hand. Stephen had that mild look of contentment he always wore around Jesse and Jesse skipped along in front, a tugboat pulling an ocean liner.

"He's here, Momma!" Jesse yelled. If there was anybody in Due East who *didn't* know they were having an affair, her son would make sure the news was broadcast.

"Jesse, hush," she said when the tugboat drew near. "Let me wipe your face now." She did not meet Stephen's eyes.

"Hi, Mary Faith," he said. "Can you believe this weather?"

She didn't answer, but rubbed away at Jesse's cheeks. Stephen always greeted her in public with a line about the weather. There was something pathetic about it.

"It's summertime," Jesse said. "Take me to the beach, Stephen."

"It's not summertime, you little urchin." Stephen plunked Jesse down on the bench and sat beside him. "It's the dead of winter, and I'm a working man."

"Oh, take me to the beach, Stephen," Jesse moaned.

"Not today, Jesse," Stephen said, and Jesse snuggled up next to him. It was amazing: Stephen said no and Jesse hushed, suddenly reverential in the face of authority. But then, it was probably Stephen's authority that had led Mary Faith to him in the first place, back when she was fifteen and pregnant. Stephen Dugan had practically presided over her pregnancy: he ran the night adult ed. classes at the high school, and she was the tutor sent by the National Honor Society to help him—the tutor whose belly grew bigger and bigger, after Michael Jagger killed himself back behind the Breeze Theatre. She'd thought sometimes that Stephen was following her, looking over her shoulder, waiting for her to ask him for help, and finally she had. She had asked.

"Where's Maureen?" Jesse asked.

"Maureen's in school," Stephen said. "Which is where you'll be next year, this time."

"With the old warthogs," Jesse said.

Stephen threw his head back and laughed. "What have you been telling him, Mary Faith?"

Mary Faith shrugged. What *had* she been telling Jesse? What did her son think this man—with another house and another child and another wife—was doing hanging around his mother?

"Maybe you could drive me to the country today, Stephen," Jesse said. "Look at the sun shining. Momma says make hay while the sun shines."

Mary Faith watched Stephen shake his head back again and hug her son close to his chest. Stephen was only in his thirties, but he looked pale and tired in the sunlight, his eyes weathered far beyond their years. He was the kind of man who probably had looked ten years older the day he stepped out of adolescence.

And she had a feeling he'd added another ten years to his face when she'd asked him for help. She had been crazy in love with Stephen Dugan at fifteen. Back then, he touched her hand so gently it frightened her, and it made her think that maybe he was crazy for her, too: crazy for her, and worn out with

☾

the craziness. He had taken her to his house and introduced her to his wife—a good-looking twit who told her where she could get an abortion—and he'd driven her home nights, so she wouldn't have to walk the John C. Calhoun Road pregnant. One night, her father gone, she'd poured him wine and tried to seduce him. He had looked old and tired, moving to kiss her, and he had let her bare her breasts and her belly, swollen big. He had looked old, and frightened, and he'd jumped three feet into the air when her father's truck pulled into the driveway. She could feel the shame of that night still red-hot on her cheeks every time she met Stephen in downtown Due East.

"Have you had lunch?" she said finally. Next to Jesse's peanut butter sandwich in the brown bag lay a flat parcel: cold crab omelettes. Mary Faith had cut the recipe out of the *Due East Courier* and started making them the minute her father left for work. There was something pathetic about that, too.

"No, I haven't."

Jesse wriggled out of Stephen's arms and jumped off the bench with an expression of utter disbelief, the same disbelief he expressed at every lunch with Stephen in the waterfront park. He was really getting very good at it.

"We have lunch!" Jesse said, and grabbed for the bag.

Mary Faith held it high in the air. "I have some omelettes," she said to Stephen. "I have enough to share. Here, Jesse, peanut butter."

"I've only got twenty minutes." Stephen's tone might have been apologetic. "I've got to get over to the City Council meeting." He was a reporter for the *Due East Courier*.

"You have time to eat something?" she said.

"Oh sure," Stephen said. The tone was not apologetic after all: it was neutral. After they pretended they'd just run into each other, he would sit back on the bench and eat the lunch and then leave, same as he had a dozen times in the last year.

It hadn't been like that when he first came back. Then he had walked into her kitchen on her eighteenth birthday with the smell of beer on him. He hadn't even knocked—he had opened the screen door at three o'clock in the afternoon, listing toward the counter where she stood chopping tomatoes, and he'd said: "Well, I waited two years. It's still crazy. I've stopped drinking mostly—"

"Ha," she said, but she had stood still, the knife in her hand.

"I've stopped drinking mostly, and I've stopped sleeping with my wife. I see

❨

you walking through town with that little boy and now I'd like to take care of the two of you."

"Good Lord, that sounds like a line from a made-for-TV movie," she had said. Mary Faith saw clearly for the first time that day that he was almost a middle-aged man, balder and skinnier than when he watched over her pregnant, and she almost choked from the surprise of his ageing and his return.

"I told you in the hospital," she started, but then stopped dead. This was a man who recited *Blake* when he was drinking. She was fifteen when he fell for her. She was eighteen when he came back. It was madness. It was pathetic.

And if it was pathetic for a married man to ask an eighteen-year-old to marry him, it was humiliating to be standing in the waterfront park on a January day, pretending they'd just run into each other, negotiating the lunch.

A month after Stephen came back, Mary Faith took the test for her high school equivalency without even studying for it, and when she had the diploma she convinced her father to let her enroll in night classes at the Due East branch of the university. Stephen got out a dissertation he'd started ten years before and defended it ten months later. She let him finish it, he said, and she told him *that* sounded like a line from a made-for-TV movie, too. He began teaching classes helter-skelter at the university: composition, business English— courses too low-level for Mary Faith, but they were night classes: she could meet him. She dressed in long cotton skirts again, and every week, while her father Jesse watched her son Jesse, she met Stephen after class and let him drive her to a field or a riverbank or a beach and made love to him until they were covered with mosquito bites or chilblains or burrs. She felt her long body hardening back into its girl's shape, and she took to looking at her sharp features in the mirror, at the narrowness of her cheeks and the roundness of her gray eyes. Her father pretended he didn't know, and her son pretended he didn't know, and Mary Faith told Stephen Dugan that he mustn't leave his wife and daughter until she was twenty-one. She didn't want to be *rescued,* she said.

But now she was almost twenty-one, and a dozen times in the last year of pretending to run into him, Mary Faith had known—with a chill that became less and less pronounced as she grew used to its presence—that Stephen Dugan had become very fond of her and her boy. Fond. Once he had been passionate. When she had been a girl, a pretty, wild girl ready to have her baby by herself,

☾

Stephen Dugan had fallen in love with her. He had been shocked with himself. She was fifteen, then sixteen, then eighteen. He had waited with his passion.

Now he had worn her down. Now he had made her agree that when she turned twenty-one he would marry her. And as soon as they knew they would marry, and the Holy Terror would have a real father, he became *fond* of her. They'd stopped making love outside. Now Stephen let them into the *Courier* offices at night, where there was a Naugahyde couch; they made love with silk palm trees brushing against them, instead of under real palmettos at the north end of the beach. He said that when she turned twenty-one, in July, he would tell his wife—who knew anyway—that he wanted a divorce and he wanted custody of their daughter, and then he would marry Mary Faith and he and she and Jesse and Maureen would live together in some hot little Due East house and never have to meet for lunch by the waterfront again.

"This is real good," Stephen said. "I don't believe I ever had cold omelettes."

"They got too rubbery."

Jesse had wandered off, bored with their eating, and Mary Faith twisted herself to see if he was challenging the Marine again. The Marine had gone. Most of the children had gone. Jesse was dipping his sandwich in the sand.

"Mary Faith, is something wrong?"

Mary Faith tried to look at Stephen's pale eyes inside his horn-rimmed glasses, but all she could see was the midday sun reflected. She had to think of a way to get him back. Today he seemed content, but there were days when he called and said he wouldn't be able to drive her home from class, days when she could hear in his voice the weariness that came with two households. If he saw her father coming on River Street, he darted into the hardware store. He probably had a closet full of lightbulbs at home, all purchased in flight.

She looked away from Stephen's shining glasses and back at her son. "There are days," she said, "when I just feel too tired to carry on being a mother." Then she smiled, so he wouldn't think her too dreary.

He smiled back, mildly: he knew she didn't mean a word of that despair talk. He knew she was crazy for Jesse.

Mary Faith was crazy for Jesse, but Stephen wasn't crazy for Mary Faith anymore. She had to think of a way to make him want her so badly that he wouldn't mention custody and marriage. He would be crazy for her again. He wouldn't meet her by the *playground.* He'd mention trips to Paris and Rome, and if he met her in town he would take her in his arms and tell the Marines who were watching to mind their own business. She and Jesse and Stephen would wander around Rome together and sit in bistros every afternoon. She and Jesse and Stephen would get out of Due East and he would write books and she would support them as an engineer and they would send her father checks from Europe. He would be crazy for her, not fond. He would be as crazy for her as she was for him.

She had to get him *back*.

((

☾

3

High Gear

"MARYGAIL, YOU GAVE ME A SCARE. WHAT you doing calling long distance in the middle of the day?"

Silence.

"Marygail? Are you all right?"

Sob. Choke.

"Marygail? What is it? What is it?"

"Stephen's got them reading a screenplay."

"What? Who?"

"Stephen got friendly with"—choke—"the assistant director of *Carpetbagging Blues,* you know, the made-for-TV movie they were shooting in Due East, I *told* you this, and then the assistant director introduced him to the director and now they're reading his screenplay and he's going to *do* it. He's going to get out of here. And I'm going to be stuck in Due East for the rest of my life."

"Marygail. For Christ's sake, slow down. Wait a minute. I thought you were having an affair with the assistant director of *Carpetbagging Blues.*"

"I slept with him once. Twice. He's married to some slick producer type."

"Marygail, what are you *talking* about?"

"I'm talking about Stephen got friendly with this guy after *I* brought him home for lunch. And Stephen's written this script, it's just ridiculous, it's called *Army of Women* and it's about these soldiers stationed out by a whorehouse so the women in town all rise up and go march on the fort and it takes place IN DUE EAST, can you *imagine?* And they're going to buy it, I know they're going to buy it and Stephen's going to be rich and try to take Maureen away from me and I'll have to go back to Columbia and live with Momma and Daddy and go to the country club every afternoon and play tennis with *lawyers'* wives. Oh god. Ohgodohgodohgodohgod."

"Marygail, are you stoned?"

"I am not stoned. I am not stonedIamnotstonedIamnot. Not stoned."

"Are you drinking? Where's Maureen?"

"Maureen's in school. Maureen doesn't come home from school, Maureen goes and looks at records with the most revolting-looking little fifth-graders you've ever seen."

"Marygail. I am getting concerned. What have you taken?"

"I haven't taken anything. I haven't taken enough to get me going and do what I have to do."

"Marygail." Ominous pause. "Marygail. You are my sister. Are you doing *crack?*"

High, hysterical laughter. "Crack? CRACK? Where do you think this is? Harlem? Hollywood? You can't *get* crack in Due East. Not that *I* know of. I've cut my last line and now the movie's gone away and my own sister, my own sister doesn't realize what is happening to me. What is *happening* to me."

"Marygail, you are disgusting."

Long pause.

"I mean, you sound like you're driving about ninety-five miles an hour."

Long rev-up. "I'm driving about a hundred miles an hour. I'm driving about a hundred and twenty miles an hour. I'm going to drive at two hundred miles an hour if that's what it takes to get him back."

"Get him back? Look, Marygail, I've got two teenage boys spreading chemicals on my front lawn and three little boys in the basement trying to find the dirty videotapes and you're whining about getting back an assistant director you barely even had an affair with. It's disgusting, Marygail."

☾

"Jiminy cricket, Grace. What do you think I am? I don't want to get the assistant director back."

"Marygail, I cannot imagine what you want."

"Oh, Jesus, Gracie. I want to get my husband back. I want to get Stephen back."

"Oh."

"Oh?"

"What am I supposed to say?"

"What are you supposed to say? Grace, you're my sister. You're supposed to say, you're young and you're good-looking and you've got time on your hands and if you want to get your husband back you just put your mind to it and you can do it! You can do it! You're supposed to say, you haven't lost him anyway, Marygail. You're *married* to him. And if he goes to Hollywood he's going to want to take a good-looking woman who knows what's what with him. He's not going to take some horse-faced unwed mother with a crazy little boy and a grease-monkey father. He's not going to take some little *girl* who wears her hair down to her ass and chews her fingernails and dresses like it's 1969. He's not going to want to go to Hollywood carting around a family of gypsies. He's going to want *you!* You're supposed to say, just go get your legs waxed, Marygail. Get yourself a pedicure and paint your toenails red. Just knock him dead. You're supposed to say, just call up momma and tell her you want to go shopping and get yourself some of the slinkiest little black dresses they sell. You're supposed to say ohshitohshitohshitohshit. Oh shit."

"Marygail?"

Sob. Choke.

"Marygail? You listen to me. You listen to me good. You call me back when you're not stoned out of your mind. You call me back when you start acting like a responsible mother and not some floozy. Because we were not Brought Up to Act the way you are Acting, Marygail. If you want some sympathy from me, you remember that you are an Easterling and not some tramp sleeping with every man who passes through Due East. Due East!"

"Thanks a lot, Grace."

Silence.

"I mean it. I mean, thanks a lot, Grace, for being such a good sister when I'm at the end of my rope. Thanks a lot for all the help and advice, Gracie. When I get to Hollywood, I'm going to slam the phone down if you ever try to call

☾

me. Because I'm getting him back, Grace. Stephen knows I always loved him. Stephen never wanted me to be some stupid housewife, waiting for him at home. Stephen knows I know what's what and I'm getting him back and don't you dare hang up the phone on me. You little bitch. Bitch. I'm getting him back."

☾

☾

4

Past Beautiful

I AM THE MOST ORDINARY WOMAN IN DUE EAST, the most ordinary woman in the world maybe, and the most ordinary thing in the world has happened to me. My husband has left me. Why that leaves with me with this extraordinary shame I can't tell you, exactly.

Look at me with my boys:

"Go on, Jack. *Don't* take another cup of coffee."

"I'll just slosh it down, Momma."

"I'll leave you, Jack. I'm leaving." That was Ethan, standing red in the doorway, his whole body heating up in the desire to propel himself outside of the house. My sad house.

"Jack, go *on,*" I said, and the younger of my twins slammed down his cup and kissed me on the cheek before he picked up his books. He kissed me longer every morning, and that drove his brother crazy: now Ethan remembered that he hadn't kissed me at all, and came back to give me a perfunctory peck on the cheek. One ordinary, unfelt kiss.

"Good-bye, you two," I said, but they were out the door, and didn't hear me, and now my day stretched ahead of me until supper-time without any of them. Nippie and Sissy didn't want to squeeze into the back of their brothers' Fiat, so they took the bus to school. They had left the house at seven-thirty.

I moved to the living room window and watched the little white car tear out of the driveway, Ethan at the wheel. There was something so male about the way the brakelights sashayed. I was almost frightened by the way I saw them: I watch men driving cars now the way men watch young girls swinging their hips at the beach.

I made myself walk back to the kitchen. Cereal bowls, coffee cups. My husband had never understood why I couldn't bear to pay a black woman four dollars an hour to scrub up my kitchen floor, the way all the other Due East housewives did. So he got me a new kitchen instead of help: we had the whole house redecorated a year ago, and now there was a cluttered island in the middle of the kitchen because the decorator said everyone was doing islands now. They made a lot of sense for big families.

They didn't make a lot of sense to me. I let Jack and the decorator talk me into an island, and now instead of a table to clear, I had an island to clear. I grew up in Due East, and as far as I'm concerned, islands were made to take boats to. Islands were made to leave you with sunburns and chiggers and ticks. They were not made to be in the middle of my kitchen, blocking my way every time I tried to make a move. But if I started thinking about the way this island irritated me, it would make me start in on how the whole house irritated me, got under my skin. My house belonged on a television set, not in Due East. I had to stop.

And I had to stop thinking of the way the boys' car shimmied out of the driveway, and I had to stop thinking about how tall Jack and Ethan had grown, Jack six feet already, and I had to stop thinking about how broad their shoulders were, because they were my own sons, and every time I started thinking about how they overnight turned into men I started thinking of men in general, starting with their chests and working my way down until I touched the real sore, which was how No One Would Ever Make Love to Me Again. I'm just an ordinary woman. It just hurts.

Besides, this obsession of mine, this business about men, started a long time before I was left alone. When I'd done something to make Jack crazy, and he couldn't rile me up in turn, he'd say: "You're cold, Becky Perdue. You're an ice cube." And I'd think: If you knew what I was dreaming. If you only knew. I watched men all the time. All the time.

☾

A couple of years ago, I talked Jack into carting the whole family to New York for a week's vacation. I'd had my fill of Due East and I was hungry to see someone walking around in a shirt that didn't have an alligator or a polo pony on it. Sometimes Due East just gets to me that way, and even though it's my own children, my own husband, wearing pink and lime-green pants day after day, I think I'll scream. Father Berkeley always said the nice thing about New York was the way it was like a costume party, saris and dashikis and fezzes in every hotel lobby. So I dragged Jack and the kids up there, and they hated it, all of them. Jack said it was dirty; Ethan said he felt hemmed in. Sissy said— I'm not kidding—there was nothing to *do*.

The last day there we were sightseeing and lost in Greenwich Village, and the whole family was miserable. The air in New York was as thick and smelly as split-pea soup, and Jack was furious with me for bringing us there, and furious with the boys, who were following homosexuals down the street to imitate their walks. Nippie was whining for something to drink, and I decided to dash into a store for juice in paper boxes. My husband and my children were a chain around my ankles.

So I popped into a little grocery store, blessedly cool, and I couldn't find the juice. I wandered the narrow aisles, just savoring those five minutes of freedom from my family, when I ran smack into a big man in a navy T-shirt. When I looked up, I saw I was surrounded by big men in navy T-shirts: the men from the local firehouse, buying their groceries. And when I blushed and said: " 'Scuse me," I felt five stubbled faces shining down on mine, flirting. I had the most inane desire to run my hand across the stubbled faces. I had a sudden need to bury my face in one of those broad, sweaty chests—any one, any chest. Any large chest. And a minute later, when Jack came to find out what was taking me so long, I realized that I'd been doing this for years, staring after men. After the size of them, after the darkness of the hair on their arms. But I'd never had such a volume in Due East. I'd never had five firefighters to lust after all at once. I felt shamed, and young, and for the first time in a real long time, I felt pretty.

The firefighters' radios crackled when they were leaving the grocery store, and we stood on the curb, real rubes from Due East, and watched them climbing aboard their engine. Jack said: "Look at that. They could get killed in this fire they're heading for and they're *still* eyeing every pretty girl on the street." And I thought: Eye me! Eye me! It was my fortieth birthday.

☾

That night, when we collapsed in our hotel rooms, I found my rosary beads in my makeup bag. I couldn't make out why they were there—I stopped saying rosaries the day I signed my mother into the state hospital—but there they were, black beads covered with a fine mist of lavender eyeshadow. So I said the sorrowful mysteries, almost in a trance, and, still not believing, asked the Blessed Virgin first to give me more patience with my children and second to stop making me feel this way about my husband and third to make me stop falling in love with big men I saw in grocery stores.

And I did stop lusting so much. I grew up with three older brothers who brought home boys I was always in love with. I was a boy-crazy girl. Now I was just a man-crazy woman. The older I got, the further away from Jack I got, the more I felt it, this need for men like my father and my brothers. And it was funny: Jack was still a good-looking man, six-one himself, with good, wide shoulders. I had no reason to complain of his beer belly, not when I'd put on an extra ten pounds. What *was* it that made those little waves of revulsion ride over me? The way his blond hair thinned? His skin, white as a flounder's belly? The sparseness of the gray hairs on his chest? The pink nipples? His very penis itself, blue-veined, flaccid? The word itself revolted me. When I was a girl, we giggled about boys' *things*. For years, I hadn't liked the way *things* were going in my bedroom. But all around me, in grocery stores in New York City, on the beach in Due East, at Our Lady of Perpetual Help on Sunday morning, there were *things* that interested me, men whose arms I wanted to wrap around me. And I was washed over with such—it's hard to find the word, because it's stuck back in my girlhood somewhere—such delight, or joy, or maybe giddiness, at the sight of those men that I thought Mary herself would intervene on my behalf to explain the innocence of my desire. Blessed innocence.

Because sure as I spent twelve years going to Our Lady of Perpetual Help Center for Religious Instruction to learn the sixth and ninth commandments, I had never made a move, raised an eyebrow, sweetened my voice, shifted my hips to call a man. It had never occurred to me that I had any business doing anything else but *looking* at these men, and looking itself had made me guilty, because I had a husband who was good and solid and steady and wouldn't let his daughters wear lipstick until they were fifteen years old. I had a husband who made more money every year, selling insurance and then getting into real estate on the islands, a husband who said there was no need for me to work when he could provide for us so well, a husband who didn't mind being Catholic in a Protestant town, who took us to mass on Sunday mornings and fried up the sausage and spooned out the grits for the Holy Name Society breakfast every year. A husband who held my hand sometimes when I didn't want him to, a husband who made love to me when I wished he'd fall asleep, a husband who yelled at my children too much, a husband who yelled at me too much, a husband who left. A husband who wasn't a husband at all anymore. A husband who was gone.

Gone and left me with cereal bowls and coffee cups.

When Ethan and Jack were little boys, I would find myself in a mood and call up one of the officers' wives who lived in Piney Woods, and we would drink coffee and laugh about our husbands. But officers' wives always moved away after a few years, and now my friends were from the Mothers' Club of Our Lady of Perpetual Help, and every one of them was as sweet as the day is long, but I couldn't bear to sit and talk with them. The only sex they ever talked about was television sex. The only men they ever talked about were television men, Tom Selleck and Don Johnson. When they talked about their husbands, they made fun of how stupid they were: they talked about how they sent their husbands off to the Piggly Wiggly to buy cooking oil and how they came back with baby oil. Because they got confused, eyeing the cute little high school checkout girls in their miniskirts.

There was no one to call anymore.

I picked up the cereal bowls and stacked them on the island and then sat down. What I wanted to do was take all the white bowls and smash them against the sliding glass door that Jack had put in himself. I wanted to see clotting milk running down the glass. I wanted to hoist up this island with my bare hands and heave the whole heavy Formica sameness of it through the sliding door. I wanted to run away and not be there when Nippie and Sissy came home at five o'clock, glaring at me in disgust for the way I'd driven their father away.

When Father Berkeley pulled into the driveway at two o'clock, the cereal bowls were still stacked on the island. I had watched television for three hours straight—the last half of the *Today* show, *The Phil Donahue Show,* and then reruns of *Leave It to Beaver.* How the mighty have fallen, my father would have said. *Leave It to Beaver* made me weep for a good twenty minutes, and

☾

when I was done crying I felt cleansed and purposeful and I went striding into the kitchen, where the sight of the cereal bowls sent me spinning into a depression deeper than the one I'd started my day with. I pulled out the *Due East Courier* from the day before, and read every column inch in it, including the legal notices. When I was a girl, the *Courier* had a section on the back page called "Items of Interest to the Colored Community," and I used to read it five and six times over, feeling that I was reading about a foreign country, an exotic place that spoke a different language. Now the whole *Courier* struck me that way. Due East was my town, and the islands were a part of my fiber, but now it was Jack who lived on Lady's Island, where I was born, and I was stuck living in a subdivision that looked like Beaver Cleaver land. Like nowhere land. Now it was Jack whose friends were on the front page of the *Courier*, while I read about real estate in my kitchen.

Now Father Berkeley—I knew who it was without even turning around on my kitchen stool—had pulled into my driveway. It was the second time that week he'd shown up in the middle of the day. On Monday he'd been potted, stewed, and I gave him three cups of coffee before I could even understand the words that came out of his mouth. He might as well have been a Holy Roller, speaking in tongues. Then he stayed for hours and asked me to teach the class for converts, knowing full well that I hadn't been in the confessional since 1969. The smell of good Scotch was so strong on him that I was overcome with a need for a strong Scotch myself. Alcoholism was very big in all those women's magazines I stacked on my coffee table and never read. I could imagine sitting alone in my house every afternoon, feeling the warmth spread through me. I could imagine lying naked on my couch, dabbing Scotch on my nipples. My father was a drunk—a sweet drunk—and I'd always been careful: it would throw the fear of God into Jack if I started drinking now.

The bell rang, finally. From the length of time it took Father Berkeley to *find* the bell, I figured he was drunker this time than the last. And he was. He swayed at my front door, and when he reached out to steady himself, he grazed my breast first, instead of my shoulder, and did not realize he had done it.

"Father Berkeley," I said, and heard in my voice the same annoyance that surfaced when I was talking to my children. Men were pathetic really, the way they reduced you to disciplining them in their middle age. I should have been able to run to Father Berkeley when I had my troubles: I should have been able to tell him, in the darkness of the confessional, how stunned I was, how

☾

murderous my rage was seething. I should have been able to count on him to hand me some inspirational book by Thomas Merton, to recite for me a psalm of woe that surpassed my own. But instead I had to mop up after him in my own living room.

His face was as white and worn as a sunbleached plank in my father's dock. "Come in," I said. "Sit down."

His hand was clammy. "Thankyebecky. I'm feeling a mite lightheaded." The voice, thick and shaky as gelatin, trembled off.

I got him to the couch. "I'll make coffee," I said, and stopped. Father Berkeley was hanging on to the rolled arm of the sofa for dear life and for a second I thought: he's going to throw up. I had a vision of spending my afternoon shampooing the living room rug while the breakfast things marinated in the kitchen, and then I had an attack of guilt that this sick old man came to me and all I could think of was the smell I would have to vanquish if he threw up. He was a dear friend, once. I could hardly forgive him.

"Hold on now, Father. Let me get you a cool cloth."

Father Berkeley's eyes were closed.

"Father. Father. I'm going to get you a cool cloth." I knew that when I came back, he would be asleep, but I made the motions of retreating to the bathroom and soaking one of the thick blue washcloths I bought in the last household buying spree intended to make me feel I had some purpose in Piney Woods.

When I tiptoed back into the living room, he was out, his breathing labored. He sounded sick on top of the liquor—he sounded the way one of my babies used to sound, struggling to sleep through croup or bronchitis. A pack of Lucky Strikes had slipped halfway out of his pants pocket, the way hidden packs of cigarettes slipped from Jack's and Ethan's pants when they threw them down on chairs. But Father Berkeley didn't smoke anymore. Father Berkeley hadn't smoked in years. I could remember him smoking twenty years ago, when everyone did, when I did, when I brought Jack home to Due East and we were newlyweds invited to Father Berkeley's cocktail parties at the rectory.

I could barely connect the rasping drunken man lying on my couch with the Father Berkeley of my girlhood. I could remember Father holding court in his tiny parlor, the parlor that was his office and his living room and his cocktail-party room. I could remember how he would gesture delicately with his cigarette, how he would let the ashes grow long and longer—catch them,

☾

Father, before they land on that old Persian rug you found in Charleston!—as he described his vacation trip to New York, what plays he'd seen, what opera he'd heard.

I could remember how heady I felt in his little parlor, how I tried to persuade Jack what an honor it was that we, the only newlyweds, the only just-graduated parishioners there, had been picked to hear Father Berkeley lecture us on art and theater and opera. Jack didn't understand: where he came from, a dusty little upcountry town called Pauls, all the Catholics stuck together and whispered about the Klan. In Due East, even if we were Catholics in a Baptist town, there were plenty of Irish, plenty of refugees from Charleston or Savannah, plenty of Marines or sailors like my father who came and fell in love with the marshlands and stayed. My father was Boston Irish, and my mother was one of those easily swayed Southern converts, and Father Berkeley *liked* them, but he never invited them to one of his cocktail parties. He invited me.

There had been rumors all through high school that Father was having an affair with one of the rich old ladies from the Point, or that he was a homosexual. All the other priests got shuffled around the diocese and dealt out to a new parish every few years, but Father Berkeley stayed at Our Lady of Perpetual Help year after year. Once they tried to transfer him to a new parish in North Charleston, a parish full of enlisted men, and he almost had a nervous breakdown. The bishop let him stay in Due East after the Parish Council got up a petition signed by every single family in the parish. Due East had gotten used to him.

And *I'd* never believed those stories for a minute. I loved the way Father Berkeley gave cocktail parties in a town where, when I was a girl, you couldn't even buy a cocktail. Father would put a manhattan in my hand when I walked into the rectory, and I would make my way around the crowded parlor, looking up at the prints he had framed. I can still tell you the way he lined them up: first Rouault's *Last Supper,* then Brueghel's *Christ Carrying the Cross,* then Rembrandt's *Crucifixion.* I had graduated from the South Carolina College for Women with my one required course in art appreciation, but no slide they ever showed me in 101 knocked me out the way those prints did. They might as well have been oils. I might as well have been in the Metropolitan Museum. When I went to the kitchen to fetch more ice there was always some new postcard stuck on Father's refrigerator. I know now that they weren't good reproductions, but back then they mesmerized me. One year he went

☾

through a Käthe Kollwitz phase—you could count the number of people in Due East who had *heard* of Käthe Kollwitz on one hand—and he kept the rectory refrigerator black and white for nine months. So I had him order some prints for me, and I put them up at home in our kitchen, and Jack said they were Unprofessional-looking.

Father Berkeley took me aside and asked me to join one of the discussion groups he led every fall, groups that read St. Augustine's *Confessions* and Pascal's *Pensées,* groups formed from the handful of families in the parish that had sent their children north to school, sent their daughters to Smith or Vassar or some solid Ursuline school. Jack said it was all phony-baloney social stuff, but I was in heaven that first year before I got pregnant, that year when I taught third grade and smoked and drank manhattans and heard about Manhattan from a priest with delicate hands and dangling cigarettes. I labored longer over the readings than I did my lesson plans and I listened in silence, feeling timid, when Dolores Rooney—who had five children and a degree in *Italian,* the most frivolous degree I ever heard of—connected the Jansenists and the Holy Rollers.

They frightened me, Dolores Rooney and Father Berkeley. I had gone to Due East Elementary with Dolores's son Tim, who played the violin and the piano and the guitar by the time we were in third grade. He probably spoke Latin by then, too. He went off to Columbia University when he was sixteen, and by the time he was twenty-three he had his Ph.D. I was frightened of them. I was no intellectual: I was the daughter of a Navy corpsman-turned-petty officer. My father brought up four children in a ramshackle house on a bluff. He had never heard of Pascal. He bought us a Boston whaler so we could learn the creeks and inlets, and he put a bamboo fishing pole in my hands when I was three. He sent me off to college because I was the only one who showed the slightest inclination to go. He was scared of the books I read the way I was scared of the Rooneys and Father Berkeley.

And while I was away at college I had found a good Catholic boy from upstate who fell in love with Due East, too, and I taught him how to crab, and we came back to settle near my parents. And Father Berkeley picked me out from the start. It frightened me. It frightened me that first year back in Due East, when I looked in the mirror and my hair shone black. When I twisted it in a braid, my eyebrows arched. Jack said I was beautiful, and I thought maybe it was true. The face in the mirror was ordinary—a full mouth, green eyes, a

☾

silly pug nose—but there was *something* that attracted him to me: something that made my brothers and their friends want to be near me when I was afraid to open my mouth to them. When I looked at my reflection, it was absolutely placid, and I couldn't connect its placidity with the fears and timidity I harbored. My mother grew up a Methodist, and she knew scripture: she named me Rebecca because she thought I would be like Isaac's wife, obedient and docile and willing to serve.

Sometimes, I had so little to say in the discussion groups that fall that I thought Father Berkeley had picked me out because I was beautiful. That frightened me most of all. He picked me out doubtfully, as if I were an occasion of sin.

But I didn't have to worry it too long. It was easy to slide out of Father Berkeley's grasp the year the twins were born, and easier still the next year, when my father was killed in Vietnam, and my brother Billy was taken prisoner. That was the year my mother fell into her first depression, the year I first began to notice that Father didn't refer to Aquinas or Augustine in his sermons anymore. He started to draw his analogies from movies: there was a sermon on Paul Newman as a Christ figure in *Cool Hand Luke* and another one on *Man of La Mancha*. One Sunday he disregarded the gospel entirely and preached about the bikinis all the girls of the parish wore on the beach. He said the girls of Due East had lost their mystery, and all of a sudden his words sounded common, like my father's or my husband's. I didn't have the nerve to ask Dolores Rooney what was happening to Father Berkeley. I didn't have the nerve, didn't have the time for intellectualizing or gossiping or worrying about Father's decline. My babies swallowed me up, and my mother was sick with grief, and I was never quite sure why Father Berkeley still sought me out after mass and held my hand so tightly.

And I wasn't sure why he had come to me now, after all these years of sliding from his grasp. Why, when I fled from his discussions and his liquor and his sermons, he came to collapse on my couch. Why he planted that crumpled pack of cigarettes in his pocket, to fall out so stagily for me. Why he came to say: Look, Becky, Rebecca, I'm committing a slow suicide. Save me. Save me.

As if I could save anyone now. As if I could do more than get myself up in the morning and clean the breakfast dishes by five o'clock. As if I were an occasion of sin for anyone. I was long past beautiful, long past staring at my

☾

own image in the bathroom mirror when I wanted to escape the hold of my
children. I watched a priest struggling on my couch, an old man grimacing like
a child in the throes of fever, and I wanted to shake him from his stupor.
Hardly knowing I was doing it, I moved to his side and took a Lucky Strike
from his pack. There: slow suicide for the two of us.

I took the cigarette to the kitchen and lit it, from the stove, and the first
drag made me want to swoon from dizziness. How familiar this dizziness was. I
had been dizzy since Jack left me for another woman.

I was in a black hole without Jack, and my black hole was sucking up more
and more light and air. I'd lived with him for twenty years, longer than I lived
with my father. I wanted Jack to repulse me again. I wanted to berate him for
the rest of my life for what he'd done to me. My parents were gone, and my
brothers had moved away from Due East: I had no family but children, children who pitied me for this shame, and their pity choked me. I had to have
Jack.

I could not imagine that he would carry this on any more than I could
imagine he'd done it in the first place. Surely that last month we'd been better,
surely that last night when we walked out in the dark he had loved me. We
had opened up the *Christmas* presents three nights before he pushed me in the
hole.

So he must have gone mad, to do this to me, to all of us, and if he'd gone
mad, then he would just have to regain his sanity. Once he regained his sanity,
I could climb out of the hole. I could stop watching *Leave It to Beaver*. I could
walk along the sand with my husband, gathering oyster shells, watching the
shrimp boats go home. I could be a wife again, and I would work hard to
overcome this revulsion that I'd been feeling for so long. I would do that, if he
would just come back.

And I could make him come back. Jack had been under my influence for so
long that I knew I could do it, by sheer force of will. Eventually he would see
just how mad he had become: much crazier than when he decided to sell those
parcels of marshland. Much crazier than when he and his son, his namesake, had
started their feud. I felt, even from the center of my swirling hole, that if I
could just control myself the same way I'd controlled myself for twenty years
of marriage, if I could just program myself to contain my hurt, Jack would
come back.

I took another drag of the cigarette, and this time it didn't dizzy me. This

☾

time I thought I could sit in my kitchen all afternoon, smoking Father Berkeley's cigarettes and waiting for my children to come home. Waiting for my husband to come home.

Then I heard a voice call from far away.

"Beck?"

I didn't answer.

"Becky?" It couldn't be Jack.

"Rebecca? Are you there?" It was my husband. It was as if I had summoned him with my cigarette and my dizziness, and I threw the cigarette into a coffee cup, as if that would make him go away. He'd been coming by with the shame money on Fridays for a month, and now for some reason he was calling into his own back door, whispering through the glass, on a Thursday afternoon. I stared at the cereal bowls in horror, but it was too late to hide them. I went instead to the back door and watched my husband, still at the bottom step. He gestured out to the front lawn as if he were talking to a deaf woman.

"I didn't want to disturb you," he said. "If somebody's here."

"You mean you didn't want Father Berkeley to see you." I almost bit my tongue. I had resolved to speak to him with dignity, to wear him down with my good grace, with all that reserve that had made him fall in love with me in the first place, and now here I was speaking to him in exactly the same snappy voice we both fell into whenever we talked about Ethan and Jack or marshland or money.

"I didn't know that was Father's car," Jack said. His voice was tight, measured.

I swung open the door and forced myself to say: "Come in." I couldn't tell if the cigarette still dizzied me or if it was just the sight of Jack, the sight of his navy blazer. His gold buttons gleamed in the cold winter light. Not gold: brass. I couldn't look at the brass buttons without picturing a redhead's long, painted white fingers unfastening them. I couldn't feel Jack brushing past me without imagining the redhead pressing her fat white breasts against Jack's chest. The redhead's name was Judi. Judi with an "i." I had seen the name in the *Courier:* "Island Paradise Realty is proud to welcome the newest member of our selling team. JudiJudiJudi." I couldn't have my husband in the house without hearing the name scream out at me from the corners of the room. From the island and the dirty dishes themselves. It chilled me so thoroughly, that name, that I'd

☾

been shutting off the television and slamming books shut when a character was named Judy.

"I'd like to say hello to Father," Jack was saying. Now that he was inside he was getting back the upper hand. He was taking his wallet and counting out hundred-dollar bills.

"Father Berkeley's asleep," I said, and Jack looked up, startled. I found myself smiling. I could picture Jack counting out hundred-dollar bills for his Judi. I could imagine Judi signing her name on a sales contract with a little heart over the "i."

"Father's asleep," I said again, and forced my smile into a smaller, sweeter shape. Did Jack imagine Father Berkeley was asleep in my *bedroom?* I wanted to hoot with glee.

"You tell him hey for me," Jack said.

This time I didn't blurt anything out. I took a long breath and said, just as slowly and deliberately and coldly as I could, "You tell him hey yourself."

Jack looked at me with his mouth open in equal measures of wonder and disgust, and then turned his back on me and walked out of his own kitchen door. He was gone.

No fight. No parting words. No squeezed hand.

My husband was gone.

My children would be home in an hour, looking for their dinner.

A drunken priest lay on my couch.

And the breakfast dishes sat in my kitchen, listening to the silence of my big house in Piney Woods. Mocking me.

I was mad to think I'd ever get him back.

☾

☾

5

Confession

I AM A MAN ABOUT TO LEAVE HIS WIFE.

Now, this is not news in Due East, the way Jack Perdue's leaving Becky for a blowsy red-haired real estate pusher was news. This information will not send the women of Our Lady of Perpetual Help clucking around my wife to express their indignation and outrage. No, this is a long-expected event, such common knowledge down at Ralph's Coffee Shop that the old geezers on their third cups of the morning will just nod, say: "Yup. *Finally,*" and get back to more timely gossip.

This leaving is not even worthy of the *Due East Courier*'s "People You Know" column. I can hardly submit an item that reads: *Stephen Dugan regrets to announce that his marriage is terminated.* I can hardly leave my wife a note that says: *One feels he must leave you now, for another woman.* There's no way to leave the *I* out of it: I am a man about to leave his wife.

I have never been comfortable in the first person, any more than I've been comfortable in this marriage or in this affair. For years I have written a hokey weekly column and daily drivel for the *Courier* without resorting to the first person. For years I have churned out I-less poems and sent them off to obscure literary quarterlies which had never before published poems not written in the first person. A dissertation, two unpublished novels, a made-for-TV movie script so bad it's *good,* so bad it scares me: pages, folders, cartons of work, all without resorting to the voice of choice in the 1980s.

For years I have believed that my wife was so unhappy in this marriage of ours that there was no need to tally in my own unhappiness. But now I am the one to make the announcement, and I am reduced to the first person after all these years of scorning its indulgence. I am the one who's leaving.

So then: let this self-consciousness, this sappy breast-beating, be my first penance for leaving her. God knows that lately I've felt a sore need for the confessional.

Marygail was nineteen years old when I met her: nut-brown, horse-faced, horse-toothed, skinny, angular, all elbows and knees. She wore micro-miniskirts and pink tank tops made of spun sugar: she looked just fine and she knew it, too. She was an Easterling, her daddy the owner of every midlands brickyard in South Carolina. Easterlings are all conceived in the womb of cold cash and Marygail, by virtue of that cash, had turned herself into what we at Carolina used to call a good-looking girl, possessed of all the drugs, psychedelic and tranquilizing, that any graduate student could ever hope to share with an equine coed. She did not belong to a sorority: she was uninterested in any female company or approval.

She was majoring in Italian, in her desultory fashion—and if you've ever heard a nineteen-year-old girl in a miniskirt say *"Miserere di me"* in a cracker Columbia accent, you know just how long it took her to seduce me.

Here's the joke she told me five minutes after we met:

A man goes to the doctor with bad headaches and the doctor finds an enormous brain tumor. Gives him twenty-four hours to live. The man goes home and tells his wife, who says, "Gee honey, let's try to make this the best twenty-four hours of your life. What'll we do?" The man makes love to his wife, and an hour later—when she asks him what she can do to ease his pain and terror—he makes love to her again. This goes on, hour after hour, until late into the night. The man has three more hours to live. He whispers to his wife, "I want to make love to you again," and she turns her back on him in the

☾

bed. "Look," she says (and the way Marygail minced this line in a cold an- noyed drawl just *slayed* me), "*I* have to get up in the morning. *You* don't."

Does that sound like a woman who can't take care of herself? Marygail repeated that joke when she told me she was pregnant—only she changed all the "made love to"s to "fuck"s—and asked for money for the abortion. Laughed like a hyena. I have to get up in the morning, she said again, and then shed large crocodile tears. Miserere di me.

If I could afford an analyst, I could proclaim from a black leather couch that the joke was on me. I married her with my eyes wide open: I could see, clear as the light that spreads over this lowcountry, that pregnancy would be the last time she'd need me.

And not only did I accept her lack of need, I was grateful for a while not to have a clinging wife. Marygail's what-the-hell attitude made her the kind of wife who slipped me a quarter tab of acid when I discovered that the Eas- terlings had arranged a dry wedding reception for their Baptist social acquain- tances. The kind of wife who amused herself by giving barbecues for the Due East Little Theatre and making fun of their earnestness as they sat hunched over leaking paper plates in our backyard. The kind of wife who worked hard at having other women see her as a good-looking shallow twit. The kind of wife who made no secret of her sleeping with the Parris Island officers who drove her home in their little sports cars. The kind of wife who made no secret of her relief that I was having an affair, too, not messing the marriage with any need of my own.

The kind of wife who could sit under the one magnolia tree that blooms in our front yard and allow its drooping pink perfection to shadow her own perfect angles: that magnolia tree could get her through a whole spring in a town she despised. The kind of mother who was so easy with her daughter she could shrug off all her little girl's tight-lipped silences and say: "She's just like me. I was *just* like that."

And I have grown so accustomed to her fierce carelessness, so admiring of her inability to hide her revulsion toward my small life in a small town, that I am unprepared for her sudden panic.

How was I to predict, as we were opening our two secret bank accounts and consulting our two gentlemanly lawyers, that she was going to pick the mo- ment of my leaving to show need again? How was I to know that she was going to spend these winter months stretched supine on the fat cushions of the

☾

sofa, no officers or assistant directors to distract her, staring out at nothing? How was I to know that this loony loneliness of hers, this string of coarse attempts to seduce me, would make me watch her swing her long brown legs off the couch and follow their curve up her lean thighs and make me want her again? How was I to know that this bald pathetic need would make me pity my wife after all these years, when I have been spending my pity elsewhere?

Mary Faith has never told me a joke. I don't believe she knows any jokes, or any songs. When she tutored at the night GED classes, she never opened her mouth, unless one of the pasty-faced Marines' wives asked her how to solve an equation. She would do the equation in her head, give the answer, stare with her gray eyes, realize she hadn't given a clue how to *solve* the damn thing, stick a pencil in her mouth, write out the steps with the damp pencil point, one numbered step at a time. And then, if the Marine wife said, "Ohhh," then she might smile: with the gray eyes again. I was in love with that one from the first, and it was as innocent as loving my daughter—she could have been my daughter—until the night she lifted her shift up above her naked belly. I could see the baby moving in her womb. She thought I ran away that night because I had some scruples about fifteen-year-old girls. She didn't know that all I could see, every time I put my hands on my wife's bony hips, was the lumpy outline of the baby in Mary Faith's belly, its fetal fist ready to punish me and her for any intrusion. Now that fetus is a child, and he unclenches his fist to put it in mine.

And that child I ran away from is a woman ready to marry me, and she knows as well as she knew how to suckle her son that I am being pulled back by my wife. She is humorless and songless and filled with such purpose, such godawful *sanity*, that she thinks hiding away her need makes it invisible. She senses that Marygail's bed is where the guilt burrows under the covers now, where I can mingle guilt with my pleasure like a good Irish Catholic. She senses that pity lies between us on the squeaking plastic couch in the *Courier* office, and she despises that pity.

So I am left to swing the scales, some days measuring my passion for Mary Faith against my pity for my wife and some days weighing my pity for Mary Faith against my newfound passion for my wife. I am a man who—arrogance of arrogances—tried to save two pregnant teenagers and who realizes he cannot even save himself from his own self-pity.

☾

All I can do is grind out a confession shameless enough to be an "About Men" column in the *New York Times,* yet another chronicle of the zeitgeist. Even Jack Perdue never kidded himself about the pleasures of guiltless adultery, or the greater pleasures of guilty adultery: even poor dumb Jack Perdue never believed he was saving anybody.

I love my wife. I love my daughter. I love Mary Faith. I love her son. There are nights when I dream a faceless woman cloaked in black sits behind the screen of a tiny confessional, eager to give absolution without ever looking me in the eye. All that is required of me is the words *I'm sorry.* I'm so sorry.

But it is way too late for that. I am a man about to leave his wife.

☾

III

☾

6

Cleaning Day

"SO WHAT YOU HEAR FROM BECKY PERDUE?"

It was cleaning day in Our Lady of Perpetual Help. Father Berkeley paid a janitor to mop up, but the ladies of the Altar Guild considered this payment charity on Father's part. As far as they were concerned, only a man could forget corners and neglect the kneelers the way the janitor did. *They* were armed with three bottles of Pine-Sol and three Scrubbee sponges, and they spritzed and scrubbed in three pews, wheezing with their efforts.

"I don't hear anything from Becky Perdue. You know, ever since she unburdened herself about Jack, she's been *distinctly* cool."

"Poor thing."

"Oh now, May, I don't know. I don't know if Becky's a poor thing or not. Jack's paying her right good, I hear. Jack moved in next door to Betsiann Mitchell out on Lady's Island, and Betsiann says that this new girlfriend is just as sweet as she can be."

"I heard she's a real cow."

"Well, she's not attractive, that's for certain. But maybe that's the *point.* Becky Perdue is a very good-looking woman. Very good-looking. And if Jack's left her for a sweet, plain girl—well, maybe there was some reason we don't know anything about.''

The spritzing and scrubbing stopped.

"You can't be saying there's some *justification* for what Jack's gone and done to Becky. To his family.''

"Good Lord, no! There's never any justification for that. All I'm saying is, cast not the first stone. You know, I saw Becky in the Piggly Wiggly the other day, and I'm sure she saw me, but she just turned her cart around the other way and pretended her head was in the clouds.''

"Maybe she *didn't* see you.''

"Maybe not, May. Maybe she didn't see me. But I *was* the one who answered the phone in the rectory when she called Father after her mother had that heart attack in the state hospital. I *was* the first one over to the house that day, with an oyster stew and a pecan pie. I *was* the one she ran into the day after her husband left her, the one she saw fit to unburden herself to.''

One sprayer, then two, then three went back to work on the gray kneelers again.

"Poor Becky.''

"Oh, I'm getting a little tired of hearing about Poor Becky.''

There was silence, but for the sound of the scrubbing and the spraying and the drawing in of breath.

"Father B. says Mrs. Stephen Dugan's been calling him at the rectory with a variety of trick questions.''

"Trick questions? Like what?''

"Like, if a Catholic marries a non-Catholic outside the Church and they have a child, but later the non-Catholic converts, does the Catholic have any grounds for an annulment?''

"Uh-oh. Looks like she's digging her heels in.''

"Yup. And the Pope's digging his heels in on this annulment business, too.''

"Looks like trouble for Mary Faith Rapple.''

"Looks like trouble . . .'' The sentence was never finished. The big front door opened, and a shaft of light fell on the pews and the kneelers and the three ladies scrubbing them. The trio all kneeled higher and peered up at the light streaming in, but they could only make out an outline in the doorway. It was only someone come in to pray.

The figure at the doorway moved into shadow, and the ladies saw that it

☾

was a tall, long-legged woman of thirty or so, wearing a sleek spiked haircut and a denim jacket with a milky blue scarf knotted around her neck. She gazed over the church and took in, one at a time, the three women scrubbing there.

"Oh! 'Scuse me!" she said, in a voice that sounded more amused than embarrassed, and then she walked languidly back out the front door.

"Speak of the devil."

"Mrs. Stephen Dugan."

"Who did she think we were, the colored maids?"

"She's got a real sense of style, though, don't you think? Who does she remind me of with that haircut? Madonna?"

"Madonna's bleached her hair blond now."

"Well, it's someone like that. She wormed her way into every crowd scene they filmed in *Carpetbagging Blues.*"

"And now she's trying to worm her way into Our Lady of Perpetual Help."

As if cued, the ladies looked front to the statue of Our Lady, who gazed back out at the little church with what appeared to be, in the half-light, deep regret. In front of the church, Marygail Dugan was revving up her engine and squealing—from inside it sounded as if she were peeling out—into the slow stream of Division Street traffic. They could picture her passing clumps of cars going the speed limit on the narrow two-lane street.

"Isn't it something how somebody like that can throw your whole day off?"

The three women turned their faces from the statue of Our Lady and back to their work, scrubbing dreamily.

☾

☾
7

Conversion

MARY FAITH RAPPLE BLINKED AT HER IN-
structor, who was standing in front of the class on top of a milk crate.
"I've set up this still life for you today," Miss Connelly was saying.
She gestured vaguely at a basket of pears perched on another milk
crate. "And sometimes I'll have a model for you to paint. But feel free
to paint out of your head, if the mood strikes you."

Mary Faith had no idea what the instructor meant by "paint out of
your head." It sounded like a quick route to insanity. She was not
quite sure how she had arrived in a painting class, anyway. She was
terrible with her hands, just terrible, and she didn't know oil from
acrylic, and since first grade she had been painfully aware that she was
one of those people who could not, would not, should not draw.

But the course list in the evening division was full of subjects she
had taken or exempted or couldn't bear to consider, like economics,
and on line at registration she had seen Crazy Tim Rooney signing up
for painting and she had just gone ahead and signed up, too.

Now her easel was next to Tim's and she didn't even know how to
hold the *brush,* much less paint the red-tinged pears in the basket. Tim

Rooney raised his eyebrows, and gave her a smile, and began to hum "Mona Lisa." Mary Faith had no idea how to mix the paints.

"I don't think I'm going to paint those pears," Tim Rooney said. "Those pears are already perfect. I think I'm going to paint Miss Eileen Connelly." And he began, with a thick green stroke of his brush, to paint a pear.

"Tim, I don't know how to do this."

"Oh, just dive in, Mary Faith," he said. "Just squeeze out some of that yellow, right on the paper, the way van Gogh did it."

Mary Faith squeezed out too much cadmium yellow and groaned. "Oh, Jesus," she said, "why did I let you talk me into this?"

"You didn't let me talk you into this. You said, Tim, what're you taking. I said, Mary Faith, I'm taking painting. You said, fine. Here we are."

"Those pears aren't yellow, anyway. They're green."

"Look again."

Mary Faith looked again at the pears and thought, after a minute, that there might be some yellow in them. She smeared the yellow around the paper doubtfully and wondered if Eileen Connelly would come around to her easel to congratulate her for putting on paper what no one else could see. There wasn't much chance of *that*, though: before Miss Connelly, or Eileen, or whatever they would be calling her, had a chance to begin making the rounds of the little studio she was surrounded by a pressing crowd of older students. She was a minor celebrity, evidently: Tim said she had made a little success in New York and had come home to be Artist in Residence at the Due East branch of the university. For the spring semester only. Mary Faith had never heard of her, but at registration, Tim showed her a year-old review in *ARTnews* and a clipping from the *Courier* and said that it was lucky Mary Faith had been scheduled to register at 9 A.M. or otherwise there never would have been an opening for her. The whole town was trying to sign up for Painting or Drawing.

Mary Faith wasn't even sure how she was supposed to clean the brush. Tim Rooney had promised to share his supplies with her, since her father couldn't be paying for tubes of exotic toxic paint on top of the course.

"Tim," Mary Faith whispered. She could not see a rag anywhere.

"Mary Faith," he said loudly, and Mary Faith went back to smearing the yellow rather than humiliating herself on the first day of painting with a Real Artist. She would *not* let anyone overhear her asking how to clean the brush.

☾

Tim grinned over at her wickedly. He was her neighbor on the Point: he and his sisters and brother had grown up next door in a big white house that always needed a paint job, but he had already left for college by the time she was conscious she had neighbors. He was two or three years older than Stephen, she thought.

She'd met him when he was recuperating from a nervous breakdown. He was a philosophy professor, he'd told her that first day they'd both been walking down O'Connor Street, but from the dull laugh he gave when he said the word *philosophy,* she'd doubted it. It was Stephen who told her it was true. Stephen knew the dirt on everyone in town.

Stephen said that Tim Rooney had come home to see his father at Christmas vacation the year before and had taken a whiz in the front pew of Our Lady of Perpetual Help on Christmas Day. His brother and three sisters had all convened to decide whether to commit him and had finally dragged him off to Due East Memorial, where he lay for a week, throwing the hospital into an uproar with his visions of the Christ child and Michael the Archangel and the Blessed Virgin and Blaise Pascal. Then one day he snapped back into normalcy, signed out of the hospital against medical advice, and returned to his father's house, announcing his intention to become a priest, maybe a monk. His youngest sister Dottie was still living at home, and after a week with Tim, whose visions came and went, she left the house in a high fury one morning and drove out to the beach. Her body washed up on the sand the same afternoon.

Mary Faith did know about the suicide, or the accident, or whatever it was the family chose to call it. She and her father did still read the *Courier:* they weren't that far removed from the society of other people. They had noticed the rows of cars parked next door the night of the drowning, and her father had even gone over to ask if there was anything he could do. "They're all nuts," Jesse said when he came back home. "Tim—is that the real crazy one?— he's playing ragtime on the piano and the others are all pretending they don't notice."

Stephen said that after his sister killed herself, Tim Rooney had been perfectly sane. At least, sane enough to maneuver Due East and make himself understood. He still wanted to be a monk, but no monastery would touch a divorced philosophy professor recuperating from a nervous breakdown. Not one whose sister had just killed herself. Not one who, in the middle of his life,

☾

had decided to live with his widowed father to prevent another suicide in the family. No one was sure whose suicide he was trying to prevent.

And from what Mary Faith could overhear, the widowed father couldn't abide his son Tim. For years, the house next door had been silent, but now that she'd met Tim, she heard him banging away at the piano while his father was at work. And ten minutes after his father pulled in the driveway, she heard Bill Rooney's bellowing and curses. He hollered at Tim as if Tim were ten years old.

And Tim Rooney, Ph.D., pushing forty, often emerged from the house in the early evening grinning ear to ear as his father's harangue followed him down the street. He was tall and lanky and had the ruddy face of a boy who'd once been freckled. Mary Faith could imagine, vaguely, that someone might find him and his high forehead good-looking if he could stop himself from flashing that unearthly grin. If he weren't whistling all the time, or hopping around on one leg as if he had to go to the bathroom.

Now, beside her, he jiggled as he painted. His pear had grown what might loosely be called breasts, and Tim was staring at Eileen Connelly, now bent over the easel of a man so old his hands trembled as he opened his tube of paint. Mary Faith watched Tim Rooney watching Eileen Connelly, and wondered how someone so sexually charged—someone walking down O'Connor Street looking as if he were on the prowl—could possibly believe he wanted to join a monastery. But then, as far as she was concerned, anyone brought up Catholic was brought up mad. Jesse's father. Tim's sister. Tim himself. Maybe Stephen. Maybe Stephen was on the brink of madness.

"That's some vivid pear you've got there, Miss Rapple," Tim said, turning back to her, and then whistled "Whistle While You Work." Mary Faith began to doubt that she could make it through the semester. She began to imagine that she would get the first F of her entire life in Painting I, and that it would throw off her grade-point ratio and throw out of whack all her plans to study engineering on a full scholarship. She would be planted in this studio next to a madman, and if she did not figure out how to clean her brush without a rag, all her paintings for the semester would be cadmium yellow.

"How's Jesse tonight?" Tim swayed and gave the pears undulating hips.

"Which one?"

"Both. What the hell."

☾

"Daddy's bored. Watches TV all night. And my little boy's been raising cain. As usual."

Tim suddenly leaned over and stared straight into her eyes. "Why don't you let *him* paint?"

Mary Faith turned her head away. Tim did this every once in a while, out of nowhere. He had decided to watch out for her son's interests. In the beginning she had been frightened to let Tim in the house—he reminded her of Michael Jagger, her son's father. She thought of them both as frayed wires, electricity coursing through them, about to burst into flames. But Tim had a better sense of humor than Jesse's father ever had: he banged on Jesse's bongos and stood on his head and brought over a guitar to do Johnny Cash imitations. So eventually she had let Jesse and Tim walk out together, in the afternoon, to play on the green or scare frogs in the pond or climb a pecan tree in Tim's father's yard.

And one day Tim had returned Jesse and sent him upstairs and looked straight into Mary Faith's eyes—the way he did now—and said, "Why do you sleep with a married man?"

She couldn't remember *what* she had said. Maybe he had left her speechless. He never mentioned her adultery again. Another time, after she had forgiven him, he said: "You shouldn't be so superior around your father. You break his heart." That time she was sure she said nothing.

And now, confused, she said: "What do you mean? I let Jesse paint."

Tim said: "Not with real paints. I've never seen real paints in your kitchen. I've never seen him drawing, except with crayons. You ought to throw away all those coloring books."

"He has a set of watercolors," Mary Faith said. Red dots were forming on her cheeks. Tim's voice was loud, and she did not dare look to see if anyone was watching them. If Eileen Connelly was listening.

"Oh, great," Tim said. It seemed to Mary Faith that he was dead serious. He couldn't be dead serious. "You mean one of those little metal boxes that you buy for seventy-nine cents?"

"Tim, for God's sake." Now Mary Faith's voice was rising. "You know I can't afford to go out and buy fancy paint sets."

"I'm not talking about a lot of money," Tim said. He waved his brush in the air. "You have enough money for those crappy little robots you buy him. I

℃

never see his paintings on the refrigerator. Never. You sit him in front of the cartoons all afternoon."

Mary Faith jerked her head away from the madman and stared at the glutinous yellow mountains on her paper. She didn't dare lift her head to see who had listened in on their conversation. What in God's name was Tim thinking of? She took care of Jesse. She let Jesse paint. She had thought of that. Even if she couldn't paint a stroke, she had bought a little watercolor set for Jesse. She stabbed away at her pears, clenching her teeth against Tim Rooney, and her pears began to resemble women, too. Why did a grown-up boy with a doctorate who hadn't lived in Due East in twenty years have to come playing around in an undergraduate painting course? Why did a man who had a doctorate from Columbia University have to hover like a cloud above her, opening up his little showers of madness? She let her son paint. She let him build towers of blocks. She spent EVERY WAKING MINUTE—except when she was allowed to escape to class—with Jesse. What had he seen, Dr. Mad Philosopher? Some moment, some millisecond, when she had let her attention slip? Some instant when she was struggling to finish her calculus on time and snapped at Jesse? Now her pears resembled yellow Amazon women, monstrous pears with monstrous hips. Now she stroked in little sleeping fetuses, yellow fetuses curled inside the yellow hips, and glared over at Tim.

Who was perfectly serene, as if he had not spoken, as if she had not answered. He had forgotten the conversation already, and was dabbing away at the new red spots on his pears. Which no longer resembled women at all.

And he had pulled a rag from his pocket.

"Tim," hissed Mary Faith. "Give me that rag." She surprised herself with the ferocity of her tone.

"Here you go," Tim said equably. Mary Faith felt she could spatter him head to foot with yellow paint. He *knew* Jesse had been kicked out of nursery school.

She pulled paint off the yellow brush and realized with horror that she still didn't know what to do: that this paint wasn't like Jesse's watercolors, that she couldn't dab it in a glass of water. And she realized at the same moment that someone stood behind her, and that it must be Eileen Connelly. She turned around, hiding the brush in the rag.

"So you see the yellow in those pears," Eileen Connelly said. Mary Faith watched her suspiciously. It sounded, on the face of it, like a sarcastic remark.

☾

But Eileen Connelly appeared to be as equable as Tim. She was a small, even-featured woman, almost nondescript: brown wispy hair, brown loose dress, brown lace-up shoes. She was not at all what Mary Faith had expected of a New York artist, and she still had a trace of Due East in her voice.

"Don't let me stop you," she said, and moved on to Tim's easel. Mary Faith almost wanted to call her back. Was that it? You see the yellow? No caustic comments on the globs? No suggestions about technique, about drawing? ABOUT HOW TO GET ALL THE PAINT OFF THE BRUSH?

Meanwhile Tim continued his swaying and whistling and painting his undulating hips, and Eileen Connelly moved on after a moment. At least she had said *something* to Mary Faith. At least Mary Faith was someone you could *talk* to. Tim Rooney was obviously somebody no one—not even an artist who lived in New York, who was probably used to nuts—dared engage in casual conversation. His whole jangly body gave off those signals: Don't Talk to Me or I Will Accuse You of Neglecting Your Child and Sleeping with a Married Man.

Now Mary Faith opened a tube of green. "Who the hell do you think you are, Tim?" She knew she was hissing again.

"Hmm?" He looked at her with wide eyes, all innocence, all little boy. She was twenty years old, and he was almost forty, and he looked at her as if he were in Sunday School waiting to hear the lesson. She couldn't bear it: that direct stare, those turquoise eyes. When she first knew him, right after Dottie was buried, his face had been puffy and his eyes glassy. Some drugs he was on, she and her father figured. But now, now that he'd been walking around Due East in the sunshine, now that he'd flushed all the medication down the toilet, his nose was sunburned and the stubble of his red beard was coarse and he managed to look completely guileless.

"I said, who the hell do you think you are?" Her own eyes were more than cast down. She cast them aside, back to her canvas. Why did men want to do that? To stare right at you?

"You got me where you want me," Tim Rooney sang softly, and then he skipped to the chorus of his song. "Chain chain chain," he sang, "chain of fools," no more embarrassed than her little boy was when she chastised him. No more guilty, either.

Mary Faith looked sideways at Tim, at the easiness of his dancing at the

☾

easel, and let out a long, disgusted sigh. A fool for you, baby. That's what her father always said: Tim Rooney was in love with her. That's what Stephen thought, too, that Tim was in love with her. He covered all his reports with a thin layer of jealousy.

But Mary Faith knew better. No man who hollered at her so, who accused her and a moment later forgot the accusation, who hummed and whistled and didn't care what a soul in Due East thought of his whistling or his humming or his wanting to be a monk—no man like that was in love with her. He never even looked at her the way he followed Eileen Connelly now, with that slight narrowing of his eyes, with that little slash of a smile as she meandered through the studio.

No. Tim Rooney was a crazy man, an oversexed man who was more attracted to a brown little artist from New York City who was obviously his Idea of an Artist than he was to a young girl he spent hours with every day. And Mary Faith knew why, too—she was another category of woman. She was a Mother. Tim Rooney could sing "Chain of Fools," but she was the one with a ball and chain on. Not that *she* would have fallen for Tim Rooney. But it was almost insulting to have him so close, so much of the day, without ever feeling from him what she had once felt from Stephen: the drawing in of his breath, the urgency. Tim Rooney's urgency would only be turned on her when he wanted to deliver instructions about how she should care for her son.

Finally she had let out all the sigh she had in her and said lamely: "You shouldn't tell me how to raise Jesse."

And Tim continued his righteous innocent look and made his voice match it. "Why not?"

Mary Faith lost all impulse to explode. It was like yelling at a child: afterwards, she felt guilty and confused and out of control. "Oh, Tim. I do the best I can."

"Well, I know *that*," Tim said. "You're a regular Madonna."

Mary Faith jerked her brush away from the easel and waved it at Tim. "Don't say that." Stephen had tried the same number. Madonna with child. It made her skin crawl.

"O.K.," Tim said. "Don't worry. I'll buy Jesse a set of real good poster paints. My momma used to drive all the way to Savannah to buy 'em for us."

☾

They were to walk home together in the dark. It was cold in Due East at last: Mary Faith piled on three sweaters while Tim stood in line to flirt with Eileen Connelly. Finally he was done with showing her his painting and calling her Eileen and chatting about impasto. Mary Faith was waiting for him in the doorway, scowling.

"No Stephen tonight?" he said, and held the door for her easily. "Isn't he teaching the illiterates?"

"They only gave him one course. On Saturday mornings."

"Oh," Tim said. "There goes the administration, blocking the path of true love again."

Mary Faith walked quickly ahead of him to push open the hall door, and the winter air pushed back at her. She let the door slam behind her. Frost tonight. The stars were raucous overhead, careening in the black sky, and she looked up so that she wouldn't have to look back at Tim.

Tim didn't hurry to catch her, outside. He stood under a streetlight, striking a match to his cigarette, and followed her gaze to the stars. Now he would sing: "Are the stars out tonight?" He would sing the *whole* song while they walked down Division Street toward O'Connor Street, and the whole way Mary Faith would want to turn round to throttle him.

But he didn't sing. He said: "At least they still give him one course. I offered my services, but my services were declined."

"Oh, Tim," Mary Faith said. "They don't give but two philosophy courses a semester, anyway. They don't *need* you."

"They're afraid I'll have visions in the middle of a lecture," Tim said. "They're afraid I'll try to convert the Baptists."

Mary Faith slowed her gait, and Tim put his arm around her shoulder, the way he did sometimes when they walked out with Jesse. When he put his arm around her shoulder, it meant that he wouldn't say anything. They would walk together in the cold, his right arm over her shoulder, his left arm swinging his paintbox. Maybe he had little visions in the dark night. Maybe as they passed under the hanging moss he would see the strands of gray turn into animals, or into monsters, or into saints. Maybe, walking under the oaks and the pecans, he would hear in the scamperings of squirrels one of those voices that called to him.

"So what are you going to do about a job?" she said. That was what her father did with her when he thought she was getting morose. He asked her about the cooking and the cleaning.

"What? Me work?"

He *seemed* perfectly normal. Mary Faith felt her shoulders tightening, though. She didn't like this talk about converting people. One of these days Tim was going to stare straight into her eyes, the way he had done in the studio, and advise her to get right with God. Maybe he would put it in more mystical terms. Maybe he would tell her about vision.

"Well," she said, "we hear your father hollering at you for not working."

"You mean you hear my father speaking. That's his normal tone of voice," Tim said. Then, for the first time since he had taken to drawing his long arm around her shoulder, he squeezed it, squeezed the tense shoulder, and Mary Faith lost her balance and turned her ankle flat onto the pavement.

"New boots," she said, and tried to wriggle out of Tim's arm. He held fast, though, and said: "Now, there's a female impulse. New *boots*. It's only going to be winter for three weeks in Due East, and then it will be spring." Mary Faith took his arm off her shoulder and walked ahead on the throbbing ankle. It had taken her six months to save up for a pair of new boots, and they were too small, and they hurt.

Tim walked along beside her as if she had not put a hand to his. A lone car, one headlight out, swayed toward them on the narrow street, and Tim guided Mary Faith to the side of the road. "What are *you* going to be doing for work, Miss Rapple?" he said suddenly. She didn't dare look at him. The car rolled past. "What are these courses in painting going to lead to for you and your son? Or are you going to let Mr. Dugan and Mr. Rapple Senior support you in your dual life as daughter and mistress?"

Mary Faith said nothing. He knew she spent her days wrestling with math and physics. He knew she was going to get a scholarship and get an engineering degree. He knew that was going to be her ticket out of Due East: that it would be a ticket for two, because by then she and Stephen would be married and he would get a teaching job, and write, and even if it was only Carolina, even if the University of *Georgia* would be the only school that would pay her way and fix her up with housing, she would pull up two sets of roots when she left town.

Tim began humming again alongside her, and at first she couldn't recognize

☾

the song. It wasn't "I Only Have Eyes for You"—it was something old: the Everly Brothers. Now, as they neared the corner where they would turn off to go into their separate white houses, he was humming "Bye bye love. Bye bye happiness." Mary Faith felt the urge to break into a run for her front door.

"All right," Tim said. "All right, so you're going to be an *engineer*. I don't believe that any more than Stephen does."

"What do you mean?" Mary Faith made a dead stop in front of the slave quarters. Behind the long, low building loomed the big brick house where the Mansard sisters lived, ominous in the dark. Up the block a hazy light spilled out of her father's den. The television. The cattails in the pond across the street swayed lazily in the breeze. In another moment, Tim would have *her* hearing voices in the night. Already she could hear Jesse shifting in his bed upstairs, calling out for her in one of his nightmares.

Tim kept walking and called back: "Trying to educate you for better things, ain't he?"

Mary Faith stamped her foot in vexation, and the foot throbbed inside the tight boot.

He must have seen.

Tim must have seen her on the front lawn, flinging the little paperback book at Stephen's car as he drove away. She had *told* Stephen. She had told him that she didn't have time now that physics took her hours. It had been all right, when Stephen was throwing himself back into the dissertation, to read the Blake he brought her. It had been all right to work her way through the piles of Dickens and Eliot that bored her to tears. He pushed them on her, and she read them all, front to back. She had *memorized* Blake. She had recited "Mock on, mock on, Voltaire, Rousseau," when she was nineteen years old and thought Voltaire and Rousseau made a hell of lot more sense than William Blake did. And she had explained to him that now, now that she had to hang on to the A's in math and science, she did not have time to go through every single book he thought would make her think the way he did: which was God-knows-what, because he never breathed a word of philosophy or belief or even literary theory but only brought her more books and more books. And she had finally taken the last slim volume he brought her, and waited until she heard him start the car, on his way to work, and flung it after him with all the energy left her after a morning of watching Jesse and fetching Stephen coffee.

Tim stopped beyond the Mansard house, stooped to unlatch the paint case,

☾

and drew out a book. The book. Mary Faith had not even stopped to read the title when Stephen brought it to her. Now Tim dangled it in front of her, jangling again, holding it up the way little boys tease little girls with stolen trinkets. Tim had her book.

"Give it back, Tim," she said. She almost expected him to say, "Come and get it," and run away from her. She advanced on him.

"It's PASCAL," Tim said with glee, waving the book like a banner in the winter breeze. "It's *THE PENSÉES.*"

"Give it back, Tim," Mary Faith said. "It's my book."

"It's Stephen Dugan's book," Tim said. "I told you. He's trying to educate you for better things. Does he send you magazine subscriptions, too?"

"Stop it, Tim."

"Poor little girl, you don't understand, do you? It's PASCAL. Stephen Dugan is trying to convert you."

Mary Faith took the book from him. She wanted to hide it in her layers of sweaters. She wanted to toss it in the pond.

"My little innocent Mary Faith," Tim said, and tried to take her hand. "Don't you see? He wants to convert you. First a little Pascal, and then—oh, let's see—then he'll throw in some modern books to confuse you. He'll have you read some sexy Catholics like Graham Greene maybe, and then if you like poetry he'll have you reading Hopkins—"

"Stop it, Tim." He must have been through her books.

"And then he'll start talking about getting you to convert. You see, he'll try to work up an annulment so his entire marriage will be canceled out, and then he'll have you baptized and you'll be able to marry him in the Church and he'll get custody of his daughter."

"Stop, Tim. He knows I don't believe in any of that crap."

"He's gone back, you know, Mary Faith. He sits in the back pew every Sunday and watches his daughter go to Communion. He can't go. And if you don't convert, the plans for the annulment will never work. He can't live with one faithless woman and then go trade her for another."

Mary Faith began to run. She was top-heavy in her sweaters, and her skirt caught between her legs. The ankle turned again, and she almost fell flat onto O'Connor Street, but managed somehow to right herself and run straight through the driveway to her father's kitchen door. Stephen could not possibly imagine that she would convert. Stephen couldn't possibly believe himself. It

☾

was for Maureen, for his little girl, that he sat in the back of the church. He never breathed a word of religion: he knew she wouldn't hear it. Couldn't bear it. She turned the screen door and heard Tim passing behind her, whistling along O'Connor Street in the dark.

Bye bye love. Bye bye happiness.

The tune hung still in the chill air.

☾

☽

☿

Dear Devoted Sister

Mardi Gras!

DEAR GRACE,

All right, I owe you an apology. But I wasn't stoned, I just had a little wine and don't worry, I don't usually drink in the middle of the day. But like I told you things had gone from bad to worse with me and Stephen and I got a little down so that's why I called you up. But I didn't mean to get so carried away so let's forget it, OK? Two girls I used to play tennis with just got orders, well their husbands got orders, so now I haven't got much company in Due East. I am so sick of doing makeup for the Due East Little Theatre I can't tell you. I had to paint everybody's face Spanish brown for *Man of La Mancha,* but you have to get out of the house, don't you?

For a long time I thought well maybe I'll just get me a job but let me tell you two years studying Italian at Carolina ain't much use here. I was thinking of going out to Hilton Head where at least people are a little snappier but the gas both ways costs a fortune and they don't pay anything and I don't want to answer somebody's phones anyway. So then I was thinking all right I'll just move, I'll just go back to Columbia, at least you and Momma and Daddy are there and I could get a job and meet somebody. And then things started to change.

I think Stephen is getting tired of his child mistress, I really do. Don't let me get started on her. But you know for a long time I figured he was going to marry her and I should just hang on for the best settlement I could get. We were hardly sleeping together at all anymore, and we were sleeping together more than we were talking to each other. The lawyer said don't leave first cause that would be desertion, so OK, so I'm sticking around here going out of my head waiting for Stephen to make the first move. And then just about the time when Stephen should be hearing one way or the other about his movie script, he started acting like he needed me. And I think he does.

First he started spending more time at home, you know with Maureen, telling his silly jokes (I bet the triplets'll know this one: Knock knock. Who's there. Dwayne. Dwayne who. Dwayne the bathtub I'm dwowning). Those two are crazy together. But then he started spending more time with me too, asking me to go to the movies and getting romantic. I figured oh no, he's hitting the bottle again, and I started to get the willies because if he doesn't sell this script we'll be as poor as we've always been and what am I doing hanging around waiting for a settlement from *him?* But no, wait, it looks like he really is getting tired of her because he asked me to read the script, which I have to tell you has as many holes as a wormy tomato. But he asked my opinion! And then in the space of a week we're falling into bed together every other night and that may not sound like much to you, but for us it's like three times a day.

So I don't know what's happening with the movie script but I think he's heard something good, I think he's really starting to think Hollywood and you know I bet he really has figured out that it would be better to have me along than her. I think he's figured out that I got on with them (maybe he figured I *got it on* with them) when they were here and I think he finally got it through his head that her and that little terror of hers would be, like, a *major embarrassment* if he's going to be working with a movie crew.

I convinced Stephen to stop wearing those nerdy Hush Puppies and he's saying funny things again and staying home at night and one night I even caught myself thinking how good he was with Maureen when she was a baby and maybe— No. Forget that. But maybe we'll have money anyway, and maybe we'll even stay together.

(

Which is what I need your help with. Momma and Daddy are going to split a gut over this one, but I decided to go and take lessons to be a Catholic. Stephen takes Maureen every Sunday now and it seems to me that if I just show a little interest and pretend like it's something I can get into then that'll help hold things together better once the movie deal comes through. Also I'll be rising in the ratings while Little Miss Earth Mother, who I happen to know never steps foot inside a church, will be falling. Anyway I don't care. The old farts at First Episcopal won't miss me, cause they only see me once every five years anyway. And Episcopal's almost Catholic anyway, it's just the Pope. It's not like it's anything offensive anyway and nobody has to know if I don't buy all that shit about purgatory and abortion. But Momma and Daddy aren't going to like it one bit, so do you think you could just mention it real casually? I mean, they let you marry a Jew so you've obviously got some way of talking to them that I never got the hang of.

So how's Jake? How're the triplets. Come see me some time. Really, you wouldn't believe how civilized our house is becoming. They'll be moving cameras in here, next thing you know.

Sorry again,
Marygail

9

Rebel Yell

I TOLD FATHER BERKELEY TIME AND AGAIN THAT I had no interest in helping him teach his convert class, but he coaxed and wheedled and begged. Finally he appealed to my mercy: he'd had no curate for ten years, he said, and he was exhausted running out to say winter mass at the mission on Distant Island. He asked me if I couldn't just fill in for the first few weeks, weeding out the candidates for baptism; he'd take over, he said, before it was even time to mention the sacraments.

He shamed me with his talk of the sacraments, and he knew it. "You'd enjoy leading the discussions, Becky," Father said, and when he said it sober, I almost believed I would. "How you used to throw yourself into the reading! I can still remember that presentation you did on the mystics and their visions—wouldn't it do converts good to hear about Catherine of Siena? Teresa of Ávila? Think about it, Becky."

So here I was, a stack of Father's books spread out before me on the dining room table. It was a cold wet Saturday afternoon, and for an hour I looked from one dreary passage to the next without registering a word. Every five minutes my son Jack popped in to shake his head and cluck his tongue.

"So Momma, you want to play a game of two-man poker? Blackjack?"

"Really, honey," I said, "you don't have to keep me amused. I have to think of something to say at this class tonight."

I pretended that I was looking at the books and taking notes, when what I was really doing was sitting at the dining room table at three o'clock in the afternoon, on the Saturday after Ash Wednesday, drunker than I could ever remember being. Drunk on bourbon I'd found in Ethan's closet: Rebel Yell.

And I was perfectly content. I had stolen a tacky bottle of bourbon from my teenage son, and now I was riding a wave of contentment at my dining room table. I felt warm and protected, and I imagined I was sitting deep in a boat carved from the tallest palmetto on the beach, and no one could see me. No one but my son Jack.

I was perfectly content, but I wished I had a pack of cigarettes. That Lucky Strike of Father's had whetted my appetite. If I just had a pack of cigarettes, and then maybe a man, a man to pull the oars for me. But that was the way it was with desires—if I began wanting, I would want more and more and more. It was better to just be content with *this* wave, and later, later when Jack wasn't looking and I could stand with just a little less effort than it would take now, I would tiptoe ever so softly upstairs, back to Ethan's closet, and pour myself just one more shot of Rebel Yell. A wee little shot, my father used to say. And the wee little shot might just give me enough courage to drive into town, to Tobias Brothers Grocery, and buy myself a pack of cigarettes. Then I could sit on the bluff downtown in the damp day and smoke Lucky Strike after Lucky Strike, and no one, not even my son Jack, would be able to see me behind my cloud of cigarette smoke.

Jack stood on one foot and thumbed through my books, snorting now and again. "Look at this, Momma. Show this one to Father Berkeley. It says, 'There are times when thinking about God separates us from him.' What does that do to his old classes? Why even give 'em? What a bunch of hooey."

"Don't you want to call somebody, Jack?" I said. "Call Rachel. Take her out. Take her out in the boat."

"I don't want to leave you alone, Momma."

"Jack, I'm alone every day of the week." With Jack chiding me, I felt myself in imminent danger of falling off this contentment wave. Falling out of this boat. Jack wasn't weaving in front of me, exactly. It was just hard to focus on him. He towered over the table, guffawing at all the convert material. If he had been five inches shorter, he would have been the image of my father: his hair dark and wavy, his face an oval, his round eyes green like my dad's, like mine. His brother's beard grew in thick already, but Jack's white face was as smooth as an egg. Girls called him up every night, giggling over the phone, and he giggled back.

"You should have gone with them," I said. Ethan and Nippie and Sissy had gone off for a barbecue with their father and his redheaded mistress. "I wouldn't have minded." I didn't even try to sound sincere.

"I don't know how they can go off like that," Jack said, and grabbed a chair, and finally sat beside me. I knew how he would get: he would pound the table, and raise his voice, and get all choked up. It always drove his father crazy, Jack's passion. Ethan didn't have any of it—if Ethan got mad, he set his mouth, grabbed a fishing pole, tramped through the woods, and came back forgetting the anger. But Jack was like his father. He wouldn't let anyone forget.

"I can't believe Ethan would share a meal with that bitch."

"Jack, don't you say that."

"All right, I can't believe Ethan would share a meal with that slut."

"Jack!"

"Come on, Momma. You know it's true. She *knows* Daddy's married. She *knows* there are four of us. What's she think she's doing?"

"Jack, you don't have to concern yourself with that. I don't want this to come between you and your father."

"Come between us! There's a distance the size of a salt marsh between us."

"Oh, Jack." What I wanted to say was: there's a distance the size of the Atlantic Ocean between you two.

"And Nippie and Sissy are little traitors, too."

"Now, come on, Jack. We can't have the whole family picking sides."

"They've already picked their sides."

"Well, listen, baby, I appreciate your being on my side, but I don't want you taking on all of them." I took his hand and squeezed it, but he dragged it back to pound the table some more. It was just as well. I wasn't sure I could have kept a grip on it, anyway.

"They've all turned on you, Momma."

Now he *was* weaving in front of me. Now that he was sitting down, he certainly was weaving. "No, they haven't, Jack, they just want to share a meal with their daddy." I was surprised that my voice came out at a normal pitch, when I felt as if I were calling to shore. "And they *should* have supper with their daddy."

"But you know what Sissy's been saying. Telling you it was because you were always taking my side against Daddy. You shouldn't ought to let her talk like that. Nippie said it was because you got *fat*—and you're not fat."

Jack had been doing this since he was a little boy. Trying to make me feel better, and making me feel worse. Oh, how very drunk I felt. Oh, how I would have loved to put my head down on that table and forget that I had to teach what I didn't believe to Father Berkeley's class that night. Oh, how I would have loved to forget that my family had left to go eat barbecue with a redheaded bitch. Slut. Whore. Jack was right. How could Ethan share a meal with her?

Jack was watching me suspiciously, protectively. How could he not smell the Rebel Yell? And even if there had been no Rebel Yell to smell, he would have smelled my need for him, the way he'd known since he was a tiny boy when I craved comfort.

For years I'd been wondering why this son and I read each other's signals so clearly, why we were the ones with antennae out for each other. Jack needed me more than his brother did from the first day in Due East Memorial: he was a greedy little piglet, slurping my milk, hanging on to my breast, while Ethan was dozing off in the middle of his feedings. One cold midnight after I'd brought them home, Jack woke me up with hysterical cries, and once I had hushed him he opened his eyes to me and smiled a shocked smile, the first smile to break from either of my boys. We were living then on the Point, in the little cottage we called the River House, and I held Jack up to the kitchen window so that he could watch a slipper moon float over the water out back. The water looked tipsy, and I felt tipsy, and I danced him around the kitchen, singing him silly little songs to go with his silly little smile. "I only have eyes for you" I sang to Jack, guilty that his quiet brother lay asleep, guilty that his brother couldn't nestle against my shoulder and feel my crazy elation, feel this moment when I forgot my fatigue and my sadness. Ethan didn't smile for another month.

Jack had always been more trouble, always the one crying in the middle of the night, always the one waking up grumpy, always the one slinging his grits at his brother. I had felt the two fetuses wrestling in my womb, and surely it was Jack picking all the fights in that watery bed. His father cuddled Ethan and told me I neglected one for the other. And the more his father held Ethan, the more I grabbed for Jack.

Now Jack was grabbing for me. He reached out and squeezed my hand, the way I had squeezed his hand a minute before. His father said he was a smoothie. His father was right. He could talk his way around anything: he'd talked his way around his bad grades, and he'd talked his way into staying home, being lazy, when his brother was out hunting or fishing or joining the football team. He didn't do anything to earn his keep, and still the girls flocked to him, and the teachers found him so—pleasant, one of them had written on a report card—that they passed him when he should have failed. It drove his father crazy. It drove his father crazy that I defended him, and called him creative, when I knew deep down that Jack had never spent more than five minutes on a creative act in his life. Unless it was with his girlfriends. Unless it was comforting me.

"*I* love you, Momma," Jack said.

I tried to sit as still as I possibly could. "I know you do, baby," I said. "And they do, too, in their way." Jack looked doubtful.

"And I have to think of something to say to all these converts tonight," I said. If Jack would just go to his room, I could see about that last shot. If Jack would just leave me be, I could just go back to my carved-out boat and my swelling wave and my need for cigarettes and men. But Jack stayed at the table and cocked his head the way one of Ethan's setters would. Together we heard the sound of shifting gravel in the driveway.

"The traitors are back," Jack said, and jumped to his feet. Now he was going to desert me too, as all the rest tramped in to smell Rebel Yell on my breath, my books open and unread before me.

"Jack?" I tried not to sound pathetic.

"I don't want to see him, Momma."

"You don't have to stay but a minute, Jack. Just say hey."

"Like hey, Dad, want a punch in the jaw? No, thanks."

"Jack?"

"Momma, I can't."

"Just one minute. Just for me."

Jack came and put his arm around my shoulder, the way I knew he would,

((

and we froze that way, Jack looking like a soldier posing for a miniature before he went off to fight the War Between the States. The front doorknob turned, and the rest of my children tramped in, one by one: Nippie, Sissy, Ethan with his red dogs. Ethan slammed the door and shooed the two setters away. Their father wasn't going to come in.

Nippie slumped into the dining room and sat at the table without a word. Nippie is a speckled redhead like her brother Ethan: her hair spirals out in wiry tendrils, and it looks like shrimp hitting the boiling water, fiery, but still flecked with black. The rest of Nippie is square and solid and—it's hard to say it about your own daughter, especially when she's twelve years old—unattractive. Drunk as I was, I could still feel the little sparks of irritation that warmed me whenever she sat slouched at the table. They'd picked out their nicknames themselves, Nippie and Sissy, when they were at Due East Elementary. Now Nippie had reached an age where the boys called her Nipples. She had little breasts that managed to look as square and as solid as the rest of her. If she lost the ten pounds she needed to, the breasts would probably disappear.

"I hate her," Nippie finally said. Sissy had already clumped up the stairs to the bedroom.

"What'd you expect?" Jack said. "Why'd y'all go?"

"We went to see Daddy," Nippie said, and stuck her tongue out at Jack. "I'm sorry I said you were fat, Momma. Now Judi—Judi's fat."

"Just hush," Jack said. "Just don't make Momma feel worse."

"You couldn't possibly make me feel worse," I said, and even as the words left my mouth, I had a vision of Judi's naked puckered belly under heavy blue-veined breasts. The thought of my husband's flab meeting Judi's flab tickled me, somehow. It was the first time I'd taken a moment's pleasure in my husband's treachery. I heard myself laughing a high, tinkly laugh that came from somewhere out of my past. I hadn't laughed that way since the children were babies.

"Oh, no," I said, and laughed at a higher and higher pitch until Nippie and Jack were staring at me with what must have been—concern? fear? I couldn't stop, though: I wasn't certain whether I wanted to keep laughing or whether it would lead to something else, whether this boat I was riding would tip over or whether I would ride this wave into hysteria. I knew, with the familiar warmth of a familiar sin, that I was frightening my own children.

"So tell us about her, Nippie," I said.

Nippie looked to Jack.

(

"She *is* a whore, isn't she, Nippie?" I couldn't believe the word had left my mouth.

Nippie yowled, "Momma!" and sat gripping the edge of the table, ready to run from the room and a mother who'd gone mad.

"Momma!" Jack echoed.

I saw them eyeing me with the contemptuous pity my children seemed to feel so often lately. I felt the smile that went with my high tinkly laugh dropping off my face, and suddenly I felt very, very sick.

An hour later I was still drunk, and Ethan carried me to bed without ever looking at my face. I couldn't believe that I could throw up for so long, or hang on to the base of the toilet as if it were the only life preserver in a raging sea, and still be drunk when it occurred to Ethan to stick a nail into the bathroom doorlock. Thank God I'd had the presence of mind to lock the door and humiliate myself in private until I managed to graduate from the toilet to the side of the tub. Thank God Sissy and Nippie hadn't seen me stretched out on the cold bathroom floor. I had tried to answer Ethan and Jack when they called through the door. I had really tried. Words had gurgled up in my throat, but the words turned into retching, and it must have been the sound of the retching that frightened them enough to call their father.

And it was just as well that I hadn't been able to answer them, because I could not possibly have explained about the boat or the wave or how, drunk as I got, I had lain on the bathroom floor and remembered my family. I had practically been able to reach out and run my hand over my father's dark head. He was just beyond me: every time I started to throw up—and I couldn't be sick again, there couldn't be anything *in* me—I caught a glimpse of him as my head bobbed down over the toilet. Now my father was strutting across the bathroom wall. Now he was lifting a pint of bourbon to his lips. Now he was gone.

Lying on the cold beige tiles in my bathroom in Piney Woods, I felt again the big faded squares of linoleum in my parents' bathroom. I closed my eyes. I was back on Lady's Island, back to the night when my brother Kevin poured me my first drink, a big water tumbler full of Jack Daniel's to match the big water tumbler he'd poured himself. My three brothers and I rolled up the braided rug in the living room and played Everly Brothers records at top volume, and my wild, shy brothers danced the shag with me just as if I were

☾

one of the girlfriends they only dreamed about dancing with. I was twelve years old. My parents were out at the Marine Corps Ball.

And I ended up sick on the linoleum in the bathroom, my brother Michael begging me to drink a cup of muddy Nescafé, Kevin bringing washrags full of ice, Billy standing in the doorway helpless. My brothers ran away when our parents came home. They cowered down in their basement bedroom while my father bent down and picked me up off the mess on the floor and carried me into bed. My father was drunk himself, drunk with his own dancing and taunting of Marines, and he knocked my head on the bedpost when he lowered me onto my sheets.

And then, when he'd tugged my socks off and pulled a quilt over me, my father laughed. He didn't berate me once, except to say, "You've got to learn to drink like a *sailor's* daughter," and he fetched a cool washrag and sat beside me to wipe my lips with a gentleness I didn't feel again until Jack was three years old and stroked my cheek.

Now it was my husband who sat at my bedside. Now I felt again the humiliation of being out of control, of smelling sickly sweet, of not being sure whether the next words out of my mouth would be my own or would come from some stranger, some stranger who came close to hallucinating in the bathroom.

"You can't let yourself go like that in front of the kids," Jack was saying. What surprised me was not that he had the nerve to say something like that after what *he'd* done in front of the kids. What surprised me was his tone of voice. He almost sounded kind. He seemed to be holding my hand, or maybe stroking it. It was hard to tell with the swirling. I'd heard Timmy Rooney say that when he went crazy the most remarkable part for him was watching himself go crazy. The hallucinations didn't scare him, he said—it was knowing they were hallucinations.

And that was what was frightening to me about being drunk for so long: there was a tiny little part of my brain or my consciousness or maybe just my soul that was watching everything I did, and in perfect control, but the rest of me was like a party gag snake let out of its can. I was flying all over the room. I couldn't even tell if my husband was stroking my hand or holding it. I closed my eyes and tried hard, with the little fraction of me that was still functioning, to stop the bed from rocking, and realized at the very minute that it *did* stop rocking that I had to teach the convert class. I opened one eye and tried to

((

make out from the bedroom window whether it was light or dark outside. It seemed to be dark. There was a sliver of moon suspended outside my bedroom window. Or maybe I was confused.

"What time is it, Jack?"

I felt my husband draw his arm away to look at his watch. "Six-thirty," he said, and I waited for his heavy hand to come back on top of mine. It didn't.

"I've got to get over to the rectory in an hour." I couldn't imagine getting out of my bed.

"Whatever for?"

"I've got to teach the convert class."

"Oh, Becky, I'll call Father and tell him you got the flu. How'd he talk you into that? You've got enough on your hands with the kids without worrying about a convert class. Look what happened. It's too much. You've always taken on too much."

He was talking to me as if I were *sober*, as if I were going to respond in some rational way, or have some little badminton hit-the-shuttlecock-back-and-forth-over-the-net conversation with him, when what I was going to do was lie there and be as nauseated by his last sentence as I was by the bourbon that was poisoning me. Jack always said I took on too much. When Nippie was finally in first grade and I went back to teaching I came down with a bronchitis that worked its way to a pneumonia that kept me flat on my back for three weeks. In Due East! In September! So after I quit teaching I tried to take courses at the university, just to keep from losing my mind, and on the night of my first big exam in philosophy, Ethan was carried bloody into the house by the friends he'd been drag racing with. It was true. Jack was right. Anything outside the borders of these split-level walls was too much for any of us. I would just have to confine my madness to this interior of plush beige carpeting for the rest of my children's lives.

"I can't stand the beige," I said. The fully conscious part of me thought that maybe I had planned to say that, but the barely conscious rest of me was taken by surprise.

"I beg your pardon?" Jack said. It was very peculiar that his voice still sounded so kind. It was very strange that his hand had come to rest on mine again: his sunburned hand, striped white where the ring had been pried off.

"I said I always hated the beige carpeting. I didn't want beige and I let you talk me into it. I didn't want an island in the kitchen."

☾

There was complete silence. Usually Jack stormed out of the room the way his namesake did. Usually I was the one who was silent, while my husband spoke his piece. The silence from him unnerved me more than my own outburst.

I opened my eyes again. Jack still rested his hand on mine, but now he was staring out the window. Surely that was a real sliver of moon out there, surely it was dropping, dropping, gobbled up by the horizon as I watched. I was used to seeing my husband angry—he rattled like a pressure cooker when he was frustrated with me, and spat out his steam. Now I could not define the look he wore. Sadness? Guilt?

"Guilt?" I said.

Jack turned farther away. He was wearing a yellow alligator shirt and his belly pressed it out in a roll over the top of his pants. His belly looked like a lump of dough and I couldn't believe that after all these years of having Jack's stomach revolt me I suddenly wanted to take this lump of pale dough and knead it. After all these years of telling him he shouldn't let his light skin get so sunburned I wanted to trace the boundary line between his white palm and the top of his hand. He slouched over the way Nippie did. He looked like a kid, like one of the third-grade kids I'd deserted when I got my pneumonia. For the last five years I'd thought he looked like every other on-the-make land-selling businessman in Due East, with his navy blazers and khaki pants and—this was the worst part, this was the part that made my skin crawl—his little tassel loafers. But now he just looked like Jack, like himself, with his long angular nose and his sun-bleached eyebrows and the hair thinning on the top of his smooth red head.

"Oh, Jack," I said. The flying-around-the-room part of me said, "Oh, Jack," with infinite disgust and disdain. I sounded as cold as the dying moon outside my bedroom window. That wasn't how it was supposed to come out. I had wanted to say, "Oh, Jack," in a voice full of remorse and longing, a voice that would summon back for him a picture of us walking our babies together in the middle of the night. A voice that would make him squeeze my hand the way our son had done not an hour before.

"Oh, Becky," Jack said, and *his* voice was pitched to remorse and longing. It was a miracle.

"I can't see straight," I said.

☾

"I can't see straight either," Jack said. "I didn't mean for you to do this. I didn't mean for you to go off the deep end."

"I didn't go off the deep end," I said. "I'm drunk. Jesus, Mary, and Joseph, what does Ethan say? Stinko. I'm stinko."

"I don't want you stinko in your bed," Jack said, and we both managed tight little smiles.

"What's the matter, Jack?" I said. I heard my voice freezing over again. I could stop it if I wanted to. I didn't have to say the next line. "What's the matter, doesn't our Miss Judi have a little drink every once in a while?" My head was clearing by the minute, and I didn't want to stop. When I was a girl standing on my father's dock to watch the morning, I had seen the sun burn a haze off the marsh in five minutes. That was what was happening to my drunkenness now: the light of my anger was burning away the haze and clearing the horizon.

"Becky," Jack said. "Becky, I know you're hurting."

If I'd had Ethan's Swiss Army knife, I would have opened up the corkscrew, the torture tool, and stuck it straight into his chest. "I'm not hurting," I said. "I'm seeing." I meant to say, "I'm seething." I was sure I formed the word *seething* in my brain, and the other word came out instead.

"Becky," Jack said, and this time he *did* squeeze my hand, squeezed it and managed to make me feel that he was squeezing the hand of a client whose land he'd just sold. "Becky," he said again, and I thought I'd scream if I heard my name once more. He sounded as rehearsed and calculating as a soap opera star. "I didn't want to hurt you. I swear I didn't. But you have to admit, Becky, there's been nothing between us for years. Nothing."

I sank back down on the pillows. If I kept my eyes closed this way, I would be sick again, and now there really was nothing left in my stomach, and the husband I intended to get back would watch me agonize through the dry heaves and go home to his real estate–selling slut and tell her how pathetic Becky was getting in her old age. Nothing between us for years. I tried to remember that last night together, when we took the walk through Piney Woods, and Jack pulled my hand up inside his to watch a satellite in the sky. A shudder passed through me. He'd been trying to tell me that night. For a whole month I'd told myself that that walk in the dark, the way he'd pulled me close when we heard a coon scurrying, were the signs that he felt something for me. But now. Now I could see. When I said: "Let's go watch the stars by the

☾

water," and tugged at his hand to make him follow me down the overgrown path to the creek, he hadn't held back because he was worried that the honeysuckle branches would pull at his sweater. He'd led me back to the front porch because he wanted to tell me. Nothing between us for years. He'd squeezed my hand that way because he was planning to tell me that we'd shared twenty years of nothing.

I was still lying on my back, and I felt warm tears streaming down my cheeks. Little rivulets. But I was a woman who didn't cry. I didn't let Jack see me cry. I didn't let the children see me cry. From the first year of my marriage, when I felt like crying most days of the week, I made a resolution that I wouldn't be like my mother. I wouldn't push Jack farther and farther away, the way my mother pushed my father. At five o'clock in the morning my brothers and I would hear my father clumping home, drunk, and my mother moaning out her misery: "Who is she? Who *is* she?" And the terrible irony was that my gentle, drunken father was never out with another woman. It was my husband, the one who never had to put up with the moans or the whines or the weeping, the one who never drank because it would take his mind off the columns of sales he was toting up, *my* husband who walked out on the family.

And I was weeping in his presence. At least the crying stopped the dizziness. "Father away," I said.

"What?" said Jack.

"I said, move farther away. I don't want you to see me crying."

"You said *father away.*"

I opened my eyes. It was better with them open: I could stop the dizziness and the weeping at once. "I didn't say *father* away." I knew I had. Seeing, seething, father, farther. It was just as Timmy Rooney said. It was realizing the lack of control that made the room pitch so violently.

Jack said: "Becky, you said *father* and I think we both know why you said it. Your daddy was a drunk and I don't want to see you getting in the same trouble. You have to get some help for this . . . problem. *I'll* pay for help."

"Oh, thank you so much," I said, and closed my eyes. "Should I go tell some counselor that I drink a glass of wine every night with my supper since my husband's left me?"

"It looks like you had more than a glass of wine, honey."

"Oh, don't you honey me. I had a bottle of Rebel Yell today and I'll have another one tomorrow if I feel like it."

☾

"And do to your kids what your father did to you?"

"Jesus God in heaven," I said, and swung myself up and sat on the side of the bed. "My father drank a beer and watched the sun go down. He sat on the dock and he watched the crabs in the water. And I'll tell you something, Jack Perdue—that beer made my father *kind*. He was a kind man. Maybe you should drink a beer now and then yourself."

Now Jack was standing. The vein on the side of his neck was just beginning to throb. "And do that to my kids? Have them go to bed not knowing where their daddy is, or when he's coming back?"

"That's the difference, Jack," I said. "My daddy *did* come back. Theirs isn't. Theirs is going to live on Lady's Island, and that's my island, damn it, that's my father's island . . ." I had lost the sentence. I had lost how I was going to finish it. I lost it just when I said, "My daddy *did* come back," because my father didn't come back, either.

I was weeping so hard I couldn't stand up, and I couldn't stand the weeping. I couldn't bear Jack seeing me that way. I'd rather he saw me lying on the bathroom floor, hallucinating. I'd rather he kept his utter contempt than put his arm around me the way he was doing.

"It's O.K.," he was saying. I buried my head in his chest and wondered whether any other man on the face of the earth would whisper, "It's O.K." to a wife he'd left.

"It's not O.K.," I said. I was making strange choking sounds I couldn't associate with my own throat.

"It's O.K.," he said again. "It's all over. It's all over."

I sobbed harder. Did he have to repeat it again and again in that uncomprehending salesman's voice? It's all over. All over. All over.

"You get back in that bed, and I'll call Father to tell him you can't make it tonight. Why don't you let me tell him to find somebody who doesn't have four kids to take care of?"

"Oh, Jack," I sobbed. I hated this. I hated what I was going to say. "Oh, Jack, please come home and take care of me. Please come home."

Now I'd done it. Now I'd driven him away forever. I couldn't stop myself from sounding like my mother, from sounding like an absolute lunatic. I couldn't stop the room from rocking and I couldn't stop the moon from disappearing and I couldn't stop myself from crying and I couldn't stop myself from needing this ordinary, ageing, faithless man.

☾

It was funny how sober I felt, driving the car. Jack my husband said he'd drive me, and Jack my son said he'd drive me, and Ethan said: "Oh, let her go. She's O.K." It was funny that Ethan was the one who knew I wasn't going to wreck the car or shame any of them.

I backed the car down the driveway in a perfect fast sweep, knowing that they watched me from the front windows. Nippie and Sissy were still hiding upstairs. Who knew how much they'd heard? Who knew if they'd heard me beg their father to come home, or if they'd heard him holding me and stroking my head as if I were some dumb puppy he had to quiet? It didn't matter: they would never hear me beg again. They would only see the same grace that now let me drive down Azalea Lane the way the boys drove it, sure of myself and not giving a good goddamn. Now that Jack had made it clear with his head-stroking that he wasn't planning on coming back, my children were going to watch their mother turn cooler by degrees.

I forgot the yield sign at the end of Azalea, but I remembered to stop before I turned out onto the John C. Calhoun Road. When I first took Jack home to Due East, we drove down the John C. Calhoun and he tried to guess how much the houses on the river cost. I should have seen real estate in his future. It bothered me even back then, in 1967, that he was a business major. I had thought I would fall in love with some graduate student who was reading Chaucer or Milton. I thought I'd fall in love with somebody who could explain to my father that I wasn't leaving him, wasn't leaving the bluff and the boats and the drinking and the television set always on full blast. I'd never wanted to leave Due East. But I had this notion that if I made it to graduate school, past all these girls who spent six hours a day teasing their hair and pushing their cuticles back, then I'd meet some man who had a room lined with books. Some man who went on a tramp steamer to Italy and came home talking about the Botticellis.

And instead I'd met Jack in the ordinary way, at a dance, and he was handsome, the sweetest business major on the face of the earth. We were Catholics, and it was 1967, and he agonized with his shame when he asked me two weeks before our wedding if he could take a *shower* with me. Not make love to me. Lather me up.

Besides, when I drove him down the John C. Calhoun Road he told me how he thought he could get my father into Alcoholics Anonymous. He liked

(

my father. He drove with him out past the packing sheds and the fields and shacks and stood on the lonely south end of the beach and said: "You picked the prettiest spot in the whole world to settle in." The next day my father and my brother Billy drove him out to Claire's Point, to an old overgrown fort they'd always loved tramping through, and Billy told him it was for sale, cheap.

That was one weekend just before we graduated. I couldn't bear Jack's talk about accounting class. I thought I'd tell him that weekend that we had to break up, but he was so sweet and my father was so proud, showing him Due East, that I told him I'd marry him instead, and he told me he would buy us the fort out at Claire's Point for a wedding present. Someday we'd build a beach house out there, and our children would have the biggest play fort in Due East.

Poor Jack. I was ashamed of his business major the way I was ashamed of my father's being an enlisted man, and I wanted to bury my shame forever. Every time I imagined telling Jack that we were through, I was overcome with pity. And now I was driving down the Calhoun Road, remembering how I had pitied Jack, and Jack was sitting in our living room, pitying me.

I managed to keep the car on the right-hand side of River Street until it took me to Division, but the Rebel Yell was overpowering me again, hypnotizing me. I could imagine parking the car outside the rectory and then slouching over the steering wheel. I realized I'd forgotten the turn signal and jerked my head around to look for a policeman. How dark and deserted Due East looked on a Saturday night. The long block of stores over my shoulder, on River Street, looked like abandoned boxcars on the Southern line. On the corner of Division and Newman was a warehouse where the Gulf station had stood until its owner was hacked to death one night with an ax. Niggers, white people said. Marines, my father said.

But up Division, Our Lady of Perpetual Help was lighted, and the university across the street had its floodlights on. I ran the rear tire up onto the sidewalk, parking the car, and tried to remember what I was supposed to do. Father Berkeley had said there would be four or five interested parties. He'd be out, saying the Saturday night mass at the mission, so I was to walk on into the rectory and set up his study for the potential converts. Except that I was twenty minutes late. The converts had beaten me there: I could see shadows in the window.

☾

I could still walk a straight line, anyway. I crossed the street and made my way up the steps, worried more about the smell of my breath than about the fact that I had nothing to say to these people. I had always charmed my way around third-graders, and I was just planning to charm my way around these poor innocents who thought the Catholic Church was going to bring them some peace. I might not have read the books Father brought me, but I could still remember my Baltimore Catechism. I could still remember the sixth commandment. Thou shalt not commit adultery. And the ninth. Thou shalt not covet thy neighbor's wife. Hooey, my son said.

I let myself in the front, feeling sober and sheepish. The sound of deliberate voices swelled out from the study, and I pushed the door open, ashamed of myself. I imagined a room full of men who looked like my husband.

"There she is," said a voice, but it took me a minute to find the face that belonged to it in the lamplight. "Come on in, Becky."

It was Tim Rooney's voice speaking to me, and I could not understand what Tim Rooney was doing in the rectory, at my convert class. Tim was appearing the same way my father's face appeared on the bathroom wall, the same way the moon appeared outside my window. Tim Rooney already was a Catholic, a Catholic crazy enough to want to be a monk and troubled enough to be turned down by every monastery in the Western world. What did he want at a convert class?

"I just got things rolling for you, Becky," Tim said, and I looked at him in wonder. He'd been a professor before the breakdown, and he sat deep in an armchair now, holding a cigarette, looking for all the world like he was holding his Kierkegaard seminar. What was he *doing* here?

"Rebecca Perdue," he said, to the class in general, and then to me: "We've just gone around the room, introducing ourselves, talking a bit about why we're here. We didn't want to start without you. Corporal Boulder, why don't you begin, just for names this time?"

Timmy Rooney was teaching my convert class. I stood in the doorway, one arm propped up to support me, while Tim directed the introductions and I met two Marines who evidently preferred Father Berkeley's rectory to the chaplain's office on base, a fireman, a policewoman—she'd be the first black parishioner in a long while—and a very good-looking, long-legged, sure-of-herself girl who introduced herself as Marygail Dugan. The name sounded familiar.

The next face around the circle was also a girl's, and when I looked at her,

((

head down in her lap practically, I realized I wasn't the only one in the room not fully there.

"Mary Faith," said Tim. "Your turn."

When Mary Faith looked up, I recognized her. She was the kind of girl who gets pregnant young and then gets involved with a married man, and everyone in town gets to recognize her. She had a long head of hair pulled back in a braid, and a sharp, bright face, and she looked ready to bolt from the room.

"Mary Faith Rapple," she mumbled, and shot a murderous look at Tim. So she knew him. Then I remembered who the married man was: Stephen Dugan. I saw Marygail Dugan crossing and recrossing her legs in a manner of perfect self-confidence, trying to get Mary Faith Rapple's attention, and I tried to fit these pieces of the puzzle together and still hold myself up in a single piece.

"I don't suppose you want to know what we're all doing here, Becky," Tim said. "Come on. Come on in. Sit yourself down."

And so I did. I made my way into a room full of embarrassed faces, and felt something crackling in there that I did not understand. I sat down next to Mary Faith Rapple in one of Father's leather loungers, and—Tim told me later —I fell sound asleep for three hours, while he lectured my convert class on the different approaches of Matthew, Mark, Luke, and John and talked about the founding of the Church on so craggy a rock as Peter. Not a mention of the mystics, or the sixth and ninth commandments.

Tim woke me by touching his cold palms to my cheeks. I had no idea where I was. The rest of the class had disappeared, and Tim Rooney was standing over me, touching me with hands that felt like water. I had the strangest notion that he was about to kiss me.

"Becky, you've got to stop hitting the bottle," he said, and laughed. "I just had to put Father to bed, too."

I could have been looking at the same Tim Rooney who was in the fifth grade with me. A giant leprechaun stood above me, giggling at my misery, at Father's misery. He had a silly little-boy's grin, all teeth and eyes.

"Timmy," I said, but by then I had remembered where I was, and I didn't know what to say next.

"Becky," he said, and grinned.

"Tim." I tried again. "How'd the class go?"

"Class went fine," he said. "Mary Faith Rapple left after fifteen minutes. You remember the stubby Marine, the corporal sitting by the lamp? He raised

☾

his furry little hand and said: 'I've been taking a course in mythology down to the university and what I'd like to know is what separates these gospels from just—myths?' That's when Mary Faith let out a big sigh and walked out the door. Mary*gail* stayed."

"What are they both doing here?" I said. "What's she doing here, with Stephen Dugan's wife?"

Tim shrugged. "Let me drive you home, Becky."

I waved him off, automatically, but when I pulled myself up out of the lounger and found that my legs were trembling, I reached out a hand for him. What a sweet boy he'd been, Tim Rooney, at age eight, at age ten. How utterly removed from the society of other children. When he was thirteen and pushed ahead to Due East High School, he was a geometry whiz, and scored third highest on the National Math Exam. The *Courier* had a picture of him, with a goofy grin. By the end of the year they were running pictures of him and his rock and roll band. By the time he left Due East for New York, he was selling mushrooms and peyote, and people had come to see him as the Due East Visionary.

"Tim," I said, impulsively, "I'll let you drive me home. But how'll *you* get back?"

Tim raised one eyebrow wickedly, and my legs trembled faster. Oh God, it was a lovely thought: that this tall, smiling man would put his arm around me, and drive me home, and then stay the night. Stay in my bed.

He had broader shoulders than I would have imagined under the ratty old sweater. He had the look of someone who, for all his craziness, knew the answer to that question the corporal put to him. He had the look of someone who would tell me to go right ahead and take him into my bed.

But he probably wouldn't mean it. He was probably just raising his eyebrow at me that way because he was kind. He was probably leaning over me to stroke my cheek because he felt sorry for me, the way my son did. Probably he felt the same pity for me that everyone else connected with Our Lady of Perpetual Help felt.

"Come on, Becky," he said, and dragged me by the hand out the rectory door.

☾

（

10

Apologia

I 'M NOT SAYING IT WAS RIGHT TO LEAVE MY WIFE.
All I can say is that it wouldn't be right to *stay* in that house, driving
each other crazy.

Because I do drive Becky crazy. I've known that for a long while.
At first, I would just embarrass her. We would come home from some
Parish Council meeting and she would say: "Jack, it's *imply,* not *infer.*"
Somebody else might look at that and say she just couldn't stop being a
third-grade teacher, couldn't stop correcting my grammar or enlarging
my vocabulary. But I knew it went loads deeper than that. She wasn't
just correcting my grammar. She was correcting me. She wanted me to
be somebody else. She'd say: "Jack, I'm biting my tongue not to say
this, but those green pants are awful country club." And she wasn't
biting her tongue at all.

She's always been embarrassed that I support us by selling land. I
don't know what she thinks is a more dignified way to earn a living.
Not being in the service like her father—she'd die before she'd let
Ethan or Jack join the Navy. And not planting the fields—whenever I
closed a deal with any of the big families in the county she'd give me

some liberal line about the plantations and the aristocracy and downtrodden blacks and never mind. I can't repeat it for you. Anyone with half a brain can figure out that if you want to help a place like Due East, you build it up.

But if I sold some big old mansion to a *writer*—and I did, on more than one occasion—or if I helped some *artist* wintering in Due East find a place to rent, that was different. Suddenly it wasn't so bad to be connected to me. She would have jumped through a hoop to meet any of *those* clients.

And I would have been proud to introduce her, if it ever came to that. She is still beautiful, even with the extra weight, and she really doesn't know it. I guess that's what makes her beautiful. In the winter her skin goes a milky color. It's tissue-paper skin, stretched thin now that she's older, crisscrossed with tiny lines. Her eyes are as green as the sea and she still opens them wide, like a girl. I feel like I'm describing some fairy-tale character here—you know, ruby-red lips and skin like the snow—but really, when I first met her, that's what I thought she was. Here was this stunning girl, with a long black braid down her back, and she didn't seem to have any boyfriends, or girlfriends even. She was shy, and her brothers all gathered around her like the honor guard.

She stood out at S.C. Women's. All the other girls there dressed alike—I can see them now, in alpaca sweaters and short, tight skirts. Bass Weejuns. Thousands of girls, all in brown Bass Weejuns. I felt like I'd dated thousands of them, too. I felt like I'd got my hand stuck in thousands of teased-up hairdos. So when I first saw Becky, she looked like she came from another planet, or another decade, with her big wide skirts and her saddle shoes. She wasn't a hippie or anything. She really didn't know who she was. The only thing she knew for sure was that she was a virgin, and even if there were girls all around her drinking gallons of milk of magnesia to make themselves self-abort, she intended to stay a virgin. And she probably thought I was, too, and I know that sounds naive, but this was 1967, and we were both Catholic, and I didn't think it would be a good idea to frighten her. I thought I'd jump out of my skin from wanting her.

I think our trouble really began that very first year we were married, when she got all caught up in those discussion groups. She came home talking about this Dolores Rooney like she was the Virgin Mary herself and she started sticking these godawful postcards all over the refrigerator, and going out to the Friends Center to hear the Quakers and joining the NAACP with Dolores. That was the year she grimaced at every word that came out of my mouth and

☾

said, "Jack, we don't say *colored* anymore. It's *black.*" That was the year I first understood that she didn't just love her father and brothers, she was ashamed of them, too, and ashamed of being ashamed. She may have had to tell me not to say *colored,* but them she had to tell not to say *nigger.* Kev and Michael both got hooked on boat building, which tickled their father no end, but Becky thought they could do better than working with their hands. I guess she wanted everybody to sit around in the rectory talking about Thomas Aquinas and civil rights. Billy she hardly spoke to anymore, because he was a Marine. She made out that it was because he'd broken his father's heart, but as far as I'm concerned, she didn't want to be reminded that she came from a family of enlisted men. And it didn't take me long to figure out that even if I'd helped her come up in the world with the money I was making, I wasn't exactly the man to please Father Berkeley or Dolores Rooney or the Virgin Mary either.

She didn't know what she wanted. And I didn't mind, in a way. I was willing to let her find her own way. I was willing to let her be embarrassed by me, for a while. But I wasn't willing to let her be embarrassed by our children. When she shoved Ethan aside like he was the runt of the litter, I wouldn't stand for it. Jack was the one who looked like her family, like a Cardigan, and she probably thought she could turn him into a man like her brothers would never be. So look what she turned him into. A lazy playboy with his head in the clouds. And I'm not sure that she didn't do worse by Cecelia and Claire. They were gorgeous little girls and Becky almost *ignored* them. Sissy's O.K., I think, but Nippie might as well be wearing a big sign that says, "Momma, *look at me.*" A little girl with a beautiful mother should not look the way Nippie does.

At Christmastime I was wavering about this leaving, thinking that maybe, maybe I could feel something again for her, because she's my *wife,* and I believe in the institution of marriage. Or I did believe in the institution of marriage, until we went to the midnight mass. God help me, I decided to leave my wife at midnight mass. That night there were three hundred bodies squeezed into Our Lady of Perpetual Help, and we were sitting in row one. And there was a big hullabaloo when Tim Rooney, who was sitting across the aisle from us, decided he had a big enough audience for his nervous breakdown. He took a pee—I mean right in row one of Our Lady of Perpetual Help—just when everybody stood to say the Creed. His father and the ushers had to drag him out, and Nippie was all upset—poor little girl, I don't think she's ever seen a

☾

man whipping it out before. We finally got everybody settled down, and Father gave a little speech about how upsetting this was and how we had to pray for Timothy Rooney (one prayer I'll never waste) and then he plowed ahead with the Offertory. And *then,* right in front of three hundred people, in the middle of the Offertory, Becky leaned over and pulled up Nippie's shoulders like she was a little rag doll. Because she was slouching over. There was this look on Becky's face that said, how can you humiliate me this way? And Nippie had *her* face all screwed up in embarrassment and I thought, you just don't do that to a twelve-year-old girl. You just don't do that. She's slouching over because she's all upset, and you for one should understand that, Rebecca, and get off her case. All these years you've been on my back for my yelling, and I've never made one of them feel bad in public. In church. Judi would know not to do that. Judi would understand we were all upset because somebody just went crazy at the midnight mass.

I couldn't believe Becky could take it out like that on Nippie. And I knew that I'd never be able to feel the same, or confess to Becky that I'd been having an affair, or do anything but escape from that look she was always casting on all of us. That look that never understands what we're going through but only says, how can you humiliate me this way?

Besides, I was worried that somebody besides Tim Rooney was going to crack up. Becky seemed bent on going as loony as her mother, too. Her mother spent all her time in the house, so what has Becky done in the past few years? Spent all her time in the house. Her mother ignored her, so what does Becky do? Ignore her own children. One time Becky told me the children were this heavy weight on her back she couldn't shake off. And I thought, Jesus Christ. They're supposed to be a heavy weight. They're your children. They're supposed to be the load you carry gladly.

After Billy was taken prisoner in Vietnam and her father bought it there, Becky's mother told us she'd only been pretending she was converted all these years. Not only was she not a Catholic anymore, she didn't believe in God anymore. So what does Becky do? She tells me one night that she's willing to go to mass until Nippie graduates from high school, and not a day longer. And what is the next step going to be? Is Becky going to start hearing voices the way her mother did? Is Becky going to lift up her dress and fall dead of a heart attack with her genitals exposed, the way her mother did?

Not while I'm around. I'm not going to let her do that to my children.

☾

Judi's willing to give them a home, and I know it'll be a shock to Becky to give them up, but it's better she get this kind of shock than an electric shock in the state hospital. Jack will probably stay home with her, anyway. She'll fight me for the other three. She'll bring up my yelling. My threats.

And I can face that. I can face a fight over the custody, and I can face making her realize what a walking zombie she's become, and I can face living the rest of my life in a different house, with a different woman, a woman who's alive and warm and breathing.

But sometimes when I go to drop the money off, I look at the way Becky's let the gray come out in her hair, and the way she still twists it back in that high braid, and I want her as bad as I did when I was twenty. For the last ten years of my life she's been rigid in my bed and she's looked at me with eyes that might as well have been marbles in her head for all the feeling in them. Now she looks at me with damp eyes and a body bowed down, as if I'd beaten her.

Once, after her brother was taken prisoner, she wanted me to hit her. She wanted me to hit her with a belt—and I thought, oh God, this is the little girl who was a virgin when I married her, this is the girl who said a rosary morning and night. Our sex had never been like that. I thought she was losing her mind.

Now she looks at me as if I went ahead and beat her that night and I think, does she *know* she's doing this to me? Does she *know* she's making me want her? After all these years of acting like I was some crass, uneducated salesman she was forced to marry, is she trying to *seduce* me back into this marriage? Maybe she can live with that kind of confusion, but I'm sorry. I can't. I certainly can't. I can't ever go back to that crazy kind of love.

If you can call it love at all.

☽

(
I₁

Red Flowers

THE FLU HAD SWEPT THROUGH DUE EAST IN February like an early hurricane. Only one member of the Altar Guild was well enough to arrange on Saturday, and she was stuffing long spikes of red gladioli in golden vases. She pushed them in quickly, glancing over her shoulder as if she might be halted at her task any minute. Glads were standard on the altar, but the Guild always reached a consensus for white or pink or orange. This week, all alone, May had ordered red—all red—and now they set the church ablaze. She jogged across the altar and then down the aisle to see them better. They were opened halfway, redder than a sunset over Chessy Creek. They were glorious.

She had chosen a handful of Peruvian lilies for Our Lady, and now her eye shifted to the left-hand side of the church to inspect them. The pink and white lilies were all wrong under the shadow of the glads. They had looked delicate and stately and graceful at the florist's, the brown speckles so subtle they must have been flecked on with the finest of brushes. Now they looked insignificant, and Mary looked shabby, the blue paint chipping away just below her folded arm. She was like an old sedan that had been dented once too often in the Piggly Wiggly parking lot.

It occurred to May that when the parish evacuated the little church, they might be leaving the statue behind. Junking Our Lady of Perpetual Help. Impulsively, she stole one glad from each of the altar vases and put the three red flowers at Mary's feet, then sped back to the aisle for a look.

Still wrong. The tall flowers looked ready to fall off the pedestal—but at least they drew the eye away from the shabbiness.

"Gorgeous," a man's voice said behind her, and May jerked her head around so quickly she thought she'd wrenched it.

It was only Father Berkeley, standing in the back of the church, nodding at the flowers on the altar.

"Father, I didn't hear the door," she said. "You like to give me a turn."

"Oh, I didn't come in through the door," said Father Berkeley. "I've been sitting in the confessional."

May eyed him queerly. He *sounded* sober, but what on earth was he doing sitting still in that dark box while she scampered about the altar? Confession didn't start for another three hours. Good Lord. Had she been tugging up her pantyhose when she came in? Could he have been watching her somehow, from behind his curtain?

"I think the glads are too tall under Mary," she said, confused.

"No, they're not," Father Berkeley said. "They're gorgeous. Gorgeous hot-house flowers. Mary deserves such."

May put a hand to her eyes as a visor and watched Father standing in the back of the church. The light streamed in high from the stained glass windows, from the strips of pastel colors Father had chosen, against the hooting and hollering of half the church, when he was going through his modern phase. Now, with pastel blue and green light arching over him, he looked old and small and round.

Once May had been frightened by Father Berkeley. Once, when they felt he regarded them as silly, twittering birds, the ladies of the Altar Guild had found him pretentious.

"Father," she said impulsively. "Are you all right?"

It seemed to her that he wavered in the back of the church, but she couldn't be sure. The light was so strange, front to back.

☾

"I'm just fine," she heard him say clearly. "You go with that red." He sounded dead sober.

"O.K., Father," May said. "If you say so." She genuflected before she made her way back onto the altar. They *were* gorgeous red flowers. Father Berkeley did seem to need them now.

☾

☾
12

Stephen Still Writes

ARY FAITH ROLLED DOWN THE WINDOW
and let her hand dangle in the breeze. She had asked Stephen to drive
her out to the beach, but he had cut off the route and headed toward
Claire's Point; now he was following a shady narrow road out past the
Friends Center. The highway wound through pines, muddy green in
the end-of-winter sun, out past fields covered against the last chance of
frost. Then the road straightened itself into a long aisle, lined on either
side with rows of mossy oaks.

This stretch of road was where carloads of high school seniors and
Marines came to wait for The Light, a foggy blue glow that was
supposed to show itself in darkest night. The side of the road was a
long open dumpster for beer cans and bourbon bottles. Mary Faith had
never waited for The Light; she'd never driven out toward Claire's
Point on a Saturday night to park on the shoulders of the narrow road
and drink peach wine or Jim Beam from a bottle; she'd never let a date
slide his arm around her in the dark. She'd been home, fussing with
Jesse.

And she could not imagine what Stephen had in mind now, driving her to the ends of the earth when she'd asked him to take her to the beach. He had both hands on the steering wheel and his eyes on the road and no matter how much she fiddled with the window he did not look in her direction. She had no radio to snap off or on: Stephen was driving a new car, a gray compact radioless Chevrolet. For years Stephen had driven a shuddering ancient Metropolitan, an antique Mary Faith thought he would nurse forever. But Stephen's little yellow car had finally died, and now she sat on a new black vinyl seat, with no radio in front of her. She couldn't believe Stephen had bought a new gray Chevrolet when he *belonged* in some old eccentric car. She was sure Marygail had picked out the new model.

"It's hard to believe they still *manufacture* cars without radios," she said.

Stephen made no answer.

So he knew what was up. He knew they were going to have it out over Marygail. Mary Faith had called him Saturday night after she walked out of the convert class, and she had heard her own voice go shrill and desperate. It wasn't that she thought Stephen really knew that Marygail was at the convert class. It wasn't that she thought he had sent his wife—he certainly had no idea *she* was going. But where the hell did he think they both were?

What the hell did he think they did when he wasn't dashing from one to the other of them? Marygail, from the looks of her, probably stayed home and painted her toenails. How could Stephen imagine what it was like, to walk into a Catholic RECTORY and come face to face with the wife, toe to toe with her red toenails? To walk in with Tim Rooney at her elbow, pushing her in the door?

And now Stephen drove beside her in contemptuous silence. He was furious with her, and she had not yet had a chance to fling her own fury at him. Down the wrong route they drove, until Stephen finally turned right onto a wide dirt road. Mary Faith clung to her door handle as the gray Chevrolet bounced and buckled its way through ruts and hollows. Branches scraped at the new gray roof. Stephen drove fast and furious past trailers and log cabins, until they could see glimpses of placid water and front lawns planted with bright winter rye. Stephen turned again, and they drove along the water, past bigger houses, white clapboard houses and beach houses. He stopped short: dead end. This stretch of road was dark, tangled with underbrush and vines. A black dog loped through the trees.

Without a glance at her, Stephen left the car and climbed a narrow dirt path.

☾

He had stopped in front of an old crumbling fort, an unused fort left from from some hundred-year-old war Due East had never been called to fight. Beer cans perched in the remains of doorways, and the names of Marines and their girlfriends shone in black spray-painted letters: Pete loves Angie. Romantic, not dirty.

Mary Faith squeezed the door handle and considered whether to crouch alone in the car. She'd seen the fort before. Claire's Point was one of those Sunday drives she remembered vaguely from her childhood. When her mother wasn't sick with a doomed pregnancy or the cancer, her father squeezed them all in the front seat and skimmed down one of these country roads. One Sunday to the Oyster Factory, one Sunday to the Toomer Plantation, one Sunday to the fort. Her mother tried to turn the trips into history lectures— "This is where they piled up the shells to burn for the tabby"—but Mary Faith and her father stood on strips of mud that stretched into marsh grass and grinned at each other while Faith babbled on about the Spanish-American War. Mary Faith and her father were smelling the salt marsh. Watching the light.

Now Stephen stood in the clear winter light at the top of the hill, light still white and thin. And Mary Faith sat below, in the dark woods road, and hugged her door handle. She had never been timid with him, not in the almost three years since he'd been back. If she was going to have it out with him about what Marygail was up to, she wasn't going to hide in a compact car. Not a Chevrolet. Not when they'd finally made it to the water. She opened the door, climbed the same dirt path Stephen had taken up to the top of the fort, and went to his side.

"I thought we were driving to the beach," she said, and tried to make it a conciliatory question.

Stephen stared at her blankly and gestured: still water, a sea of sapphires, stretched out beyond them. Tiny green islands bobbed in the river, and on the shore mud flats glistened damp in the light. It was low tide, and Mary Faith watched columns of fiddler crabs scurrying like wavy lines on her father's television set. Gulls swooped out toward the horizon.

Mary Faith felt a chill, standing up above the littered shore. It was almost March, and the sun was warm in the middle of the day, but the breeze laid a damp clammy hand on her. She always got chills when she'd left Jesse behind —and today he was with Tim.

"Stephen?" she said. "What are we doing on the river?"

☾

Stephen pointed calmly off to the left, where the land curved and the water continued. "The sound starts out there," he said, even-toned, "and if you follow it down in a boat you're not far to the ocean."

Mary Faith had lost her sense of what water they were headed to when they left the beach road for Claire's Point. She supposed Stephen was right. She supposed he would manage that flat tone of voice indefinitely.

She looked around helplessly at the fort. Most of it was still standing, but she couldn't help being reminded of her high school Latin books; she might as well have been standing in the Roman Coliseum, for all this ruin. They stood on huge tabby slabs, and the fort seemed to go down several stories, down to subterranean passages, down to bats and snakes, probably. She supposed there was some point to their being there.

"I guess you could tell how upset I was," she said finally. "On the phone."

Stephen turned toward her and glared with his thin strip of mouth set in disbelief. Mary Faith glared back—*he* was the one who was married, *he* was the one whose wife was faking a conversion—until they both cracked smiles and Stephen shook his head back to laugh.

"Happens all the time," he said. "Women call me up all the time and say I can just forget about marrying them. Happens every Saturday night."

"I'm sorry," Mary Faith said. "I tried to say I was sorry this morning, but it was hard in front of Tim."

"I guess so. I guess Tim Rooney's just about moved into your father's house."

"He's there a lot. For Jesse, you know."

Stephen shrugged. "Yup. For Jesse."

"Oh, come on, Stephen. Tim thinks I'm Little Miss Earth Mother."

Stephen widened his eyes and coughed. "Little Miss *Earth* Mother?"

Now Mary Faith shrugged. She had pictured them all the way out at the south end of the beach, walking hand in hand by the surf, not standing atop the bastions of an unused fort from the Spanish-American War. Now she could feel snakes slithering up from below to creep over their feet, and she shook her sneaker impatiently. The mud below the fort was a thick glop strewn with sharp shells. She had pictured a bluff for them to sit on, a downed palmetto at least. Here she had nothing but slabs of stone. She plopped herself down, and felt grit beneath her hand.

Stephen stood above her. "I don't suppose you have any inclination to tell me what made you call on Saturday night. Something you ate? Something you read?"

Mary Faith stared down and out at the water. She and Stephen never fought: if she was going to fling a paperback Pascal at him, she waited until he was out of sight.

She kept her voice on the same even keel as his. "Do you know where Marygail was Saturday night?"

Stephen paused—a count of ten—before he answered. "My wife was at the auditorium Saturday night for rehearsal. If you saw her with another man, you can hardly blame her. I'm surprised you've resorted to tattling on her."

Mary Faith set her jaw and counted to ten herself. "Marygail was at Our Lady of Perpetual Help rectory," she said softly. "Taking religious instruction."

Stephen looked down blankly into her eyes. "How do you know that?"

Mary Faith blinked. "I was there, too," she whispered.

Stephen sat—a gun emplacement between them—and snorted. Mary Faith reached to take his hand, but he was too far away. The snorting sounded ominous. She watched him slowly and deliberately unlace his shoes, take off his socks, roll up his khaki pants. He made his way down the stony path, over a flat expanse of sandy grass to the mud flats, stubbing his bare toes every few steps. Finally he rounded an old shack and picked his way around the oyster shells to the shallow water's edge. He stood there a moment and then turned back, just as slowly and deliberately.

When he had crossed the flat land and made his climb back up to the bluff and the fort, he sat down wearily beside her and said, as if he had never left for the water: "What were you doing at Our Lady of Perpetual Help taking religious instruction?"

She had memorized this explanation, but she could barely call back the lines.

"After you gave me the Pascal," she said slowly, "it occurred to me that you might like it if I were more interested in your . . . religion." She would *not* say the word faith.

Stephen took her hand and held it lightly. "Mary Faith?" he said. "You sound awful—ingenuous right now, but the last word you applied to religion, as far as I can recall, was *crap.*"

Mary Faith took a long breath. She had anticipated this. She had worked this out.

(

"I have to be perfectly honest," she said. "I don't have the slightest intention of ever becoming a Catholic. But I'd like to know what you're thinking sometimes. Tim said—"

He cut her off. "Oh. Tim said. Don't tell me. Tim is running the convert class. Tim Rooney and the Catholic Loonies."

"It has nothing to do with Tim! It has to do with you and me. Who do you think you are, going on about Tim when you're cramming every book you ever taught down my throat and then not even letting me discuss them with you? You think I'm some Galatea—"

"It's a good thing I had you reading. Now you can fling that back at me."

"Christ, Stephen. I'd know who Galatea was without you. I'd read without you. Maybe not Dickens and *Eliot.*"

Stephen grinned suddenly. "Those aren't *my* favorites. *I* don't go for that sap. Why'd you keep asking me for them?"

Mary Faith's blush paled. *Romola* had taken her a month. By the end she was just skimming the pages in case Stephen questioned her. "I guess I was just trying to be polite," she said. She couldn't *bear* it when her voice went high like that. "I mean, isn't that your period? The nineteenth century?"

Now Stephen shook his head back and laughed so hard that Mary Faith was sure she'd named the wrong time. Could he possibly be eighteenth? Could she have been so uninterested that she misplaced an entire century?

But Stephen's laugh pealed out full of pleasure. "You slay me, Mary Faith," he said.

Mary Faith thrust her head between her knees. Stephen had managed to make her feel twelve years old. Twelve, or maybe fifteen again: fifteen and humiliated, with nowhere to turn, no one to look to but a kind teacher. A kind, married teacher.

She refused to look in his direction. She couldn't let him make her feel like a kid. She had to remind herself that she'd had a child by herself, that she was *raising* a child by herself. That she could understand physics Stephen couldn't even read. He didn't have the faintest notion what Boolean algebra was. She wasn't fifteen anymore.

"So what was the purpose of the Pascal?" she said, from between her knees.

Stephen kneeled down behind her and put his hands on her shoulders. "He's a mathematician, Mary Faith. I thought he'd be right up your alley."

Mary Faith groaned.

☾

A mathematician. How could she have let Tim throw such dark fears into her? How *could* she have let him convince her that she had to go to a convert class to know what to resist? She pictured Tim grinning on O'Connor Street, dangling the book in front of her. How he must have relished her torment. He must have known then that Marygail had signed up for the convert course. The monster. The next day he had suggested she come to the class—to do the reading. If only she'd had the sense to trust this man she meant to marry. If only she hadn't mistaken his kindness for pity.

Stephen hugged her from behind. "It's O.K., Mary Faith," he said. "It's going to be O.K."

Suddenly she felt as if she could fold back into his arms, as if she could collapse like a paper fan under his touch. What a fool she had been, waiting for passion from him when he'd been searching out books he thought would appeal to her, when he'd found a mathematician for her. How childish of her to resist the presents that represented his passion.

Suddenly the white light, the blue light that curved around the Due East River to the south, reminded her of the light she and her father had stood under on those Sunday drives. Suddenly this view of mud and scrappy shells filled her with a blessed contentment. She could let Stephen hold her up forever on the walls of this crumbling fort.

"Oh, Stephen," she said. "I'm sorry. I've been a baby. Spoiled rotten."

He held her. "Must have scared you. Scares me."

"What was she doing there, Stephen?"

"I don't know," he said, and she heard in the flatness of his voice that he knew exactly what his wife had been doing in that class. Marygail wanted to get Stephen back. She was going to convert; then she was going to refuse him a divorce.

Mary Faith swung her braid round her shoulder, unplaited it, braided it up again. She never asked Stephen about Marygail. Try as she might, it was hard to picture Marygail as a woman Stephen had once fallen in love with, as the mother of the little girl he was so crazy for. When she pictured Marygail, she summoned a cartoon figure blown up large on the screen of the Breeze Theatre: a good-looking shallow twit who was somehow still grabbing Stephen by the ankles, pulling him back from this marriage Mary Faith wanted so badly now. She *did* want to marry Stephen: she wanted to lift the weariness from his

☾

shoulders. She did not want to lie alone at night anymore, picturing Stephen in bed with a wife he'd sworn he never touched.

She disentangled herself from Stephen and rose. "Oh, Stephen," she said. "What are we doing here?" *This* is nineteenth-century, this slinking around Due East, she wanted to say.

But Stephen misunderstood. "I have good news—I think."

Mary Faith's mind raced ahead. He was buying one of these low, rambling houses that stood near the water. They were going to live in the bright light of Claire's Point, away from Due East. He was not going to wait for her birthday. He was going to marry her right away.

But he said: "I've sold a script."

"A script?" She tried not to sound stunned. From time to time she saw one of Stephen's poems, dense as this mud was dense and just as appealing. A year before, he had been working on a play. "What script?" she said.

"I didn't want to tell you until I saw whether I could sell it," he said. "It seemed like a long shot. Come on."

Stephen dragged her down the path, and let her hand go when they reached the bottom of the bluff. He turned a full circle around the mud and the water, like a little boy dizzying himself, and when he tottered to a standstill, he shook his head back and howled with laughter. "It's the most godawful script," he said, and then he sputtered off into giggles again. He ran down to the water, laughing, and Mary Faith ran after him. He sounded silly and boyish, as young as Tim managed to sound with Jesse: she had never heard him this way.

"Stephen!" she called. He was running in the water's edge, oblivious to the cold.

"Stephen!" she called again. He looked back at her on the mud and raised his shoulders in a magnificent shrug. He looked like a demented prophet, knee-deep in water, his glasses slipping down his nose and his pants slipping down his stomach.

"But, Stephen," she called, and his boyishness made her grin like a girl. "What are we *doing* here?"

Finally Stephen retreated from the cold river and came to put his arms around her on the beach. The sun shone high, and Mary Faith looked through prisms when she looked up at his glasses.

"We're scouting locations," he said, and doubled up with maniacal laughter. "They're going to make my TV movie on Claire's Point."

☾

Mary Faith curled up in the front seat on the ride home and slept with her head on Stephen's lap. She drifted in and out of dreams: her mother in the sunlight, her father driving Marygail to the beach. Each time she woke, the steering wheel grazed her ear, and she was not sure whether she heard Stephen saying "Hush" in her dreams or in her waking.

When they pulled into the driveway of her father's house, she woke suddenly, disoriented by the fading light. Stephen must have been driving around the islands for hours. His hand brushed her shoulder.

"Mary Faith," he whispered. "You're home. Hush, now."

She lay still for a moment, savoring the waking, and sat up slowly. Her eyes met dusk, and then her father's old pickup, parked in front of them in the driveway.

"Oh no. He's home."

"Hush," Stephen said again. "Say I drove you to the library."

"What time is it?"

Stephen came around and opened her door. The kitchen light was on, and through the window she could see Tim's tall torso bobbing like a marionette.

"I lost half a day with you," she whispered in the driveway—they were always whispering in front of her house. "I'm sorry I fell asleep."

Stephen smiled, barely.

"Well. 'Bye, then," she said. "Tell me more about the movie tomorrow?"

"I'll walk you in."

"Stephen—no. Jesse'll give it away."

Stephen hesitated. "I'd like to see him. We'll say I *met* you at the library. Gave you a ride home."

"Three blocks?"

Stephen shrugged, and Mary Faith thought he might retreat to his car, but he walked beside her up to the kitchen steps.

Stephen had sold a movie script, and this would be the first time in almost three years that he had come inside with her father there. Her knee was shaking, and she felt the tightness of his hand on the small of her back. What would she say? Hello, Daddy. Hey, Daddy. You know Stephen. She couldn't get any further than that before she pushed open the door. They would probably stand crowded in the kitchen, choking with embarrassment.

☾

But her father wasn't in the kitchen; Tim Rooney waited for them alone, by the sink.

"Hey, Mary Faith," he said, and came at Stephen like a loony bird crashing into a landing. "Stephen. How're you *doing?*"

Stephen coughed and scowled and shook Tim's hand.

"Don't get to see you too often, Stephen. I mean, when you drop Mary Faith off."

Mary Faith brushed behind him. "Thanks for watching Jesse, Tim," she said. Anyone with the sensitivity of a slab of tabby could see she meant for him to leave. But not Tim: he stood planted where he was. He seemed to be rinsing supper plates. How long had they been gone? Where had Stephen driven her after they left the fort, after she fell asleep?

"Where's Jesse, Tim? Where's Daddy?"

"Your daddy's watching *Wheel of Fortune* in the den. Ogling Vanna. And Jesse's upstairs with his new easel. Eileen's helping him set everything up."

"Eileen who?" Behind her, Stephen shifted from foot to foot. Tim was delighted, of course—Tim was watching them squirm.

"Eileen Connelly," Tim said, and turned the faucet up. "Our professor."

Mary Faith knew she held her mouth open in a grimace of disgust. Why in God's name did Tim have to invite the little brown woman into her house? He probably stayed awake nights, thinking of ways to make her twitch. Why did Tim have to send her father—who OWNED the house, poor man—into his den to hide? And why did he have to pick the first night Stephen had come in to say hello? Standing outside her father's house, she'd thought for a minute that Stephen had meant to take it all in a leap: that he aimed to tell her father tonight that he had sold a movie script, that he was divorcing his wife, that they would be married in four months. But with Tim washing the dishes and her art teacher upstairs ingratiating herself with Jesse, she didn't have a prayer that Stephen would come clean. He'd probably flee immediately, before she separated her father from *Wheel of Fortune.*

Then Stephen said: "I haven't seen Eileen since she's been in Due East. You think she'll be coming down in a minute?"

She left Stephen and Tim to glare at each other over the supper plates. This was just perfect. Stephen knew Eileen Connelly. Stephen and Tim and Eileen would stand in the kitchen over the dirty dishes, drinking beer and talking about art, and Jesse would run wild through the house, hours past his bedtime, and her father would sit silent and peeved in front of five hours of game shows. They would never have a chance to tell him about the movie script. Tim Rooney would spend the night trying to show Stephen up as a married asshole and Eileen Connelly would see how harried girls got when they had their babies at sixteen and—

"Daddy?" The den had no door, but it was dark inside, no light on but the glow from the black-and-white TV. It was an old console, and her father had dragged his green recliner up so close that the footrest met the screen. Mary Faith couldn't tell for sure in the hazy light, but she thought her father's eyes were closed.

"Daddy?" she said again.

He pushed down the footrest and smiled halfheartedly.

"Hey," he said.

"How come you're hiding out here?" she said. "Did you and Tim *eat* together?"

Her father grinned. "He fried us up some grouper he caught this morning. It was pretty terrible. Fell apart all over the plate."

"Fried? Daddy, did you let him use butter?"

"Crisco, Miss Smarty-Pants."

"You shouldn't be eating fried."

"Mary Faith! Give me a break. Bad enough you leave Jesse the whole blame day."

"I just don't want you getting in the habit of eating fried fish. Let's not get off the subject." But she was already off the subject: the subject was Stephen and she was already harping on the diet. Her father had had heart attacks, at least two before her son was born, a small one a year later. The more Mary Faith hounded him about food, the more he made a point of sneaking out to Ralph's for a cup of real coffee or eating a whole unheated sausage in his bedroom. When she married Stephen, he would probably start smoking again, and then he'd buy butter and eggs and bacon, and he'd die of heart disease before the honeymoon year was out.

"Anyway," she said. "I've been promising Tim for weeks he could take Jesse for an afternoon."

Her father kept his eyes on the screen. Sometimes he wore wire-rimmed glasses now, but he didn't put them on if he was planning to drift in and out of sleep in front of the television. He looked even older without the glasses: there

☾

were ruts around his eyes and a hard deep line that curved down the left side of his mouth. Before Jesse was born, his hair was a slicked-back black skullcap. Now it was gray and sparse. He was not yet fifty—he had maybe five or six years on Tim, and they looked more like father and son than contemporaries. Tim Rooney had had nervous breakdowns that left him looking like a boy, and her father had had heart attacks that left him looking like an old man.

"Work O.K.? You get home early?"

Her father grunted, which could have meant not too bad, or not too good, or not too special. He ran the Plaid King gas station on the Savannah Highway, and he still did most of the repairs himself. Mary Faith could not remember a night when he did not fall asleep before he went to bed. Some nights when he played with his grandson he took his tired look off, as if he were hanging up his hat, but it always slid back down on his head after Jesse was asleep.

"What's Eileen Connelly doing in our house?"

Now her father sat up tall and looked her straight in the eye, interested. "Beats me, honey. She was here when I got home. Playing with Jesse."

"I hadn't even hugged him yet," said Mary Faith. "I better go on up. She's my *art* teacher."

Her father's eyes were still on her.

"Did she eat with y'all?"

Her father nodded. "I guess Tim's finally got him a girlfriend," he said. His next sentence hung in the air.

"Praise the Lord," said Mary Faith. "Only maybe Tim'll start bringing his girlfriend to *his* daddy's house instead of my daddy's house."

"Oh, it's nice to have us some young people here," Jesse said vaguely, and Mary Faith watched him focus back on the TV. Young people. Tim and Eileen and Stephen were practically the same age as her father. She'd never even gotten around to telling her father that Stephen was in the house, and now her father's eyes were closing again.

"Night, Daddy," she said. She could hear the Holy Terror giggling and stomping upstairs, and she could hear silence and static electricity crackling out from the kitchen.

She clumped up the stairs deliberately, hoping Jesse would spring out at the sound of her. No such luck: his door was still shut tight when she reached the landing. Jesse had a tiny room just off the stairway, her mother's old sewing room. Sometimes she thought she should switch rooms with him, but there was

☾

a pecan tree just outside his window, and the way its gray branches scraped and caressed the glass gave her so much comfort that she thought the sound must comfort Jesse, too.

She stopped at his door and listened to him bouncing off the walls: and the bed and the ceiling, probably. He was screeching with delight, but there was no hint that another person was in the room with him.

When she turned the knob the door wouldn't budge, the new easel blocking her way. She heard it being pushed across the floor to let her in. She hoped Eileen Connelly would leave as soon as the door was sprung open. She hoped Eileen Connelly would slide down the pecan tree *before* the door was sprung open.

"Momma!" Jesse screamed, when the easel was out of the way. "Momma, look!" He was jumping on the bed, pointing, and Eileen Connelly smiled—she looked *proud*, Mary Faith thought—as Mary Faith stood in the doorway and surveyed a dozen—no, fifteen, twenty—long sheets of newsprint covered with muddy red and blue abstractions and taped on the bedroom walls with scrappy little bits of masking tape. In the corner stood the new easel, wood and chalkboard and metal, another piece of newsprint attached.

"That's nice, Jesse," Mary Faith said. Nice. Great. She pictured herself in the morning, scrubbing the walls where the tape left sticky bits. There were five plastic containers of paint in the easel's tray, and five fat brushes. A lifetime supply. She'd painted Jesse's room white herself so that the morning light would shine in bright and clear, so the leaves outside would shimmer. She'd put the only framed picture she had of her mother on his dresser. She'd never considered all this mess working its way into the picture.

"Hi, Mary Faith," Eileen Connelly said.

Mary Faith tried to smile. She'd only taken three classes with Eileen Connelly, and she was scared to death of her. The woman's economy was terrifying: she could get through the three hours in the studio on a dozen sentences, half of them answers to questions. Her drab shapeless shifts made Mary Faith's long skirts look garish. At first Mary Faith had thought her plain, her heart-shaped face childish. But now, in Jesse's room at dusk, Eileen Connelly looked almost exotic: her wispy hair was pinned back on top of her head, and her white skin shone translucent. Round brass rings dangled effortlessly from her ears, leaves on a tree.

"Momma, come paint a picture with me," Jesse said.

☾

"No, Jesse, it's getting late. I've got to get you to bed."

"*Eileen* painted pictures with me," Jesse said.

Mary Faith wanted to fling the easel out the window. Naturally, Ms. New York Artist painted pictures with her son. Naturally, Ms. Childless and Successful could spare an hour to amuse a little boy she'd never see again. Eileen Connelly wouldn't have to wrestle him into the bathroom and read a story to him and lie beside him, holding his foot until he fell into sleep. Eileen Connelly wouldn't be getting up at six to make sure Jesse didn't dump the sugar bowl into his breakfast cereal.

"He's great," Eileen said, and Mary Faith tried to smile again. This time it took more effort. *She* knew Jesse was great. Eileen probably thought she hadn't noticed in the last four years.

"Good night, Jesse," Eileen said, and Jesse yowled out DON'T GO and PLEASE STAY and JUST ONE MORE. When Mary Faith told him she had to get him into the bathtub, he bounced on the bed and worked up crocodile tears and Mary Faith felt utterly powerless to stop his tantrum. When they were alone, she could hush him with one sharp word and then draw him close, cradling him until he stopped his sobbing. In front of the art teacher who knew she couldn't even clean a brush and didn't know yellow pears from green ones, she couldn't even imagine what that one quieting word was. She felt herself blushing and she had an impulse that almost never overtook her: she wanted to slap Jesse silly.

"I'm making this worse," Eileen said, and slipped out the door before Mary Faith could answer her. Jesse yowled louder, and Mary Faith reddened deeper. Now she remembered what she said to him.

"Stop," she said, as if she were quieting a puppy. "Stop."

Jesse collapsed in a heap on the bed, and Mary Faith let him have his fill of sobbing before she went and covered his skinny little back with kisses. She had to stop seeing herself as a single mother, pitied by all the independent women in the world who happened to look in on them.

"Come on, Jesse," she said. "You can take all your boats into the tub. You can take your jumping lobster."

Jesse flipped onto his back and took her face in his two little hands until he had pulled it close to his wet cheeks; then he stared at her relentlessly, as if he meant to mesmerize her.

☾

"Don't leave me like that," he said, and he sounded like a grown man. "Don't go away and leave me like that, with strangers."

It was nine o'clock before Mary Faith came downstairs. She had strained so hard to hear the conversation below when she ran the bathwater that afterwards she let herself drift into sleep, lying next to Jesse. Voices still floated up from the kitchen. She had two chapters of astronomy to get through before Tuesday night's class and a load of socks and underwear to hang out back in the morning.

She checked the den first. Her father lay exactly as before, in front of the television set, but now his snoring drowned out the hum. If she turned it off, he would wake and pretend he hadn't.

In the kitchen, Stephen and Eileen and Tim sat at the dinette table, a bank of empty brown bottles in front of them. Stephen and Tim were sloshed: Tim's eyes had opened wide and bright, and he looked ready to dash through the house; Stephen's eyes were narrow slits. Only his eyebrows raised when she came in.

"I've been telling them we should get out and leave you be," Eileen said, but she sipped contentedly from a full bottle of beer. She did not appear to have any intention of rising.

"No," Mary Faith said, and stopped. "Daddy's asleep. Should I make coffee?"

Tim giggled.

"I guess not." Mary Faith stood at the refrigerator door and debated whether to pull out a beer. She could do the wash sleepy, but the astronomy would be hell to get through. The three of them had been talking for two hours, nonstop, and now the kitchen was silent.

"Eileen's been telling us about life in the big city," Tim said, finally.

"I have not. There's nothing to tell."

"She's been telling us about the godless streets she roams at three A.M.," Tim said.

Mary Faith pulled out a beer and sat with them. When Eileen smiled at her, Mary Faith realized why she had looked exotic upstairs: her mouth was wide, and when she pulled its corners up, her face was transformed, lightened. She looked like one of those beatific round-cheeked peasant women in—oh God.

☾

Was it Brueghel she was thinking of? Mary Faith didn't know anything about art. She prayed Tim wouldn't start talking about art.

"Tim's full of shit," Eileen said, still smiling. "Some things never change."

Mary Faith looked to Stephen for help, but he was watching Eileen.

"I didn't know you all knew each other," she said. The wrong thing to say: Stephen turned to her with one eyebrow raised.

"Tim and I went to Camp Our Lady of Perpetual Help every summer," Eileen said, and then she giggled, and Tim giggled.

"An army of youth
Flying standards of truth
We're fighting for Christ the Lord," Tim sang.

"Shh! You'll wake Jesse," Eileen said, and then she giggled again. She was sloshed, too. "The Catholic Action Song," she said to Mary Faith. "Tim used to plug in his electric guitar in the canteen every night and lead a hundred campers in the Catholic Action Song."

"Heads lifted high
Catholic Action our cry
And the cross our only sword," Tim sang, more softly.

"He was about thirteen," Eileen said. "I must have been nine or ten. God, I had a crush on you, Tim."

"Nobody ever had a crush on me."

Stephen scowled, and Mary Faith drank her beer down fast. There was something—sweet, maybe—about Eileen Connelly. She seemed comfortable in Mary Faith's father's kitchen, sitting at the old chipped dinette. Maybe they wouldn't talk about art at all.

"Didn't you get married for a while, Tim?" Eileen said. "Didn't I hear you were in love with some Barnard girl?"

"Tim was married for six days," Stephen said. Mary Faith was startled by the tightness of his voice: she had never heard him mean before. She had never seen his face twisted with such a venomous concentration.

"Now, Stephen, let's get our statistics straight. I was married for six *months*. We *lived* together for six days."

☾

Eileen was giggling still. "That's not bad," she said. "Six days. Did you sing the Catholic Action Song every night?"

"I ascended into heaven for six nights," Tim said, and Mary Faith watched Stephen slug down the rest of his beer. She was afraid he would crash the bottle down on Tim's head.

"Stephen used to come and read me poetry," Eileen said.

Tim howled with laughter and banged the table.

"Really," Eileen said. "He used to walk down Stearns Street when I was in high school and read me poetry while I was out hosing down the azaleas."

"Tell me he read you Pound. The *Cantos,*" Tim squealed. Beer squirted out of the corners of his mouth. "Tell me he read you T. S. Eliot."

Stephen rose and threw his beer bottle across the room. It teetered off the edge of the trash can and rolled across the linoleum floor. Mary Faith almost rose to reach a hand onto his but Eileen said, "Oh, I'm sorry, Stephen." She and Tim sputtered off into hysterics again. "It *was* pretty funny. The *Preludes,* and your pants all wet with the spray."

Stephen stood still, staring out over Eileen's head, and the room was perfectly still. Mary Faith heard branches scraping the roof. Stephen had never told her any of this. He had never told her he knew Eileen Connelly.

Eileen's laughter trailed off, and she looked up at Stephen with her wide smile. "You were the sweetest twelve-year-old boy in all Due East," she said.

Stephen sat down then, and Mary Faith watched him breathe deeply. He and Tim were little boys, with a line drawn in the dirt before them. And she hadn't even been born when Stephen was twelve years old, when Eileen Connelly was hosing her azaleas on Stearns Street. When Tim Rooney was playing his electric guitar and dropping acid.

"Stephen still writes," she said, and Stephen shot her a warning look.

"Oh, I know," Eileen said. "My mother sends up a packet of *Due East Couriers* every month. I don't know how you get away with half you say, Stephen."

Stephen did not answer, and the silence swelled up again. Was that Jesse shifting in his bed upstairs, or only the trees again? Mary Faith had finished her beer, and now she looked around at Eileen's smile and Tim's vacant gaze.

"Stephen's written a movie script," she said, knowing it was wrong: knowing what would happen. Stephen rose and grabbed the jacket off the back of his chair.

☾

"My wife'll be wondering where I am," he said, and his voice was calm. His eyes had opened from their slits. "It's good to see you again, Eileen. You look very pretty. Tim." Then he looked at Mary Faith with an expression so blank that even his eyebrows stretched flat across his forehead.

"You tell your father I'm sorry I missed him," he said to Mary Faith, and pushed his chair in and walked a straight line to the kitchen door, and pulled it tight behind him.

Mary Faith sat in her chair, trying not to rise.

"Nasty son of a bitch," Tim said cheerfully.

"He is not," Eileen said, and Mary Faith knew that her knee was shaking again. Stephen had never brought her Eliot or Pound. There hadn't been any time for poetry when Jesse was a baby: only the Blake, so that when she saw snatches of his dissertation notes in his car and caught sight of phrases like "the wedding of prophecy and despair"—the most godawful phrase she could remember catching sight of—she could connect them to the simple raw verses. She had been willing to suffer Blake as long as she believed there were two passions in Stephen's life, but there hadn't been time for more.

And now he had spoken with a cruelty she didn't know he possessed: his wife would be wondering where he was. His WIFE, as if their three years together had been erased.

"*Real* nasty son of a bitch," Tim said absently.

Maybe she had dreamt up the movie script. Maybe she had dreamt up a marriage.

((

☽

13

Marygail Writes, Too

DEAR STEPHEN,
I never showed you these because I thought you'd laugh at me, writing poetry. Now I'll just leave them in a drawer and maybe you'll find them. I know they're not very good, but I wanted to try *something* you're interested in. I haven't had a lot to do.

Maureen and Stephen
You stroked our baby's
curls and I remembered what I
Used to say.
Miserare di me. (Sp???)
　　　　　—Marygail Dugan

Untitled
When you touched my face again
In the moonlight
And said
Your legs are as long as a summer night
I thought
I'd melt.

—M.D.

Nights Without You
I was wondering where you were last night
I was wondering if you lay on her sheets
I was wondering if I should come after you
I was wondering if I should tell you

—M.D.

Peace
Sometimes I walk into the church and sit in the dark.
Sometimes I think the door will open and you will walk in.
Sometimes I wonder if I should pray.

—M.D.

the end
i hope
this is not the end
because
without you i would
lose
my
mind

—m.d.

☾

Stephen, I don't know whether you will find these or not. If you do, Bunny Moses from the Little Theatre is putting together a poetry magazine she's going to offset down at Easy Printer and she thinks "Untitled" is pretty good. She would use it on the first page after the Table of Contents. I said it was pretty personal and I'd have to ask you, so do you think it's O.K.? Maureen would be so proud.

Love you (I really do)
Marygail

P.S. First page after the Table of Contents! She's already got stuff from the whole English dept. down at the Univ. Can you remember how to spell that Italian?

☾

14

Braided Hair

I HAD TWO HOURS BEFORE MY HAIRCUT APPOINT-
ment at Myrt's Beauty Salon, and I couldn't settle down to read or to
get ready for the next convert class or even to sit and daydream. I
rinsed a few coffee cups and stacked them in the top rack of the
dishwasher, but as soon as the cups were done I raced into the downstairs bathroom to look at my hair in the mirror.

Every morning for twenty years I have twisted my hair into a
French braid, or plaited it flat and pinned it high; every morning for
twenty years I have pulled my hair back to get it out of the way of
nursing babies with drool on their chins, and toddlers with pureed
peaches on their bibs, and ten-year-olds with melted Tootsie Rolls on
their fingers. Maybe I have twisted it back to get it out of Jack's reach.
I don't know. But now I had it loose for the haircut.

Loose, I could see more of the gray, and I swept it back behind my
ears to watch the streaks of black and white gleaming under the fluo-
rescent light. Every time I complained how fast it was turning, Jack
would say, "Just put a rinse in it. *Everybody* does that." I wondered
sometimes if he put a rinse in his own blond hair to slow its ageing.

But I'd never wanted my hair to go back to pitch-black—even if Jack did finally get himself a woman who looked like she threw a vat of chemicals on her head every morning.

On Saturday night, Timmy Rooney had looked at my hair with such a sweet expression on his face that I thought gray was the most beautiful color in creation. I thought for a minute that I was the most beautiful woman on the face of the earth. Tim pulled the bobby pins out of my head one at a time, and when he had my braid down to my shoulder he unplaited it and shook it loose. His fingers barely touched it: he was skimming it, the way he would skim his hand through water, and not just my hair but my whole body was willing to be pushed one way or the other. When my hair had all fallen, he pushed it back off my forehead, and then he took my face in his two big smooth hands and kissed me on the lips. Lightly. Once.

That was in my bedroom, where he followed me without my even asking him, after he drove me home from the convert class. I had gone upstairs to get him a blanket for the couch, and I looked up from the hope chest to see him slinking into the room. I was still drunk—I was drunk for the next two days from that Rebel Yell—and I believe I would have let Timmy Rooney unbutton my blouse and unzip my skirt and tug my pantyhose down my legs, if he'd wanted to. But as soon as he had fingered my hair and kissed me, he turned around, slow as you please, humming some old Everly Brothers song, and walked out of my bedroom and down the stairs. Lightly. Once. I didn't understand. We hadn't heard the children. I hadn't gone stiff, the way I did with Jack. I'd been so willing to take Tim into my bed, even with my children asleep off the same hallway, that maybe I frightened him away.

And once he was gone, I wasn't sure that I had ever been kissed. Tim had soft lips and a stubbled beard, just the opposite of Jack: Jack shaved twice a day, and his lips were always blistered from the sun. When Jack kissed me it was either absentminded or rough, rough because he'd already decided I wouldn't want him.

Tim's kiss wasn't physical. It melted into the rest of my drunken Saturday like ice in a glass of whisky: a kiss half there, like the moon, like my father, like the convert class I couldn't stay awake for. Sunday morning I lay in bed for an hour, trying to figure out if I had finally lost my mind the way my mother had lost hers. If I had imagined that kiss.

But when I made myself get up and stand in front of the dresser mirror, I saw my hair spreading out like a fan because someone had spread it. Timmy *had* been in my bedroom. I had never thought that a man would follow me in there so soon, or at all, ever again, because Jack Perdue was the only man who had ever shared my bed, and no one since the firemen in New York had noticed how tightly I had been holding myself in.

And now I had decided to go to Myrt's to get my hair trimmed. I wouldn't give up my braid—you don't just give up twenty years when a would-be monk follows you into the bedroom—but I wanted Myrt to cut off the old dead ends so that my hair would fan out twice as wide, so that I could swing it loose for Tim Rooney. I wanted his fingers running through my hair, feeling how thick it was, how wiry: hair that reminded me, no matter how far I felt from Ethan and Nippie, that I had given them part of me.

I felt a tug for Nippie. What a sweet misshapen angel she was, what a lumpy, doughy little girl. I could see her slumped at the table, telling me how she hated Judi, and I wished I had taken her hand then, even hugged her. What if she had heard Tim following me up the stairs? She was still crazy for her father.

I couldn't spend the morning staring in the mirror and feeling tugs for Nippie, though. And I couldn't bear to go back to the kitchen or the laundry or Sissy's bedroom, where I would find her journal accidentally open to the page where she'd written that I treated her like a prisoner. No, Sissy, I wanted to write underneath her round backhand. *I'm* the prisoner.

I wanted to get out of the house. I wanted to run into Tim Rooney on River Street. I wanted to run into Jack and Judi on River Street while I was walking hand in hand with Tim. And I wouldn't let Tim's wild eyes bother me: if Jack ever said one word to me about how crazy Tim looked sometimes, I would make him remember that Tim had a doctorate in philosophy, when all Jack had was real estate and his own infidelity.

But I wouldn't run into Tim or Jack on River Street. I never ran into anyone but other housewives in the middle of the week, and besides, I had two hours to kill. If I went downtown I could spend twenty minutes at Ralph's drinking coffee, another twenty in the bookstore. I could walk in the river-front park for twenty minutes, ducking away if I saw anyone from the Mothers' Club.

I didn't want to go be lonely on River Street, but I had to get out; in my house I was like a champagne bottle with the cork pulled up halfway. So I

☾

decided to do what I hadn't done in years—I decided to get in the car and drive out to the country. Not to Lady's Island, and not to the beach: there were still places I couldn't see without remembering Jack. I decided to drive clear in the other direction, toward Savannah, to find some place from my girlhood that Jack had never touched. Some land he'd never stood on.

By the time I'd grabbed a jacket and started the car, the cork had flown right out of the bottle, and in a flash I decided that I would run out to see Camp Our Lady of Perpetual Help, where I'd spent all my summers when I was a girl. Jack Perdue had never set foot in Camp Our Lady of Perpetual Help. It was just outside Due East: I could drive out there and look around at My Life Before Jack Perdue and be back in time for my appointment at Myrt's.

And once I was backing out of the driveway it didn't take me long to figure out what had put the camp in my head; by the time I turned left on the Calhoun Road, I realized that I'd been there with Tim Rooney. Timmy Rooney and his brother and all his sisters had been packed off for three weeks every summer, just the way Billy and Michael and Kevin and I were. Camp OLPH was full of families named Rooney and Cardigan and Connelly and Burke, families with four children, or six, or ten or thirteen.

I sped up on my way out to the Savannah Highway. It was the first day of March, warm as springtime, but the sky had clouded over and the day had a gray, sticky cast. I didn't mind. When I was a girl, I spent March days watching the gray of the sky bleed into the gray of the moss on the trees, and I waited for the clouds to pour down gray rains as soft as the moss, as soft as the sky.

It rained at Camp OLPH, too: once a day, on schedule. We were always there in July and August, when the heat was fierce. The counselors would wake us at six-thirty, to a day already bright and hot and sticky. After we'd made our way through mass and morning catechism class and swimming, we'd spend the afternoon rest time lying on our bunks, feeling the pressure build around us. We peeked through the cracks in the wooden barracks and watched the sky bruise gray and then purple. By midafternoon, it was pouring, and sometimes —if it had been just too hot that day—the sky would crackle over with electricity. It was always over by the time afternoon catechism started, and we thought the Sisters prayed the storm away so that we would not miss our classes.

Camp OLPH was only fifteen miles from Due East, and I was halfway

☾

across Chessy Creek, watching whitecaps curling up in the water, when I noticed a car in back of me. It was one of those nondescript sedans, as gray as the day, and it wasn't following me closely. But every time I sped up, it sped up; and if I slowed, it slowed too, instead of passing me. A man was driving, but the car wasn't close enough for me to see his face.

I tried to shake off any notion that the car was following me. I'd been noticing, since Jack left, how little things frightened me. A branch would sway outside my window, and I'd worry that someone was in the yard. One of my children would get up in the night, and I'd tremble in my bed, waiting to be murdered. Now I imagined that a man was following me. It wasn't as if there were anyplace else for him to be—the road was long and straight, and unless he turned off for gas, or down some dirt road, he'd be following me all the way to the camp's turnoff.

So I tried to forget the car behind me and remember Camp OLPH instead. I tried to remember the feel of the air after the summer rains had stopped, how clear and light it was for an hour under the oak trees, until the temperature rose again and we were wrapped in the sticky sheet of a Carolina summer.

The camp sat on a bluff over the Okatee River, and every activity of the day—mass, the three sessions of catechism, evening prayers, even the Catholic Action Song before we went to sleep—had to be timed around the river rising and falling. We could only swim at high tide, and every day Father Glowski posted a new swimming schedule.

The river was a pale blue, muddy near the shore but clear as it stretched out toward the sea. Not a hundred yards from the dock we would see a little island, and fifty yards away, another. The river was checkered with green and brown islands, and the seminarians would load up the motorboats with campers and take us crashing through underbrush on some other shore. Angela Alighieri was bitten by a rattler on Devil's Island, but Brother Patrick sucked the venom and spat it out, the way we all knew to do; by the time he'd gotten her to Savannah in the motorboat there was no more poison in her blood, and Father Glowski reminded us in evening chapel that Brother Patrick's namesake had surely interceded for him. He said that we must all call on our patron saints when we were in harm's way, and I ducked my head in shame that I had been given an Old Testament name.

I'd forgotten all that. I'd forgotten the look of the green wooden chapel, set between the boys' and the girls' barracks. The girls had to pass in front of

☾

church to get to the dock or canteen or class, and we made a sign of the cross at every passing. The Sisters said we should offer up indulgences, too, and there were days when I said: "Mary, Mother of Mercy, intercede for us" forty times. A hundred times. Every Catholic girl raised in Due East knew to ask her favors through Mary, but some of the boys—the ones who were altar boys and thinking already of the seminary—had a special devotion to her, too. Tim Rooney was famous for the shrines to the Blessed Virgin he built around the baseball field. He'd won most of his statues of Mary in Catequizzes—he walked around with his nose poked into *Lives of the Saints*—and he recrowned Mary every day in little grottoes he dug around the baselines, grottoes he lined with moss and pine cones. Every day he'd pick black-eyed Susans or whatever clumps of honeysuckle he could find and lay them at Mary's feet. Father Glowski donated little girls' bracelets from the lost and found for her coronations.

But one summer—the summer before we turned ten, I think, the summer just before Tim was skipped ahead—even the seminarians started to tease Tim about his statues, and the baseball teams were relentless. The older boys called Tim *fairy,* and I felt for the first time the terrible thrill that came with hearing a gentle word turned foul. Tim didn't give up his statues that summer, but by the next year there were no more grottoes, and suddenly Tim was the pitcher on the St. Joseph's team.

I never had much to do with Tim at Camp OLPH. The boys and girls sat on opposite sides of the picnic tables for catechism class, and on opposite sides of the chapel, and at alternating tables in the cafeteria. The bolder ones sat mixed together every night at Entertainment, but Tim wasn't bold when it came to girls: by the time he was old enough to notice us, he was all wrapped up in the cord to his electric guitar. Every night Father let him plug it in and lead us in the Catholic Action Song. At the end of the song there was a little staccato verse:

> Christ lifts his hand
> The King commands
> His challenge: Come and follow me

and Tim would mime the whole scene between his chord strums. It was always hard to tell if he was kidding; no one ever knew what to make of him. By the time I was thirteen, my last summer at camp, his guitar playing had gotten so loud and so discordant that Father Glowski shut his eyes when Tim played, and I knew it wouldn't be long before they'd all make fun of that, too.

I was trying to summon up a picture of Tim Rooney at age thirteen when I realized that I was almost on top of the turnoff for the camp. It had taken me fifteen minutes. When I was a child, it seemed a hundred miles away, and I had time to say three rosaries on the car ride from Lady's Island. My children would scream bloody murder if anyone asked them to say a rosary in the car— Jack even quit catechism in town right after his First Communion: right after he reached the age of reason.

I was still smiling at the notion of asking my son Jack to say a rosary when I made the turn, still anticipating the look of the clump of pines, the oaks around the gate. I knew there was a swimming pool now; they'd dug one in the last days of the camp, the summer before Father Glowski discovered that three counselors were pregnant, by three different seminarians: the summer before the bishop decided to shut it down. For a while Camp Our Lady of Perpetual Help was a Job Corps camp, and then the Sisters of Charity arrived to turn it into a home for unwed mothers. The wooden barracks were gone, replaced by green cinderblock. I hoped the Sisters would let me walk around. I wanted to stand on the dock, where we used to crowd together at spring tide, waiting for the porpoises to come by and feed.

But as soon as I made my turn, I realized that the gray sedan had turned after me, and my hands iced over on the steering wheel. Maybe the car was going out to the camp, too. Or maybe he was pulling into one of the driveways before the camp. I saw two houses in the quarter-mile stretch, and by the time I passed the second there was no place to turn around.

There was nothing to do but drive on into the camp, and the moment I passed through the gate and saw the empty parking spaces in front of the priests' house, I realized that the Sisters of Mercy were not there. No one was there. When was the last time I had heard about the camp being a home for unwed mothers? Three years? Five years?

The trees still reached down low, mossy and covered with green buds, and I had to follow the drive through all the overhang. There was still no place to turn around. The gray car still followed me. By now my hands were trembling on the wheel. I pressed the lock on the driver's side down with my elbow, but all the other doors were unlocked. I still could not make out a face on the driver behind me, but he was pulling up closer. Suddenly he tooted his horn, and waved, and I panicked. I tried to pull my car around into a U-turn, but I was going too fast and the car veered out of control and spun back in the wrong direction. The driver behind me braked and blocked my path, and I imagined him leaping out, pulling me out of the passenger seat, and raping me on the banks of the Okatee River. I imagined him throwing my body into the pale blue water.

But he only rolled down the window and called out: "Rebecca!"

I barely had the courage to look in his direction. When I did, and saw that it was Father Berkeley, I wanted to throw my arms around him. Of course. He was driving the silver car the parish gave him for his twenty-fifth anniversary in Due East.

I left the driver's seat and went to him with my cheeks flaming. "Father," I said. "I feel like an utter fool. I thought you were a stranger following me."

His eyebrows went up at the word *stranger*, and an odd smile broke from him. "I've been trying to get your attention since Chessy Creek," he said. "I thought maybe you were driving to Savannah."

"No," I said, "I wanted to see the camp again."

"Funny." I realized he was perfectly sober: his face had a pinched, serious look. "The Sisters asked me to come out today and take a look around. They're driving down from Charleston over the weekend to see about making it a home for battered women."

"Battered women?" Father sensed my confusion—*at least Jack never hit me*—and he said: "Come on in. I'll make you a drink."

He didn't seem at all self-conscious about saying he'd make me a drink, and I hated the pity I felt for him. "No thanks, Father. I have to get back to Due East."

"Oh, come on in for a little minute. You drove all the way out here."

What was it in his voice? Surely it wasn't pity for *me*. I felt again that Father wanted something from me: I felt like a young mother again, when I thought Father Berkeley looked at me with more than spiritual concern. But at least he was sober. At least I didn't have to worry about what would slip from his lips in his drunkenness. And I would not go into the priests' house and be party to his losing another afternoon of his life.

"Really, Father, I have to go." Over the roof of his car, I saw the big open canteen where Tim sang, where my brothers used to tease me when it was time

☾

to dance. How I wished that Father had not followed me in, that I could spend the morning alone, walking by the river.

"Becky, I have to talk to you," Father said suddenly. He laid a hand on my hand with an insistence that I wanted to shake off, and I was terrified that Father Berkeley was tired of hearing everyone else's confessions. That he wanted to make a confession to me.

"Oh, Father," I said, "I'm sorry to be in a rush, but I've got an appointment back in town." I hated my cowardice even more than my pity.

Grim and weary, Father Berkeley watched me. His face had aged twenty years in the last twelve months, in the time he'd been drinking: the pouches beneath his eyes hung heavy and loose and full of despair.

"You go on back to town now," he said, looking straight through my lie. "But you call me soon. I don't want you to let your husband take the children. You don't need that pain just yet."

I had a crazy desire to lean close to him and make sure there wasn't liquor on his breath, after all. "Oh, Father," I said. "I know Jack's been acting cruel, but he wouldn't do that. He wouldn't take my children."

Still he watched me. "You have that son of yours call me, too," he said, and finally he smiled. "Have young Jack call me. Tell him it doesn't have a thing in the world to do with church. Tell him it has to do with money."

I smiled, too. When my son was ten years old he went to see Father Berkeley on his own, to tell him that he thought the whole church business was mumbo-jumbo and he didn't want to put half his allowance in the collection anymore. When Father told the story to my husband, as a joke, he didn't laugh. He pinned his son against the wall and hit him with a belt, and I barely spoke to him for a week.

"I'm sorry to leave, Father," I said, and the way Father refused to acknowledge my words reminded me of how he had been in the old days: he never bothered with small talk back then, either. He waved instead—a brisk dismissive wave—and pulled his car away from mine.

When I drove out toward the gate, I looked back at him in the rearview and saw him mount the steps to the priests' house slowly and deliberately. I could not imagine what had gotten into him, to warn me about Jack that way. I wondered, the way we all had when the drinking started, if he was sick on top of the liquor. For the first time, I wondered if maybe Father Berkeley thought

☾

he was going to die, and then I wondered what had put such a soap opera notion in my head.

All the way back to town I worried about leaving Father Berkeley alone at the camp to watch the spring rain spitting down, but I paid for my desertion by getting to Myrt's half an hour early for my appointment. She sat me down with a stack of horrible hairdo magazines, but even if I'd had the slightest inclination to look at them, I couldn't concentrate on anything but Father's words about Jack. It was such a strange idea, so unlike anything Jack would ever dream of doing—but then, wasn't leaving us unlike anything Jack would ever dream of doing?

In Myrt's little shop, I sat in a pink plastic chair with chrome armrests, magazines in my lap and magazines at my elbow. I smelled the sweet candied fragrance of hairsprays and mousses and nail polish, and I tried to imagine Jack telling a judge that I should not keep my children.

I came into Myrt's twice a year for a trim, and I hated it more each time I came, now that the town was so crowded with BMWs and Mercedes-Benzes, now that the women who drove the BMWs came in to have their hair silvered and pouffed. They were women who lived in the condominiums and town-houses Jack sold them, identical modern townhouses that looked out over their golf courses. Sleek women, women with subtle brown eyeshadow, women whose husbands wouldn't dare leave them. Women whose children wouldn't dare consider living with their fathers. I looked like an uninvited guest sitting in their midst, my own hair hanging down half-gray and shapeless. I wished I had worn a braid.

"Miz Perdue?"

I looked up from my magazine, full of regret that I had to talk to someone, and saw a familiar face staring down at me. It was not a Due East face: it was young and hard and made up like an ad in a French magazine, the eyes shadowed almost black and lined thickly, the lips pale. It was Marygail Dugan, I realized, the girl from the convert class. She'd just had her dark hair streaked with white, and it stood up in funny bristles all over her head. She must have brought in a picture to show Myrt how to do it: the retired generals' wives in Due East had never dreamed up haircuts like that.

"I hope you're feeling better," she said, and I flushed to the roots of my own streaked hair. For a second I thought she was being sarcastic, trying to shame

☾

me with the memory of my sleep in the convert class, but as she moved along to the cashier I realized it was just a vacuous beauty shop greeting.

I tucked my head back down in the magazine. It was ridiculous that I allowed such a young woman to embarrass me. I remembered her self-satisfied look in the class, when she watched the little Rapple girl squirming, and I realized that the revulsion I felt for Marygail Dugan was physical, that I trembled again in my plastic seat. I could picture her sharing gossip with Judi: maybe it was their dyed hair, their pale pouty mouths.

It didn't make any sense: Tim said Marygail Dugan was in the convert class to get her husband back, so I should have been on her side. She was the wife. But I watched her count her change, and sashay back to tip Myrt, and I said a sudden prayer—a prayer like a hex—that her husband would leave her. I couldn't believe the words had formed in my mouth: Dear Lord, give that woman's husband the strength to leave her.

What was the matter with me? Had Father Berkeley's nonsense shaken me up that much? Was I filled with such a terrible bitterness?

I tried to picture the other one, the girlfriend, but I could barely remember her presence. They were similar in their outlines, Mary Faith and Marygail: both tall and thin, their faces long and narrow. But the way Mary Faith had sat in the rectory, her braid hanging down so sadly over her shoulder, almost into her lap, had drawn me toward her. I wanted her to win. I wanted her to get the man in the end.

And I almost smiled at the wickedness of my desire. Her braid. Of course: Mary Faith reminded me of myself. We had to be the only two women in Due East to wear our hair swept back so plainly. We were probably the only two women in Due East who hadn't cut our hair off.

Mary Faith Rapple had sat in the rectory wearing all the fear on her face that I had felt in my drunkenness. And her lover's wife waltzed around Myrt's Beauty Salon as if she owned it. Asking me if I felt better. I wished Mary Faith Rapple would come back to my class, though I knew she wouldn't. I wished I could take her aside and tell her to go ahead, to erase the wife from the picture the same way I'd wanted to erase Judi from my picture of Jack.

I smiled the coldest smile I could force when Marygail Dugan left the salon; she waved good-bye like Miss South Carolina, trying to catch the camera's eye. I waved back as dismissively as Father Berkeley had waved out at the camp, and his words chilled me again. I wanted to jump from my pink plastic chair

(

and run to Island Paradise Realty to find Jack and make him tell me that he would never try to have the children live with him. I couldn't let Nippie's sagging little shoulders move into a house with him and Judi. He wouldn't ask me to do that.

I wished I still believed in prayer—the other kind, the decent kind. If I had still believed in it, I would have asked that I be allowed to keep my children. I would have asked that Father Berkeley not come after me, with strange looks and strange notions. I would have asked that Tim Rooney call me up and take me on a drive out to the Okatee River.

Or maybe I would have asked that I could go backward, not forward, with my life, that I could forget these dyed heads and braids and mistresses and wives and just drive Jack out to Camp OLPH one day, and tell him what I was like, when I was a girl.

☾

15

Prayer

O H MY BLACK HEART.

Becky Perdue is soft: no other word for her. Soft eyes, soft voice, big soft breasts. Soft enough to sink into—but whoa, dude, she's drunk and deserted and begging you to save her. Her skirt rode up when she slept in Father's study, her thighs exposed: white, soft.

White and soft: my sisters all had those fleshy white thighs. Did Becky Perdue grow up in a house like ours? Did anyone on God's earth grow up in a house like ours? My sisters let their white thighs spill out on hammocks and couches and beds all summer long. The other girls in Due East were busy bleaching their hair blond and roasting themselves on spits out at the beach, but the Rooney girls were lolling and drooping in the shade of the Rooney house. They were reading *Mad* magazine until lunchtime, and then—if Mother was on one of her poetry kicks—they were memorizing whatever she had lined up for them.

He is stark mad, whoever sayes
That he hath been in love an houre

and

Batter my heart, three person'd God

and

Oh my black Soule! now thou art summoned
By sicknesse, deaths herald, and champion.

The Rooney *boys* only learned the first few lines, and drove Mother crazy. But oh, my white-thighed sisters were the best of obedient little girls and they got their John Donne by heart, and I came to think of them as otherworldly, with their comic books and their metaphysical poets and their soft uncared-for bodies. Lovely white girls. Lovely white thighs.

When I was a boy, I dreamed my sisters ran naked on the grass, and I woke up covered with sweat and semen and shame.

Tonight I can almost hear their sweet reedy voices. Tonight I lie on my little sister's bed and I can almost remember her. Tonight I can almost hear the Blessed Virgin call out my name, the way she did when I was a boy. The way she did when I was mad. What signals is *she* sending? Messages from a little sister? If I could crawl toward her, off Dottie's bed, I would. If I could believe with any of the smugness I possessed when I lived in those self-righteous radical Catholic communes dotted all over the dirty South, I would. I would call out to her—a vision in blue, the innocent vision of my boyhood—and I would ask her to stop me. Stop me summoning these white thighs, I would say. Stop me summoning Dottie and Becky and

Intercede for me, I would say, or my black Soule is damned.

Mother of Mercy, I would say, if I am so undeserving of your help, help that sad little girl. I'm not asking that you keep her away from me: only that you give me the courage—for the love of Christ give my body the peace it

☾

needs—to stay away from her. Keep her just as cold, just as rational, as she is this very day. Keep her in the cold light of reason until she sees that no one is coming to marry her. No one is coming to save her.

And for the love of your son, I would say, stop me when *I* go to save her. Would you have me fucking Mary Faith the way I fuck Eileen? Forgive me the word in a hypothetical prayer, but while I am still sinning—while I am still functioning with my will if not my reason—what other word is there? Would you have that little girl asking me, the way Eileen asks me, to pull her hair back until it strains from its roots? In my pride I pretend that it is mercy I show when I pin Eileen's arms back and fuck her. Should I pretend to show Mary Faith mercy?

Sweet mother of Jesus, it would be more merciful to keep me in Rebecca Perdue's bedroom where she is withering from the want of human love, the want of a human hand to touch her soft white thigh.

Stop me from pretending there is kindness in this black heart. Stop me from pretending I believe. Stop me from this need to lie in darkness, reciting all my doubt in stilted words while I look out across the yard to watch a girl put her son to sleep. A scholar and a Peeping Tom: stop this man. Stop me from thinking I can recapture the ritual of a boyhood, when I believed with all my fear and passion and trembling and sweet innocent love that you were the mother of my Lord and you would summon your mercy to save the world, and me in it.

And me in it.

Oh my black soul.

(

IV

☾

16

Graveyard in Daylight

"GO SEE."

"What if he's out there with a *bottle?* Mercy."

"All right. I'll go see."

The three faithful of the Altar Guild had been surprised at their work by keening from the churchyard, wails set midway between male and female pitch. They assumed that Father Berkeley had gone berserk among the little green graves and that one of them would have to do something about it.

Now May led them single file past the altar, through the tiny sacristy to the back door. The trio peeked out, one head over the other. Nothing. No one. An empty graveyard: two pecan trees, one stunted palmetto, one wrought-iron garden seat painted white, one browning statue of Mary, forty weathered headstones standing guard over the bones of forty Due East Catholics: forty stillborn babies and paralyzed grandmothers, forty of the chosen whose families had elected burial under the shadow of the tiny white clapboard church.

The cry commenced again, lower this time.

"Jesus, Mary, and Joseph," whispered May, in the doorway. "That's not a human being. That's an animal. There's a *wildcat* out there."

"Hush. Listen."

The sound came from behind the church, from the little corner where priests and benefactors were buried, their graves and florid tombstones enclosed in austere black ironwork fences.

"That's no wildcat. He's out there. I know he is."

"One of us has to go."

"Let's all go together."

"We can't let on that the three of us heard him *crying.*"

They watched each other warily in the dark doorway, their faces lined and cracked like the stones outside. Beyond them the March sun was brilliant and clear: two o'clock, the first day of spring.

"Look," whispered May, and pointed up past the little palmetto, where a full moon stood in dim relief against the pale sky.

"Oh my God. And there's a spring tide this week, too. I wonder if Father'll grow *fur.*" They started giggles, but swallowed them up.

Then the sobbing outside subsided, and they heard instead heavy gasps and thuds that sounded for all the world like someone stomping on the ground.

"I'm going," May said. "I'm going to him."

She dashed from the doorway, tripped down the steps, and rounded the corner of the church without glancing over her shoulder to see if the other two followed her. She knew they would not. They hadn't convinced themselves yet that Father Berkeley wasn't anybody to be afraid of anymore.

"Father Berkeley?" May called, in a voice that came out high and unsure; she was *trying* to sound concerned and maternal. But as soon as she was past Ignatius McGarrigle's tomb she knew it was not Father Berkeley in the grave-yard.

It was Marygail Dugan, hanging on to the high black spikes at the far side of the McGarrigle plot, swinging herself to and from the tall fence and thrusting her head close enough to the iron bars that May was moved to call out.

"Stop that now!"

Marygail Dugan looked at her blankly through the bars, but quit her rocking and then let out a long, windy shudder. May stood uncertainly, trying to see through the bars, without staring her down, if Marygail Dugan wore a drug-crazed look. Finally she said:

☾

"What's the matter, honey?"

Marygail stared at her, her long face a blank sheet with only the words *complete disdain* written on her swollen, pouting lips. She was dressed in a white tennis getup, her legs already tanned dark. Heavy earrings dangled under her streaked hair: how was she supposed to play tennis with all that gold pulling down her earlobes? Why was she leaning her little white flouncy skirt against the dirty old bars? Her face was mascara-streaked, but she didn't hide it or avert her eyes. She didn't blink, and she didn't answer.

"Let me help you, sweetheart," May tried again, and this time she heard her voice an octave higher than when she thought Father Berkeley was in the graveyard. This Marygail Dugan was unnerving.

But Marygail finally answered: "I wouldn't have come here to cry if I thought anybody was around."

"Well," said May, and she began to circle the fence. "Well, we *are* around, and it looks like you could use some unburdening."

Marygail shook her head and leaned down to pick up a tennis racket from the ground. She held her body stiff: another set of bars.

"There's times we could just use a little help—"

Marygail dismissed her with one long swing of the racket. "Oh no," she said, brushing past May, smoothing her skirt as she went. "You can't help a nobody. You can't help a nothing."

May heard a million phrases forming: *Oh, no, sugar, everybody's somebody* and *We all need to let out a little steam* and *Don't you look down your nose at me, you little snit,* but she said nothing.

Marygail made her way through the forty graves and past the browning statue of Mary and May stood stock still, watching her, until she had gone out through the open gate and shut it behind her without looking back once.

May moved to watch her head bobbing over the brick churchyard fence along Division Street until she was out of sight, and then she scampered to the sacristy door, where the other two were waiting.

"Did you *hear* that girl?" she said, climbing the steps.

The other two nodded grimly.

"Out of her head."

"Pff. She's not out of her head. She knows just what she wants. She wants the whole world to pay attention to her."

"She didn't know anybody was here."

☾

"May, don't tell me you *swallowed* that line. She saw the cars parked outside and the lights on inside and she came back here so somebody in Our Lady of Perpetual Help would be witness to that crying jag. Oh, she's a slick little devil."

"Those were real tears. I know they were. She was trying to smash her head against the bars."

"She was trying to cause a scene. And she did."

"I guess she did."

"And I guess we better get started—we want to finish before that moon's lighting the night sky."

"Well, I guess we better had."

Single file, the ladies of the Altar Guild made their way back to the altar. May started to say: *That girl needs help,* but the silence of the church stopped her—the silence of the church, and the little asters they had spread out by the gold vases. The asters looked frail and sickly, and May gathered them up by the handful, and thought how very insignificant they looked compared to the red glads she had picked out when she was on her own.

☾

☾

17

Sick and Hurting

IT WAS THE FIRST DAY OF SPRING, BUT MARY FAITH Rapple had been inside her dark house for three days. Her only company—if you could call it company—was her father at night and Jesse, sick with a cold that was worsening.

The house had become a cave for her. She wandered from the kitchen into the hallway, a narrow cool tunnel, and when she finally emerged in the parlor, where no one ever sat, she stretched herself on her grandmother's faded velvet couch and imagined light outside and the sound of water dripping somewhere above her.

Not that she had any need to imagine sound: all night she had slept by Jesse's side, sleeping more fitfully than he did, listening to the rattle of his breath. Croup. Her father said she had never had croup as a child; she was the one who looked it up in Dr. Spock and ran the shower for steam and held Jesse up over her shoulder as he struggled for breath at midnight. Her father had stood in the bathroom door, close to tears himself and ready to race Jesse to the emergency room. But there was no fever. They'd waited it out.

Now, in the early afternoon, Jesse slept in his room overhead and

Mary Faith tried to close her eyes in the dark cave downstairs. Next door Tim Rooney was playing the piano, as if to lull her into sleep: the *Moonlight* Sonata, the only piece she could recognize after all these months of Tim's chiding her —she never *could* remember which Beethoven was which. The notes came in plangent gusts, riding the breeze outside, and Mary Faith tried to relax her stiff neck, her tense shoulders. It was no use. She wouldn't be able to sleep in the afternoon, and she wouldn't be able to sleep tonight: Dr. Black had said on the phone to expect another night of wheezing at least.

Tim finished the *Moonlight* with a crash of mad passion and began a new piece. A rumbling start, trilling—it had to be the *Appassionata,* though that was the one she always guessed wrong. Tim laughed at her ignorance and never had the patience to play it through when she sat with him. She just had passion on her mind, he said; she just liked to roll that word *Appassionata* off her tongue.

And Tim had to know how cruel it was to tease her about her musical ignorance: her family never had a working *record* player when she was growing up. Her mother never so much as hummed a Baptist hymn in the kitchen; when Mary Faith was six or seven, wheedling for a piano, her mother jerked her head in the direction of the house next door. Expensive pianos were for crazy families like the Rooneys, Faith Rapple said in a cold fury, families where the mother was content to let five children tumble out of a dilapidated house while she—a white woman!—was out joining the NAACP and neglecting her husband.

Mary Faith could not recall another time when her mother had carped at the neighbors or worked up an interest that went beyond spying on their backyard fights from the kitchen window. But the word *piano* had left even-tempered Faith Rapple choking with rage at the woman next door, the mother who'd managed to have a Rooney baby for every Rapple that had been miscarried. Mary Faith had never asked for a piano again, and her mother never again mentioned the Rooneys by name.

And she and her father weren't likely to be exchanging small talk about the Rooneys either, if Tim kept the same distance he'd been keeping for a month: skulking in and out of his house, setting up his easel across the floor from her in painting class. When he decided to judge her—when he stopped coming by for Jesse, stopped dropping by with crabs for supper, stopped walking her home from class—she told her father that Tim was too busy with Eileen Connelly, that he was carrying on like a moonstruck teenager.

☾

But she knew that it wasn't Eileen Connelly who had come between them. The day after Tim called Stephen a nasty son of a bitch, Mary Faith told him that she was going to marry Stephen on July the first, her twenty-first birthday, and she didn't give a shit what he thought about it. She had flounced off, too, as if she were seven and sassing her father.

And Tim, Mr.—no, *Doctor*—High and Mighty Philosophy Professor, had cut her off. Now he didn't know that Jesse was sick, or that she had been up all night, or that she lay in the parlor listening to him play the *Appassionata,* sure for the first time that she recognized the right piece. Tim didn't know that when she told Stephen she wanted to marry him on the first of July, he had asked for more time. Stephen said you couldn't just tell a wife and a ten-year-old daughter and a lawyer and the courts that you wanted to get married on your girlfriend's birthday. They would marry soon, Stephen said. Maybe by fall. Certainly by Christmas. But they had to postpone a twenty-first birthday wedding.

The unemployed philosophy professor next door didn't know anything about her life for the last month: he was so damn superior about her breaking up a marriage—a pitiful marriage to *begin* with—that he acted as if she were morally infected and morally infectious. Tim had put her in moral quarantine.

The irony was that he was still sending messages, still beaming in the *Appassionata* over the airwaves. The irony was that now—with all her ignorance about music, all her fury at his desertion—now her body relaxed, as he bore on with his Beethoven.

She closed her eyes, drifting off, and let her jaw go slack. She was remembering her aproned mother on tiptoe at the kitchen window, straining to see next door. She imagined a scene in the Rooneys' bright backyard—Tim and his sisters staging a pageant—and by the time she was asleep she was dreaming that a film crew had moved into the Rooneys'; she was dreaming Stephen directing a movie with a bullhorn at his mouth. Her mother stretched taller and taller at the kitchen window to catch a glimpse of Stephen.

"Momma?"

Jesse's little hand was pressed to her forehead, and she made herself lie very still before she opened her eyes. She knew her son, but she didn't know where they were: for a moment she was still at the Rooneys', starring in a movie. The hand on her head was fiercely hot, and when she opened her eyes her son stood

☾

watching her with a strange pale patience. His eyes were unfocused, and two perfect red circles stood out on his white cheeks.

"Jesse, you're burning up. How long you been standing there?"

He put his head down on her breast as if he couldn't hold it up another minute and breathed heavily, his larynx coated again. God, she hated the sound of his struggle; she wanted to will every breath he took and make the next one —all right, the next, or the one after that—come out cleanly. He was frightened of his own rasping, and she lifted his legs up after him so that he could lie nestled inside the curve of her body. This curled-up little creature, flaming with fever and frightened that his throat would narrow tighter and tighter until there was no passage left: this was the son she called a Holy Terror.

"Hey, little sweetheart," she said, and raised herself on an elbow. "I got to take your temperature. I got to get you some aspirin."

"No!" he cried, and began to shiver; she drew a leg over his legs and tried to think through carrying him into the bathroom to get the thermometer. He was almost never sick, and now he was so heavy that she wasn't sure he would *let* her take his temperature. He would raise holy hell when Dr. Black came by after office hours, too: the last time he'd looked the old man right in the eye, and then he'd spat.

"Jesse, I got to carry you in there. Come on, little watermelon." She lost her balance, trying to stand up with him in her arms: he curled back on the couch, afraid to move, and consumed himself in a spasm of coughing. This wasn't the little night croup Dr. Spock talked about. This was something bad. This was her son, who didn't know *how* to take a nap, sleeping in the middle of the day and then frightened of his own cough. He could be coming down with pneumonia or—she tried to remember delivering Jesse and whether she could have possibly been given a blood transfusion she didn't remember, whether she could have passed on AIDS to his poor innocent blood. Whether Jesse's father could have been shooting up without her ever knowing about it, sticking himself with dirty needles that contaminated the son five years after the father ceased to exist. Whether whatever predisposed her mother to the miscarriages and the cancer had been passed on to this child, this Jesse who was doomed to leukemia, who stared at her so *strangely*.

"Hush now," she said, though he hadn't made a sound after the coughing stopped. It was the most comforting phrase she could summon—and if he didn't need hushing, she did: letting her imagination go like that. Leukemia.

☾

AIDS. She was getting to be like one of those desperate housewives who sat around with nothing better to do than imagine diseases for their children. Even Tim was telling her, from next door, to calm down: he had started the second movement of the *Appassionata* and his playing was cool and controlled and mathematical.

"O.K., darlin', you lie there and I'll go fetch you something to drink. Hear?"

Jesse moaned.

"Jess? Anything else you want?" It seemed to her that his lips had gone whiter since he'd come downstairs, that even underneath his dark thick hair she could see his scalp livid.

"I feel *bad,*" Jesse said, and tried to raise himself up to see her. She reached an arm out to help him; before either of them knew what was happening, Jesse had spewed forth a pool of pink liquid. She thought he was hemorrhaging, and then realized that he was vomiting the cherry cough medicine from the night before and that the smell of it made her faint and nauseous, too.

She tried to run to the kitchen for paper towels, but Jesse caught at her arm. "It's coming out my *nose,*" he cried, and she saw that he had begun again. She swooped him up in her arms and ran to the bathroom, hearing the plop of his sickness falling on the plank floor behind her.

"Hang on, baby," she said, and he clung to her shoulders, his fingernails digging through her blouse to her skin.

When she stood him up over the toilet his knees buckled, so she leaned her body against his to support him. He had always been sturdy; now his very bones felt frail. She breathed deeply, hoping to conceal her pounding heart: her son was a wobbling spinning top looking for a place to stop and fall over. He was frightened of throwing up, frightened of standing up, frightened of the cough that started up again now out of his constricted throat.

"It's all right. Hush now." She picked him up to rub his back. He was panicking, and whistled a high note of fear when she tottered forward with him to get the steam on in the shower.

The steam didn't help: he shook his fist at the shower curtain, meaning for her to turn it off, and still his little body trembled and gasped. He couldn't possibly be taking in enough air. That white face, those rouged cheeks would go purple in a minute. Half a minute.

"*Hush* now, Jesse." Her voice had gone high and harsh, as if she were hollering at him for leaving his toys all over the floor. She squeezed him tighter, then lessened her squeeze. She turned the steam up; she turned the water off. Her son was gasping for air. Her son could not breathe.

She had to call an ambulance. She had to call an ambulance and her father. She ran from the bathroom, Jesse's fingernails digging again, digging into her as he rattled and growled for air.

But she didn't run toward the kitchen and the telephone as she'd planned: she ran instead to the front door, which they never used, and fumbled it open with a hand that was moving, against her will, in slow motion. She was running down the wooden steps, crossing her front lawn, scraping her bare feet against the pebbled road that took her around the Rapple fence and into the Rooney yard. She was tripping over the oak roots, stubbing her toes on acorns; it was as bad as traveling through marshland, with the soft damp earth pulling her down, down, and all the while she struggled to pull her legs up faster she could hear Tim finishing the *Appassionata*. It cascaded as she ran, its notes streaming down clear and pure and fast, the way she should have been running. She knew there was something very wrong with her because—even though she could not hear Jesse gasping anymore, even though she thought he had stopped breathing altogether—she could not make herself move any faster, and her only clear image was of the dried pink mess on her bare forearms. Her son was choking to death, and she was imagining how terrible she would smell when Tim came close.

She pulled open the Rooneys' screen door, never thinking of knocking or ringing, and stumbled through the dark hallway into Tim's living room. He had heard them, or sensed them: the playing had stopped, and he sat expectantly on the piano bench. When he saw her face he rose and took Jesse from her in the first motion she could identify as quick since she started her flight.

Tim cradled Jesse as if he were an infant and peered down at the pinched face. "You're burning up," he said.

Mary Faith wanted to scream: "No! Hold him up, so he can breathe!"—but Jesse smiled up at Tim and coughed weakly. He was breathing. He was breathing normally. His cotton pajamas fluttered up and down, a pale blue flag waving from the force of his breath.

Mary Faith held her arms out to take Jesse back, but Tim shifted him and backed into a dingy wing chair. Jesse's head and legs trailed from Tim the way stuffing trailed from the chair.

☾

Mary Faith stood by helplessly. "Croup," she said, feeling again the caked sickness on her arms, its dampness on her blouse. "He spat up. He couldn't breathe."

Tim settled into the armchair, stroking the little boy's forehead and humming "Silent Night." Jesse's eyes darted from Tim to his mother—even sick he knew it wasn't *Christmas*—and then closed magically, all at once. Mary Faith could see his toes relaxing, his legs, his belly. His chest. He was all right.

Tim tapered off his humming. "Sit down, Mary Faith," he said. "You did the right thing to run him out. The change of temperature shocks the breath right back into 'em."

Mary Faith sat, weakly, on the piano bench. "How do you know that?" she said. "How in God's name do you know that? I've been running the shower."

"That's why outside worked. It was cooler than the steam."

"But how'd you know anything about croup?"

Tim smiled. "The baby had croup. Dottie," he said. "My momma used to line us up for croup duty."

Mary Faith clamped her jaw shut at the mention of Dottie's name, at the sight of Jesse falling back into sleep in Tim Rooney's arms. Dottie was the youngest Rooney, the one who'd driven out to the beach to drown herself. Tim had run her outside when she was Jesse's age, chasing away the croup, and Dottie had forgotten how he had saved her. How could Tim bear to say her name like that, with no pause, no choke in his voice, no mention of the irony? Dottie had deserted Tim the same way Jesse's father Michael had deserted her, after she'd tried to give him some comfort. You tried to save someone and he left you in the swamp of his own despair, the muck of it pulling you down.

Mary Faith trembled at the memory of her flight from the house, of the second she thought Jesse had stopped breathing. Was that moment of doubt her own desertion? But no: she could not dream, not for a minute, that she would ever leave this fevered child, not in any sense of the word *leave*. Leaving was the guilt-induced hysteria that had led Michael and her mother and Dottie to pills and cancers and long swims out into the ocean.

She watched her son, limp and pink. Already he slipped away from her: already he eased into sleep, into erasure. Already he had done away with the fear, while she was left shaking on the piano bench. There was a tight-braided bloodrope that stretched from her to Jesse, stronger than the umbilical cord had ever been; and if it chafed her sometimes, if it left her a prisoner in her own

☾

bed at night, still it meant that she would always honor his claims on her. She had managed to get him outside. She took a deep breath.

Tim sat easily, his head settled into the back of the old golden chair, watching her try to calm herself.

"It probably wasn't near as serious as you thought. He was probably just scared."

Mary Faith was sure that he could see her shaking. Oh, it wasn't *near* as serious as she thought. Little boys just choke themselves to death every day of the week.

"I'm sorry to trouble you." She tried to make her voice as cold as a night sky. "If you'll just put him in my arms, we'll go on home now. Dr. Black's coming by at five."

Tim didn't answer, or move to hand over Jesse, but watched her twitching. She couldn't remember ever seeing Tim this still: when she and Jesse were visiting in the afternoons a month ago, Tim jumped from the piano to the guitar to the kitchen for a beer. He was always dangling quotes that were just beyond her reach—if he brushed her breast accidentally, he would mug and say: "Oh my black soul"; and how was she supposed to know who said that? What was it supposed to kindle in her but flames of resentment? He was too bored to stay with one subject, too bored to identify the quote, too bored to play the *Appassionata* all the way through for her. Now he was watchful and quiet.

She couldn't help herself: the idea of Tim Rooney with his wires unplugged made her smile.

"What you laughing at?" He grinned back, and looked more like himself.

"Nothing," she said.

He grinned wider. "You walk in here after three weeks—"

"A month."

"Three weeks, and you expect me to save you and your son and then you laugh at how I look holding him."

"You look still, Tim. You look peaceful, holding him." She knew she was smiling wider.

Tim managed to shrug.

"I'll probably have to wait for the next crisis to see him. I might as well hold him while I've got him."

☾

She couldn't *believe* he could turn the situation inside out like that. *"I haven't been keeping him from you,"* she said.

But he didn't answer: he watched her, and waited.

So she let her eyes wander, buying time before Tim started up again. The Rooney living room was not like any Due East living room Mary Faith knew; the Rapple parlor was probably as stuffed with old furniture as this one, but her mother had never let theirs go this shabby. The Rapples didn't have bald spots in their rugs, or a plastic armchair sitting next to the frayed wing chair. Years before, Tim's mother had put some old gilt-framed prints on the far wall; they would have been almost elegant if it weren't for their religious fervor— the Book of Kells, Tim said. It was a real Rooney touch, prints scissored out of a book of cheap reproductions and then gussied up in golden frames.

The piano took up the back half of the room: Tim's mother had bought him a Steinway baby grand one year when the father made a big real estate killing. She gave the rest of the money away to some Indian reservation schools, Tim said, when his father wanted a new car. Just gave it away. It was a schizoid room, and there was no wonder that a schizophrenic had been bred there.

"I better get on home," Mary Faith said finally. "I have to get him some aspirin until the doctor comes."

"He's cooling off," Tim said. "Let him sleep. You go on up and wash—get yourself a clean shirt from my dresser."

Mary Faith hesitated, then walked over to lay a hand on Jesse's arms. They *were* cooler. And Tim was holding him with an older brother's authority. "I'll just be a minute," she said.

She didn't need directions from Tim: she'd chased Jesse through this whole house in the winter. Now she made her way up the bare back stairway and along a corridor of Sacred Hearts and framed snapshots of Rooneys. When she pushed open the bathroom door, sunlight streamed down on her through the narrow window. Paint peeled around the frame, but the windows glistened clean, and the chipped white tiles were scrubbed and waxed. No scum or dustballs in this bathroom. It annoyed her that Tim kept immaculate house for his father: there was something womanish about the scoured tub and sink. He *would* be a good monk.

She lathered her arms up and washed them with a thick clean washcloth from the wicker shelf, imagining Tim laundering the linen and fluffing it out.

☾

What was he *doing* here, in an old man's house? Her blouse was stuck to her chest like a gummed label and she peeled it off slowly, listening for Jesse. Not a sound from below: so there was time to really wash. She soaped her breasts and rinsed them languorously, a weary female intruder in this bathroom shared by men.

Then, damp and smelling of cheap scented soap, she wrapped a towel around her nakedness and crept down the hallway to Tim's closed bedroom door, waiting for him to sneak up on her as she stood half clothed and still shaky with worry for Jesse. She entered quickly, but only Tim's unmade bed faced her. At least he kept *some* disorder for himself: the floor was strewn with magazines and papers. She stopped still, aching to rifle through the magazines and discover what Tim did with his long days, but Jesse was waiting downstairs. It was a clean shirt she'd come for.

She made her way through the dim room to the old double dresser, scratched with initials left over from the days Tim had shared this bedroom with a brother: BVM was gouged into the pine on top, and underneath, lightly scratched, Timothy Michael Joseph Rooney. It gave her the willies. She felt the towel slipping and her cheeks flushing when she opened the top drawer and found graying underwear; men's underwear had always meant her father's old boxer shorts, the elastic wearing out. She'd never even had the pleasure of doing a load of wash for Stephen.

Tim's T-shirts were in the next drawer, underneath, crammed in with old flannel shirts and worn sweaters. She pulled one out and grinned at the sight of it—U.S. Out of Central America, it said, red letters on a black background. It was a T-shirt that had never been worn. Even on his way to the trestle and fishing, Tim wore an unpressed button-down professor's shirt with a pair of baggy corduroys. She couldn't imagine him in a T-shirt, even when the weather turned sticky. She couldn't imagine him in gray underwear.

She took up another T-shirt: War Resisters League in spartan print, the black ink still vivid and unwashed. Did he get these shirts from Eileen Connelly and stash them away for another life? She pulled on the War Resisters shirt and looked around for a mirror—Tim would be sure to comment loud and long if her bare breasts showed through the thin white cotton—but there was no glass to see her reflection. She listened again at the door: still no sound from below. There was no time to look through the papers, not with Jesse needing a drink and a cover downstairs, but now that she had this monk's cell to herself she didn't want to leave it. She would just peek out his window, to see what Tim looked out on when he bothered to view the outside world.

The old plaid curtains, little boys' curtains hanging on rings, were pulled almost straight across the double windows, but she circled the bed and lifted one aside to see her own house across the side yards. Her family's pecan tree stretched out in a graceful Y, and between the two big branches was a clear view of Jesse's bedroom windows. At night, with the lights on, Tim would be able to see her wrestling her son into his pajamas. She let the curtain droop back down to cover the sunlight and felt a twinge of guilt: if Tim *was* a spy, she was the counterspy. She skipped away from his bed and shut the door tight.

Downstairs, Tim and Jesse were still intertwined, but Tim had closed his eyes and his chest heaved up and down in rhythm with her son's. She stood in the doorway watching them, wishing that she could sleep too, that she could blank out Jesse's sickness for just one hour of this long day. But Tim blinked his eyes open and yawned: no rest for the weary.

"You look scrubbed clean," he said. Nothing about her nipples showing through the white shirt.

She stood awkwardly again. If she insisted on taking Jesse home, he might wake, the cough might start up again. She pictured the steam running in the downstairs bathroom, and she pictured herself, solitary, holding her choking son.

"Stay awhile," Tim said.

So she sat cross-legged on the rug next to Tim's chair and leaned back against it, feeling the cricks that had twisted into place the night before, in Jesse's narrow bed. But sitting silent next to Tim, after all the weeks of silence, was unbearable.

Finally she said: "Jesse looked so helpless, spitting up." At least Tim couldn't see her face; she was sure she was wearing a dusty powder of panic. "It was like watching him when he was a baby."

"You had to deal with that ole baby mess again," Tim answered. She could *hear* him smiling.

She smiled, too, and one of Stephen's phrases flashed bright: "Inter faeces et urinam nascimur," she said. We're born between the piss and the shit. Stephen had been watching her unload a tub of Jesse's nighttime diapers and she had glowed with pleasure that he did not need to translate for her.

☾

"Mary Faith!" Tim feigned indignation.

She should have known not to let one of Stephen's lines slip from her lips. "I won the state Latin award," she said, knowing she sounded prim. "Sophomore year."

"They never taught you *that* at Due East High School," he said, and laughed as raucously as he could, holding a sick and hurting child. She imagined he'd keep needling her about Stephen, but instead he said: "My wife was a Latin scholar. Lord save us. A Medievalist."

Mary Faith was careful not to turn around, careful not to let him see her face. Tim never talked about his wife—he'd been in his twenties. She'd never heard a word about the marriage until Eileen Connelly dug up that ground.

"Well," she said finally, *"I'*m not a Latin scholar anymore."

"And why not, Miss Rapple? Why are you giving up all the hard things?"

Hard things: as if physics and astronomy and advanced calculus were not enough to keep her amused. She *did* miss the Latin, she *did* wish she'd been able to work the Existentialism seminar into her night classes so she could conduct a conversation with Tim that did not involve his complete condescension, but she was already a year behind, and you had to choose: she still didn't have the vaguest notion of what an electrical engineer *did* all day, but she was sponging up the physics and the calculus. It came easily to her; her first year at night school, she had discovered that she could watch her son in the playground and prove the convergence of a series at the same time. Now she was at the stage where she could imagine understanding relativity—and if she could get to that point studying part-time at the Due East branch of the university, she could manage electrical engineering, however plodding it might be.

Once she'd pictured herself curled around the Great Books for four years; now she was curled up around her son in the cave next door, a cave where she might as well have been entombed for the past three days, as far as Tim Rooney was concerned. So she'd given up Latin. She gave up the idea of a dormitory in Harvard Yard or even Chapel Hill the day her drugstore pregnancy test ringed positive in its tube; she gave up the idea of trying for a scholarship at MIT—even though she'd hit 779 on the math SATs, twenty-one points shy of perfect—when Stephen said Marygail would never in a million years let Maureen that far away from her.

So she gave up things. She gave up nights of sleep, too. This was what Tim

((

always came back to: telling her how to run her life. As if *he*'d been pregnant in graduate school. Her anger brimmed.

"Why'd your wife the Latin scholar leave you?"

Tim answered with silence.

Why did she let herself get so peeved at him? After all these weeks he was beside her, holding her son, saving her from her solitude, and she'd let him needle her into an anger she felt no desire of possessing. She swiveled around— she could make *some* sort of apology, put a hand on his knee—and saw that he was watching her with the same intensity that blazed when he was about to give her a moral lecture.

She shriveled back, waiting for it, and watched him narrow his eyes and take in his breath.

"My wife left me because I had an almost uncontrollable urge to beat her."

She almost laughed from the relief of it. He looked dead serious, too. "Oh, Tim," she said. "I thought y'all lived together for six days."

He was watching her with that uncanny focus that could have meant madness or contempt or wait-'til-you-hear-this-one. She remembered her father's words in the first weeks she'd known Tim—"He's crazy in love with you, honey"—and suddenly she thought: He is. He's warning me off. He's pretending to be a monster.

But Tim danced his eyes to laughing, rolled them as if they were shoes sliding across a polished floor, and grinned and said:

"She'd finished her dissertation. She'd *defended* it, for Christ's sake, and every time I sat down at the typewriter she came in and ruffled the hair at the back of my neck."

"But you didn't beat her."

"No, my dear. I said I had an *urge*. The day she walked out on me, I was tripping and I decided it would be fun to tie her up."

"You tied her up when you were on drugs?" Sweet Jesus, what did she sound like to him? Like somebody who'd been buried in Due East all her life, somebody who'd missed a whole world of drugs and wife-beating. Someone who couldn't figure out how Tim seemed to know all her secrets, from Stephen's giving her the Pascal to Stephen's tying her up.

How could Tim *possibly* know? —It was a year ago already: it was the last time they were naked at the beach, before Stephen had moved them indoors forever. Stephen had dragged his pants off slowly, and she had looked away;

☾

even in the dark, he was a startling white, and his loose skinny belly almost repulsed her. Someone had left a long piece of rope behind on the damp sand, and while Stephen peeled his socks off, she reached over to fondle it absently. It was coarse on her fingertips, thick and moist; when she handed it to him and whispered that he should tie her hands back with it, her voice was as high and fluttery as a little girl's. He smiled, almost solemnly, and stretched her out on the damp sand. He tied her hands up high over her head: when he kneeled over her, he held his white belly tight, and she no longer felt the need to avert her eyes.

But how could Tim know that she'd asked Stephen to do that? How could he know how delicious it had been, to pretend she had no will, to let Stephen pretend that he was forcing himself on her, that she was no party to his hungry sucking at her breasts? Afterwards he'd been so tender that she'd imagined a whole future of ropes and belts and giving up. But two nights later, he'd suggested the couch in the *Courier* office, where there were no fat abandoned strands of rope, where they made love on a Naugahyde couch under a silk palm tree. No wonder passion dwindled.

"Thank your lucky stars, Mary Faith, that you didn't live through the days when newlyweds dropped a tab and a half of acid and went to work on their dissertations."

So it was a joke? She didn't know whether to smile up at him or grab Jesse from his arms and flee back down the route that brought her here. Tim looked *serious* suddenly: he was playing back the memory. This was like Jesse's sickness, starting out as a cold and congesting itself into trouble.

"I was sitting at the typewriter, *way* beyond reason. I was meditating on my favorite line: 'Faith begins precisely where thought stops.' " He laughed shortly. "Thought had surely stopped on my part. One minute I was in ecstatic union with the East-West Jesus-Buddha Wildflower-God-of-the-Sixties and the next minute I was trying to remember all my Boy Scout knots."

He was still waiting for her to react.

"She did not have the same sexual proclivities. She was not amused."

What did he want her to say: that those were *her* sexual proclivities?

"Anyway, she didn't like all the drugs. I got weepy tripping—women hate weepy men. She didn't mind getting a doctorate out of visionaries, but she didn't want to spend her life with one. She had the sense to get out, honey lamb."

☾

HONEY LAMB? Her own father had never called her honey lamb. Tim's face looked childlike—he had flushed with that line about women hating weepy men—and suddenly she could imagine his breakdown. She could imagine him in Due East Memorial, holding in his guilt, waiting to make his confession until he had taken the right wide-eyed girl prisoner. Her father was right: he was watching her with a mad passion. He had chosen her—her braid and her son and the loneliness that drove her next door—and she was not about to be chosen. She could honor Jesse's claims. Tim's claims she'd just as soon flush down the toilet.

"You are some whited sepulchre, Tim." She knew she was hissing the words more than saying them. He had reduced her to quoting *Scripture.* "Listen to you, condemning me for marrying Stephen and then telling me tales from God knows how long ago. I have no interest in that part of your life whatsoever."

"I beg your pardon, Miss Rapple. I thought you asked."

He smiled ironically again. He flustered her completely: she *had* asked. And if she hadn't asked, he'd still be sweet crazy Tim and she could have let him hold her son all afternoon while she rested at his feet.

"All right," she said. "All right, I asked. But I just don't want to *hear* about you—"

Suddenly she was aware of another presence in the room; a shadow crossed her back. She whirled her head around to see an ancient slip of a black woman making her way into the living room. She'd seen the woman before, limping down O'Connor Street on her way to a housecleaning job, carrying a cudgel to ward off the dogs who made a career of barking at garbagemen and maids.

"Hey Lily," Tim said. He had switched off his this-is-my-sordid-past routine and now he was master of the plantation, leaning back in his chair and smiling indulgently at the old woman. Mary Faith had never heard the front door turn open. She felt as if she'd taken a tab and a half of acid herself, watching this scene.

"Hey youself," the woman said. She walked woodenly, her gnarled shoulders hunched forward, and her hair floated above her, a translucent halo as white as her name.

"Lily Lightsey, this is Mary Faith Rapple. And the sleeping one's her baby Jesse."

"How-do," the woman mumbled, still progressing forward. Her face betrayed no expression.

☾

Mary Faith murmured hello, trying to reason out the presence of an old black woman in the Rooney living room. Years before, her own father had hired a maid to help her sick mother with the bathroom and the kitchen and the laundry. The woman had been as dour as Faith Rapple and the two of them outdid each other, shooing Mary Faith off the newly waxed floors. Faith had ended up accusing the woman of taking a silver teaspoon—they found it later in the refrigerator, in an iced-tea glass.

But this woman wouldn't be a *maid:* not in the Rooney household. Dolores Rooney, first white member of the Due East NAACP, must have spent a lifetime working to get black women out of white women's kitchens.

"Where you going, Lily?" Tim asked. She was almost up to them and looked as if she might hobble right up to them, and through them, and past them.

Lily stopped and put a hand on her hip and grinned at Tim—she made contact with *him,* all right. "I be aiming to start in here," she said, only she said *hi-uh* in a Charleston accent, and she laughed at Tim in a light high tinkle that took Mary Faith by surprise.

Tim said: "Oh, all right. C'mon, Mary Faith," and rose with Jesse. He was already passing through the dining room to the swinging kitchen door, and there was nothing to do but follow him. Jesse was twitching in his arms, but still asleep, and in the kitchen Tim pulled out a chair as if he planned to hold Jesse all day. As if his I-Want-to-Tie-Women-Up Confession had not been interrupted by what might as well have been another vision.

"Wait," Mary Faith said, and tugged her son from behind.

"What you doing?"

"I'm taking Jesse," she said. It was like loosening Jesse from plastic wrapping, Tim clung to him so. She thought she might pop him free, but Tim held tight, and Jesse stirred, and finally she threw up her arms in defeat.

"Sit down, Mary Faith. Stay 'til he wakes up on his own."

"I've got to get going." She pointed a finger toward the living room. "What is that woman *doing* in there?"

Tim affected puzzlement. "She's cleaning the house."

"She's been walking down O'Connor Street to clean *your* house?"

"For forty-odd years."

"She cleans your bathrooms?"

☾

Now Tim hooted with utter disregard for the sleeping boy in his arms. "Don't worry. We pay her."

Mary Faith pictured the white tiles upstairs and sat down across from Tim. She had been *sure* that Tim got down on his hands and knees to scrub that floor. She had been *sure* Tim kept house for his father.

Tim tipped his chair back, holding Jesse tight with one hand while he used the other to reach into the refrigerator for a beer.

"I guess I don't know so much about you," she said.

"No," Tim said. "You want a beer?"

"I never thought your family would have a maid."

Tim shrugged. "We didn't have a *mammy* or anything."

She watched him chugging his beer. She had to get Jesse out of his arms and back home, but Tim was watching her out of the corner of his eye, waiting to see if she'd resume the living room conversation: if she'd bring up his Confession. She'd be damned.

Tim put his beer down. "Look. You and Stephen going ahead with a July wedding?"

She was taken aback and shook her head in circles, yes and no at once. She should have known he'd turn things around. If she told him right out that the wedding was postponed, he'd grin knowingly. She'd rather go back to the sordid details of his marriage.

"You been to see Father Berkeley?"

Now she shook her head *no* vigorously. Even if Stephen could convince the Pope himself that his ten-year-old marriage had never really existed, even if his whole history with Marygail were wiped from the records of the Catholic Church forever, she had no intention of being married by a priest.

"You know," Tim said, "Becky Perdue called me to ask after you."

"Who's Becky Perdue?"

"The pretty drunk lady from the convert class."

"Why was she calling about me?" Mary Faith felt her color rising. Stephen would not have set some church lady after her. He wouldn't. "Jesus Christ," she said, "there is no such thing as a private act in Due East."

"She wanted to know if you were coming back to the convert class. I told her not to count on it."

"She better not," Mary Faith snorted. "Some lonely housewife with nothing better to do than track down people she saw for five minutes once in her life.

When she was so plastered she couldn't find a chair, much less a reason for converting."

Tim watched her. "How much are you willing to make him go through?" he said softly.

By now Mary Faith was so used to Tim's switching his interrogations on her like this, so used to feeling like a political prisoner just before the torture session, that she almost answered him. But she didn't answer: she stopped herself, and rose from her chair, and lifted Jesse out of his arms. This time Tim did not hang on to the child.

"Are you willing to convert?"

"He's never asked me to convert, Tim, never once!" She whispered it, so Jesse wouldn't wake.

"He's stalling, right?"

Mary Faith felt that she might tip over from the combined weights of Jesse and Tim's question. Her son's presence in her arms was all that stopped her from reaching over and throttling Tim. If only she did not have to cross by Tim's chair to make her way back through the swinging door and the dining room: she did not trust herself to come near him.

"Tim, you have to stop hounding me. I'm marrying Stephen, for Christ's sake. I'm in love with him. All Right? ALL RIGHT?"

Tim smiled sweetly at her and tapped his fingers lightly against the beer bottle. "ALL RIGHT, Mary Faith," he said, and winked—WINKED—at her before she turned around. "I just want you to remember one thing. You may think you're 'in love with him,' but love don't wash over you like a spring tide, little girl. Love is an act of will."

Mary Faith let out a long spray of disgust—LITTLE GIRL—and brushed past him. As she pushed open the swinging door, she saw Jesse shudder, still asleep in her arms. It was a wonder that her quivering did not wake him with a start.

Tim did not call or follow after her. In the living room, Lily Lightsey was hunched over the vacuum cleaner, fiddling with the hose. Mary Faith tried to guess her age: seventy-five? eighty? Tim said Lily needed the job, when any fool could see that what she needed was a retirement check so that she wouldn't have to cope with lazy men's broken-down machines.

"G'bye," Mary Faith said softly, and she heard Lily grunt without raising her head.

☾

"Don't you be letting that crazy boy fool you," Lily Lightsey said, in her soft, high voice; and Mary Faith almost wanted her to repeat it, to make sure she'd heard right. What boy? Jesse? Tim? TIM? But Tim wasn't a boy—he couldn't seem a boy, even to an old woman—any more than she was still a girl. She hesitated, but there was no other word from Lily.

She struggled alone with the screen door and kicked it closed behind her. She could feel her son sliding down, down her chest, and she shifted him up higher, listening to him breathe. The rasping was gone now, and she made her way slowly and heavily across her own front yard.

All afternoon Tim's reprimand echoed in her own dark house: love is an act of will. Was she supposed to recognize the author of *that,* too? Did Tim think that the idea had never occurred to her before?

Jesse was awake, watching cartoons in the den, his fever at bay and his cough looser. It was still half an hour before Dr. Black would come. She couldn't bear to imagine the doctor hearing water in Jesse's lungs, and she couldn't bear the scraping screeching noises of the cartoons, and she couldn't bear to hover over her son. So she hovered over the kitchen phone instead, holding herself back from calling Stephen again.

She had tried phoning him at the *Courier* office three times already—it was reckless, but the knowing little honey-voiced receptionist wouldn't tell her where he was—and in her longing to share her outrage with him, to have Stephen reassure her that Jesse was really all right, she heard the other half of what Tim had said: love doesn't wash over you like a spring tide.

But that was where Tim was wrong. Love was an act of will *and* it washed over her. It had washed over Stephen, too. Standing at the telephone, ready to try him again, she called back a picture of Stephen watching her lift her dress over her naked pregnant belly. She couldn't recollect his face, but she remembered his pale sinewy arms, rigid with wanting her. She could hear the choke in his throat, too, the way he'd struggled to control his breathing.

Finally she dialed warily—one last try—ready to hang up the receiver if she heard the receptionist's voice again. But he answered the call himself: "Stephen Dugan."

His good deep voice poured over her. There was none of Tim's snideness in his tone—and if there was a weariness, that was no wonder: he'd been running around, out of the office all day.

☾

"Slow down, Mary Faith," he said. "Slow down. Tell me about Tim later. Tell me about Jesse first."

So she did, starting with the long night before and working her way through the run to Tim's house. "Tim *helped,*" she said. "I don't want to make it sound like he wasn't good to Jesse. But Stephen, I can't bear it anymore. He won't lay off about you and me. He doesn't believe we're getting married."

"Well," Stephen said, and then there was a long pause. The quiet at the other end of the line was so very still that Mary Faith found herself darting her eyes around her father's kitchen. She knew that she was planning how she would put new curtains up, new pictures of Jesse on the wall, if she didn't marry Stephen soon. If there was a longer wait than she had planned.

"When's your father coming home?" Stephen said, finally.

"He's trying to get here by five, to talk to the doctor."

"I can't see you two tonight, then."

She stopped scanning the kitchen walls. "I guess not."

"I miss you, Mary Faith." His voice was dim, and tired, and he didn't really sound as if he *meant* the words. Still, her whole body eased. She had lived this way for three years. She could wait a few more months.

"Maybe tomorrow?" she said.

"I'll drop by in the morning. I'll bring Jesse a book."

"I miss *you,* Stephen," she said. A year ago, she would have said: I want you, Stephen, but now there were whole weeks when they didn't make love, and her body didn't strain for him the way it once did. The way it had the night she'd asked him to tie her up.

"I miss you, Stephen," she said again. She might as well have been calling from outer space.

Dr. Black said she'd been at least half right about Jesse's sickness: it wasn't just a little night croup. The cold was moving down from the little boy's throat to his chest; he had a bad bronchitis now. They'd have to get him on antibiotics, and keep him still—"Oh, sure," Mary Faith said—and pour as much juice down him as he could swallow. He'd be at least another three days in the house, the doctor said, and then they'd get him out in the sunshine and burn off whatever was left in his bronchial tubes.

She stayed beside Jesse while he fell asleep, holding his foot and watching the light fading outside. Her father had gone to get the prescription filled: she

☾

almost wished *Wheel of Fortune* were blaring out from the den below. Jesse's quietness would last while the fever burned, and the rooms of the house would once more form tunnels around her. While he was getting better, he would fret, anxious and rowdy, and Stephen would only be able to look in on them every few days.

A light went on across the yards, and Mary Faith remembered peeking out of Tim's plaid curtains. The afternoon seemed a week away.

She let go of Jesse's foot and leaned her head back against the wall. Someone —Lily?—had pulled Tim's curtains wide open, and she could see straight into his room. The overhead light was glaring, and the shadow of Tim's back looked naked through his screen. She imagined him sifting through the stacks of papers from the floor, and though she could hear Jesse breathing deeply in sleep, she lay still, watching Tim.

After a minute the shadow formed stark silhouette. Her eyes adjusted and she could see Tim clearly: he was not alone. He was no longer standing with his back to her—now he stood at the side of his bed with a woman, and the woman was naked. Mary Faith knew, without even seeing her clearly, that it was Eileen Connelly in Tim's bedroom. Her small breasts dangled low on her chest and her wispy hair hung loose, a ball of Spanish moss in the glow of the light.

Mary Faith could not believe that Tim was not putting on this show for her benefit, the way he and his brothers and sisters staged religious pageants in their backyard for the benefit of the whole Protestant neighborhood. She had never even *noticed* Tim's room across the way—never seen more than rows of plaid and floral curtains—in a whole year of putting Jesse to bed. Now he and his girlfriend were putting on a live sex act, and she was the audience.

She rose to leave the room and saw Tim slide his belt out of its loops. Mary Faith pressed herself flat against Jesse's wall and watched Tim twirl Eileen around, arms behind her. He twisted the belt tight around her hands, slowly and meticulously: he *was* staging the show for her, the very night of his confession.

Mary Faith watched him guide Eileen back into profile. He leaned close to kiss her neck and—Mary Faith slid down the wall—pulled Eileen's head back by the ball of hair. They were too far away for her to see an expression on Eileen's face, but the profile let out a long silent moan, and Mary Faith felt in her own shiver the practiced pleasure of it. Eileen's head tipped back farther

☾

and farther until her breasts rose up erect, and Mary Faith ran from her son's room.

She was as directionless as she had been when Jesse was choking: she began to run down the stairs for the kitchen and remembered, halfway down the flight, that Stephen would have left work long ago, that there was no sense trying to call him again. She retraced her steps on the stairs and retreated to her own room, on the other side of the house. She lay down on her own bed, her breath coming in shallow spurts.

There was no erasing the picture of Tim and Eileen. In another second, he would drag his pants off: maybe she *should* have stayed to watch.

She had a sudden desire to run out of the house and stand in the driveway, waiting there to divert her father when he came home clutching the bag of medicines. She couldn't bear the thought of her father looking up the side of the Rooney's house and seeing Tim—with Godknowswhat, whips and chains —and his prisoner.

It was too late for that, though: she heard the scrape of the kitchen door downstairs, and knew her father was back. She roused herself and made her way back downstairs. This time Stephen's line, *Inter faeces et urinam nascimur,* echoed through the cave walls. She wished that she could breathe it out loud to her father, and sigh, and have him understand.

☾

C

18

Letter to My Daughter

DEAR MAUREEN,

I don't think I'm going to *die* or anything, but I've been feeling funny so I had a photograph made and I decided to write out these things so that you would remember who I was, or maybe so *I* would remember who I was. I don't know what's happening, little girl, it's not just you slipping away from my reach and recoiling when I go to touch you, it's every day slipping away from me. I can't get anything done. I lie down on the couch all the time. I look at the same magazines over and over, and sometimes I think I see a shadow crossing behind me, but when I turn around, it was just my imagination. So I try to write a little poem or do a watercolor of the azaleas splashing open all over Due East, but it's hard to keep my attention when the sunlight gets so bright.

I decided some day you might want to know what I was like when I was a girl, whether I was ever different from the momma drinking too many wine coolers every night when the clock strikes five. And once I decided to tell you what I was like back then, the first thing I remembered was the morning I went over to your father's house to tell him I was pregnant with you. Because I was still a girl then. I was.

But your daddy was already old, his skin already looked gray. He was already older than everybody else in graduate school, and I thought it was kind of pathetic for him to be dating a *sophomore*. I never could figure out why I was going out with him—he was a funny-looking guy, always skinny like now and moody sometimes, and shy. He was your Uncle Jake's best friend and he was mad as hell that Jake married my sister when she is such an airhead, so he used to be over at their house all the time, trying to break their marriage up, and smiling a tight smile when Gracie screeched at Jake.

He was always telling jokes. The first day I met him over at Gracie's he said, "What's the shortest verse in the Bible?" and I thought oh no, a Jesus freak, so I said, "Damned if *I* know," and he said: " 'Jesus wept.' By Christ, he must have had some of the same relatives I do." So I laughed and told him my own joke which I don't remember now and he laughed and I rolled him a joint and we got drunk and I went to bed with him about an hour after I met him and then Jesus *really* wept. I guess you better not read this till you're about sixteen, baby!!

The funny thing was, he seemed to have girlfriends floating all over. He had a girlfriend from Due East, but she was living in New York, Miss Career Girl or something I guess. And they had broken up, sort of, but he told me about her—just the way he told me about little Miss Rapple. I guess once he left the Church and didn't have the confessional anymore he thought he could just piss on me whenever he needed a little relief.

Anyway, I can't say I wasn't warned about the girlfriends. And I wasn't serious about him anyway, he liked to do coke with me and back then it was *real* expensive and *real* dangerous and it made him so happy to stay up wired and work all night that I'd just as soon share it with him as one of those asshole Alpha and Omega guys.

The girlfriend from New York was visiting the morning I went over to tell him I was pregnant. I told him right in front of her that I wanted money for an abortion and he had the nerve to say he wouldn't let me get rid of the baby and *now* I remember the joke, I said to him: "Well, *I* have to get up in the morning. *You* don't." And his fat girlfriend was watching me, her hair all weedy down her face, and I burst into tears. Which I never do, as you know. And Maureen, I guess I wasn't going to scrape you out of my womb. I don't know, you just

☾

can't imagine how lonely you feel, the whole world spinning on you and all the dorky Alphas after you for drugs and the father, your father, with these dumpy girlfriends on the side.

And he did the right thing after he knocked me up but it was just this *burden* and this *duty* and I could see he sucked in his breath and went ahead with it because his father'd just died and his girlfriend went back to New York. He was real sweet, and he'd pat my belly and tell me more jokes. That used to drive me really crazy, especially after you were born, his being so kind. He used to come in at six o'clock looking ready to weep from all the claims on him and taking that crappy job with the *Courier* but then if I was blue he'd pick you up out of the crib and tell me to get out of the house and have some fun and he would really try. Really try.

And I wouldn't try at all, buried in Due East. I was just like Scarlett O'Hara —well, I can't help it, we were *raised* on that book—I thought my life was over at twenty. So I got involved with a captain from Parris Island, god, he was a good-looking man, and it wasn't shallow or anything, I mean he had a lot of scars from Vietnam and I knew I was healing him. What really got to me then was the way Stephen just forgave me. After I told him he just put his arms around me and forgave me. He never once hollered and I couldn't stand that freedom to do whatever I wanted, I mean he was asking for it, wasn't he? Asking for the freedom to do whatever *he* wanted. So then there was a lieutenant and so on and so on but I didn't ever move down to enlisted men, I want you to know! Just a little joke.

But couldn't your daddy have said, Don't do that again? or I'll leave you if you do that, no he just acted like it didn't bother him and drank a fifth a night and sometimes disappeared with you. And then one year that goddamned pathetic little slut who drove her *boyfriend* to suicide came around here whimpering for help and now what have I got? What have I got, Maureen?

I said to him, Please stay with us. For the first time I said that, the night after he took you out to Claire's Point to see where they're going to make the movie. I said, Please stay. It's getting better. Please give her up, and stay with me and Maureen. And you know what he said? He said, "Well."

Well well well. Well what about us? What about me? I don't want any Marine lieutenants or captains anymore, I don't want to do makeup for the Little Theatre anymore, I don't want to write these stupid crappy little poems anymore, I don't want to lie here on the couch writing words you can't ever

☾

read, I don't want these shadows to pass over me and this chill, I don't want it, I don't want it. Last night in the breeze that live oak out back was whispering and I thought it was calling my name. I'm hearing my name in the trees and I'm trying not to drink before five o'clock, I am trying, but do you want me to have the screaming heebiejeebies? Do you want me to start tripping without the acid? Do you remember the time you told me you saw yourself driving another car down the Savannah Highway? Do you want me to start seeing visions too? Do you, Stephen? If you would just stay with us, if you would just forgive me, really forgive me this time for those Marines I would forgive you anything, even that other little family of yours, I would forget they ever walked the face of the earth. I would go to your church, I swear it, I would name every one of those affairs to the priest, I would, I would, I would go back to school, I would learn *Italian* again, I would read your dissertation, I would do anything. But don't leave me alone at night like this, when you go out with that producer. Don't leave me with the breeze and the live oaks and the shadows falling quicker and quicker until I'm afraid they're falling down on me and choking me and calling out my poor miserable name. Don't leave me alone in the dark. The moss is moving out there in the funniest way, like i was little creatures hanging from the trees. Little babies, dangling from the oa branches, trying to catch their breath. Don't leave me alone with those litt babies. Don't leave me alone.

(

☾

19

State of Shock

WHEN JACK FINALLY GOT AROUND TO TELLing me that he wanted custody of my children, I said—more to myself than to him—"I haven't felt this numb since Daddy died."

I was out front feeding the azaleas and the roses when Jack pulled up with the week's money. Judi-with-an-i was with him, but she stayed behind in the car. From across the yard I could see her red hair shining in the sunlight, as high and fluffy as cotton candy.

Jack had never brought Judi by the house, and if seeing her hair flaming in his car hadn't told me something was wrong, I would have known from the guilty way he crept up toward me. I was a sight: my hair was sprouting out of its braid, weedier than my front lawn, and I was wearing a pair of Ethan's jeans, the legs rolled up and the waist slipping down my belly. I had looked that unkempt since a week ago, when I'd called Tim Rooney and pretended I was asking about Mary Faith Rapple. He'd sounded sweet and distant and unaware that he'd ever made a move in my direction—so it didn't matter that my hair was unwashed, or that I'd taken to wearing my sons' clothing.

"Becky, I got the money," Jack said; so I put down the hose and wiped my hand on Ethan's back pocket.

"I've got some news, too," he said. Those were the very words my mother used when she called me up about my brother's being missing in Vietnam. "I've got some news," she said. It never even occurred to her to say, "I've got some *bad* news." So when Jack used the selfsame sentence, I thought that something had happened to one of my children. I wiped my hand again and again against Ethan's back pocket, waiting for the blow.

"I know this is going to be a bad surprise," Jack said, and cast his eyes down while he made his voice low and mournful. "I told Lamarr I want custody of the chidrun." Lamarr Fisher was his lawyer: he'd been my lawyer too, five months before.

I watched Judi's red cotton candy hair bobbing in the shaft of light that had opened up in Jack's car. "The word is not *chidrun,*" I said. By now my hand was in a fist.

"Rebecca, do you understand what I'm telling you?"

I stared down at the fat spray bottle of Miracle-Gro solution for a long while, and then I finally looked my husband in the eye and shoved my hands in my son's pockets. That was when I said: "I haven't felt this numb since Daddy died."

In 1969, the year my boys were born and my brother was taken prisoner and my father died, I didn't think I could sustain any more shocks to my system. Every night I nursed Jack and then Ethan and sang them the song my father sang when he was drunk and maudlin:

> If I had the wings of an angel
> O'er these prison walls I would fly

Then, when the boys were asleep and their father was busy flossing his teeth in his painstaking way, I would slip out the back door of the River House and walk barefoot through the damp grass down to the river's edge. Sometimes, without even knowing I was doing it, I skated a foot back and forth against the low tabby seawall, stabbing deeper at my sole with each sliding motion. I looked down at my bloodied foot in wonder: I didn't know why I couldn't feel my sole, and I didn't know why I couldn't cry.

☾

My feet grew calluses that year, and my heart grew calluses, too. By the time my mother settled herself in a gray fog and spent her days sitting and staring out, I wasn't concerned about shocks to my system anymore. I had my babies to care for, and now I had my mother to care for, too.

Besides, I knew what burden of grief *she* carried. My mother had betrayed my father twice: she signed the papers for Billy to join the Marines when he was seventeen and my father said he'd never stand for a Marine in the family; and then she stood by without a word when the MPs came to the house and dragged my father off, drunk and hollering that he didn't have anything against those Vietcong. He'd heard Muhammad Ali say the same thing on the television news. He'd never had politics in his life, but he'd started to pay attention when he was on leave and Dolores Rooney handed out War Resisters pamphlets after the twelve-thirty mass. He was scared, scared like a baby, and he wanted my mother to hide him out.

But my mother was scared, too. Daddy was a forty-seven-year-old man with no other trade but the Navy. He'd gone AWOL from his home port, which was Jacksonville then, and sent the fear of the Lord into my mother when he showed up in Due East.

I even thought that she might have tipped off the MPs, though it didn't take much of a military brain to figure out where Daddy might be laying low. He went AWOL on Friday night, and they came for him Monday morning. He only served a couple of weeks in the brig, and then sailed off to Haiphong to mine the harbor there. He got word that Billy was missing the third week into his tour, before he'd ever had the time and the inclination to forgive his son, and six weeks later he was dead himself.

My mother was sure that Billy was dead, too, that he'd left her just as sure as my father had, and she didn't know how to mourn them. She was left with a pension and free medical care at the naval station, and about a month after Daddy's ship was hit she started going to the Navy doctors. First she complained of headaches and then, when she was driving there every other day, dizziness. Soon she couldn't get herself to the naval station at all. I had to drive by her house on Lady's Island, laying my babies like cartons of eggs on the back seat of the car and crawling at twenty miles an hour, to make sure she got at least one meal a day. She never said, "I blame myself" or "I could have saved him." She only stopped talking, and looked at the twins as if they were two gooey pecan pies I'd brought to set out on the table.

☾

My brothers Michael and Kevin had settled in Charleston, but even if they'd lived closer I knew I would have been the one seeing to my mother every day. We'd none of us ever been very close to her. She wasn't humorless, exactly, but she was hard-working, and she didn't like to chatter. When we were children, her first chore every day was to get us all out of the house, so we wouldn't mess it up; and once that was accomplished, she was happy to piddle around, dusting and scraping vegetables that would stew all day and fill the house with a rich dank smell. If my brothers got too wild, she waved a carving knife around the kitchen, though it never occurred to any of us that she was threatening to use it. By the time I was ten or so, she seemed as unrelated to me as a Mother Superior is to the novices in a cloister. If I asked to have friends over, she always said no, there was too much cleaning to be done; then, an hour or two later, she'd call me in to say she'd changed her mind, and she'd push my bangs back out of my eyes.

It was Billy who really made her laugh. He was a skinny little blond runt, full of the devil; he used to come up behind her and pinch her backside until she shook her head with laughter and frustration. If she was in a temper about my father's drinking, Billy would tell her a string of terrible knock-knock jokes and elephant jokes and even dead baby jokes, and she would smile in spite of herself: Knock knock. Who's there? Dwayne. Dwayne who? Dwayne the bathtub, I'm dwowning. Billy had choked purple once, when he was three and had asthma, and she'd held him and massaged him and pounded his chest until the ambulance got across the bridge.

So after Billy was gone, and my father with him, my mother stopped talking at all. She went a whole week without answering a single question I put to her, and I begged Father Berkeley to go see her.

Father had her talking five minutes after he stepped foot in the house. "I'm sick to death of your church," she told him, and ranted on about the Pope, the way she must have been taught to when she was growing up Methodist. She had always been shy and reverent around Father, who'd given her convert lessons himself; now she said she wouldn't have anything to do with a church ruled from Rome and she wouldn't have anything to do with a god whose sport was tormenting people. What about Abraham, she said, being asked to sacrifice his own son? Was it a God of Comfort who asked Abraham to climb that mountain? Either there was no god at all, she told Father Berkeley, or the God running the universe set up the Pope and the bishops and the parish priests

☾

right comfy and didn't give a thought to the sorrow of mothers. Father began to speak of the Sorrowful Mysteries, and she told him she'd run a knife through his chest if he drove up in the front yard again.

But at least Father got her talking, and for a while she seemed to be functioning. She dressed herself in the morning, and she picked at the food I brought her. She let out little sighs that sounded strangely familiar to me, and one day I realized that they were the same little sighs I'd heard wafting from her bedroom when my father was out carousing.

I got Kevin and Michael to come down to Due East when she started talking to Daddy as if he were there. Jack said she was having visions, but I never believed she was hallucinating: she was more like a child with an imaginary playmate. Her pleasure was to pretend that he was sitting slouched over the kitchen table, drunk again, and to holler at him about girlfriends and never being home and the drool that slid down his chin. At first it seemed like an improvement over the silence, but after a time she got worked up in her talks with him, and started bringing out the carving knives to threaten him. I couldn't have the babies around that, and I thought that one day she might turn a knife on herself, so I called my brothers down and we had her committed to the state hospital in Columbia.

I was the one who admitted her. After the big steel door on the locked ward clanged shut, I was filled with such a sinking guilt that I wanted to change my mind, but Jack said no, she had to have treatment—besides, she was committed by court order now—and my brothers agreed. I suppose I stood by and let the state take her the same way she'd let the Navy take my father.

She was only three weeks on the locked ward: I think seeing people who were really crazy gave her the will to be sane. That and Thorazine, maybe. When they released her, the doctors told her she'd have to take the drug for the rest of her life, and she did stay on it for a good long while—until they told us that Billy was alive, in a prison somewhere in the North. She was so crazy happy at the news that she flushed all her pills down the toilet, and she even went back to the Church to say prayers of thanksgiving. She acted like a normal grandmother for the better part of a year.

Maybe it was the waiting for Billy to be released that sent her spinning again, or maybe it was the imagining what was happening to him. She drove herself up to the state hospital the second time and signed herself in. She stayed three weeks again, and then one night—a Friday night, the night before I was

☾

supposed to drive up to see her—she lost control. The nurses told me later that she lay down on the floor and lifted her nightgown, imagining that she was giving birth, and she cursed my father and God and the imaginary child. The other patients all skittered out of the way of her fragile white-skinned naked-ness, and the nurses called for a doctor to come change her medication, but somewhere between the time she lifted her nightgown and the time the doctors got there, she suffered a heart attack. Nobody recognized it: they all thought the gasping for air was part of her crazy labor. I remember talking on the phone to the psychiatrist from Columbia as if I'd been expecting her dying, when I hadn't been expecting it at all; and I remember thinking that she'd change her mind in an hour, and call me in, and brush the bangs out of my eyes.

I had let the state of South Carolina care for my mother in a hospital where she didn't even have the comfort of the marsh to look at, and I had worshiped a God who gave and took back the gift of reason with utter indifference. I put away my rosary beads, and I quit the Church, and I was sure for a while that I would lose my own reason. Jack told me over and over that it wasn't my fault, that it was Momma's sin to leave me, not my sin. His voice grew sterner each time he told me not to blame myself, and I could see that he was frightened I'd sink into the same grayness my mother had sunk into. Even when I tried to picture Billy, skinny and hurting but *alive,* as alive as my parents were dead, I couldn't bear any more of Jack's preaching to me. My husband's words made me despise him—men are always trying to hide guilt away, always trying to kick it under the bed like an old pair of slippers—and after a time the only comfort I could imagine was having a daughter. I thought that I could really talk to a daughter, not just watch her tumble out of the house the way I watched Jack and Ethan, not just tune her out the way I did Jack. If I had a daughter, I thought, I would let her have her friends over seven days a week.

"Becky, I *know* it's a shock." Jack was using a voice he'd practiced for twenty years of marriage, a definite sensible voice: he'd talked himself into believing that what he was doing was right. "The girls need more attention," he was saying. "We can give them that attention, while you're getting on your feet."

I looked down at those feet I would be getting on.

"Becky, say something to me. *React,* at least."

☾

I reacted: I stared at my feet some more. In those early years, when Jack berated me for my guilt over my mother, I had learned to stare at my feet for long hours on end. Back then, I was angry at Jack for so long—for his logic and his wanting to return to normalcy, when nothing would ever be normal or logical for me again—that it didn't seem possible that I would ever have another child. Now I let my eyes wander beyond my feet, out over the grass coming in lush and weedy, and tried to remember wanting Cecelia.

Cecelia was the easiest of all the babies, and the smartest: she pretty much taught herself to read by the time she was four, and when she came to me with the poems and the prayers she'd written I thought I'd given birth to a little girl who'd be attentive to all the things I'd put aside. I framed one of the drawings of the Blessed Mother she did in second-grade catechism, and hung it in the kitchen where it berated me for my own disbelief. Over Mary she had drawn a floating banner with the words: "Oh, Mary, For Joy, For Joy." I looked at it twenty times a day, every time I washed a dish or scraped a carrot into the sink or remembered my mother giving up control like that, and I hoped it would work on me like a magic charm.

But Cecelia didn't know I looked at her drawing twenty times a day. Claire had been born when she was still in diapers, and she resented every minute I gave to her little sister: she knew how to stiffen her shoulders and stare beyond me when I tried to make up a slight. I was always tired with the four of them needing so much from me, the four of them not knowing how I resented every grandparent living and breathing in Due East, and sometimes I spoke to Cecelia with the same sharp despair that prisoners must feel when they hear their sentences called out. My sentence was to care for these four lovely little ones, four little bubbles of light, and watch myself fade and shrink, bleaker than my gray mother had ever been.

One year—the same year she changed her name to Sissy—I saw all at once what a wild streak Cecelia had. I caught her doing a striptease in front of her brothers, who were ten already and shamed by the way she liked to sneak up on them in their baths, and I smacked her right on the side of her narrow spiteful face. It was the only time I ever hit her, and she never let me forget it. She took to prissing around the boys at school, and I could see her resentment festering into the same despising for me that I had once felt for her father.

It was bad between us for a long time—there were days when we didn't exchange more than two sentences—but still I thought I could reclaim her.

☾

One night last year, when the rest of the family was out shopping for a Halloween party, I went into Sissy's room to make her a present of my mother's picture. She was growing to resemble my mother, with her Roman nose and her high cheekbones, and God knows Sissy had heard little enough about her grandmother: I didn't want the children to know she'd died in the state hospital.

So I went to the jewelers for a narrow silver frame I thought Sissy would like, and wrapped up my present, and waited for a minute when Nippie wasn't around. I knocked on her door the minute Jack's car left the driveway.

She called out "What" in that flat bored voice that makes a mother wonder why she ever went through childbirth, and when I turned the handle of her door the stench of cigarettes rolled out into the hallway. I decided to ignore the smell, and I handed her the ribboned package without a word. She grinned and unwrapped it in a rush—I could see that she wanted to be pleased—and then she stared at my mother's image, blankly. We were both so consumed with puzzlement and embarrassment that I wanted to fill up the silence between us, so all in a single breath I said: "After your grandmother died we prayed so hard for you to be born." Sissy looked up at me and smirked, as if to say, you haven't prayed in fifteen years, and we both know it. I wanted to smack her as hard as I had when she undulated her naked hips in front of her brothers.

I decided then and there to stop trying with Sissy. I felt powerless against all her bitterness and what's more, I didn't blame her. There were times when I almost admired all the spite she could twist into her pouting mouth, and I thought that someday she would come round again, the way I came round with her father, the way I'd come round to forgiving my own mother.

But Sissy hadn't come round yet—she hated me more than ever, if that was possible, now that her father was gone. If Jack took her off, there might never be a time for her to come round. Already she was slicking her hair down with gel and drooping her shirt off her shoulder: she looked like one of those California mall girls you see on the television. God in Heaven, what would her hair look like if she moved in with Judi and her cotton candy dye job? Jack would take back his no-lipstick-until-fifteen rule, and Sissy would go through the rest of eighth grade with lurid blue eyeshadow on her lids.

☾

I was still in the front yard. My husband had stood over me, measuring my words, and I had gone back to my spraying as if he weren't even there. I let him purse his lips, and stare at me worried, and finally walk off toward his car and his girlfriend with his shoulders hunched, as if he had a lifetime of loneliness facing him—when loneliness was the package he'd left on my front lawn. I hated myself for the way I held back. I wished I had turned the spray on him and the Miracle-Gro had splattered all over his maroon jacket. I wished I'd berated him for not leaving me sooner, for not leaving me alone with my grief when at least I'd had grief to keep me company.

At that moment I didn't even have my children to keep me company. Ethan and Jack and Sissy always came home as late as they could get away with; that meant that Nippie would straggle in alone off the bus, grumpy and hungry, and I would have to sit at the kitchen table to tell her that her father wanted her to move out of my house and into his. And then I would have to repeat the scene with Sissy, and then with Ethan and Jack.

It wasn't that I was frightened of telling them. It was only that I felt so tired, so chilled to the marrow standing out on my front lawn on the first day of spring. The first day of spring! What timing Jack had. What grace.

It was three-thirty. Nippie would be home in ten minutes.

I ripped the fertilizer bottle off the nozzle and tried to wind the hose up, but it was snakelike and went its own way, splattering me the way I should have splattered Jack. I could barely keep a grip on it, and I knew that I was in a state of shock again, the same shock that used to send me out to the river's edge when my boys were babies.

When my boys were babies. All of a sudden I wanted nothing more than to go downtown and stand in the little triangular park that looked out over the bridge at the end of River Street. All of a sudden I wanted to balance on the edge of the seawall, watching the bridge swing open and shut. I wanted to see a spring sky above me, perfect and pale, a sky as endless and indifferent as that God my mother believed had taken her son and her husband.

I didn't want to watch Nippie's face grow pale with the news. I didn't want to watch her try to hide her guilt when she realized that she'd rather be with her father, who never straightened her shoulders or proofread her homework or saw to it that she read poetry for half an hour before she went to bed.

So I went inside and made myself find a pen, and I scrawled out a note: "Dear Nippie, Had to see about some church business. You & Sissy can put on

☾

some corn dogs if you're hungry. I love you. Mother." I propped the note up on the cleared-off island and I read it through in a daze. Dear Nippie. I love you. Mother: I hadn't written a note to my daughters in five years that hadn't told them to pick up their clothes. I love you. Mother. Mother! Not Momma, or Mom. How strange that I had seen *my* mother as the Mother Superior, when at least she had seen to it that the house was filled with the deep rich smell of her vegetables cooking. At least she had waved knives back and forth to catch the light, and let us know that she still lived and breathed.

And I wasn't living and breathing at all. I was a woman in a state of shock.

I grabbed the keys and ran to the car, hoping I wouldn't pass the old yellow school bus turning into Piney Woods, hoping Nippie wouldn't see me frozen rigid. Look at you, I said to the reflection in the rearview. Just look at you. The lines around my eyes looked as if they'd been made by whiplashes, and I could see in my reflection what I must have looked like at twenty-four, out by the river in a floating robe, trying to feel grief.

I started the engine, and the way the car surged back down the driveway made me think: my son will stay with me. Jack will tell a judge that he can't abide his father, and his father will let him stay with me. The car slid down the street, some power of its own propelling it to the John C. Calhoun Road, and I watched as the big front yards on the side of the road curved into a kaleidoscope of pink and white. The yards shifted their colors, blurred and melted and merged: the azaleas had opened up everywhere, all in a day, and Due East was transformed with light and snowy stamen. What a wonder that all the flowers should blaze open, that women should stand in front of their big white houses —just as I'd stood, not an hour before—sending down streams of water on their fecund bushes, while Jack was driving home with Judi, plotting to take my children. It was just like the day when my brother was reported missing, and the bridge still opened for the shrimp boats; like the day my father died, and I still had to take my children to my breast and feed them and burp them and change their smelly diapers. When my mother died, and every busybody in Our Lady of Perpetual Help came by with a casserole so that she could see for herself if I'd collapse under the weight of my parents' deaths, Dolores Rooney sent me a smudged copy of "On Anothers Sorrow":

> Can a mother sit and hear,
> An infant groan an infant fear—

☾

I read, and Dolores Rooney's poem finally released for me the tears I'd been holding in for a father and a mother and a brother. First I cried with my grief; and then I cried with frustration and white rage that Dolores Rooney hadn't come by herself with a tuna noodle casserole, like all the other women, instead of sending me an anthologized poem so perfect for the occasion. I hated Dolores Rooney and her apt poems with all my soul. I hated how easily she went on with her life.

And now, driving down the Calhoun Road, I hated how all these women in Due East went on with their lives, with their watering and their azaleas. It seemed to me that my hatred was pushing the car too fast down the road, but I was afraid to look at the speedometer, afraid to see that I wasn't moving too fast at all, that I was coping with Jack's betrayal just as well as I had coped with my brother's and my father's and my mother's and Dolores Rooney's. So I let the car spin me down the Calhoun Road to River Street, and I rode through town just like everybody else, stopping for red lights and waving at people I knew.

By the time I parked in front of the little triangle of land down by the water, I was sure that I looked just as normal as every other soul in Due East, sure that I would be able to sit for two hours, maybe three—with my shoulders straight, the way Momma used to holler at us to sit—feeling nothing but the breeze and the light on my face, seeing nothing but the flowers blooming everywhere Due East had left a piece of earth unpaved.

And somehow I did. I sat rigid in the little park and focused on Lady's Island, across the bay, where Jack and Judi sold land and birthrights. I pictured the two of them going home: how surprised I had been to learn that they lived in a house, and not a condo with a pool. I imagined them drinking Diet Cokes in their beige kitchen and cutting on the TV while Judi chattered on about fixing up the girls' rooms: "Ooooh," I could hear her saying, bobbing her red hair, "it'll be so-o-o much fun to have KIDS in the house." Now Judi was blow-drying Sissy's hair and showing Nippie her thirty-year-old collection of Barbie Dolls. Now she was putting her arm around Ethan, who never let anyone touch him. Now I was putting my arms around my brother Billy—

But no. Blankness again. I focused on a pine tree just the other side of the bridge: during labor, the nurses used to tell us to stare our way through childbirth. Just look at one little spot, they'd say, until you know every square inch of it. But the pine tree was so far away that I knew only that it darkened

☾

in the wavering light. The air was cold even against my own cold skin. I stared at the tree until my eyes were numb in their sockets, and I made myself sit very, very still, dreaming of Judi in a bubble bath, her white belly billowing in the froth.

The smell of the salt air and the coming of evening finally brought me back. I made myself wake from my dream very slowly—my mother had lost control, but I couldn't lose it—and I made my eyes slide away from the pine tree and Judi's bath and focus instead on Nippie in the kitchen in Piney Woods, burning corn dogs and leaving the mayonnaise to go bad on the counter.

I made myself stand up and bend my back: my very skin had ossified, sitting on the bench for four hours. It was so dark, so suddenly, that I had to make myself walk back to the car as slowly and deliberately as I'd wakened from my dream. I couldn't afford to walk into my house looking frightened. Hadn't I stopped drinking after the night Jack found me incoherent? Hadn't I been managing?

Still, I had to sit behind the wheel to let my eyes adjust. I couldn't imagine that I had focused on the tree across the bay for so long: it was invisible now, as invisible as I felt behind the wheel. It was too dim even to see my face in the rearview.

I turned the headlights on and made myself move the car forward. I should have turned around the block, and gone back down to River Street, but I felt myself drawn the other way. All my resolution to go home and face my children was faltering. I was weak and watery, disappearing like the light, and I let myself float through the back streets of town.

I found myself driving through the Point, the finger of land that jutted out into the river. Jack and I had started our marriage in a little cottage on those narrow streets, and after they razed the cottage I stopped driving back this way.

Now I wanted to drive through the Point all night. Back here there were no new streetlights like the tall silver ones in Piney Woods: the old oak trees stood guard, and the moon gave off her light over the marsh. My father used to drive us to the Point every year for Halloween, back when Lady's Island didn't have enough houses for trick-or-treating. When we were small, the moss beckoned on the trees above us, and the big brick Mansard house, the slave quarters abutting it, was a grim dungeon. Even the low buildings—the cottages and bungalows they tore down later, when they tore down the River House— were daunting.

☾

The Point still daunted me. I told myself that I would only drive round the old neighborhood once, but I felt myself slowing the car and looking up at the grand houses as if I were one of the tourists off a boat down at the marina. When I was a girl more of the houses had looked modest: the Rooney house was close to ramshackle sometimes, when Dolores's husband was having a bad year with real estate. Now all the houses looked wealthy, all the oleanders trimmed, all the crape myrtle draped artfully. I found myself wondering if Tim kept up the old house any better now that he'd moved in with his father. My car crept down past O'Connor Street, and I turned in, knowing all the while that I should be heading home.

I could barely remember where the Rooneys' would be, or even if I had the right block; but then I saw a single light blazing out of a second-story window, and I knew at once the house where I'd come for Father Berkeley's discussion group the year I graduated from college.

I inched the car forward and stared: surely the house wasn't as sunbeaten as it had been when Dolores was alive. Surely that was fresh green paint on the shutters. Dolores was gone three years now, and even in the dark her house— an eyesore while she lived and breathed—looked as fit as the rest of the gussied-up Point. What irony that her house should stand there looking up- right and respectable when her family had caved in on itself: Tim breaking down; Dottie drowning out at Hunting Island; Bill Rooney stumbling into mass, a drunk like Father Berkeley. Sometimes they drank together.

My car rolled past the Rooney yard slowly, past the big pecan trees in front of the semicircular driveway, and finally—when I had crossed half the house's shadow—I shifted the car into park right in the middle of O'Connor Street and ogled Dolores Rooney's house. I must have still been in my state of shock. It never occurred to me that Tim Rooney was inside, or that he might look out and see me watching his house. It never occurred to me that he might think I was a pathetic middle-aged woman running after him. It only occurred to me that when I was twenty-two years old, in the first year of my marriage, Father Berkeley had chosen the Rooney house for his discussion groups, and I had run up those front steps as if I were running for air to breathe.

Now I stared at the front door as if I could see right into the hallway, and I pictured Dolores, brisk and smiling, ushering us all into her shabby parlor. She never apologized for the Betsy-Wetsys and the Sears guitars and the piles of books we'd have to step over; she never apologized for her husband when we

☾

could hear him hollering down the stairs. She never shooed her children out of the room once Father blessed himself and began our meeting with a Hail Mary. I found myself sitting next to her more than once, watching the way she leaned forward when she formulated an idea, and by the time she suggested that she drive me out to the Friends Center to hear a Quaker lecture on nonviolence, I didn't care what Jack thought of her or her ideas.

Suddenly I could feel, like a hand from the back seat pressing down on my shoulder, the memory of my mother's jealousy the year I got close to Dolores. I never even mentioned one to the other, but Momma must have felt me shrinking away from her as I sat in her kitchen on a chrome-and-plastic straight-backed chair. She must have sensed somehow that I had been sitting in another chair, a lumpy ripped armchair sprouting stuffing, and she must have resented its comfort.

Surely my mother must have known that year how I recoiled from her, how I preferred to have Dolores Rooney sling one of the twins over her hip, hardly remembering he was there, to having my mother fuss with the little white sweaters she buttoned up to the babies' chins. Surely Momma must have seen me close my eyes when she went on about Daddy. Dolores Rooney had a tall handsome paunchy husband who flirted with all the women from the church right in front of her, squeezing them around the shoulder in his coarse way. But Dolores never complained of him, though there were always stories about his hitting the children: Tim said his father had smashed two guitars right down over his head. He was a man who sang loud enough some nights to cause the neighbors to make discreet calls to the police, but Dolores never took me aside, the way my mother did, to whisper how he hurt her. She only rolled her eyes sometimes and looked out past him. After a while I could see that she did the same thing I did with Jack: I cut him off, the way I would a car radio, never hearing a word he said once I'd turned the volume down.

It wasn't that we became girlfriends, the way women in Due East do, going out to the country club to sit by the pool together. It was just that if Dolores said, "Oh, that's as dark as the *Purgatorio*," I would run off to the library, shamed at how little I knew. She had cast a cold eye on me, on my reading and my politics, and she didn't know that she was as brisk as a broom in my own mother's hands. She probably didn't even know that she forgot sometimes that I was waiting for her downstairs, my boys indistinguishable from the other stuffed toys strewn on the parlor rug. She probably didn't know how awkward

☾

I was when we were with Father Berkeley: Dolores talked to him as if they were lovers sharing a secret, and when she left the room his eyes followed.

I had to pull myself away from her, the way I pulled myself away from the Church's reach after my parents were both dead. I forgave her sending me the poem instead of putting her arms around me, but I couldn't spend a lifetime waiting for Xeroxed pieces of edification to arrive in the mail. I couldn't spend a lifetime waiting for her hints about the holes in my reading.

Now, sitting and eyeing her house, I felt guilt pressing down on both shoulders, and I wanted to lean my head forward into the steering wheel and let guilt take over the driving. My mother hadn't been smart enough for me. Dolores Rooney hadn't been warm enough for me. There hadn't been anyone whose comfort I was willing to accept after my father died—and when my father was alive, he himself had made me blush with shame when he was high and ungrammatical. I had always looked down on my own husband, on my own children, to see a list of deficiencies pinned to the fronts of their shirts: there was no one in my tiny claustrophobic world, not even Father Berkeley himself, who'd ever stayed good enough for me. I deserved the tiny cell of this car, of my shame and disappointment. I deserved to be locked in it forever.

I turned the motor on, slipping the car into gear but not realizing at first that I was rolling in reverse. I slid down the grade until I was back to the side of the Rooneys', and when I looked up at the lighted window—*now* I thought of Tim, of his looking out to see me gazing up—I thought for a split second that I was hallucinating, or dreaming again.

A naked man and woman were illuminated in the upstairs windows: I was stunned and then exhilarated, feeling part of some blue movie scene. It took me a moment to realize that the naked rolling back in the window must belong to Tim Rooney, that those were the same broad shoulders I'd hoped to keep in my own bedroom. He was holding a skinny woman who looked for all the world as if she had her hands tied behind her back. My exhilaration fizzled and flew around the car like a deflated balloon, and in another instant I was watching Tim Rooney pull the woman back by the hair, her head a floating orb in the window.

Had they opened the curtains on purpose? For God's sake! I could see down to just below her waist, could see that her breasts were tiny and girlish. I watched Tim lean his mouth down to suck those nipples. My own nipples stung, and my own mouth hung open as I sat there, unable to put the car into

☾

drive and flee until I heard a low hum behind me. In the rearview I could see
the double beams of a pickup truck turning into O'Connor Street. By the time
it pulled into the driveway behind me, I had taken my eyes off the two blue
movie stars and willed myself into action.

So Tim Rooney took lovers and tied them up while he pretended he was
waiting to join a monastery. I sped down O'Connor Street and made three left
turns, finding my way to River Street with my foot glued to the accelerator. I
wasn't seeing that movie image of Tim Rooney and the woman anymore; I
wasn't even sure I'd seen it in the first place. I was seeing myself slapping at
Sissy, the time I caught her dancing naked in front of her brothers. Guilt
popped up from the back seat to sit with me again, and I remembered Sissy's
shame, and mine, our cheeks dotted pink with a shared and wild resentment.
Then I summoned up another shame, another night when my face flushed a
high color: now I could see myself when I was seven years old, sneaking into
my brother Billy's basement bedroom late at night. I watched myself slink in
next to him in his cold bed: I watched myself put my arms around his neck and
kiss him full on his sleeping mouth. He kissed me back, dreamy and surprised,
and I was tugging at the elastic waist of his pajama bottoms when the overhead
bulb flashed on and my mother stared down on us with all her majesty and
horror. I could feel the soft flannel of Billy's red pajamas and I could smell his
musty socks on the concrete floor, but I wasn't sure whether it was real
memory or imagination. I hadn't thought of loving Billy in all these years. I
had wanted Jack to beat me senseless when I thought he was dead.

Now I wanted to speed the car home to my children. I didn't care what
lovers Tim Rooney was taking. I didn't care what women he tied up. By the
time I reached the Calhoun Road I didn't need to look down at the speedometer to know that I was twenty miles over the speed limit. I had to get home to
tell Sissy—what?

A police car pulled out of the Depot Road behind me and its red light
swiveled around lazily in slow motion, following me up the street. I was in
slow motion, too: I saw in the red reflector the MPs come for my father.
Attendants come to put my mother in a straitjacket. Jack and his lawyer, come
to arrest me for child neglect. The siren set off an angry whine, as insistent as a
baby's cry, and I felt a surge of excitement pump clear through to my fingertips on the wheel. I wasn't going to pull over. I wasn't going to stop the car.
Nobody was going to drag my father off to Vietnam. Nobody was going to

☾

put my mother on a locked ward. Nobody was going to take my children away from me. I slammed down the accelerator, daring myself, and watched the needle go to fifty, fifty-five, sixty, sixty-five before any degree of rationality returned. The needle dangled at seventy, and I dangled between reason and madness, wanting to speed through the night. I felt myself sliding past the tech school, breezing past the hospital: the police car behind me was pulling out, getting ready to come up alongside and force me over to the side of the road. I made myself brake—slowly, slowly—and I steered the car over without once leaning my head down on the wheel to cry that I had flouted the law for the first time in my life. I sat as tall and rigid as I had in the park.

Then I watched the police car pass me by, off to bigger crimes than stopping a crazy lady. I wanted the cop to come back and slap handcuffs on my wrists. I wanted to go back to Tim Rooney's and let him tie *me* up. I wanted someone to beat me senseless.

The next morning I woke feeling as cotton-mouthed and hung over as if I *had* been drunk and pulled over to the side of the road by the police. I had slept the sleep of the dead, to blot out the night before: by the time I'd walked into my kitchen, I could see that my husband had already told my children what he intended to do. The four of them were all sitting slouched at the island in the kitchen, the only time I'd seen them together since the family Christmas picture. They were clicking knives against the inside of the mayonnaise jar and brushing away crumbs from the Formica top and looking at me—even Sissy—as if I were eighty years old and they'd just decided to put me away in a nursing home.

None of them said they'd move in with their father, but I knew from the way Jack averted his eyes that they'd already talked it out. He would be my only defender. There was nothing to say after Nippie said: "Daddy told us what he's doing," so I said nothing. I kissed them, one at a time, on their foreheads, and let Ethan put his big red-haired arms around me and hold me for a good long while. I deserved to lose him.

I went upstairs with nothing on my stomach and nothing on my mind, not bitterness at Jack, not lust after Tim, not plans to get Sissy back. I slept for twelve hours. Maybe I was hoping for a vision to come to me in my sleep, but all that came was a dream of police cars carting pink azaleas in their back seats.

☾

The police cars were lined up for a funeral procession: there was no sign to help me.

By the time I regained consciousness, the children had all left for school. I was so leaden and groggy with the extra sleep that I didn't even know I walked naked to the top of the stairs to call for them: I had a start, seeing my white breasts in the hall mirror. I had come to the point where my body got out of bed before my mind. What if Ethan had still been home? I never slept naked, not with four children in the house. What had come over me? I tried to remember undressing the night before, after I toiled up the stairs, but all I could remember was a lighted window on O'Connor Street and the sight of Tim Rooney's naked back.

And then I remembered my children's faces circled around the kitchen island. I ran to the bathroom as if one of them were still in the house, about to see me naked, about to tell me the truth. It would be all right without them. I said it out loud to the empty house: "It'll be all right without them." It would be better without Sissy: better for her, better for me. I turned the shower on and tried to calculate what money Jack would give me once the children were gone: how much if Ethan went, how much if Ethan and Sissy, how much if Ethan and Sissy and Nippie. I tallied up what a teacher's take-home pay must be nowadays, and then I tried on the idea of moving to Charleston, having Sunday dinner with one of my brothers' wives around a picnic table in a cramped kitchen.

I thought at first that it was the steam filling the bathroom that made me breathe so heavily, but then in the fog I looked down at my nakedness and saw what a coward I was. Why didn't I just go to Jack? Why didn't I just say: No, no you can't have my children? Why didn't I find myself a lawyer who could outharangue his lawyer?

I forced myself into the hot shower and wanted to lie right down in the tub, giving myself up to the force of it. My head was bowed against the beating down of the hot water and I remembered again the way that little Rapple girl's head was bowed down in convert class. I was sick to death of my own fears. I was sick to death of my own whining. I was sick to death of having my head bowed down.

The force of the water on the back of my neck made me vow that I would drive myself over to Island Paradise that very morning, before I even found a lawyer. I would march into Jack's business with fire on my breath this time,

☾

not ice. I would tell Jack to his face that he could not have the children. I would let Judi strain to hear every word I spoke to my husband behind his closed door.

The new day was as clotted with sunshine as the day before had been and the azaleas, like peacocks preening, were still flaunting themselves all over town. I crossed the bridge with my eyes on the speedometer, completely in control, and kept five miles under the limit.

Jack's office was just beyond the first curve of the beach road; he'd built Island Paradise Realty out of cinderblock early in the seventies, when everything in Due East was going up in cinderblock. But then in the eighties he'd realized that all the new brokers had classy wood facades, so he covered up the green cinderblock with cedar shingles painted blue-gray. Now Island Paradise was a squat stockade, with walls so thick no hurricane would even try to knock it down.

Jack covered over his business the same year he sold a huge parcel of marshland out on Isaacs Island—land my father told him to buy, twenty years before—for a development of time-sharing condominiums that half Due East County was dead set against. His own son, Jack, told his father that the apartments would sink into the mud before ten years were up; his father said that would be the developers' problem, not his. Ethan stayed out of it, though he was the one who'd fished at the end of that land, but Jack kept it up until he and his father weren't speaking: "I can't believe we're going to get rich," he would say, "off some damn apartment complex spilling its sewage into Grand-daddy's marsh."

But we didn't get rich anyway, we just got comfortable: and that should have been my first clue that Jack was spending his money somewhere else besides home. I should have figured out three years ago that he wasn't traveling alone to Florida for all those time-share conferences. I should have put together the late nights and the vague answers and the crazy way he yelled if the okra was overcooked, and I should have known he was seeing someone. It never crossed my mind: I was so busy pulling back from him it never occurred to me that he was running away from me.

Now, turning into the parking lot, the years of cheating Jack must have accumulated blazoned themselves out as clearly as the palmetto tree on his Island Paradise sign. The tree was a big green cutout that stretched out over

☽

LAND • HOUSES • WATERFRONT PROPERTY, and I saw in every one of its spiked branches the ways Jack must have deceived me. For years. For all the years I was feeling guilty for staring at the broad shoulders on a *fireman:* those were the years Jack must have been pulling down Judi's Frederick's of Hollywood red panties, lifting up her black garters, sliding his hand between her fat white thighs.

I parked the car as close to Jack's gold Cadillac as I could without actually peeling paint off his doors. Now I wondered if Judi were the only one, or if there'd been a string of little realty helpers he'd been sleeping with all these years. Jack thought, when I married him, that I believed him to be a virgin. I never believed any such thing: you could smell in the Jade East he slapped all over his face how many girls he'd had. But I believed him when he said—with the same clear-eyed look he wore to recite the Credo—that a man picked a wife for life. When the sheriff made a raid on a plain little frame house near the fort at Claire's Point, and it turned out to be a whorehouse, Jack joined every other man in the Holy Name Society, shaking his head along with theirs to say: "I can't believe it. Right by the fort." They probably all knew! They were probably all out there on Holy Name Society nights.

I knew I was getting hysterical in Jack's parking lot, but hysteria felt like a brand-new party dress, unfamiliar and silky next to my skin, and I didn't want to unzip it just yet. I swung my pocketbook over my shoulder and checked my braid: I planned to look as fierce as a Gorgon when I passed Judi's desk.

But Judi wasn't at her desk when I flung open the door to Island Paradise Realty; the outer office, where there were usually two or three pert little ladies in red blazers and navy-blue pumps, was cleared of salespeople. Two men sat on wooden folding chairs in the waiting area.

Ordinarily I would have sat down myself to wait, but now I was picturing red panties and whorehouses and years of cheating, and I walked right up to Jack's office door, ready to pound out my rage. At the last minute, I held my fist back: I wouldn't let Judi see me crazy.

"Do you know if Mr. Perdue is in?" I turned to look for an answer from the two waiting men, and recognized one of them as Stephen Dugan. He had on his reporter's outfit—laced Hush Puppies, chinos, narrow tie—and I wanted to straighten his shoulders the way I straightened Nippie's. How dare he keep that little Rapple girl waiting for him! He probably had no intention of marrying her.

☾

"He's in. We're waiting on him too, Miz Perdue," Stephen said. I could have wrung his scrawny neck for calling me "Miz," as if I were ten or twenty years older than he. He used to call me Becky, when we waited for our children every Thursday afternoon in the parking lot at Our Lady of Perpetual Help Center for Religious Instruction. Back then, when I thought he was a lonely father chauffeuring his daughter to catechism classes against her mother's will, I'd almost found him attractive. I thought that Dolores Rooney would have approved of all the series he did for the *Courier,* the long pieces on migrant workers getting the tomatoes in, on Marine wives working for less than minimum wage around town. The long piece on Jack Perdue selling Isaacs Island.

Now when I looked at him I thought of two women making fools of themselves over him. How dingy and tired he looked, especially set off by the man sitting next to him: it was a wonder *any* woman bothered, much less two.

The other man was younger, or more possessed of energy, maybe: he wore boat shoes without any socks and he tapped his ankle on his knee as if he were not used to waiting—not in Due East, anyway. He didn't look Due East. He had long thick curly dark hair on the top of his head, and on his chest too: there was one too many buttons unbuttoned on his shirt. He sat up a little straighter when he heard Stephen call me "Miz Perdue."

"Miz Perdue?"

Stephen said: "Eliot Purser, Becky Perdue."

Stephen's neighbor clumped his foot down and turned a round cherubic eye on me. He smiled cagily.

"So you're Mrs. Island Paradise Realty." His voice was as slick as the oil Jack's motorboat left in the creeks, but it was pleasant somehow, too. He was distracting me from my rage—from my vision of Jack's hand and Judi's thigh —and I almost turned my back on him.

"I'm separated from Mr. Island Paradise," I said. "Excuse me. I have some business with him."

I turned back to rap on Jack's door, but heard from within low intense voices. One of them, I was sure, was Judi's. My hand was caught midair: I couldn't have Stephen Dugan and some stranger watch me go confront Jack *and* Judi. I turned back in confusion to the rows of folding chairs, and sat down to wait behind the two men. I felt diminished already. I felt defeated already. Why couldn't I sustain my one hour of rage?

☾

Eliot Purser turned a tanned face on me and said: "I hope your husband isn't as difficult in his dealings with you as he is in his dealings with us." Somehow he kept his tone pleasant.

Stephen Dugan turned around too, not with any hurry but with apologetic eyes, as if to say, He wasn't raised in Due East. He doesn't know any better. "Mr. Purser is here to make a movie," he said. "He's a producer."

The voices behind Jack's door accelerated and hummed louder. I could hear my husband saying: "Damned if I will! Damned if I will!" His old clenched-teeth voice.

Eliot Purser let out a low whistle. "Doesn't bode well for us."

I felt the blood rush to my temples. Doesn't bode well for *me*. Doesn't bode well for me that Jack is so distracted with somebody else's business that he won't even hear me when I make the first real demand I'd made in all our years of marriage. I had barely registered the word *movie:* a year ago, I would have been as giggly as a girl that I sat behind a producer come to Due East to make a movie.

I twisted in my chair, trying to see past this Eliot Purser to my husband's door. I couldn't pay any mind to their movies. It was my children I had to concentrate on. It was my rage.

Mr. Purser turned toward me again. "We're set to start shooting in two weeks."

I tried to smile the least smile a good Due East girl could get away with smiling. I did not want to hear about his movie. I had to keep my fires fueled.

"Your husband is being pretty pigheaded about the whole thing." Mr. Purser, I realized, was leaning his body toward me now, and there was a faint musky smell about him.

What did I care for movie deals in Due East when I was losing my children? Finally I said: "What's Jack got to do with shooting a movie?"

"We scouted it months ago," he went on, oblivious. "He knows the whole budget's based on shooting at the fort. Now he's trying to pull a real estate sale at the last minute! You have to tell your husband this isn't how it's done, Mrs. Perdue. We can't buy his fort."

I stared at this Hollywood producer come to Due East and couldn't remember a word I meant to say to Jack. The fort. The minute Eliot Purser mouthed the word *fort,* my mind was wiped clean of all my plans. Jack still held the deed to our old crumbling fort at Claire's Point, the land my father and brother

☾

showed him the weekend I decided to marry him. It sat on the river, near the sound, and one day we were going to build a beach house out there. It was a piece of property we'd talked about handing down to Ethan or Jack.

Stephen Dugan looked at my twisted face and tried to explain. "I've written a script," he said. "It's a TV movie—most of it takes place at an old fort. I had Claire's Point in mind, so Eliot flew the director down, and *he* thought it was perfect. Everybody liked it just fine."

"I went to see your husband on my own," Purser said, "and he was all for it. Signed the contracts."

Stephen Dugan smiled a rueful smile. "But when he heard *I* wrote the script he remembered those articles I wrote about Isaacs Island."

"And now he's got his lawyer trying to declare the contract null and void. Now he's threatening that we'll have to buy the fort to shoot out there! For a million dollars!" Mr. Purser's voice was poised between outrage and amusement.

"A million dollars," I said, still keeping my voice cool. I couldn't believe Jack could form the words *million dollars* so coolly in his mind: a million dollars for a fort my father found him, for land we were going to hand down to one of our sons. Jack was a regular bulldozer, crushing down the family, clearing out the past. I could almost feel myself rising with the heat of my anger, but in front of me sat two grown men, vying for my attention like boys at a dance.

"You've got to understand, Mrs. Perdue, that the budget for a two-hour television movie does not exceed a million dollars by very much in the first place," said Purser. "We're not talking major stars here—"

"The shot list is finished," Stephen said.

"Stephen's *designed* this screenplay around that fort, Mrs. Perdue—"

"If we hadn't counted on it in the first place. If he hadn't made a commitment—"

"The million dollars is just a joke. I *think*. He can't be that naive, to think we're made of that kind of money. Can he? What do you suppose he really wants?"

If I weren't still in my state of shock, I would have laughed at them, leaning forward like little boys, trying to trick me into helping them. Me. I was the one he left in the first place. The one whose children he was taking away.

"Can't you just shoot somewhere else?"

☾

Mr. Purchase let out a practiced Hollywood sigh. "I suppose we can find another fort," he said, but I saw Stephen stiffen. "The question is whether, at this stage of the game, it's worth it—"

I shrugged at them finally, as if to say, you two are looking to the wrong intercessor, but as I lowered my shoulders the door to Jack's office opened and Judi stepped out, fat and red-mouthed, her makeup color-coordinated with her Island Paradise jacket. She was taken aback to see me, but she smiled anyway and held out an arm to usher Stephen and Eliot into Jack's office. I stared hard at her red fingernails: she had painted little gold glitter hearts on them, and they glimmered in relief.

"He's ready to see you now," she told them, sweet and efficient. Her voice was as squeaky as a rubber mouse's, and I realized I'd never heard her speak before.

Behind her I could just make out Jack at his desk, and as the men in front of me rose, I could see Jack rising, too. He had seen me in the outer office.

"Just a minute," he barked to Judi, and he slipped on his own red blazer as he came to his door.

"Becky," he said, looking straight at me, ignoring the two men. "Becky, are you here to see me?"

"Oh no," I said. "Oh *no*. I just came to file my nails at Island Paradise." Then I looked around behind me. Whose voice was coming from my mouth? I had never once sassed him the way the children did.

"Come on in, Becky," he said, betraying himself: his voice was casual, but his white hands vibrated in embarrassment. "I'll be with you two gentlemen in a moment."

Judi glared at him and then at me, and I made a point of waiting for her to clear her large protruding body out of the doorway before I went through to see Jack. Then I closed the door slowly. Seeing Jack alone in his office, fluttering his hands, had a strange effect on me: I could feel my foot on the accelerator from the night before. I could feel the same surge of power. I pictured the gold glitter hearts on Judi's fingernails.

"Sit down, Jack," I said.

There was a long moment of silence. Then he sat behind his desk. "I reckon I know what you've come about," he said, his voice pitched high and guilty.

"I've come to talk about the children," I said. "The chidrun."

He tapped a pencil on the desk, unwilling to look me in the eye. "Becky,"

☾

he said, "I know you want to talk about that. I understand how you feel, honey. But you know I wasn't even supposed to come by the house yesterday. Lamarr told me specially not to *do* that." He paused for drama, something he learned to do in sales conferences.

"I had to do that, though. We were married for twenty years. I had to tell you face to face what I was looking to do."

"And you had to bring your girlfriend along to witness the proceedings."

"Well, surely you can understand how—"

"I don't understand, Jack."

"Becky, I know you don't like it. I knew you wouldn't like it. But Lamarr says I'm not supposed to talk about it. He told us—"

"He told US? He told you and that harpy outside what to do about MY children?"

Jack could not keep his hands still on the desk: he was a pinned butterfly. "Lamarr says I'm not to discuss it with you."

"Well of course he does." I wasn't screaming, or even yelling—I was projecting the way a stage actor does, and I heard my voice bouncing off the seats in the back of the house. *"Of course he tells you not to talk to me.* He does not want you to have to face the consequences of this act."

I could see Jack listening for the men and the woman outside. We were both picturing them leaned forward, straining to hear my new actor's voice.

"He wants to make this a *legal* matter. Not a moral one," I said.

Jack shut his eyes, and I saw the color rising in his white cheeks: soon his face would bruise purple with his guilt and confusion. "I guess he told you not to discuss it with Father Berkeley either," I said. "I guess he told you not to discuss it with your own conscience."

My husband actually squirmed in front of me. In twenty years of marriage, he had never *squirmed* in front of me.

"You are not going to try to take the children," I said.

He sank his face into his hands.

"You are going to tell Lamarr that you've thought it over, and you're not going to ask for custody of the children."

Still he said nothing.

I looked down on his hunched shoulders and realized I could drive right over him if I felt the inclination. I was speeding way past seventy miles an hour

☾

now. I was going to push the speedometer past a hundred if I kept going: past two hundred. I was going to fly into orbit.

"And you are not going to talk about selling that fort!"

Now he looked up at me.

"How dare you manipulate anyone with that land! You never would have known that fort existed if it hadn't been for my father. You are going to tell those men out there that they can use my fort to shoot their movie. My son is going to get that land someday."

Jack half rose from the chair. I could see he was frightened. "Becky, get ahold of yourself," he said. He hissed the words, trying to whisper. "I was just giving Dugan a hard time, paying him back. I was going to tell them they could use the fort after a while." He sounded as much a little boy as the men outside had. Little boys with million-dollar toys: forts and movies and

"You are going to tell Judi not to bring up the subject of the children again. She cannot have my daughters."

Jack slammed his fist down, and for one terrible moment I thought I might be losing my power over him. I thought he was going to defy me. Then I saw that the fist he clenched was trembling.

I could get him to do anything I wanted.

I could get him back, if I wanted.

"Don't ever bring her by the house again, Jack," I said. He stood trembling over his desk, and I swiveled down to pick my pocketbook up. I could feel my braid swish against my shoulder, and I sashayed out of Jack's office with enough hip-swinging to win me a part in Eliot Purser's movie.

Judi and Stephen were studying their cuticles when I opened Jack's door, but Eliot Purser followed my march with anticipation. I stopped in front of the men until Stephen Dugan had to look up at me.

"You've got the fort," I said to Stephen. "You can shoot your movie." The two men looked at me with horror and delight: Mrs. Island Paradise came out of her husband's office with a new identity. Now I was someone they were afraid to talk to: the ex-wife emerging renewed from the sunshower of vengeance. The ex-wife from hell. I didn't turn around to see the look on Judi's face.

Outside I glided to my car, sunlight drenching me, air currents pushing me. I was all light, all power. From behind the steering wheel I watched Stephen shuffling into Jack's office in those horrible beige Hush Puppies, and I realized

☾

in a flash that I wasn't going to let him get away with it any more than I was going to let Jack get away with it. I thought: I'll go see that Mary Faith Rapple. I'll tell her not to squander her young life on a faithless man. I'll *save* her.

Then I turned the motor over, though it seemed a waste of energy to have another engine on when the one propelling me was moving with so much power. I wasn't driving down the beach road, I was flying over it, flying on my way back to Due East and the Point. I was going to go back to the Rooney house, only this time nobody was going to keep me waiting in the parlor. I was going to seduce Tim Rooney, and just when he was ready to *die* from wanting to tie me up, I was going to get him to tell me where Mary Faith Rapple lived. Then I could save her the same way I had saved myself.

The car hit a little bump as it eased onto the bridge, but I kept my foot on the accelerator and sped up when I saw the bridge tender lowering the barrier to stop traffic. He was going to open the bridge for a shrimp boat, but he wasn't going to stop me. I scooted my white car through just as the stop sign was lowered, and I heard a dull *clunk* as it hit the roof. I drove fast under the tender's watchpost, and saw him shake a fist down at me; he had no choice but to open the other side to let me out. The drivers in the waiting cars leaned their heads out to stare at the fool speeding over the bridge, and I waved a sweet hello at them. I passed a silver car on line, and I dreamed for a moment that Father Berkeley was driving, that my son Jack sat in the passenger seat. I waved again, and then I heard my mother's voice whispering from the back seat. "Now you know what it's like to lose control," she said.

And I heard myself answer back: I'M NOT LOSING CONTROL. I jammed the accelerator again, coming up to the red light, and swung the steering wheel around. Right turn on red. I AM NOT LOSING CONTROL. I was turning onto the Point again, screeching my old white car around the corners, talking out loud to myself. Timmy said he could see the hallucinations coming. What was that shadow in the street? An old black woman limped by my big car, and her fist was raised too, raised at me as I almost brushed against her. I was turning onto O'Connor Street, imagining old women with haloes of white hair and masklike immobile faces.

Where did Timmy Rooney go when he knew he was losing his mind? Did he go to Father Berkeley to ask for help? No wonder I imagined Father's car on the bridge: I was looking for him. I was looking for anyone to tell me that I

☾

wasn't losing my mind. But Father couldn't help me any more than he could have helped my mother. We weren't believers: we only believed in black holes and betrayals. Now I heard myself whispering down O'Connor Street.

"Please don't let me lose control," I heard, only it wasn't my voice speaking. It was a little girl's voice.

"Oh God, please don't let me lose control."

☾

20

Father Berkeley Prepares

MY DEAR LADIES OF THE MOTHERS' CLUB
—*and will that company include Becky Perdue? Will Rebecca come to hear
me present a talk I have no inclination to prepare? She looked distracted
beyond reason on the bridge today, as distracted as I am sitting down to write
these empty words.*

*They want an address on the Decline of Faith in the Modern Age, these
women. They want to know why their children are down in the basement
watching blue movies instead of out in God's sunshine spreading the gospel
and giving the Baptists a good run for the money. They have certainly chosen
the right man to discuss the decline of faith. But I will be perfectly sober: not
so much as a glass of sherry, not to face THESE women.*

*These women, innocent as babes, want only to indulge in spiritual nostal-
gia. They want only to recall the years when the schoolchildren wakened in
the dark every First Friday for early mass; when the lowliest uneducated
enlisted man called out the Latin responses loud and clear; when Will
Lumiere brought in the smudgepots from Toomer Plantation so we could say
midnight mass down by the bluff; when the whole parish crowded into church*

*for the Stations of the Cross, weeping right along with the Blessed Mother at the end
of that long walk to Golgotha.*

*These women want only to believe that they are not hopeless anachronisms at the
end of the twentieth century. And why not offer them hope, after the years of service
they have given this little church?*

*If they were more inclined to forgive desecrations on the order of urinating in the
first pew, it might be Tim Rooney's story I'd tell them: the young man returned to the
fold after years of drink and drugs.* My dear ladies, *I would say,* faith manifests
itself in the strangest ways. *I would tell them how Tim came to me the Christmas
after his mother died with two file boxes and a system to explain man's relationship
with God as one of mutual betrayal. But they would only be fuddled by Tim and his
strange cries for help. They are not any more interested in Tim's cries than they are in
Job's or Abraham's.*

*And the wonder of it, besides, was not that Tim Rooney went mad at Our Lady of
Perpetual Help. The wonder of it was that Tim could still call out at all, after the
years of punishment he gave his brain cells. When he was sixteen years old and went
off to New York on his own, I doubted he'd be able to keep up with his studies if he
kept up with the drugs. I begged Dolores to send him to the Jesuits, where they could
keep an eye on him, but there was not a Jesuit school she would accept as good enough
for Timmy. She had to make him a secular scholar, and he had to prove her right.
And when he decided to major in philosophy, he mailed me grocery boxes full of
books, as if I'd never heard of Christian existentialism before, as if I wanted to follow
his intellectual development book by book, the way his mother did. I can hardly blame
him for that bit of condescension, when his mother made condescension her lifetime
occupation. What a family for sending Xeroxes and books and magazine subscriptions! for thinking that I was in need of theological education, because I took MY
graduate degree in counseling.*

*Leave the psychology to the family therapists, Dolores would say, meaning there
was nothing I could tell her about her family. There was only too much I could have
told her about her family, and tried to, but I doubt if a single admonition registered.
Oh no, she had more important business than seeing to the children who followed her
with their tongues hanging out of their mouths, so hungry were they for a moment of
her attention. And when she did attend to them, it was to their "education," and not to
their needs. Not to the needs Tim put on like a hair shirt every morning. Poor little
fellow, with his hand on his crotch all his boyhood. Didn't his mother see the other
children smirking at him and his hymns played on an electric guitar? Didn't she*

☾

understand that when his father walloped him, Bill at least could see that something was wrong? He could at least summon some emotion for the child, even if it was only rage. But for Dolores Timothy was only a social experiment and a wall she built to shut out a husband who never did understand why she condescended to marry him.

Ah Dolores. Ah mercy me. Forgive me.

How you would have laughed to read the typewritten note I found at the bottom of the collection basket: "Dear Father, I am ashamed to send you this but there is something you should be made aware of, there is talk about the way you look at Dolores Rooney, the way your eyes follow her." Mary, merciful mother of Christ our Lord, grant me patience as I recall the words. My eyes were always trying to catch her attention! trying to shepherd her back to her children! to beg her to listen to her husband when he opened his mouth, not to pretend he didn't exist!

When she latched on to Rebecca, and Rebecca was still an impressionable girl herself, I tried to warn Dolores off, but she'd have none of it. She was too busy enlightening Southerners in the joys of liberalism, and only too glad to have another young woman read her lessons on the art of cold judgment.

And so at the end of her life I was judging her, and what she made of Tim. But these women don't need to hear my prideful judgment of Dolores Rooney. They all saw Tim on Christmas Eve; they were all present when he reverted to infantilism at midnight mass. And they all see him still, haunting church meetings, looking not for God to show him mercy, but for a woman to show him the mercy his mother never possessed.

These women don't want to hear of Tim Rooney's muddled faith: it is their own faith, their own constancy, they want to hear praised.

And dare I tell them what I think of their faith? Their breast-beating? Their scrubbing the church cleaner than Martha dared scrub her household for Christ's visit? Dare I tell them how little charity there is in my heart for their endless piety, for the way they have scrubbed the church clean of men, too?

Why do I turn my anger so easily onto these silly twittering women? Dolores wasn't one of them—there wasn't a clean coffee cup in her kitchen for the seventeen years I knew her—but wasn't she up to the same tidying? Wasn't she tuning out Bill until he was desperate to find another woman to notice he was alive? She led her family to church the same way these women lead theirs: oh, there are men at every Sunday mass, following their wives the way their children follow them. And the women give the men the same attention they give the children: "That's very funny, darlin', now how about bringing the car around?" They pay no mind to their hus-

☾

bands' needs until one day the sheriff makes a raid on a brothel at Claire's Point and then they close ranks together, an army of women betrayed by the men.

They are all such faithful wives, such faithful mothers, that they think the very priests standing before them are sexless, to match their own sexlessness: shall I remind them that the seminaries are scrubbed clean of men now, too? Shall I tell them of the young men who studied with me? They think Tim Rooney is crazy—well! There was not a man studying for the priesthood in my seminary who did not blink or stutter or crack up before he took his final vows. But the men I studied with were not sexless, only determined not to live in the chains of their sexual desires, desires they sublimated in their blinking and stuttering and, when they were holy men, their veneration of the Blessed Mother. And those are the very priests they treat as they treat their own husbands, laughing at their little jokes and then going home to typewrite anonymous notes accusing them of infidelity to the Church.

Infidelity! I have stayed faithful to a priesthood for which I have no talent and precious little vocation. I stand in judgment of all of them, when what I should like is the privilege of releasing myself from this judgment. I should like the privilege, ladies, of cracking up like Tim Rooney, instead of taking my brandy too early in the afternoon. I should like the privilege of walking away from it all, like Jack Perdue. I should like the privilege of telling Becky Perdue that when she learned Dolores Rooney's lessons in coldness she deprived me of what may have been my last chance to counsel a woman of virtue.

How Dolores would have smirked at that phrase: a woman of virtue. If Dolores were alive she would be recruiting Becky to join the army of women marching on the Pope, demanding priesthood for their sex. She would not remember the young Becky Cardigan I remember, the one shining with her passion and her faith. Dolores never saw Rebecca shining with the mercy she showed to that shrewd husband of hers, shining with the mercy she showed to her whining mother. She never saw Rebecca shining with the mercy she showed to a priest looking for one merciful woman. She came to the rectory one morning to borrow the Confessions *of St. Augustine and said, her eyes cast down, "I wish I could be a Monica for my sons, Father"—not knowing then that it would be Jack who kept the faith and she who would turn on every person in her life who tried to love her.*

Does she think today that I don't see Dolores Rooney's cold contempt in her eyes if I drive to her house after one of those afternoon brandies? Does she think she is the first soul on earth to lose her faith? She has called Jack unfaithful, but Jack by Christ has never doubted for a moment of his life on earth; his is the Old Testament God who

☾

will grant him another wife if the first wife is barren and empty inside. Oh yes, Becky Perdue is empty inside, and she is not the only one.

Will she show up for this little Mothers' Club meeting, for the tea and powdered cookies afterwards? Will she sit on the porch at the Center, her eyes turned to the night and the river, while I dryheave my judgment at these women, a judgment that is nothing but bile now, after twenty years?

Will she look up with those empty lined eyes if I ask these women: Do you want to know how to get it back, ladies? Do you want to know how to get your faith back, in Due East, in the last years of the twentieth century? Are you asking an old drunk such a question?

Perhaps, ladies, you have chosen the wrong man to address you. Perhaps you do not require a man's insight at all. Certainly you do not require the sad insights of an aging parish priest who does not even have the courage to deny his own paltry faith.

☽

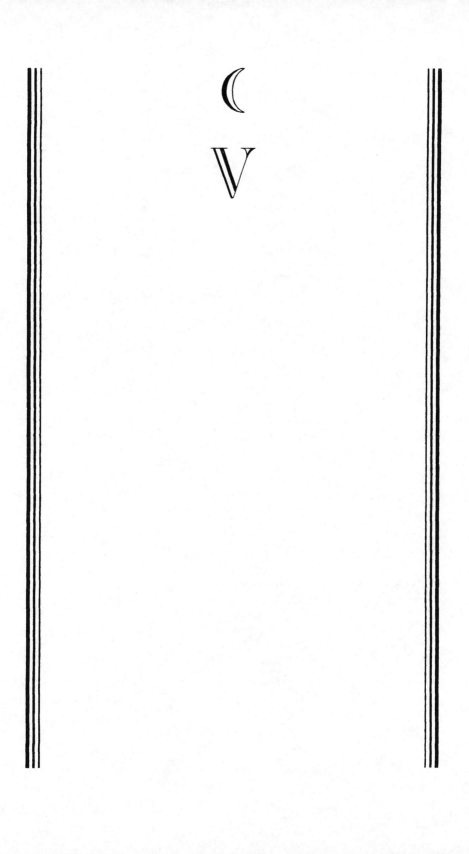

V

(

2|

May

For TWENTY-FOUR HOURS, MAY HAD AGONIZED over Marygail Dugan swinging her head so close to the graveyard fence. Her friends had pooh-poohed her, made her feel an old fool for fretting, but a day and a night of scrubbing her own kitchen had not relieved May of the distinct impression that she had been made witness to the girl's breakdown, and now God expected her to *do* something. So she left supper out for the three cats and for her husband, who was out fishing on Chessy Creek, and she drove back downtown to talk to Father Berkeley.

Now she stood on the rectory steps smoothing her hot pink pantsuit and wondering what had possessed her, when she took the trouble to change her clothes, to choose hot pink and to wear *trousers* when she had heard Father Berkeley say forty times if he'd said it once that he missed the days when bishops and priests and nuns and husbands and wives and children wore different robes, and you could tell one from the other.

Well. There. She'd promised herself not to work herself into that little-girl simpering she'd always pulled around Father—holy moley, she was sixty-five years old!—and already, just waiting on his steps, she was slipping into it. It had always been hard for her to look any priest in the eye— *he* had heard the darkest of your secrets in the confessional, but if *you* so much as imagined his private life, you already had another sin to confess—and this priest had heard thirty years of her troubles and her sinning. He had always been so impatient, so short with her, too: "Say the Sorrowful Mysteries for goodness' sake and stop imagining that good provider of yours is doing anything other than working as hard as he can for his family!"

But she was not here to talk to Father Berkeley about her guilt or her suspicions; she was here to warn him that a young woman was going mad. She didn't know *how* to explain to Father Berkeley why she had such a tingly breath-quickening sensation that Marygail Dugan was going to submerge herself in madness right at Our Lady of Perpetual Help, but someone had to tell him. Hadn't Tim Rooney picked the midnight mass? And with Holy Week right around the corner, why shouldn't Marygail Dugan just pick the Easter Vigil for *her* final plunge? Lordhavemercy: it was one thing for Tim Rooney to take a tinkle in the front pew, but what if Marygail got the same loony idea? She could picture herself putting a hand over her husband's eyes as Marygail lifted a leather miniskirt. They shouldn't ought to let this sort of thing go on: it could become a tradition at Our Lady of Perpetual Help. They could become a pilgrimage site for people on the brink.

Besides, coming to warn Father this time wasn't like agreeing to be the one to type the note putting him wise to the gossip. She'd *never* felt good about sneaking the use of her daughter's Selectric. And anyway, this time she'd come completely on her own, not only to save Father Berkeley's reputation but maybe to save that Dugan girl from bringing such sadness and pain on her whole family. Maybe she would be saving Marygail herself, saving her from doing something as plumb crazy as what Dottie Rooney had done when she drove out to the sea and let her family and her parish wonder forever after if it was just that terrible riptide rolling down or whether she had really meant to do away with herself.

It was better to act, May was certain, better to save people from themselves than to let them go on sliding down their slippery banks to craziness. And Father Berkeley, no matter how annoyed he made himself out to be, would know what to do. He just needed May to prompt him.

She was beginning to wonder if he would ever come to the door, but the

☾

study light was on, and she'd made out his shadow at the desk when she drove up. He was there, and working, probably on Sunday's sermon. It seemed to May that the sermons were getting back to normal, that he was pulling the thread of them through better than he had six months ago. But his face was still that horrible marbleized moony white, his eyes sunk into their muddy pouches and bubbling open like fiddler crabs' holes when he thought someone was watching him.

A little shiver ran up the back of May's legs as she heard him approaching the rectory door, and she could feel her pantsuit clinging to her, cold and silky. Why did she feel like a servant, ringing the bell?

Father opened the door briskly and stared down at her with what May felt sure was pure indifference.

"I'm real sorry to disturb you, Father," she said quickly.

He brushed her sentence aside with a long sweep of his hand. "Did I forget that heat again, May?" He sounded pleasant, almost warm, in his distraction.

"No, Father," she said in a rush. "No, Father, we finished up in the church *yes*terday."

He stood patiently at the door, blinking open the dark holes that were his eyes and waiting on her.

"There's something I think you ought to be made aware of," May said quickly, and when Father's white skin pinkened for a moment she thought: OhmyGod, did I use those selfsame words to write the note about Dolores and Father all these years ago? There's something I think you ought to be made aware of.

"Come on in, May," Father said, and when he turned away she thought: ohyes, ohmyLordyes, it *is* how I started the note, made aware of, and now he knows and this will be worse than the dark confessional; this will be like a husband's scolding. But then, May was not afraid of her husband, only sick to death of his grocery money lectures; and she did not need to be afraid of Father anymore—not even if he knew finally that she was the one who warned him about the way it looked between him and Dolores. If he knew she was the one, well. There. It was out finally, and all she had been doing in the *first* place was trying to save him from trouble, and now she could go about the business of saving Marygail Dugan.

Still, the little walk to Father Berkeley's study was a trial, the possibility that he had found her out hovering in the dark and airless hallway. "Father, I'm real

☾

sorry to disturb you at your work," she said again, trying with all the breath in her body to sound like a sixty-five-year-old woman. To sound like Father's elder, though you'd never know it from the ruts around his eyes.

"Oh, never you mind," Father said graciously, and May started at the paternal pitch to his voice. He turned around to smile at her over his shoulder, and she nearly tripped on his heel: Father smiling. He wasn't annoyed with her; he hadn't connected her to the note she'd dropped in the collection basket. He ushered her into his study, and waved her into the plump blue armchair opposite his desk.

May felt a familiar little twinge of resentment at the heavy old patterned rug under her feet, the warm blue plush of the chair beneath her: how nicely Father Berkeley had set himself up in this rectory. He sat himself behind a massive modern desk strewn all over with sheets of yellow legal pad, the pages crossed through in dark slashes. He looked comfortable here in the rectory; behind him, in the bookshelves, bottles of brandy and cognac and sherry were clustered. Right comfy.

" 'Scuse me, May," he said, shuffling the yellow pages into a stack. "I've been preparing a little talk for the Mothers' Club." He winked at her— WINKED! Father Berkeley!—and said: "At least I won't embarrass myself in front of you this year. I imagine it's a relief to have your children grown and your Mothers' Club days behind you."

May felt a wave of confusion wash over her. He was sober—she'd made sure of that at his first breath—but he was speaking to her in the easy charming self-deprecating way he spoke to his oldest allies in the church: the way he'd spoken once to Dolores Rooney or Becky Perdue.

"Um-hum," she said cautiously. "That's right, Father, it's a welcome relief not to have to get out to *those* meetings"—though the truth of it was that she sorely missed the good gossip of middle-aged mothers.

"Now May, what's this something I should be aware of?"

She hesitated. "Father," she said, trying hard to keep her eyes off the brandy bottles—off the variety, the *quantity* of them—"Father, there's a young girl been hanging around the church, and I am sick to death with worry for her."

He did not look in the least surprised, only mildly interested, and May remembered a sermon he'd given years ago, exhorting the congregation to return to confession. Father Berkeley had said from the pulpit that it was just plain silly to be ashamed of anything you had to tell in the darkness of the confessional, when a parish priest in a little town like Due East had already heard all the darkest secrets of human nature. Now he waited for her to go on.

"It's that Marygail Dugan," May started. "Stephen Dugan's wife, with the little girl. The one who never converted."

Father smiled encouragement. "I know her well," he said. "Why has she got you losing sleep, May?"

He had reduced her to feeling like a little girl already: saying she was *losing sleep,* putting words in her mouth that never would have formed in her mind. What she'd said was that she was *sick to death.* With worry.

"I'm afraid she's going to have a breakdown, Father." That was plain enough.

Father Berkeley stared down at the yellow pieces of paper without answering for so long that May was sure he was still composing his speech, and not listening to her at all. She began to hear the sound of her own breathing.

Finally he looked up and said: "I doubt it, really," but she could read in his eyes that he considered it a possibility, at least.

"I have this awful funny feeling, Father," she said, gentle and persistent as she could be.

"Did you know Mrs. Dugan is taking lessons?" Father Berkeley said. "She's to be baptized come Easter."

"I knew it!" May couldn't help herself: she knew she shouldn't have burst out with it, but this was un*can*ny.

"Knew what?"

"I knew it would be Easter! That she'd pick for the breakdown."

Father Berkeley smiled. "People don't pick the times for their breakdowns, May."

May smiled back as sweetly as she could manage. She knew better, and Father Berkeley knew better, too. "Father," she said, "I think I've been called to do something about it."

"And what might that be, May?"

May walked this minefield delicately. "Why, I've been called to let you know, so that you can counsel her. Before it's too late."

Father stared down again at the yellow sheaf, and May saw how stooped he had become, even sitting. She imagined him here at his desk, deep into the night, a brandy bottle on the desk top; suddenly she felt the quiet, the stillness —the absence—in the little rectory on Division Street.

☾

But he broke the stillness with an emphatic gravelly cough and peered up at her. "May," he said, "it was good of you to come."

Father always told the Altar Guild that it was good of them to choose the flowers, good of them to scrub the kneelers. May did not intend to be dismissed so easily this time.

"Will you talk to her, Father?" She leaned a hand on his big desk to press home the urgency, and saw Father Berkeley shrink back a little.

"I'll see to it, May," he said, and his shoulders sank lower.

May was satisfied with his answer: Father always kept his word, and if he said he'd see to it, well then, he would, no matter how miserable and resentful he looked. She had discharged her responsibility, anyway, and now this whole salvage operation had been put into motion.

Standing to wait for his dismissal, she found herself towering over the priest. He had shrunk, surely, in the last year: maybe he was even developing that bone disease that left people diminished and bent, though wasn't it usually women who fell prey? May was almost revolted by the idea of a man catching a woman's disease: if there was anything she didn't want to feel for Father, it was pity.

"Thank you kindly, Father," she said now, briskly, "thank you for your time." Her friends were silly fools to tremble before him.

"Thank *you*, May," he answered, "thank you for your concern." She looked down to see him twinkling up at her, almost smirking, taking his time. Making fun of her, maybe.

And at the thought of Father Berkeley making fun of her, she was almost trembling herself. After all these years, he had still found a way to get the upper hand.

☾

☾

2₂

At Eye Level

THE EVENING SUN WAS HOVERING ON THE HO-
rizon somewhere outside the Rapple house, and still Mrs. Perdue
reclined, half sitting, half lying, on Mary Faith's grandmother's couch
in the parlor. Mary Faith was in the kitchen, fixed in her determination
not to call the woman Becky and fixing her yet another cup of coffee
—though God knew Becky Perdue appeared wired enough without it.

Tim and his girlfriend had gone back home an hour ago. The three
of them—Mary Faith, Tim, and Eileen—had come tumbling out of
the two houses at three o'clock in the afternoon, when Becky Perdue
ran her big white car off the road and smack into the only live oak on
O'Connor Street. Mary Faith, faced with the sight of a smashed-in
front end and a dark-haired figure slumped over a steering wheel, had
turned back to the house where her coughing son was watching cartoons and had screeched up at the indifferent window:

"I told you not to leave the wagon by the side of the road! I told
you that!"

And then, shocked at her own outburst, she had held back on her
side of the road while Tim and Eileen crossed over to the mossy oak

tree; and she had hung back, still, when Tim opened the driver's seat to discover that Becky Perdue was not dead or even hurt but in some strange agitated state of shock and humiliation manifested by her inability to look anyone in the eye. Jesse's wagon—it had been Mary Faith's wagon, fifteen years before—lay twisted into a jagged priapic form in the middle of the road, its black handle pointed straight up to the sky, and Mary Faith could barely summon the decency to go see how bad Mrs. Perdue was feeling. All she could picture was Jesse, if he had been pulling the wagon. The woman must have been traveling at some speed.

Maybe it was her initial disinclination to cross the road and stretch out a hand to Rebecca Perdue that had made her insist so vehemently that the woman should come lie down in her house, not Tim's: "It's our fault, leaving the wagon lying there," she said, knowing full well that anyone traveling the speed limit, which was twenty-five on the Point, would have been able to stop before the rear wheels passed over the rest of the wagon.

Anyway, Mrs. Perdue had appeared to sorely need a resting place, whether it was in Tim's house or hers; her green eyes went from Tim to Eileen to Mary Faith as if they were taking inventory, or doing a reality check: they were strange eyes, their color as bright and pure as the color of the buds just coming out on the big old tree.

Tim had wanted to call an ambulance, but Mrs. Perdue looked terrified at the idea, and Eileen dismissed the notion with a single rude guffaw. There wasn't a mark on Becky, she pointed out—and when Tim said there might be internal bleeding or heavenonlyknew, Eileen raised one eyebrow and shook her head in disbelief.

So they'd helped Becky into Mary Faith's mother's parlor, and after Mary Faith had checked in on Jesse, now watching his third hour of cartoons with glazed eyes, she retreated to the kitchen to do what her mother had always done in emergencies: she made coffee and brought out a tin of pecan short-bread. *That* would be good for a woman with internal bleeding.

Then she and Tim and Eileen had sat on the worn parlor chairs, their hands awkward on their knees, while Becky Perdue assured them in a voice full of vibrato that she was fine and that she really just needed to get home to her daughter. Her three rescuers did not consult one another, but Mary Faith jumped up to call the daughter and Tim went outside to see if he could turn the engine over and back up the car; as they left the room Becky Perdue sat

☾

very still—all but her hands, which approached each other in little knitting motions. Coming back from the kitchen phone, Mary Faith heard her say to Eileen that the experience was like a bad dream, almost like a hallucination, and by the time the coffee was brewed, Mrs. Perdue had leaned her head back on the rolled sofa arm and commenced *wringing* her hands.

Now, three hours later, Tim and Eileen had said doubtful good-byes and Mary Faith's father had come home with the Plaid King tow truck: he'd pulled the big white car into his own driveway and decided to tinker with it right there, to see if he could get it running so that Mrs. Perdue would have it overnight, before she turned it over to a body shop. Mary Faith had called the Perdue house three times in three hours, and none of the children had answered; as she traveled back and forth with new cups of coffee she heard the woman sighing strangely, as if to say: "I *knew* they wouldn't be home. I *knew* they wouldn't be around."

And it wasn't just the sighs that made Mary Faith dislike this braided woman stretched out on the old velvet couch; it wasn't just that she'd destroyed a fifteen-year-old red wagon; it wasn't just that she'd flushed Eileen out of Tim's bedroom in the middle of the day. Mary Faith had decided to dislike her that Saturday night when she'd been fool enough to make her way to the convert class. Mary Faith could not abide vague women, or women unfixed on what they wanted, and it seemed to her that a woman who could walk tipsy into a class she was supposed to teach was as vague and as unfocused as she could get. The sighs were just flourishes: momma's-a-martyr flourishes.

But Mary Faith and her martyred guest would just have to wait for Jesse, who said he'd have the Buick running in half an hour. That was an hour ago. Now Mary Faith, trying to time dinner so she wouldn't have to set it out while Mrs. Perdue was still there, had the oyster stew simmering away, clotting up too thick and—once she had brought in the last cup of coffee—nothing to do but sit down with the woman, who had refused so much as a magazine to look at.

If Becky Perdue wasn't hurt, why was she still reclining?

Mary Faith settled on the edge of the old plaid ottoman so she could leave the room in a rush. "My son's got bronchitis," she said flatly: God, she hated this small talk with older women. With anyone. She wouldn't have sat down at all if she thought there was the slightest chance that this Becky Perdue

☾

would ask why she didn't come back to convert class. But she wouldn't, today. She was too shook up by the crash.

Becky Perdue turned the corners of her mouth up into what Mary Faith figured must be an attempt at a sympathetic smile. Jesus, the woman was a mess: it was hard to even interpret her facial expressions.

Jesse coughed in the TV room. "There he goes!" Mary Faith exclaimed in a false voice, hoping that the little boy's hack would be bad enough to send her fleeing again, but the sound died down directly: she was a prisoner on the ottoman. "Can I get you something? Some Bayer? Or Pepto-Bismol?"

Becky Perdue narrowed her eyes—maybe she was insulted at being offered Pepto-Bismol—and looked out through the dark window in the direction of the Rooney house. Finally she said: "I had no idea you lived next door."

Now Mary Faith could read her expression. The woman couldn't say no thanks, I don't need any aspirin, but she could admit what she'd been doing on O'Connor Street in the first place. Driving by Tim Rooney's house. Mary Faith wanted to hoot at Mrs. Perdue's transparency: what did she and Eileen see in Tim? She could understand their finding him sweet, after they got past all his interrogations—but what in God's name did they see in him sexually? What would Mrs. Perdue think of the belts Tim liked to use?

She studied the woman's face while it was set in profile: she was old, her face as lined as Stephen's. What was she doing running after Tim?—she was a married woman, a mother. Mary Faith thought three children had been mentioned, at least.

"I'm sorry," Becky Perdue said suddenly, and for a moment she turned full face to Mary Faith. At least she wasn't a starer: she looked, and then she looked away. Old-fashioned manners, old-fashioned braid. Mary Faith had been trying to figure out all afternoon whether the braid was a vestige of this woman's Joan Baez days or whether Becky Perdue had just never noticed that nobody between the ages of twenty-five and sixty-five wore her hair that way in Due East. It made her feel distinctly self-conscious about her own braid, and now, sitting on the ottoman, she found herself wondering if Stephen ever thought Marygail's streaked spikes were attractive. Sexy.

That was the effect this strangely silent woman had on her: here she was, in her own mother's parlor, floating away with jealous fantasies about Stephen and Marygail when she'd started out looking at the woman's profile. She looked again and saw that Becky Perdue was good-looking, after all, in that

☾

fifties or sixties sort of way: that sheer jutting chin and the very whiteness of her skin: her dark lipstick. Her nose was funny, though, pug and red at the tip. Mary Faith was willing to bet that the woman was a regular drinker, a serious drinker. Like Stephen.

"How 'bout a beer?" she said, trying to cover up Mrs. Perdue's floating apology. They could both pretend it had never been said.

"Oh," Becky Perdue said, with a start, "oh, no thanks." Then she began to cry.

Mary Faith suppressed her own sigh of martyrdom. She did *not* want to stand up and go comfort this old woman, this mother whose children did not stick around their house waiting to hear that she was hurt, this Catholic proselytizer lusting after Tim Rooney. She found herself pushing her own hands through the air, mocking the knitting motions Becky Perdue had started after the crash. She wanted this woman to go home, not fall to pieces on her. She wanted to nurse her bronchitis boy and to coax her father in out of the driveway and to serve them up some warm food. She wanted to write a note to Stephen. She wanted to take care of *them,* not Becky Perdue.

But here she was, rising, making her way to the velvet couch, putting a hand that rebelled against the motion onto Becky Perdue's pathetic slumping shoulder.

"There now," she heard herself whispering. She'd never said *there now* in her life.

Becky Perdue pulled her shoulder out from under Mary Faith's hand and sat up straight, as if she were fighting an impulse to shove the comfort away. So Mary Faith backed off, all the way back to her ottoman, and Becky Perdue said:

"Please forgive me. I'm so sorry. I don't *do* this sort of thing."

Mary Faith had no idea how to answer *that.*

"It's just been such a strange day. I'm just having a good hard time sorting out what's real and: can you imagine, driving to see Tim, I thought I saw a wizened little figure by the side of the road. An old black woman, stooped over like the laundresses when I was a girl. She had a halo like the guardian angels' haloes in the *Messenger*s my mother used to read to us—oh, my word! I was thinking of my mother and I must have imagined that old woman. I can't tell you how disconcerting that is. Seeing pictures from my childhood on the side of the road."

((

"Wait," Mary Faith said. She could see that Mrs. Perdue would be off on a talking jag followed by another crying jag if she didn't hush her up. "Wait up now," she said.

Becky Perdue looked up with her strange green eyes—they looked clouded over, like agates, in the dim light of the parlor—and murmured another apology.

"That woman—" Mary Faith said.

Mrs. Perdue shivered in the dark room, and Mary Faith could see her fear. Did she think she was having the DTs?

"I mean," Mary Faith said. "I mean, that woman is real. There's an old black woman with white hair who walks down O'Connor Street to do people's houses—she's Tim's maid."

Becky Perdue looked as if she'd been slapped hard on her back. She jerked forward and said: "Tim's MAID?" and when Mary Faith nodded, she broke into a faint pixilated smile that Mary Faith found irresistible; she knew she mirrored it when she answered:

"I know he doesn't seem the likeliest person to hire an old woman. To clean his daddy's house."

Becky Perdue shook her head back and forth. "I am so embarrassed," she said. "I am so ashamed. That woman is real?"

Mary Faith smiled again. "Tim says she's been working for the family for forty years."

"Oh dear," Becky Perdue said. "Oh gracious. Forty years? Could that be?" She smiled again, abashed and confused. "I mean to tell you, that house has always looked like the day after the hurricane. I can't believe there was somebody keeping order there."

Mary Faith shrugged. "You know the Rooney family?"

"I was best friends with Tim's mama fifteen or sixteen years ago. Oh, I don't know if best friends is the word. But she took me in, under her wing, and—"

"They were always putting on pageants in the backyard."

"The Rooneys were always putting on pageants all over the house!" Becky Perdue said. "They were always in a state of complete upheaval. Oh, I don't mean to run on at the mouth. I'm so sorry."

Mary Faith wondered if Mrs. Perdue was on the verge of hysteria, opening up this way after three hours of silence. If it wasn't the crash that shook her up,

☾

maybe she had been this loopy driving down O'Connor Street: "You were driving over to Tim's?" she said.

"Actually," Becky Perdue answered her, eyes down to the floor, "actually, I was on my way to see you."

Mary Faith felt her jaw dropping open and made no move to close it. Becky Perdue *was* a church lady, and if Tim was right—if Stephen was sending this crazy stranger over to convince her to convert and get married in the Church —he could just forget about a wedding. He could just go back to Marygail: to Ms. Streaky Spikes, Ms. Flat-chested Miniskirt, Ms. Sleep-Around-with-Soldiers.

Mrs. Perdue shifted on the couch. "It's been a *real* strange day," she said, and then stopped. Mary Faith closed her mouth, finally, and waited.

"I was on my way to see Tim, to get your address, because I ran into Stephen Dugan today and—" She obviously didn't know how to go on. She was peeking up at Mary Faith.

This woman knew Stephen, and this woman knew Tim, and she had known Tim's mother, and: who *was* she, with her strange hairdo and strange eyes and strange clothes? She was dressed in a long cotton skirt the color of seaweed and a big loose jacket with padded shoulders that could have come right out of *Vogue* or right out of the Our Lady of Perpetual Help secondhand shop, it was so wrong for a middle-aged woman in Due East. And Mary Faith felt that she was losing her breath, that she didn't want to hear the next line—that Stephen had asked someone else, some stranger, some forty-five-year-old woman who WORE HER HAIR THE SAME WAY SHE DID, WHO WORE THE SAME LONG SKIRTS—that Stephen had asked someone like that to intervene when religion had to be the biggest barrier between them. The biggest. The only.

Her voice came out flat and dull again. "Stephen asked you to—"

"Oh, no!" Becky Perdue said. "Oh, no. I'm embarrassed. This is such a strange idea I had. It's like that old woman, that guardian angel in the street. I don't know if I should . . ."

Mary Faith wanted to take her by the shoulders and shake her. What*ever* was she going on about?

"You came by my house," she prompted, knowing her voice was laced with contempt.

Mrs. Perdue could have been the younger of the two women, the way she

☾

was twisting the gold button on her jacket. "I was going to come talk to you—" She was stuck again.

By now Mary Faith was sitting on a quarter-inch strip at the edge of the ottoman. She felt ready to propel herself through the dark window and over to Tim's house. She felt ready to shake Tim by the collar, and Stephen, and especially this woman. Especially this Becky Perdue.

"You wanted to talk to me about converting," she said. She couldn't *help* it if she sounded snippety. She was more than snippety.

But Becky Perdue said: "Oh, no."

And when Mary Faith looked at her with obvious, hateful disbelief, she repeated it: "Oh, no. I *knew* you'd never turn Catholic."

Finally Mary Faith rose from the seat that was barely holding her. "What then?" she said, and she ironed out the flatness of her voice into unwavering, unwrinkled smoothness. "What'd you want to talk to me about?"

Mrs. Perdue blinked and swallowed. "I wanted to say . . . Oh, this seems so *wrong* now. You see, this is what I mean about this strange day, and sorting out what's real. My husband is trying to get custody of the children and when I went to see him, and Stephen was there, I got this crazy idea in my head that— I realize I don't even *know* you—but I thought I could"—her voice twisted off to shame, or embarrassment—"save you."

Mary Faith did not wait to see whether Becky Perdue expected a reaction. She shot from the room and through the hall into the kitchen, where she brought her fist down onto the counter with a furious thud. Save her. SAVE HER. So Stephen had sent her, after all. That was their code word: I'm going to *save* you. Becky Perdue and Stephen Dugan were the Billy Grahams of the Catholic set, only they had to arrange car crashes and twisted wagons instead of revivals and baptismal pools to sucker souls in.

Now what was she supposed to do? Was she supposed to go get saved? Was she supposed to pretend the woman wasn't there, and call her father in to eat a stew that had congealed itself into a solid mass in the saucepan? Was she supposed to try calling the Perdue house again in hope that the children could come and pick up their ranting mother? Was she supposed to call Stephen and tell him what she thought of this madness? She was certainly not going to go back into the parlor and *talk* to Becky Perdue. She was not going to talk to the lunatic. She could hear her father outside the kitchen door, singing to himself. He would be hours over the car, caressing it as if it were a hopeless woman.

☾

Hopeless. She had thought the word *hopeless* because that was the way she felt, staring at her ruined oyster stew, listening to the news blaring out from the TV room. The *news*. The sound of the Savannah anchorman's thick slick accent vibrated in her quiet kitchen: Jesse knew she didn't want him listening to the news, didn't want him memorizing pictures of airplane crashes and children consumed in flames and AIDS and

She made her way back down the hallway, flashing past the parlor without a thought for what Becky Perdue might think of her running through the house. But Jesse wasn't in the den: he wasn't lying on the couch: his comforter lay crumpled on the floor, his Coca-Cola glass overturned beside it. Mary Faith clicked off the old console, stooped over to pick up the tumbler, and watched black gooey Coke pool at her feet. This was too much. This was way too much.

"Jess!" she called, clutching the glass to her midriff in the hallway. "Jess?"

His dark curly head peered out of the parlor door, across the hall, his face flushed with pleasure at his own disappearing act. "You said not to watch the news, Momma." He ducked back into the parlor.

"Jesse David Rapple, you get back here this instant."

There was no sound from the parlor.

"Jes-se. I mean now."

Still there was silence, until Mary Faith heard Mrs. Perdue's soft voice: "You better mind, honey."

You better mind, honey. The voice was as gooey as the Coke on the floor of the TV room. Where was her father—where were this woman's children? Mary Faith could not bear going back in to face her; she heard Jesse's high wild giggles from behind the open parlor doorway. She stomped back down to the kitchen, slammed the plastic Coke glass on the counter, and swung open the kitchen door to see her father's back bent over the smoothly idling engine of Becky Perdue's white car.

Idling: the car was working. "Praise the Lord!" she said. "Can she go home now?"

Her father could not—or pretended he could not—hear her over the hum of the car.

"Daddy!"

Still no response.

(

"Daddy!" she hollered, progressing down the steps, and when he turned around and straightened himself slowly: "You might could answer."

Jesse scowled at her and put a greasy hand to the small of his back. "I beg your *pardon,* Missy," he said.

"Oh, I'm sorry," Mary Faith said, "but she's driving me goofy. Is it fixed? Can she go home now?"

"I've got her running," Jesse said, "but I've got to see to this right headlight if Miz Perdue's going to pull out of here in the dark."

"Oh, Daddy. It's light out."

Jesse squinted out at the twilight on O'Connor Street. "It's not *light* out," he said pointedly, and leaned back down to fiddle with the radiator cap.

"Daddy," Mary Faith tried again, but she could tell from the fixed angle of her father's back that he would not be straightening up again until he had the car to his satisfaction. Probably not until he had personally hammered out the whole crushed front grille.

She climbed the three steps to the kitchen slowly, and when she was back in the bright room she sat helplessly at the kitchen table. Now she could hear Jesse singing from the parlor: putting on one of his acts for Becky Perdue. Now she could hear Jesse singing "Joy to the World."

"That's *enough,*" she said out loud, and then she rose wearily and returned to the parlor, stepping deliberately and holding her breath back so that it would not come out at hurricane force when she finally hushed Jesse and asked Rebecca Perdue to get out of her parlor and out of her house and out of this idea that she was going to save her from anything.

"Jesse!" she said at the doorway, but Jesse was singing out his own version of the hymn his grandfather had taught him:

> "Joy to the world
> The Lord is dead"

Becky Perdue was sitting up rigid on the couch, her hand clutching the arched arm and her face a study in bewilderment: Mary Faith didn't suppose any of Mrs. Perdue's children ever sang out "The Lord is dead."

"Daddy and I have a slight disagreement about whether my son ought to be singing hymns," she said, knowing that her voice had gone past sarcasm: it had traveled all the way to *nasty.* "That's enough, Jesse."

☾

"Look here, I'm sorry," Becky Perdue said. Mary Faith thought she'd scream at the top of her lungs, louder than Jesse sang, if the woman said she was sorry one more time.

Jesse cocked his head back, calculating how far he could go, and hummed the tune, his face maddeningly beatific, no trace of the bronchitis in his sweet high voice.

Mary Faith finally let out her own sigh. "I didn't tell him to come in here and offend you," she said.

"No, no, he's a darling," Becky Perdue said: now Mary Faith could not tell whether Becky's voice shook because she thought she was hallucinating, or whether the caffeine from the three cups of coffee had set it to quivering.

"I don't know whether I'd call him a *darling*," Mary Faith said, letting the tone of her voice fly where it might. "He's our little Nietzsche." Her tone had settled past nasty and lingered somewhere between the sound of Stephen's haughty voice and Tim's snide routine.

To her amazement, Becky threw her head back and laughed at her haughty snideness, and the laugh did not sound shaky at all, but full and resonant.

Jesse laughed along and sang, "Knee-she, Knee-she," and for one long moment the two women looked at each other, Mary Faith daring the older woman to smile.

She did smile faintly, and said softly: "Your father wants to bring him up with some religion?"

Mary Faith stiffened. "Daddy wants to baptize him." She didn't know why she bothered to answer. "But I won't let him step foot in any church: not after what they did to me."

Becky Perdue nodded vigorously, as if she knew the whole story of the Baptist preacher sermonizing on teenage pregnancies when Mary Faith sat in the congregation, big with her child: she had to remind herself that *everybody* in Due East knew her whole story.

"He reminds me of my son Jack," Becky said, her voice still delicate, almost slurred. "One minute you think they're full of the divil, and the next they're little saints."

FULL OF THE DIVIL? WHAT WAS THIS BROGUE BUSINESS? "Look," Mary Faith said, "my father's got the car running. Maybe you could go on out and look at it."

"I'll go look at it!" Jesse threw himself backwards off the ottoman.

☾

"No, Jesse—go get your slippers on."

"I've *got* my slippers on," he bellowed, and kicked them off his feet high into the air.

"Jesse Rapple," Mary Faith started.

"Jesse," Becky Perdue repeated after her, and Mary Faith saw that she was pulling herself together, speaking quietly in a schoolteacher's voice and leaning forward off the couch with determination. "Jesse," she said again, in a lower octave, "I'd like you to do me a special favor."

Jesse sat straight up on the ottoman and watched her suspiciously. "What?" At least he had stopped shrieking.

"I'll bet you're pretty good at finding things."

"Yeah," Jesse said, still mistrustful.

"You mean yes," she said briskly. She was transforming herself by the minute from a woman suffering an anxiety attack to a classroom teacher dealing with a fractious child. "You mean yes, ma'am."

"Yes, ma'am," he said doubtfully.

"I'd like you to find me my pocketbook."

"Your pocketbook—" Mary Faith started, but Mrs. Perdue fixed her with a dull quieting eye.

"I can find it!" Jesse said. "Let me find it, Momma," and he scampered off to the kitchen.

Mary Faith took a breath. "Look here," she said. "I don't know how long you think you can get rid of Jesse. He sticks like chewing gum on the bottom of your shoe. He'll be back in a—"

Becky Perdue interrupted. "I know I've been an awful bother." No more trembling in the voice, no more doubts about her sanity: she had transformed herself completely. "I know that suppertime's just about the worst time to be overstaying your welcome in somebody's house."

Mary Faith shrugged: this was a queer manipulative woman, talking herself out of her fragility while she held Mary Faith prisoner in her own house.

"I could see I scared you out of your wits with my talk about saving you, and I want you to know the truth." Becky Perdue allowed herself a pause. "I don't want you to go back to that convert class. I don't even believe myself, anymore."

Mary Faith swallowed back the question of what an alleged nonbeliever was doing teaching a convert class. She waited.

☾

"I probably have no business saying this," Becky Perdue said, and Mary Faith nodded—that's right, Mrs. Perdue—but the woman droned on.

"I've just been hurt badly myself, and I thought for one moment that I could protect you from having the same thing happen."

"Stephen and I are not having a custody fight," Mary Faith said sharply.

"No," Mrs. Perdue said. "No, you're not. I guess I *don't* have any business saying it, or coming by your house." She smiled the faint smile again. "Especially coming by in *that* fashion. But I was drawn to you the minute I saw you in the rectory. I don't know why, exactly: I just was. I'm sorry. I'll go see to my car now and thank your father for all his help." She pulled her pocketbook out from underneath the couch and rose, unsteady at first, leaning on the arm of the sofa as Jesse came back into the room.

He scowled. "You've *got* your pocketbook."

"I just this minute found it, little watermelon." Becky Perdue smiled easily at the boy, and Mary Faith almost raised a hand to cover her own face or shut her own mouth. Little watermelon was what *she* called Jesse. "Whenever I ask one of my children where something is, I find it directly."

"You're too old to have children," Jesse said.

"Jess!"

"It's all right," Becky said briskly. "I am too old to have children like you. My children are nearly grown."

"Got any boys? How many boys?"

"Jesse—Mrs. Perdue is just fixing to go."

"What about supper? I'm *hungry*, Momma. How many boys?"

"Two," said Becky Perdue. "Two boys almost men. It was real nice to meet you, Jesse. I'll bet you can't show me the way out to the car."

"Ha!" said Jesse. "She thinks I don't even know where the back door is. In my own . . . House!"

Jesse wiped his nose with the back of his hand and then held the hand out to Becky Perdue, who pulled a handkerchief from her pocketbook, wiped the hand and then the nose, and let Jesse lead her into the hallway. Mary Faith followed them, her fury muffled. She just wanted to sit down. She just wanted to sit her father and her son down to supper and go up to her room and sit on the edge of the bed and look out of her window at the night falling.

Mrs. Perdue was so self-possessed now that she looked around the kitchen as if she were taking the Due East Spring House Tour, and Mary Faith peered through the kitchen door at her father, sorting his tools back into their box.

"Looks like he's got it going good," she said. Even relief had been stripped from her voice.

"Hurray!" shouted Jesse. "Hurray, he's got it *going*."

"I'll just walk on out there and thank him for all that trouble," said Becky Perdue.

"But aren't you staying? For supper?" Jesse said.

"No," Mary Faith said. "No, she can't."

"I can't," Becky repeated. "But thanks for asking. He's a fine boy," she said, almost wistfully, and turned to Mary Faith.

Mary Faith knew that she should say *yes, he is,* knew she should praise her son in front of this stranger, but she said nothing. She tapped her foot on the linoleum, and even the tapping sounded contemptuous.

"I am a fine boy?" Jesse said.

"Of course you are!" Now pure exasperation spluttered out. "Mrs. Perdue, if you don't mind, I'm going to dish out this food and get my son off to bed. He's been sick. He *is* sick."

Mrs. Perdue nodded—a pathetic little nod—and Mary Faith turned to stir up the pot. For a long moment, the kitchen filled up with silence, even Jesse's, and then Becky Perdue spoke to Mary Faith's back:

"I hope you'll excuse this. I wouldn't even say this to my own daughters. I'm not so good with my own flesh and blood. But even if I can't *save* you"— she was very good at that self-deprecating tone—"even if I can't save you, I can leave you with something to contemplate. I heard the way you talked to your father when he came in before, and now I've heard you talk to your son. You must see the way they depend on you. You can't be dismissing them all the time."

Mary Faith knew that the heat from the simmering burner could not possibly make her cheeks flush up the way they were doing. DISMISSING THEM. She had only been trying to fix a meal for them half the afternoon. She only played mother to both of them, a forty-five-year-old man and a four-year-old boy. She did not trust herself to turn around. If anyone was leaning on her, it was this woman, who must have taken lessons in hypocritical lectures from Tim Rooney himself.

"Thank you for your hospitality," Becky Perdue said, as if she had not been chastising the minute before. "Thanks to *both* of you." Mary Faith knew that she was leaning over to kiss Jesse, or squeeze his hand, and still she did not turn around to acknowledge Becky Perdue's words. She heard the woman turn the kitchen doorknob and disappear into the twilight.

What Mary Faith found hard to believe was not just that Jesse dragged a chair over to the sink to wash his hands, without a word, or that Becky Perdue did not return to say *I'm so sorry* one more time. What surprised her was that the color of her cheeks paled down and that she—unable to smooth out any of the floury lumps in the pot, or even concentrate on doing it—was so conscious of the emptiness of the house once Becky Perdue had left it. What she found hard to believe was that there was such a pervasive quality of absence, now that the woman was finally gone.

The night stars were subdued at ten o'clock, when Mary Faith went to walk down O'Connor Street: they were hushed in the sky by a blanket of lumpy dark clouds, and Mary Faith was subdued with them. She was remembering the night Tim had brought Eileen over to sit at the kitchen table to drink beer, and how she had stayed awake in her bed later, trying to retrace the woman's wide smile and wispy hair; the need to remember Eileen—to make the image photographic and permanent—had frightened her. Wasn't she a girl who'd missed out on the years of marking boys' images and fixing them in her mind?

Now she wanted to remember Becky Perdue's face, the imagined dignity of it when she'd told Mary Faith off, and surely there was something perverse about that. Hadn't Eileen's image been twisted into a grotesque the night before, when she saw Tim tying her hands up? At least she could not imagine Becky Perdue letting anyone tie her up, not unless it was attendants in a mental hospital.

Mary Faith followed the same route walking she followed every night: it was not what you could call exercise, not the goose-stepping thick-soled walk of all the retired officers in Due East who subscribed to *The Walking Magazine*. Mary Faith meandered every night, once Jesse was down and the dishes were dried and her coursework was done; she followed O'Connor down to Faulk and walked past the Percy house and the green and the big cluster of pecan trees by the water. She followed it in an exhausted daze, usually, letting the silky night come between her and any fantasies about what Stephen might be doing with Marygail. He'd promised.

☾

And every night she turned around at the end of Warren Street to retrace her steps, knowing that the Parrishes' Irish setter would howl as mournfully at her when she was returning as when she was leaving. By the time she opened her kitchen door, her father would have pulled himself up off the lounger in the TV room to say good night and she would lock up, solitary downstairs.

Tonight, though, there were silhouettes in the dark. A group, a trio—a regular shamrock of dark figures—was saying good night at the Rooneys' door: Tim and his father, sending Eileen off. Mary Faith couldn't *believe* she could laugh and wave so easily in the doorway with the old man when she'd been upstairs half the day with her S & M games. She slunk back near the live oak, across the street, until she had passed the Rooneys' safely.

Or almost safely: before she had crossed over into her own yard, she heard a skipping along the pavement behind her and knew before she had turned to look that Eileen had come after her.

"Mary Faith!"

There was nothing to do but wait for her to catch up. Eileen was awkward running, breathless and bedraggled.

"Tim just called your father to find out if Becky Perdue was all right. Your father was kind of vague—what'd you think?"

Mary Faith considered: not the answer, but how to phrase it. She let Eileen catch her breath. "I think Mrs. Perdue's crackers."

"How long'd she stay?"

"Forever."

"I *told* Tim we shouldn't have walked out on you. But with Jesse sick and all—"

"Oh, that's all right." Mary Faith found it hard to look this woman in the eye, seeing what she'd seen of her. "She was just rambling on. She said she was coming by to see me and *save* me."

Eileen's eyes lighted up with a mischief visible even in the dark. "*Save* you. Is she trying to bring you into the Church?"

Mary Faith wanted to erase her answer and start again. What had she been thinking of, using that word aloud? "I guess," she said. "I guess that's what she was after. I think she needs a good psychiatrist."

Eileen hooted. "Don't we all?"

"Not me," Mary Faith said. "I just need some peace from all the nuts in this town."

☾

"You prob'ly just need some rest," Eileen said. "I prob'ly shouldn't be keeping you out here in the night. I swear, I don't know how you do all you do, with a child."

Mary Faith wanted to weep from the relief of someone *seeing* it: seeing her fatigue and her despair. She wanted to weep from the someone seeing being Eileen, who would be gone from Due East in two months, back to New York and her work and her childless studio. She hung her head down, childlike as Jesse.

"Tim told me he's been sick for a good while. Would you let me come by tomorrow afternoon and sit for him? So you could get some work done, or just drive out to the beach?"

Later, Mary Faith decided that it was the words *drive out to the beach* that made her say something so crazy to Eileen. She couldn't drive: her father had given her three lessons and then made excuses about how hard it was to learn in the truck, how he'd teach her when they bought a regular sedan with an automatic transmission. She was a prisoner in her house, with only the streets of the Point and the waterfront park as her exercise yard—surely it was those words *drive out to the beach* that made her say what she did.

"I couldn't let you do that. I don't want to take you away from Tim," she started, knowing already how wrong it was coming out. "I don't want to take you away from all that pleasure." And by then she'd gone so far that she rolled ahead, imitating Tim when he was grilling her, or maybe imitating Becky Perdue telling her off. She fixed her sights on Eileen, right at eye level. "Why do you let him do that to you? Don't you know he's off his rocker, too?"

Eileen stared at her puzzled; there was a pause, and then she scraped a foot on the road. "Oh, I don't know," she said softly. "I'm real fond of Tim."

And when Mary Faith shook her head back and forth, aghast at what she'd said, Eileen went on: "Tim's a sweet guy. I guess he needs as much—I don't know, mercy—as any of us."

Mary Faith nodded stupidly, wanting to apologize and not knowing how to form the words, wanting not to sound like Becky Perdue with her pathetic *I'm sorry*s. Eileen smiled a broad smile and waved: "G'night. I'll call tomorrow. To see if I can spell you," as if Mary Faith had not rejected her offer, as if she had not said anything out of the ordinary.

Mary Faith watched her walk back to the Rooneys' driveway to get into her car, and then listened for the sound of it starting. She couldn't imagine that

☾

Eileen's sweet nature wouldn't sour, that she would still forgive Mary Faith in the morning. Surely Eileen would replay their conversation until she seethed with anger at Mary Faith's nerve.

She couldn't imagine that she would ever go back to the art studio now, not with Tim and Eileen both in the room, not when Tim would hear by the morning what Mary Faith had gone and said.

She walked right by her own house, quickly, and kept moving down the road, speeding her pace until it was almost a run. There was a pay phone outside the bank, and she could call Stephen's house. If he answered, she would have to think of an excuse for waking his household deep in the night. She could not tell him about Becky Perdue's visit. She could not humiliate herself that way.

Suddenly she knew what she would tell him, and when she knew she broke into a real run, a determined breathless dash through the streets of the Point.

She would tell Stephen that this was it. If she couldn't be married on her birthday, they had to set a new date. A new, definite date.

She couldn't bear it anymore.

☾

$$\left(\begin{array}{c}\end{array}\right.$$

23

Wits' End

"MARYGAIL? WERE YOU SLEEPING?"

"Who's this?"

"It's Grace, hon. You let the phone ring twenty times."

"I don't want to talk. To him."

"Who? Stephen?"

"No." Pause. "Stephen doesn't call in the middle of the day. That old man. The priest."

"Well, that's what *I'm* calling about. I've been trying you for days. Momma said you told her you were getting baptized. She said you sounded real strange and she thinks you've been brainwashed. Know what else she said? She said they could try to bring you into that Church, but the first water that wet your head was your real birthmark. They are *real* upset, Marygail. He promised when he married you that he wasn't going to ask you to *do* that."

"He."

"What? Why d'you sound so strange? You *were* sleeping, weren't you?"

Silence.

"He what, Marygail? Are you all right?"

Silence.

"Marygail, you are frightening me good now. Are you doing coke again? No, not coke—are you back on all that Valium?"

Silence.

"Marygail. I am at my wits' end. Are you all right?"

A sudden definite defiant answer: "No."

"Is it the drugs, honey?"

"No."

"What? Is Stephen leaving you?"

"Well."

"I can't believe it. I can't believe he finally got up the courage to do it."

"I." Pause. "Won't let him."

A long sigh from the big sister. "Marygail, I don't want to sound *cruel* or anything, but after all these years and all those affairs—I don't just mean you now, I mean him and that little girl, too—I can't say but that it wouldn't be a blessed relief for the two of you. You belong back in Columbia, I have always said this even to Jake who as you know was Stephen's best *friend* for years. You have always deserved better than that sweltering little house even if it is on the water."

Silence.

"All right, I know that's hard to take from me, I know I haven't been an angel either, but Jake and I got way past that, and we had triplets to deal with which puts it on a different level. That's a lot more pressure."

Silence.

"Come on now, Marygail. I don't want to preach at you. I just think it's something you ought to consider. When you're calculating. And what's this old priest doing calling you? Are they all putting pressure on you now, to turn Catholic? They are out of their heads, Marygail. I mean, the *Pope*. It's just a song and dance the Irish and the Italians feel comfortable with, but you know, it's not *our* song and dance. Those are Stephen's people, not yours. If Jake made me bring up the boys Jewish I don't know what I'd do, I swear. I'd leave him, that's all. Can you imagine? Bar *Mitz* vahs? So you just tell that old priest to quit calling you before you have to go to some Polish fair. You just come on up and spend a few days with me."

"He's taking over."

☾

"He's taking over what? What's Stephen taking over?"

"Not Stephen. The priest."

"YOU CAN'T LET A PRIEST TAKE YOU OVER. Momma's right, they are brainwashing you."

"He's taking over the convert class. For the ones who want to get baptized."

"But you don't want *that*. You don't really want that."

A slurpy sound. "Iwannagethim back."

"Oh, Marygail." A long whewwwwwww into the receiver. "I think maybe I am beginning to lose my patience. I think maybe I better call you back later when you are speaking like a grown woman."

"No!"

"All right. All right, I won't call you back. You sit in that hot little house and you think about it, and I guarantee before the sun has set you'll be dialing *my* number."

"No Gracie, don't hang up, no Gracie, I need you, I need someone, Gracie. Don't hang up now, not now. No. Please."

"Well goodness gracious. Slow down. I'll talk to you if you really want to talk. You just don't sound right at all. You don't sound like the Marygail Easterling Dugan I know."

Silence.

"Grace?"

"What, honey? Try to make some *sense.*"

"Grace?"

"*What,* Marygail?"

"Grace, did you ever hear a shhshing sound in your house? We always had a shhshing sound in the house when we were little, remember, but it was the fans, or the air conditioner. But I can hear that shhshing sound all day. And it's not summer yet. Grace, we don't *have* an air conditioner."

"Ohmygod."

"Do you hear that sound in your house, Gracie?"

"Ohmygod tell me this is not what I think it is. Marygail, is this some drug you're taking?"

Silence.

"Shit. Marygail, I am not coming down there just to throw away your stash again, I have three little boys and the maid does *not* like to take care of them, she says I pay her to clean, not to babysit, and I'll have to give her forty dollars

☾

a day if I come down there. And that will put me in a real bad mood. If it's drugs, I swear I won't forgive you this time."

"Grace. Oh please. Ohpleasepleaseplease."

"Ohmygod. It's not drugs. Is it, honey?"

"Grace, don't hang up. I can hear it on the phone—do you hear that now? You can hear it, can't you?"

"Ohmygod in heaven. What do I do? All right, I'll just talk to Ettamae, I'll just tell her she has *got* to watch them. I'll say this is a medical emergency and Jake can just come home early. I'll just tell Daddy he's got to let him off early. And Momma'll come down, no you don't want Momma, I'll just drive down myself. This very morning. I just will. Marygail? You have got to call Stephen on the phone and tell him to sit with you until I get there. Who in God's name do I know who's got the name of a shrink in Due East? Never mind, honey. Don't call Stephen. *I'll* call Stephen. Sonofabitch. Hasn't he *noticed* anything?"

"Grace, don't hang up."

"I won't hang up, Marygail. You're my sister. I'm going to take care of you."

"Don't hang up."

"I'm going to rock you in my arms if you need me to."

"Grace?"

"It's all right, Marygail. It's all *right."*

"Don'thangupI'm goingtogethimback and tellthatoldmannottocall me anymore. He says I need some help and. I don't need help. You're coming and. I'm going to get him back."

"That's right, Marygail. That's right."

"Oh, Grace."

Breath intake.

"Oh, Grace, I sounded real crazy for a minute there, didn't I? I mean, you heard that sound, it's just fuzz on the wire, isn't it?"

"That's right, Marygail. That's all right. It's just some old fuzz on the wire and now I'll hang up and call Stephen. Will you let me hang up so I can call your husband now? So I can call him and tell him to get home where he belongs?"

"Will you tell him I'm not going to let him go?"

"You're damn right I'll tell him that, Marygail. I sure as hell will tell that man you are not going to let him go."

((

"Grace?"

"Yes."

"You can hang up now. You're coming, right, even if I don't sound crazy anymore?"

"You swear you're not on something?"

"I swear. I swear. I swear. I love you, Gracie." A whimper.

"Oh, my sweet lord Jesus. I haven't heard you say that in twenty years. I love you too, Marygail. I'm coming. I'm coming. You just sit tight, baby. I'm coming."

☾

☾
24

April Fools

IT WAS ONLY A WEEK TO EASTER, AND ONE NIGHT close to dawn I had a dream that I'd bought myself a pair of red shoes with silky fluffy rosettes and heels three inches higher than any I'd ever worn. Like a movie star arriving at the Oscars, I made my entrance at the Easter Vigil: it was dark night, and the church was ablaze with candles. I walked down the aisle of Our Lady of Perpetual Help with my red spikes and a low-cut dress so garish that everyone turned to look and wonder what had brought about the transformation of Becky Perdue.

I woke slowly from the dream, drifting in and out of it, and somewhere on the borders of sleep I saw Jack's Judi up on the altar, her face floating in a golden bucket filled with wilting wildflowers. When I dressed that morning, I could still hear the click of my dream heels on the cold tile floor, and I found myself a red scarf to tie in my loose hair. I decided to celebrate the spring and Jack's leaving. I decided to celebrate my sanity.

For ten days I had known I was sane. After I saw Mary Faith Rapple I couldn't pretend anymore that I was imagining things: "That woman is real," she'd told me at her house, and with that word—the one she meant to dismiss me with—she had brought me to my senses. A twenty-year-old girl who was bored to tears by my confession told me I wasn't hallucinating, and her sharp words could have been a slap to my face.

That woman was real. Now when I was frightened in the cool afternoon, when I pictured black holes opening up to strangle me, when I began to miss Jack's paunch and his crochety presence, I threw myself into physical labor, real work. I'd scrubbed and polished and weeded so much over the course of ten days that the very flower beds dreaded my approach. I'd made myself a model of sanity: sane enough to dream of buying clothes that would make Jack's Judi look like a pitiful wildflower, dried out by the glow of candles.

And every morning for a week—I was my sanest with the new daybreak—I'd been sending the children off and then driving downtown in the white car with its front end bashed in so meanly. I'd been wearing sandals, though it was still early for bare feet: I wiggled my toes on the River Street sidewalks and waited for ten o'clock to come. Once a shop's doors were thrown open to me, I spent Jack's money as fast as I could think of ways to spend it. Some days I'd have lunch out, alone with a solitary beer and still celebrating. One morning I ordered three new azalea bushes for the front of the house.

On the morning of the first of April, I intended to go buy myself a tape to play in the car: the "Ode to Joy." If I started to feel myself suffocating at four o'clock in the afternoon, I would remember Dolores Rooney putting on that old scratched Beethoven record in her house, and I would grab Nippie and Sissy by the elbows and have them drive around some old country road with me while I played the "Ode to Joy" at full volume.

I had made it through a whole winter, hadn't I? In nineteen years and nine months more, I would have spent as much of my life without him as I had with him.

I parked the car right on River Street at eleven o'clock in the morning and walked toward the little record store, window shopping and eyeing more ways to get rid of Jack's money: I could buy a new gold watch, and count out the nineteen years. I could get myself a permanent and streak my hair to look like Marygail Dugan's.

Marygail Dugan. Now there was a woman who'd never doubted her sanity, a woman who knew how to control things in her life. Any fool could see that

Stephen Dugan was going to stay with her; he wasn't going to marry a sharp-voiced weary little mother and take her away. But there wasn't anything I could do about that now: Mary Faith Rapple had said plainly enough that she didn't want my advice or my touch, and I'd given up on helping her the same way I'd given up on Sissy. I pictured Mary Faith's daddy, with his slicked-back hair and his shy smile and his not knowing the right words: poor man, he knew his daughter was ashamed of him. At least Mary Faith Rapple would have the chance, growing old, to let her shame wear thin until the fabric of it tore and then disintegrated.

I let the shop door slam behind me and looked around at the posters on the wall: Black Sabbath and Madonna. Evidently no one from the Mothers' Club had taken note of *that* juxtaposition.

I hadn't bought a record in years, and the store was new. I stood close to the doorway, getting my bearings and imagining my sons and daughters spending their afternoons here. I tried to think what Ethan listened to now: the only clue I had was that too much screeching guitar vibrated out of his room some nights.

But I meant to open Ethan's door that very night, and play him my new tape. I meant to show him I wasn't fading anymore.

I stood still in the entrance; just beyond me, a little boy was trying to grab down book-and-tape packages from a hook, and the speakers on the wall drummed out a relentless droning accompaniment to his reaching. I had a start when I recognized Mary Faith Rapple's child: surely that meant his mother was in the store.

I thought I'd better back out before he caught sight of me. Jesse Rapple was a beautiful child: his black curls had straightened out in the dryness of the day and his bangs hung down lank over his eyes, but the dark size of the eyes over the narrowness of his cheeks made him look otherworldly. I'd come back later for my "Ode to Joy": I had a feeling seeing his mother would put an end to my celebrating.

Just as I made my decision to retreat, the woman behind the cash register darted out to hold Jesse Rapple back from upsetting the whole pegboard wall, and then she turned to me for help. It was too late to back out. I lifted my palm up to help the clerk out and turned my face away, so that Jesse wouldn't recognize it. I could see a vertical half of Mary Faith poring over records in the back.

☾

"Where's your momma?" the clerk said to Jesse. "They let their fool children run all *over* the place." She turned to the back of the store and the only customer in it: "Ma'am! Ma'am! Can you come get your child, please?"

Mary Faith Rapple stuffed a record back into its bin and marched forward without a glance in my direction.

"Jesse!" she said sharply. "You put that down!"

But Jesse Rapple had nothing to put down; the clerk had one firm hand on his shoulder, and he squirmed underneath.

"You can't let him run off in the store," she said to Mary Faith. "We can't have him reaching up for things."

Mary Faith took Jesse gently by the hand. She had let her hair loose that day, too, and she was wearing tight jeans; she looked like a child herself. She fixed a cold eye on the clerk, and then she walked out of the store slowly. Jesse turned to look over his shoulder, but he was perfectly quiet; she still hadn't seen my face, or else she had chosen to ignore me. She took her time, turning the knob, and pulled Jesse out deliberately.

"Some people!" the clerk said, and I nodded my head miserably. Some people were just beyond reach.

The clerk tightened a screw in the pegboard with a long red fingernail, and once my palm wasn't needed anymore I made my way back to the one sad little bin of classical records. I was sure now that my luck had turned, that I wouldn't find the "Ode to Joy." I tried not to let the shadow of Mary Faith's presence cast itself on my spirits. She'd already done her part; she'd already told me I wasn't losing my mind.

The bin I looked through must have been the same one Mary Faith Rapple had been fingering: there was a copy of Beethoven's piano sonatas standing higher than the other records. But there was no Ninth Symphony, no "Ode to Joy." Slowly I realized that it wasn't a record I'd come for, but a tape, a tape to play in the car on long narrow country roads—what was the matter with me, spying on Mary Faith Rapple, going through a dusty bin to see what her taste in music was?

I asked the clerk about tapes, but she said: "Oh no ma'am, we don't have *any* classical tapes. It's mostly teenagers and Marines buying car tapes." When I asked if I could order the music, she looked doubtful; and I left before she'd worked out in her mind whether that clerical problem was insurmountable. I wouldn't have it tonight, anyway, to play for Ethan.

☾

I pushed at the door, and the brass knob felt cold and heavy against my hand. I felt I could barely summon the strength to swing the door out into the street, and my breath came a little quicker—here was one, here was a little panic attack.

How quickly my moods swung now, now that I was truly and finally on my own. Like an old lady catching her breath, I made myself stand still on the sidewalk before I moved ahead. I tried to remember if I had spent five minutes celebrating and then five minutes cast down in mists of despair while Jack was still there.

I wouldn't have been surprised to see a mist covering River Street itself, but the day was still bright and dry and warm. I would *not* be anxious while the morning sun still shone. That woman is real, I said to myself. I could breathe more slowly now, and I started a lingering walk back to my car. I couldn't face another lunch alone at Ralph's, not with all the old men laughing over their newspapers and flirting, their palsied jaws tremulous when I looked up at their gaiety. I did not even have the heart for window shopping, for facing all the spring pastels—peach and mint and sky-blue—in the dress shops. I fingered the red silk scarf in my hair.

I was passing the little alley and eyeing the green of the park beyond when I heard her call me.

"Mrs. Perdue?"

There was no mistaking that sharp tongue, sharp enough to make the sound of a name called from an alleyway sound halfway to a curse.

I peered down into the shadows: Mary Faith Rapple was kneeling there, helping Jesse zipper his fly, and looking up at me on the street with a blank face. We couldn't have been more than ten yards apart.

"It's the car crash lady!" Jesse said. "Momma, let me pee in the alley. But just this once."

"O.K., Jesse," his mother said, and then—after hiding her face from me—"It's O.K." He scampered out onto the sidewalk and his mother followed, twisting her long brown hair over one shoulder, working it into a thick rope.

"I just wanted to say hello," she said, still sharp: it sounded more like an accusation than a greeting.

"Hello," I said, sounding foolish. "Hello, Jesse."

We stood there, my breath coming fast again.

"Tim said—" she started, but she must have seen my look of horror. What

☾

had Tim told her? That my husband had left me? That she should be more delicate with me? "Tim said we should find out if your car's running all right," she said.

"It's running fine." I didn't want to stop talking: I wanted to find out what Tim really said, or tell her how she'd freed me from all my crazy fears. But my lungs were still working the air out too fast. "The body shop tells me I'm going to have to spend a thousand dollars to get that front end back in shape, so I'm driving it the way it is. You have to thank your father again for me."

"I will," she said, breaking off the conversation. That was it: I will. Already she was turning away from me.

We smiled awkwardly—a sharp little *smile* she had too, from a mouth almost as small as her son's—and then we backed off in different directions, Jesse babbling away a mile a minute and Mary Faith trying to hush him.

She rambled off to her own solitary domestic life. Only nineteen years to go. What I wanted to do was stop time just at the moment when Mary Faith said she wanted to say hello. But time was just going to keep rolling, right up until four o'clock, and at four o'clock I would forget any celebrations. I would forget the "Ode to Joy." I would remember Jack again, and I would lie on the couch and picture him squeezing that woman's breast. Then the air outside my house would turn chill with the coming of evening, and I would remember my mother and father—not their faces, but their bitterness, their two souls locked in one long refusal to forgive—and I would find myself losing my balance and waiting for black holes to suck me up and worrying for my sanity once more.

All around me spring showed itself on River Street: down in the bay, I knew, a few sailboats would already be winging along in the dry breeze. I could have called out after them: I could have just said "Wait" to the girl; but I wasn't a woman who asked anyone to wait, and so I went on alone. I missed Jack with all my heart: I missed how he would measure out the distance between the azalea bushes and turn the best blossoms out to the street, where the neighbors driving by would see them. I missed the way he took my hand and told me the truth, that there had been nothing between us for years. I missed the way he had defied me without my even knowing it.

I shook my head, trying to shake out the knowledge that the afternoon was coming, and then the evening, and I made myself keep walking, one sandal leading the other. I was celebrating. I had to remember that.

☾

I was celebrating my freedom. I would have to drive on home and plant those azalea bushes by myself.

The phone was ringing when I opened the door to my house, and I ran to the kitchen to catch it, imagining Mary Faith or Jack on the other side of the wire. But there was no sound when I picked it up.

I was about to lay the receiver down in its cradle when I heard a peculiar hissing sound. I picked it back up to my ear and thought I could hear someone saying: "Shhh, shhh," soft and high and girlish. Was it a child's voice? I was done with thinking that I imagined voices; it didn't occur to me until later to be frightened. Meanwhile the soft voice spoke a single clear sentence:

"Tell him not to call me."

There was a click, and I held the receiver to my chest for a minute, feeling the heavy black weight of it close to my heart. Tell him not to call me. Could it have been a child calling? A prank? Or one of Jack's girlfriends?

Maybe it was my *husband's* girlfriend who was phoning me: Judi's voice had been pitched high that day at their Paradise Realty. I could see her sneaking out at lunchtime, using the pay phone down by the bank to call me up and torment me.

I shook my head back and laughed out loud at the idea. I imagined a headline in the *Midnight Globe* at the Piggly Wiggly checkout counter: "Woman receives mystery call from outer space."

I was rummaging for my gardening apron when the telephone rang again. I ignored it for three rings, and then for five, but the keening went on to ten rings, and finally I decided to pick it up. If there was another shhshhing sound, I would laugh right into the receiver, and take out my vengeance with another dream about Judi.

I picked up the receiver, held my breath, and said nothing; finally there was a confused cough and a man's voice I'd know anywhere:

"Becky?"

It was Father Berkeley. I tried not to sigh with the confusion of my surprise and my relief and my frustration. I'd given Father back his convert class. What more could he want from me?

"Hello, Father."

"Becky, are you all right?"

"I'm fine, Father." I tried to sound brisk and efficient. "I just ran in."

☾

"Oh," he said. I could picture him considering on the other end of the line. "How would you like to just run out again?"

"Whatever do you mean, Father?"

"I mean I have something I'd like to show you."

"Well, Father . . ." I remembered now where I had left the plastic apron. I wanted the relief of digging my hands into the cool damp earth, of getting those azalea's roots into the ground finally, and forgetting Jack and Mary Faith and the mystery call. "My children are coming home soon," I said, and I knew it sounded lame.

Now Father decided to be brisk and efficient. "I can have you home by three o'clock, Becky. I'd like to talk to you."

Could it be that he was lonely? Poor Father: I wondered if all the women in the parish brushed off his phone calls this way. "O.K., Father," I said, and this time I let the sigh out. "I'll drive down to the rectory in fifteen minutes."

"You'll do no such thing, Becky. I'll be by the house in ten minutes. I just want to drive you out over the bridge."

"Oh, Father, it's not to see Jack—"

He spluttered into the wire. "Of course not. Good heavens, do you think I'd be scheming behind your back?"

I didn't answer him.

"No, I'm *not* driving you to see Jack. Will you be ready?"

"I will, Father."

"Oh, and look here—"

Really, this was too much. Father was speaking to me as if I were a child. "Look here, Becky, do you know Stephen Dugan?"

The name made me fix my jaw at the phone. Father's call was becoming stranger than my mystery call from outer space. "I do, Father. I guess. Not real well."

"That's no good, then."

"What's no good?"

"I need someone to talk to him, but if you don't know him—no, never mind. I'll be by directly."

He hung up without a good-bye and I put the receiver mouth up on the island: there would be no more phone calls for me today. I'd have a long enough trial getting through my drive with Father Berkeley. I didn't need to listen to any more shhshhing sounds, or to hear voices called from alleys.

☾

I pulled the red scarf from my hair, fingering its rich crimson color again, and sat at the island to wait.

Father Berkeley was smoking Lucky Strikes like a truck driver, down to a half inch; he didn't put the butts out in the ashtray so much as drop them in and wait for them to dissolve. He was wheezing from the effort, too, and I felt his lighting them up one after another was a dare: he wanted me to ask him why he'd gone back to cigarettes after all these years. I didn't ask. Tim Rooney had said, chain-smoking, that cigarettes were a death wish wrapped around a mother's nipple. I breathed in the thick rich smoke and longed for one myself, a Lucky Strike I could dangle while I waited for Father to finally show me this surprise he was being so secretive about.

We'd passed Island Paradise two miles before, and now we were driving out farther along the beach road. In six more weeks the fields by the side of the road would be dotted with migrant workers stooping over to pull tomatoes off a vine: now, irrigated, the fields were the shimmering color of spring. Father drove another three miles or so and turned right, down the road to Claire's Point. I held my breath. I knew this was something to do with Jack: he'd bought up so much land out here he'd stopped showing it to me years ago. Now Father Berkeley was going to show me.

Father's face was flushed from the cigarettes. When he turned it in my direction he said: "Figured it out?"

"I haven't got a clue, Father Berkeley. Where are you taking me?"

"Hold on," he said, and made another sharp right down a dirt road. We jostled along under low-hanging trees for a quarter mile, moss swishing down over the car's roof, and then Father jerked on the brakes at the border of an empty field, overgrown and patchy. He had driven me out to an empty field: suddenly, in the quiet of our stopping, I got my old shivers back. I could sense water somewhere down at the end of this road, and I had a terrible premonition that Father was going to tell me this was where he wanted to be buried when he died: out in a desolate field.

"This is it," he said. He could hardly hold the glee back from his voice, and he lit another Lucky Strike.

"This is what?" The land was nearly the size of two football fields and bordered by sparse woods—pine and scrub oak—on two sides, by a ragged barbed wire fence on the third. The rest of Due East County was green, but

(

Father's field was yellow, mostly: a field full of brambles. Crows picked it over lazily. Poor Father: now I wanted to lay a hand on *his* arm. I should have been watching over him when he started down this long decline; I shouldn't have been so wrapped up in my own troubles.

"This is what Jack found me!"

"What's it for?" I said, flat. "How much is he going to charge you for this miserable field? And why'd you go to Jack, Father?—he'd gouge the Holy Father himself."

"Young Jack, Becky. Your *son*. You know, the apostate." I stared at his chuckling as if he were the one losing his mind. Maybe he was better able to hide his drinking these days: I couldn't smell a whiff of brandy on his breath.

"Becky, Becky, why do you look at me that way? I thought you'd be tickled we finally found us some land for the new church! Do you know that atheist son of yours has used his cunning to get it out of his father for next to nothing?"

"So it's Jack's land after all." First I stared at him, and then I took a cigarette from the pack he'd left on the dashboard. He lit it for me in a flash, with a golden lighter he pulled from his pocket.

Father, I wanted to say, Father, nobody in the parish is going to drive to the ends of the earth to hear mass said in a barren field. Father, I wanted to say, nobody in the parish is going to contribute another dime to your building fund once they find out how much Jack wants for this land.

"I didn't know Jack was even speaking to his father."

Father chortled, beside himself at the unveiling of his new land. "Oh, I told him I'd manage a small commission for him if he could find a piece his father didn't want to put to use. We've been driving all over this island for a month now!"

For a month: so it had been my son sitting in Father's car when I passed them on the bridge and thought they were figures in my imagination. And now I was sitting in Father's car and the sight of the dry abandoned land, miles out of town, was worse than imagination: it was real.

"Look at the size of it, Becky! We'll have a parking lot for two hundred cars."

"I don't know what to say, Father."

He coughed a false polite cough. "Say you'll be the one to talk it up around the parish, Becky. That's why I brought you out here. You know the first thing

☾

they'll all say: Father, we have to build the new church in town. They'll say: Father, we can't drive out this far. Talk it up, Becky. Tell them there's a bluff a quarter mile down the road where we can say midnight mass by the water again. Tell them there's no more land to build on in town: not anything the parish can afford. Tell them the retired generals are buying all the Due East plots from your husband. They'll listen to you."

I rolled down my window and watched the Lucky Strike hit the dirt below. There was a desperate edge to Father's voice: the parish council hadn't approved any of the sites he had found in the last five years. There had been whispers about his retirement, about how he could be eased into it if the bishop were only made aware how bad the drinking had become.

"Father, I can't."

Now it was as if I were the one slapping someone's face, but I hadn't brought him back to his senses. He sat scrunched behind the steering wheel and gripped it as if he were still driving: his face was the same yellow as the brambles in the field. The pouches around his eyes were soft old leather, and he blinked them open and shut.

"I see," he said softly, and now the diminishment of his voice made me move to put a hand to his arm, to the shiny black cloth covering the old flesh underneath. He closed his eyes, and I drew my hand back.

"I think this is what you've put off telling me for years."

I took a deep breath.

"I think you're going to say you can't talk up a new church because you're past believing now. You've been past believing for a good long while."

It wasn't fair of him to bring the confessional into his silver anniversary car. I didn't have to answer that: not yet.

Then he opened his eyes and said: "Don't you know there are days—months, Becky, years sometimes—when I'm past believing, too? I rounded that curve long before it even occurred to you."

I turned my face away. I didn't need company in *this*. I didn't need one of his sweet pretending sermons.

His voice was absolutely toneless, but now he raised the volume a decibel. "I imagine you're one of the few parishioners who've figured out that priests are the worst doubters. The very worst. Dolores knew, of course. Dolores could see through me. But what she couldn't see—and she stopped taking the sacraments near the end, did you know that, Becky?—what she couldn't see was

☾

that this road we're on just might be a circular one. If we wait long enough, Becky, maybe this car we're driving will just come back to that same curve."

I wanted to hear his confession even less than I wanted to give my own. Still I said nothing, and looked out at the crows in the field, tearing whatever new growth there was from the earth.

"Maybe faith is like a marriage, Becky. Maybe you just wait in it. Maybe you just wait *on* it."

My patience with all of them—sons, priests, my husband's lovers—had worn away. "I think that may be the wrong analogy for *me*, Father."

He shifted his body in the driver's seat and turned toward me the way he must have turned toward a hundred parishioners, the troubled ones he called on after suppertime. He must have sat on a hundred sofas and turned his body to them at just that degree, trying to save them when they didn't even want his help.

"Becky," he said, eagerness escaping. "I meant it from the heart when I said on the phone that I would never sneak around behind your back. But there's another reason for this drive besides the new church. Your husband's come to ask my help. He wants to come back home."

The field beyond him, beyond the driver's seat, shifted in my vision: the land stood higher against the horizon, and the crows on the ground plumped up bigger and blacker. I tried to run it back through: Mary Faith, Mystery Caller, Father Berkeley. There was something I had been trying to concentrate on all day, something they kept interrupting me at. What was it? My mind was wiped clean. What was it?

A crow flew off to a green patch of land and I remembered what I had been trying to concentrate on. Celebrating. I had meant to spend the day celebrating my freedom.

I looked down at my hands folded in my lap and said: "Father, you have to take me home now."

He started to speak—I could feel him straining toward me—but then he shifted his body back to the steering wheel and started the car up. I closed my eyes against the sunlight and Father's empty field, closed them against my vision of Jack and Judi alone in the Island Paradise office. Jack had closed his door, and she leaned against his desk, hitching her skirt up. I felt the car rolling forward down the dirt road, and I didn't open my eyes until we made a stop. Father made a wide left turn and I stole a glance at him, steering the car with

☾

his left hand and groping for the Lucky Strikes with his right. I reached the cigarettes for him and said:

"I'm sorry, Father."

He dismissed me with a wave of his lighter. "Nothing to be sorry about, Becky. Dolores always said I should leave the family counseling to the family counselors. I should have told Jack I have no talent for this."

We were on a real back road now, a narrow road close to the water but dark under the archways of trees and gray moss. It stretched out forever. More than anything now I wanted to get back to Piney Woods and the azaleas: on this dark road I was seeing nothing but Judi peeling off layers of her Island Paradise uniform, peeling her shirt off to lift out her soft clay nipples. Father's cigarette was making me woozy. We passed one dirt road we could have turned down, then another; but Father kept driving, urging the car faster the farther we left his field behind.

"Shouldn't we be turning back around now, Father?"

He kept his eyes ahead of him. "Jack showed me a big road we can turn on." He showed the strain now of trying to drive and smoke at the same time, and he craned his neck up to see over the steering wheel.

The path was rutted from all the spring rains, and we took enough hard bounces that I was almost moved to ask him if I should drive, but still he kept his foot pressed to the gas. Jack wants to come home. I found myself wondering where he was sleeping, nights: probably he was still sleeping in Judi's bed. One night he would take her for a walk through the honeysuckle and tell her that there had really been nothing between them these four months.

Finally we came to a wider smoother dirt road, and Father turned unsteadily. We were back on our way to the Claire's Point road, back on our way to the beach road, back on our way to Due East. I wanted to go home. Jack wanted to go home.

We passed along through an aisle of big pines resting on sheets of brown-gold needles and came at last to the old yellow stop sign before the state road. A caravan of Winnebagos, five or six of them, passed us by on their way out to Claire's Point.

Father pointed to them, the cigarette in his hand shaking. "I guess they're started up in earnest now."

I had no idea what he meant: there were no campgrounds out this way, only

☾

farms and shacks and a few beach houses at the end of the land. Or had Jack set up a new vacation paradise outside our fort?

"There's the future of Due East rolling out before us," Father said, and laughed a bitter dry laugh. "We're a movie set now."

Of course; now I saw. Those trucks were going out to our fort: a big orange truck that said "Evening Sun Lighting Company" was coming up behind them. A long string of cars stretched out taut on the Claire's Point highway: now we would never be able to turn out of our dirt road. The cars would be filled with county development people, reporters from Charleston and Savannah, Chamber of Commerce types, all following the production company out to the fort in a procession longer than the bishop's on ordination day.

"So they're making their movie after all."

"Ah, yes," Father said. "Jack tells me it's Stephen Dugan's screenplay."

"It's our fort they're using for a set."

In silence, we watched the cars inch by, and now I remembered the rest of Father's phone call. "Father, why'd you want to know if I knew Stephen Dugan? Is it something to do with the movie? The fort? Did Jack ask you—"

"No, no, Becky." Now he wasn't even looking at me out of the corner of his eye, just watching the procession of cars march before us. In the distance I saw a big gold car and waited for its approach with horror. It was Jack's Cadillac: Jack was going out there to escort the movie people. I wanted to slide down low next to Father. Jack wanted to come home.

"Why did you want me to talk to Stephen Dugan, Father?"

Father turned a stern eye on me, telling me to hush. Jack's car would be driving right in front of us soon. Now. Now he'd be passing us by.

"What was it, Father?"

Father Berkeley tapped his fingers on the steering wheel in exasperation. "I'm sorry I brought it up, Becky. More bad judgment on my part. You knew his wife from the convert group—I thought you might have been able to talk to the man. But now, with the movie starting, I'll have to go beyond him. He won't *see* what kind of trouble she's in."

"What kind of trouble, Father?" Surely the gold Cadillac had passed us by. Surely Jack hadn't seen me.

"Marygail Dugan is having a breakdown, Becky. I thought, after your mother, that you might be able to help the family out."

Marygail Dugan: a breakdown? I didn't believe it for a minute. With those

☾

streaks in her hair? Those miniskirts? That mincing walk through Myrt's Beauty Salon? Oh, she was a slick cold devil. She was putting on her own show just as the movie was beginning, and Father was the first member of the audience to sit down before her. How could Father think that woman could have any connection to my mother, to an old woman sitting at a plastic dinette set talking to an imaginary man?

"Father," I said, "I doubt there's anything you can do."

He turned his haggard eyes to me, and they lighted up with a terrible resentment. "There is most certainly something I can do, Rebecca. There is most certainly something."

"Father—"

"Becky, would you like another family to go through what you went through, signing your mother onto a locked ward? No. I won't have it. I don't expect any help from you—it was foolish to ask it—but I cannot sit back and let the man continue an affair the whole town knows about while his wife descends into madness. Any more than I could let Jack go on with his." He shut his mouth with the realization of what he'd said, but it was too late.

Father Berkeley must have gone to Jack. Father must have told Jack that he had to come home. Maybe he talked to him the day after I sashayed through Jack's office, sure of myself and my braided hair. Maybe Jack had been looking at the little gold hearts on Judi's fingernails, feeling revulsion for them. Maybe she painted her lips too red and glossy for him, and when Father pointed it out, when I told him he couldn't have the children, he'd given up. He'd decided to come back home.

"And how are you going to get Stephen Dugan back home, Father?"

He could hear my contempt; I knew he could. He tooted his horn and pulled the silver car out into a tiny space that had opened up in the movie caravan. We edged by the approaching car, and I braced my hand against the dashboard.

"I'll have to speak to the other woman, I suppose, Becky," he said, raising his voice over the horn blasts behind us. He laced his line with a contempt colder than my own.

What did he mean? Had he gone to Judi then, and not Jack at all? Had he been calling Judi up, telling her to let Jack go? Had Father Berkeley gone to a fat floozy with gold hearts on her fingernails and told her to give my husband up?

☾

How could he have? I could see Judi weeping a black mascara-drenched tear for me, for the wife left at home going crazy because she had taken a man away from his family. I could see Jack coming back home to holler at us for overcooked vegetables, remembering at every meal that he could have been sipping champagne with his Judi.

"You're not going to speak to Mary Faith, Father!"

"I may have to," he said coldly.

My hand was still braced against the dashboard, and I watched the road swallow us up. Father was racing to get us back home, to deliver me from his car.

"Father Berkeley," I said, "that young woman is not going to give you the time of day."

He ignored me.

"Father Berkeley," I said, my voice going shrill, "that girl knows better than to be left dangling by your God! You told my mother when my father died that that was a God of *comfort,* Father. How's he going to comfort that little girl? You just told me you didn't even believe in that God yourself."

He did not so much as wince, but kept driving the way men drive down country roads, punishing the very pavement with their heat.

I had to get back to town. I had to get back to Piney Woods. I had to put my azaleas in the ground and call Mary Faith Rapple to tell her what was coming. Faith is like a marriage, Father Berkeley? That's right, Father. You've seen that much of marriage in your days in Due East. Faith is the chokehold that ruined your life and Dolores Rooney's life and my mother's life. But that Rapple girl knew better than to let it put its hands around her slender neck. That girl knew how to get away.

"Take me home, Father Berkeley," I said, and my voice was a spring frost, a sparkle that would settle down on every pore of my skin and save me from ever letting Jack Perdue, the scent of another woman moist on his fingers, into my bed.

Please just take me home and leave me be.

☾

25

Tail Between My Legs

I TOLD FATHER NOT TO TELL BECKY I'D GONE TO him, I told him please just be kind enough to drop hints while I'm struggling back to her—and then what do I see on my way out to the fort? Father and Becky snuggled up nice and cozy, coming back from looking at the new church site. I can imagine what he told her in the front seat of that car. Jack is just about donating this land to Our Lady of Perpetual Help, he probably said, on account of wanting you back so bad.

Which Becky'll spit on, for a while at least. I can see her looking around that land all snooty, saying: Father, nobody'll want to come this far to hear mass said. She'll say: Father, it's penned in between farms. We won't be able to hear your sermons in June, she'll say, when they're harvesting the crops.

But Father Berkeley is the shrewdest old wheeler-dealer I've come across in all my days selling land—he got *Jack* to come do his dirty work and beg for the land, didn't he, Jack acting like it's the only decent thing I could do after walking out on the family. And then, then Father made out that he didn't want to talk to Becky until just coincidentally the price came down three thousand dollars, and then five, and then ten. Ten thousand dollars off a parcel of land to get your family back! I have to hand it to him.

He'll talk the parish into it. He'll get them thinking he's a doddering old fool and then he'll lay off the bottle for a month and come thundering in to tell them they've got to stand behind him. He'll start a sermon out all meek and folksy and then—boom!—right when he's got everybody misty-eyed about how nice it is to have Father Berkeley back to his old self, he'll look them in the eye, one by one, and tell them they can't let him down. I bet he'll say *Don't desert me this time*. I bet he'll say *Don't run off now, not when I'm back on my feet again*. He'll have the whole parish feeling so guilty they ever considered going to the bishop that they'll run on out to the island and decide it's not so bad after all. They'll remember he started drinking when they turned down the last five sites, and they'll end up praying for forgiveness. They'll do it for a parking lot.

And Becky will come round, too. I understand, I understand the psychology of it: I shamed her, and now's she's got to shame me back a little bit. She already has shamed me. That afternoon she came into the office, I caught a glimpse of her sitting up so straight and sad and dignified, that faraway look in her eye, and then I caught the glimmer of the gold hearts on Judi's nails. Becky must have loved seeing those. I *told* Judi they were tacky two nights before and still she hadn't scrubbed them off.

And on top of the nails and the little white go-go boots, Judi thought she could take over the office the way she'd taken over my life, telling Stephen Dugan to go to hell on the phone and making me talk to Lamarr about snaking out of the movie contract, too. "I'll chop off Dugan's head he calls one more time about that movie!" she was always saying, and I'd been thinking *Whatever in God's name possessed me? I must have been out of my mind* long before Becky ever showed up furious. She was right to be furious, and I'll just have to wait and let that storm die down.

I left Judi for the condos on Isaacs Island, and it looks like I'll have to spend a few more months living out there alone (Jack's right, the buildings are just about sinking into the sea. They're built on *marshland*). My tail's between my legs, half my records are missing from Judi's vengeful clearing out, and I can see that the rains are going to be washing down for a good long while. Ethan tells me she'll never let me back, and he's sticking by his momma, and Sissy

☾

tells me she *liked* Judi, why can't I make up my mind, and then Jack tells me if I give the land to the church cheap maybe Becky'll consider my moving back in. Though prob'ly not, he says.

Then Stephen Dugan tells me I'm a fool. It's not bad enough to have my whole family and my parish priest punishing me for my sins, that hypocritical two-timer's got to bless me out, too.

I've got to hand it to Dugan. He's got the whole town, the whole county, jumping to the snap of his fingers now this movie's rolling. He's got the *Courier* assigning other reporters to interview *him,* and to take pictures of his wife and child. He's got a line of cars and trucks longer than a funeral procession following him out to Claire's Point, and when he gets to the fort he acts like the king of the hill.

What a scene it was, that first afternoon. They'd been casting for extras all week down at the high school gym, and they must have had five hundred Marines and high school kids and housewives show up. They had twenty-five actors holed up in the Due East Motor Court, reading their lines out by the pool and walking through town like it's the cutest little movie set they ever had the pleasure to work on.

Then they go to set up the fort for the first day's shoot, and Dugan's leading the parade. First half the rented equipment trucks are three hours late coming in from Florida—they've run into an electrical storm that has them all pulled off the interstate—and then when we finally get out there they discover the floor of the fort is knee-deep in puddles from the rain the night before. The DP, the guy running the lighting show, is tearing his hair out and hollering like a fishwife at the best boy and the gaffers, trying to get the scaffolding up before the sun goes down.

Best boy. Gaffers. I love it, it's a real movie. And there's Dugan, up on the ramparts, looking oh so amused at the sight of all these techies running around busting their humps. The director's reading with the actors out by the pool, back in Due East, and now the best boy is trying to winch the generator truck up the side of the hill. They had to cut down a dozen saplings to even roll it up that way. Some other assistant is trying to park six honeywagons, a kitchen truck, three or four more forty-foot equipment trucks that have to get up a slippy-slidy unpaved road and back down the other side to park on the flat land by the river. That's why they had me out there, to show them the quickest routes in, and once they got me there they didn't want to *know* about shoveling

☾

sand out the way. So one of the honeywagons got its rear wheels stuck in that sand, and *that* stopped everything for a while. They needed all the hands they could get to haul her back onto the road again.

Somebody's yelling he's got to get his hands on the pump to clear out all the water before they run a single cable, and in the middle of all the chaos I walk on up to Dugan, standing up high on the fort and looking out at the river, making fifty thousand dollars if he's making a dime—to polish his glasses every now and again up on the lookout.

"Some show, huh?" I say to him. I'm willing to let bygones be bygones—it was Judi dealing with him, mostly—even if he damn near blew a million-dollar deal for me when he ran those pieces on Isaacs Island. I even stick my hand out to him, but he makes like he doesn't notice, takes out a dirty handkerchief, and wipes off his hornrims again.

They don't need me down below—hell, they don't *want* me down below—so I try again. "Look here," I say, "with all the excitement going on, I don't even know what the movie's *about.*"

And the skinny pretentious little bastard yawns and says, "Why, it's about women coming to stop men from taking their pleasure."

Son of a skunk bitch. Does he think I don't know like everybody else in Due East that he seduced a fifteen-year-old *girl* and he's been carrying on with her ever since? While he maintains a separate residence with a damn good-looking woman—she could have been a *model* and God knows what she sees in him—and anyway at least I had the decency for Christ's sake to haul my ass out of the house before I destroyed Becky with what was going on behind her back. And now I'm trying to drag my belly back there, slinking along the ground to Father Berkeley, while he's perched up on top of a twenty-foot wall.

So I say, "Why, whatever gave you the idea for that?" I say, "What was your inspiration?"

And Stephen Dugan raises one eyebrow over the hornrims and laughs at me and says, "You 'member that raid the sheriff made last year on the whorehouse out here? Right when they were shooting *Carpetbagging Blues.*"

I stiffen up a little. He has to know I owned that property—he's a *reporter.*

But I just nod, thoughtful-looking, when what I want to say is "Look, Dugan, I had no idea what was going on in that house, they paid the rent three days before it was due every month." I don't say it, because he knew and I knew and every male over the age of twelve in Due East County—every male with his eyes in his head and ears glued to the side—knew the goings-on out there. And I never got charged with a thing.

"So how you working the fort into the story?" I say. "This another War-Between-the-States saga?"

"No, sir," he says, extra polite. "This fort wasn't standing during that war. They built this fort for the Spanish-American War, and they brought a company of federal troops out here. The troops were supposed to be watching the water night and day. They got mighty bored."

"I see," I say. I can't believe the man thinks he has to tell me which war they built *my* fort for. "They brought whores out here, is that it? They gonna let that on television?"

"Mr. Perdue," he says, still laughing at me, "we are practically in the twilight of the twentieth century. Do you watch TV movies?"

"I guess you're right," I say. The scaffolding's going up below us, and the afternoon sun is setting on the water. They're setting up two tents down by the shack, the shack we were going to tear down to build a beach house. The shack we *are* going to tear down, once Becky and I are back together.

"So how do these women trying to stop the men from taking their pleasure get into the picture?" Jack and Ethan used to play right down below from where we're standing. They used to run down the underground passage to the dungeon, to play they were taken prisoner in Vietnam like their Uncle Billy. They never played that game if Becky was here.

"The women come from town," Dugan says, bored. "Church women. They sail a salvation boat up through the sound, and they land it right on the beach. It's a comedy, of sorts."

"Dugan," I say, "I hope you didn't make that *Catholic* church women. Father Berkeley'll have a heart attack I let you use this fort to make fun of Catholic women."

"No sir," he says, and now he laughs out loud. The sky's darkening a little behind him, and not just with the coming of evening. You can see the dark clouds coming in from the west. "I made 'em nondenominational Protestant women. We have to worry about lawsuits, y'see."

Nice little jab about the lawsuits. I don't like the turn of this conversation, but there's a little electricity in the air from all the excitement of having a

☾

movie company scurrying down below us, and I feel like staying put while the sun gets fiery on the horizon.

Then Dugan says, "I don't know that they need us here now, Mr. Perdue. They'll be putting up the lights within the hour."

"It's going to rain on those lights, Dugan," I say, and we both look out to the sea.

"They'll wrap the casings. They don't put the lights themselves in until daybreak," he says—a real movie *expert* now. He starts moving down the path, sliding a little on all the loose tabby. "We'd best be getting home to our wives."

He knows damn well I'm separated from my wife. That's his way of making me a fool—he's going home to his wife, all the while he's cheating on her, and I'm locked out of my bedroom because I haven't said my act of contrition properly yet. Because I didn't lie to Becky when I took up with another woman.

"What are you going to do," I call after him, "if it rains tomorrow?"

He doesn't turn around—he's got his hands stuck in his chinos, walking down the steep incline—but he calls back, "We're going to get nervous, I reckon. We're paying you a thousand dollars a day."

And he leaves me on top of my own fort, on top of my own land, with his little parting shot. If I'd just been smart enough to lie to my wife the way he did, I'd have a warm bed to crawl into tonight.

The meal tent's all the way up now, so the actors and the extras and the crew can take their supper on the front lawn of my fort, and I've got a lonely supper of my own to look forward to. I look at the clouds, crisping on the edges, and I find myself thinking of Becky coming to give me what-for in my own office. "My *son's* going to get that land someday," she said, and I look down at the muddy beach and the dilapidated shack I've had no time to tear down. I'm going to tear it down. I bought her this fort for a wedding present, and I'm going to build her a beach house once she decides to have me back.

☾

VI

☾

26

Spring Tide

ON HOLY THURSDAY, MAY DROVE THROUGH
Due East at fifteen miles an hour, top speed. The rain was sheeting
down, unwinding itself through the blanket of clouds in shades of
purple, then shades of gold when the sun broke out. Rainbows teased
and disappeared at the edge of the sky, but this was more than a little
sun shower: it had been raining off and on for three days, and it was
spring tide besides. Nobody had seen the new moon being born in the
last three nights, and no one had seen stars in the night sky. All Due
East had seen was rain and lightning and more rain.

The puddles on River Street were three feet deep in spots, and May
was convinced that plowing through one more would cause the car's
electrical system to go up in a shower of sparks. It was too early for
hurricane season, but the wind was whipping off the water at close to
gale force.

May had fled her house in vexation; her husband was lost without
his fishing, and she was thwarted at every turn with him underfoot.
The Easter flowers had been ordered a month before, but she decided
to go walk through the empty church once more to see what they'd

forgotten *this* time around. It was still midmorning, and she'd have a few hours
before the services began, before the twenty-four-hour Adoration. This would
be her last chance: after the Stations of the Cross tomorrow, the church would
be draped in purple and black, and the florist's truck wouldn't be delivering
until five o'clock Saturday. She had the sudden inspiration that a garland of
flowers over Mary's head would be nice—they'd done that some year past, but
she couldn't remember what they'd used. Wildflowers, she thought, but there
would be no wildflowers in Due East on this rainy day. They'd all have been
bent and broken by the force of the sudden rains. Maybe the rain would quit
by Holy Saturday. Maybe there would be wildflowers, protected at the edge of
some wood on Lady's Island, that she would be able to pick.

When she turned off River Street onto Division she could see whitecaps
spuming in the bay, the water licking up almost to the top of the tabby wall in
the little triangular park. The headline in the *Courier* that morning had said,
"Production Company Weighs Pulling Out"—if they didn't get sun before the
end of the week, they'd be too far over budget, what with the rented equipment and the big cast they were putting up in the Due East Motor Court.

"Serve them right," May said, right out loud. They wanted to use an
outdoor set for their low-budget extravaganza, and now the wind and the rain
and the patchy sky had conspired to stop them. They'd never thought to
include Due East's tempestuous nature in their calculations: maybe they'd
planned for a day or two of rain, but not for this onslaught. She for one had
just about had it with movie companies pulling into town, pretending they
were here to shoot historical dramas, and then making trash no better than soap
operas. She hadn't let her own grandchildren watch *Carpetbagging Blues* all the
way through: they let the three little girls see themselves on the edge of a
crowd scene, dressed in floor-length gingham dresses and straw bonnets, and
then they shut the television off. Marygail Dugan had appeared in a long close-
up shot in that one, and now May had read that she'd been cast in the new
movie as a mysterious woman in white who walked along the shore at night.
The *Courier*'s feature on the Dugan family was titled "Local Family Doubly
Blessed with Talent."

So it appeared that Marygail Dugan was not going to have a breakdown
after all, not after the director had been so inspired by her that he'd had
Stephen Dugan write in an extra scene just for her. She would have to wear a
wig over the spiked haircut—if the rain ever stopped long enough to shoot a

☾

moonlight scene. May hated herself for even reading the *Courier* articles; she could picture Father Berkeley reading them too, and chortling over her foolish fears for the girl.

There were no cars parked on the church's end of Division Street. May slid hers in directly in front of the church doors, but had to huddle inside, waiting for the wind to die down. Finally there was a break, and she dashed across the pavement and the sidewalk and up the brick steps, hanging on to the iron banister at the top. The umbrella was turned inside out by the rain and she brought it, twisted and soaked through, right into Our Lady of Perpetual Help with her.

The church was dark and silent, and May pulled the spokes of the umbrella right before she groped for the light switches in back. They'd warned Father to start locking the front doors, but he'd have none of it—he wanted an *open* church—and now May imagined AWOL Marines and escaped convicts loitering in the dark, waiting. Served *her* right, she supposed for sneaking down here on her own, without the rest of the Altar Guild, when the Easter arrangements were debated and voted on as if they were articles of war.

The recessed spotlights in the ceiling flicked on, and when May surveyed the church she almost turned on her heels back into the storm. There in the front pew, opposite the blue and white statue of Mary, a lone figure knelt. Had been kneeling, in the dark. The punishing rain overhead sounded like a barrage of cannonballs coming down.

May stood still in the dark, waiting for the figure to turn around—but the back she faced, covered by a yellow slicker, stayed slumped over the front of the pew. May knew who it was without stopping to think it through: it was Marygail Dugan. They didn't need her for the movie if the movie crew was pulling out of town. She was coming to have her nervous breakdown instead.

May slipped into the last pew and studied the statue, Mary's hands clasped so placidly, the plaster rosary beads dropping down between her fingers. The graceful curve of the beads triggered her memory of the wildflower crown they'd made so many years before: a diadem of violets and Queen Anne's lace. Wouldn't *that* be lovely, with the red roses at Mary's feet?

How long could the girl stay like that? It occurred to May that she might be sleeping up there in the front pew, sleeping off a drinking spree or her disappointment over the movie. She considered tiptoeing up to lay a hand on Marygail's shoulder, but watched instead as the long neck above the slicker

☾

lifted itself. The girl's right hand was rising now too, and May saw her make a sign of the cross the way converts do: big and wide and slow.

Finally Marygail Dugan pushed herself up, both hands on the front of the pew, and turned to face her. She smiled back at May, tentatively, and then she waved as if she were facing the cameras already.

"Hi, honey," May said softly. "What you doing here in the dark?"

Marygail still clung to the pew with one hand. "I'm getting baptized Sunday," she said; and May saw even from a distance that her face was wiped clean of makeup. Even the hair, streaked through with platinum, lay flat and wet on her head like a little boy's. She looked so very slight in the big slicker.

"Are you feeling all right?"

Marygail studied the front of her slicker and fiddled with a clasp. "My sister's here," she said, and her voice was so distant that May had to strain to make out the words. "My sister's here to take care of me."

"Well, that's *fine*," May said, forcing heartiness into her voice. "She coming to the Easter Vigil?"

Marygail shrugged and hobbled out, one hand on each new pew as she made her way down the aisle to May. She didn't look like a little boy now: she looked like an old world-weary woman, her eyes ringed with black puffs.

She came right up to May and stopped, her mouth contorting itself, trying out different grimaces. "I *had* to get out of the house," she said ferociously.

May drew back and heard a nervous giggle come from her own mouth. "Me too," she said. "My husband like to drove me crazy."

Those were the wrong words, but Marygail did not seem to hear them. She settled her mouth into a wondering pout, and her eyes wandered to the back door. "I can't stay in one place too long." She turned to May. "*I can't stay.*"

"Well, I can understand that feeling," May said. Father Berkeley should be here now, to see those eyes darting back and forth! And he thought she'd overreacted, asking him to help Marygail.

"Look here," she said quickly—the girl was surely drifting back out of the church door, and May could hear the rain lashing it—"look here, are they going to be shooting that movie or not?"

Marygail seemed to snap all her bones back into position; her shoulders raised up, and her eyes focused sharply on May.

"Oh yes," she said. "Oh yes, the rain's letting up directly. Hear?"

May could hear the wind and the steady pelt of the rain. "Why *certainly* it'll

☾

let up," she said, and watched Marygail move to the door. The girl waved again, and drew her hood up against the storm.

"You need a ride home?" May said suddenly, but it was too late for Marygail to hear her: the door was ajar and the rain was angling into the church as she was slipping out. May watched the door pushed shut from the outside and shivered from the currents of cool air drifting her way.

So she had been right, after all. Marygail had picked Easter to get baptized, and Easter to let go of her reason. And here she'd been worried about how to sneak in a crown of purple flowers before the vigil began.

May picked up her umbrella and moved back to the light switches. By three o'clock tomorrow the Stations would be over, and Father would be bringing out the bolts of purple cloth to swathe the statues and the Blessed Sacrament. The whole church would be covered in purple mourning, and Marygail Dugan would be losing her mind. May clicked off the lights. If only Father Berkeley had listened to her.

☾

☾
27

New Morning

ARY FAITH HEARD A RAPPING ON HER kitchen door at seven-thirty in the morning, and turned to see Tim Rooney grinning in through the glass pane. She was washing up the cereal bowls, and she wasn't wearing so much as a robe: she was wearing, in fact, the War Resisters T-shirt Tim had let her borrow when Jesse was sick. It hung halfway down her thighs, and her legs—untouched by the sun since last September—were white beneath it.

She let him in, and he hooted at the sight of his shirt. Thank God she'd slipped a pair of bikinis on underneath.

"Taken over our neighbors' shirts, have we? Come on, Mary Faith. Get dressed. Get Jesse dressed."

She eyed him suspiciously and wiped a soapy hand on his shirt. She felt no inclination to go fishing with him today of all days, with the midnight phone call still on her mind. "What you doing here this hour of the morning? You're lucky you didn't wake us all up."

"*I* was summoned from bed at the crack of dawn, my dear. Lily Lightsey called me at six A.M. to beg a ride out to the fort."

The fort? For the movie? But Stephen had called her from the

Rebel Tavern in the dead of night, hopeless with the incessant rain. The crew had been drinking and listening to the weather report on the late-night news, confirming what they already knew: the forecast called for another week of cloudy skies and high winds—a fifty percent chance of showers in the next two days—and the rumor was that the producer had decided to cut his losses. The worst part, Stephen said, was not the movie left unmade. The movie was trash, he said, picked up by such a fly-by-night production company that they'd gambled against weather insurance: but he didn't get a penny until the cameras started rolling, and without the money—

"Come on, Mary Faith, we're going to watch them shoot a movie. I told you you should have brought Jesse by for the tryouts."

"They're shooting?" she said. She couldn't help but break into a wide grin herself.

"They're shooting to*day*. The weather fooled everybody, and now they've called all the extras in to shoot on the beach while they patch the fort back together. And I'm bringing you out there." Tim grabbed her by a wet hand, but Mary Faith pulled back. The morning had dawned so bright and clear that she had not known whether she was wakened by the light or by the terrible irony that Stephen had missed getting paid by one day. And then she had lain in bed letting the sun pour in and letting her whole body swell up with the relief that Stephen might yet be poor, but at least Marygail wouldn't get her big moment on film. Stephen had said there was nothing he could do about that—the director thought she was a natural for the camera and it couldn't hurt with the locals—but still. Family doubly blessed with talent. She'd had to read about it in the *Courier,* and she and Stephen bickered over it as if they were married already. The strain of waiting had them battling, these days.

And now the movie was on after all. Stephen hadn't called this morning to tell her: so he must have left his own house at dawn; he must have stayed up all night with the movie people, watching the sky change on them. He must be at Claire's Point that very minute, hung over and giddy with relief. Now he would get his money and there would be enough—surely there'd be enough to settle the divorce.

"Come on, Mary Faith, they need her at eight A.M. We'll have fifteen minutes to tear out there the time you put yourself in some decent clothing."

"Tim, no." Mary Faith turned back to the kitchen sink and picked up a soggy sponge to wipe the counter. Long before the three-day rain, long before

☾

the call that the production company was ready to pull out of town, she and Stephen had agreed that it would be better for her not to show up at the fort. Stephen said he was going to make his announcement, once and for all, when the fifty-thousand-dollar check was in his wallet.

Now Tim grabbed the sponge from her hand and looped around the kitchen, dripping gray water over the stove and the refrigerator. He was *dancing*. "Come on," he sang. "Come on, time's awasting." Jesse and his grandfather chose that moment—the long yodel of time's awasting—to walk hand in hand into the kitchen and laugh up at Tim.

"Mary Faith, put some clothes on." At least her father was still smiling. "What's up, Rooney? You look bright and chipper. You getting married or something?"

"Ooh, yuck," the little boy said, and went to tackle Tim by the legs.

"I'm not getting married, I'm going to watch them shoot a movie. If her royal highness here will consent to get some clothing on. Get your shoes on, Jesse. Quit wrassling me."

"Well, it's nice some people can spend their leisure time out on movie sets. Me, I got to get to work."

"Come on, Grandpa. Come on out to the movie."

"Nah, I'm too old for that nonsense. Take your momma, honey."

"I'm not going," Mary Faith said, and grabbed the sponge back from Tim. It was slimy in her hand, and she turned her back on all of them to wring it out in the sink.

"Oh, go on," her father said. "You been carrying on for three days how you got to get out of the house."

"Come on, Momma," Jesse squealed. "Come on, I'm going." Then he stopped. "They don't shoot people, do they? They wouldn't shoot a kid."

"No, no, Jesse, they shoot the cameras. With film inside. And I'd be a crazy fool to drive your son out there and have to keep him from pulling all the plugs by my*self*," Tim said. "Come on, Mary Faith."

"Go on, sweetheart." Her father came up behind her to squeeze her shoulder. He had caught the movie bug himself, grinning the way he was, and he leaned down—she couldn't believe it: her father never kissed her—to graze her shortly on the cheek. "Go on. I've got to get out to the station, but you owe Jesse a day at the movies."

Mary Faith leaned back for a moment on her father's chest, disconcerted by

☾

the two of them touching each other that way, and looked out through the kitchen window at the bright yard beyond the sink. The sun was shining on the dogwoods—the sun was *burning*—and maybe there was a sign in the light and those pink-flowering trees. Maybe there was a sign in her father's touch. It was a new morning, and Stephen would be seeing the whole day in a new light. Marygail would get her moment on camera—Marygail could *have* her moment on film—but she and Stephen would get better. Now they could set the date.

Surely Stephen wouldn't mind if she showed up now, in the new light. It was time to stop hiding in the kitchen. Time to marry Stephen at last.

Tim was driving his sister's old car, a tiny blue subcompact, and Mary Faith threatened Jesse with staying home after all if he didn't let her buckle him into the seatbelt. Her own shoulder harness was twisted up beyond use, and she swung her long legs back and forth, trying to escape her torture position behind the driver's seat. Lily Lightsey sat next to Tim, a lacy web of bobbing white hair the only visible sign to the back seat that she was there at all. She hadn't spoken a word but "Hey" since they'd picked her up down at the corner.

Tim was driving the beach road the way he walked through a house—like a loon—and every now and again Mary Faith put a hand around Jesse's shoulder, as if that would protect him when Tim ran off the shoulder. She was still wearing the black and white T-shirt: Tim had only given her five minutes to get dressed, and she'd thrown on and off jeans and her blue flowery dress before she'd finally settled on a long black skirt with the T-shirt over it. Marygail would be dressed to kill, costumed and wigged and painted on the hard lines of her face—but her own face was scrubbed clean, and she'd combed her long hair loose. She knew she looked fifteen again.

"Hang on, everybody," Tim said, and sped up to catch the green light before he turned off on the road to Claire's Point. Jesse put his hand to the window, peering out, and Mary Faith heard a high tinkling of laughter from Lily in the front seat.

"You gonna kill us all," Lily Lightsey said, but they caught the light and made the turn: Mary Faith could see between the two bucket seats in front that traffic was thick on the road ahead of them.

Tim pulled back from passing—the double yellow line was swimming

☾

around the curve—and they fell in behind a cavalcade of station wagons and sedans on their way out to Claire's Point.

"I thought they brought in their own actors," Mary Faith said. "How many people did they *hire?*"

"Hundreds, from the look of this road!" Tim said. "It's an epic. It'll be bigger than *The Ten Commandments.* Bigger than *The Bible.*"

Jesse laughed his high excited laugh, and Mary Faith watched him ogle the fields and the patches of wood the same way she did when she was set free from the house.

"A bull!" Jesse hollered, and Mary Faith looked out on a narrow pasture of cows grazing, not a bull among them. Poor little boy, shut up in the house all winter. Maybe Stephen would have time to show them around: maybe he'd be able to carry Jesse on his shoulders around the movie set.

They meandered along, Tim settling into the slow steady rhythm of traffic, and came finally to a road block set out before the turnoff to the fort. A sheriff's deputy manned it, leaning down into every car as if he were searching for terrorists. There were ten or eleven cars ahead of them.

Jesse fidgeted, waiting, and Tim tried to settle him by describing what they'd see: "The director'll have a bullhorn, Jess, and he'll be wearing a French beret."

"He will not." Mary Faith laughed, but Jesse strained forward with his anticipation.

"They don't shoot kids," he said.

"They don't shoot *anybody,*" Mary Faith said. "Tim told you: they're shooting a movie. They shoot the film with the cameras."

"And the film wouldn't hit nobody," Jesse said.

"The film won't hit *any*body. That's right. The film just takes the picture."

"What's a bullhorn? That a cow?"

Lily Lightsey laughed shortly and twisted around the front of her seat to get a good look at Jesse in back. She gazed at him from black watery eyes set deep in a dark face that was tiny—shrunken-looking—despite its high wide cheekbones. Her forehead was stretched taut, and for all her years, she had fewer lines around her eyes than Mary Faith's father. The golden hoops in her ears glinted in shafts of sunlight.

"Precious boy," she said, finally.

Jesse shrank back from the little old woman and hissed at Mary Faith: "Momma, is she wearing a mask?"

☾

Mary Faith felt her cheeks flame up and squeezed her son's shoulders. The old woman turned back around without a word.

Now Tim inched the car forward to the front of the line, and the deputy swaggered over and leaned down into the driver's window: Mary Faith could feel Jesse quivering beside her.

"They don't shoot anybody," she whispered. The deputy's chubby tanned face looked familiar: somebody she'd gone to high school with, probably—somebody from a million years ago.

"Can I help you folks?" he said importantly.

"We're delivering the star," Tim said.

"Somebody here for the crowd scene? I got to move this line."

"Here she is," Tim said, with a grand sweeping gesture toward Lily.

"Just one?"

"Just the one."

"Well, I can't let all of y'all stay. You're going to have to drop her off—drive straight down this road and turn left. They'll have somebody directing traffic down there, but you'll have to leave her and drive on out the back way. They don't want an audience this morning."

Tim gunned his motor and said: "We'll see about *that*," winking into the back seat at Jesse.

Mary Faith watched the dirt road flash by, the same road Stephen had taken her down the day he told her the movie was sold. The trailers and cabins had been lifeless that day, but now their driveways were filled up with cars, and she watched whole families trooping down the road with coolers, going to a picnic. Going to watch the movie. Half of Due East had shown up, and Mary Faith didn't know whether to breathe out relief or panic that they wouldn't be able to stay. The effort it had taken to choose going, to choose seeing the look on Stephen's face when she showed up, had tightened every muscle in her body. Now she couldn't loose them all at once.

They made their left turn, and were stopped dead in a parking lot lining both sides of the road for a quarter mile. A boy not older than Mary Faith, a baseball cap over his ponytail and a clipboard in his hand, was waving cars over to the side to park. The clipboard, Mary Faith figured, listed the names of the extras, but the boy was too busy directing cars to consult it. Tim threw the gearshift in reverse and sped backwards until he eased into a spot on the embankment.

☾

"Tim, we're supposed to drop her off," Mary Faith said. Suddenly the idea of showing up to surprise Stephen seemed childish. He'd be caught up in this rush of activity. He'd have no time to carry Jesse around on his shoulders: and if his wife was here, it would be worse than awkward.

"Oh, I reckon we can slip right in. Everybody out."

"Lily can't walk that far. Look—see that patch of trees, with the hill? That's where the fort is, way over yonder."

"So let's walk on up there."

"It's too far to walk, Tim." Mary Faith clung to the seatbelt Jesse was trying to unlatch.

"Where my stick be?" Lily was already opening her door, already squeezing between the car and the thorny branches that pressed up against it. She could have been a wraith.

Tim drew a stout wooden cudgel out from under his seat and went round to help her, but Lily chose the stick over his hand and hobbled on off down the road.

"Come on." Tim leaned into the back and held his arms open for Jesse. The little boy finally found the button on the belt—click—that released him, and Mary Faith watched him push the seat in front of him and clamber out.

"Come on, Miss Rapple. Don't be shy. I'll protect you."

"Tim, they're going to kick us out."

"So let's see what we can see until they do. Come on, Jesse."

Suddenly Mary Faith remembered the way she had lingered in Stephen's car that day he'd driven her out to Claire's Point. And hadn't he wanted her out there after all: hadn't he *wanted* her to be the first to hear about his movie? He had waded out into the muddy water and twirled around like a boy. He would understand when he saw her today—maybe he would throw his arms up and dance in the water again—and maybe she would let a slow-breaking smile dance on her own face, while a director shot the movie that was setting them both free.

She struggled out of the car and ran off after Tim and her son, Lily Lightsey already far beyond the three of them. The sky was still banked with clouds up beyond the trees, but the clouds were high and white and fluffy. Downed branches and clumps of gray moss littered the dirt road, but they circled the debris and the mud puddles giddily, moving to catch up with the crowd.

"There's a bullhorn, Jesse!" Tim said, and they watched a woman halfway up the road calling out to the stragglers: "Extras up this pathway. Costumes in the tent. Extras up this pathway." Breezes floated in toward the woman, inflating her windbreaker: she was dressed in grubby jeans and sneakers, and Mary Faith looked down at her own long black skirt and sandals before she eyed the path they were to climb. She'd worn the wrong clothes after all.

They were still far in front of the fort: Lily bobbed along in the midst of the fifteen or twenty other townspeople preceding them on the dirt path, picking their way around palmetto stumps and thorns. When they reached the top of the low hill, Mary Faith saw below them a neighboring beach house on stilts and, over toward the water, a rickety shack. The movie company had set up two white tents that looked ready for a wedding reception, and now more men or boys—or *whatever* they were, in their long hair and caps—were ushering them in the direction of the tents. "Women to the left, men to the right. Women left, men right," they chanted. The path had changed from dirt to sand, and Mary Faith stumbled in her flimsy sandals. Could Stephen be watching her through a long lens, seeing her trip and right herself?

Over her left shoulder was the fort, the crumbling ramparts rising up over spindly trees. She could hear a racket of hammering and equipment hauling, and below her she saw jacketed crew members gathered at the pulled-back tent flaps. She strained to read the jacket lettering when a back was turned toward her: "New Morning Productions" it said, yellow script on sky-blue shine, and she blinked to read the words through again. The jackets actually said "New Morning." The sunlight on the dogwoods *had* been a sign.

"Mary Faith!" she heard from behind. "Tim!"

She stopped to look in the direction she'd come from and watched a woman wading through the dune, following a teenage girl and waving. It was Becky Perdue, looking perfectly sane. She'd even known how to dress for the movie down by the water: she was wearing old baggy dungarees splattered with bleach stains, and a crimson kerchief was tied around her head.

Jesse was still racing ahead, Tim on his heels; Mary Faith watched them flit away and held herself back to wait for Becky Perdue. She couldn't *believe* she was letting the crazy church lady intrude yet again: the woman—the lunatic— had called her up Monday afternoon with the hysterical message that Mary Faith was not to let Father Berkeley talk her into anything. Mary Faith had never spoken to Father Berkeley in her life, but when she hung up the phone that afternoon she'd been cold with fear—what if the priest was trying to save

☾

Stephen's marriage? The week had passed, though, with no phone call from any priest, and she'd decided that Becky Perdue's warning was only a response to the foolish way she'd stopped to say hello on River Street. Just a madwoman's way of being friendly. Becky Perdue was lonely, just inventing excuses to talk, and ever since Tim told her how the husband had left her with four children while he ran around town with a redheaded divorcee, Mary Faith had been inclined to forgive her the strange phone calls and even her car rammed into a live oak tree. If she was being left behind—

Now, seeing the breezy way Becky hurried up the path, she realized that it was almost relief she felt at the sight of the woman. They had been moving along so quickly that she'd barely had time to register how unreal it felt to be here, on Claire's Point, surrounded by a production company flown in from California or Florida or God knows where, surrounded by old ladies in pedal pushers and mesh golfing caps, old ladies on the arms of retired officers: strangers who'd moved in while she'd been holed up on the Point. It *was* relief she felt at seeing Becky Perdue's face, relief that she could pretend to be connected to someone other than Tim. If Stephen were watching from high up on the fort. If Stephen had seen her black skirt slipping along the way. She didn't want to shame him, showing up this way.

"You in the movie?"

"Oh, no," Becky Perdue said, and her smile was as bright and clear as the day around them. "My daughter. Wait up, Sissy!"

A sulky teenager with dirty-blond hair drooping down into one eye put an impatient hand to her hip and waited for Mary Faith and Becky to approach together.

"This is my daughter Sissy, Mary Faith." Becky was taking her time, making a formal introduction—where did she think she was? "Cecelia. This is Mary Faith Rapple."

"Hey," the girl said. "Come *on,* Momma."

They hurried along, and Mary Faith caught a glimpse of Tim and Jesse seeing Lily into the tent on the left. They turned toward her—Tim mugged and pointed a finger at Jesse's head—and then they darted off toward the men's tent.

"I've got to go after Tim and Jesse," she said, watching them disappear for good. "They're not supposed to be here."

"Well, hold on," Becky said. "I don't know who-all showed up, they called

☾

us in so suddenly. It's Good Friday, and Due East just about shuts down for Good Friday. Maybe they could use your little boy."

"He didn't go to the tryouts." What if Stephen were in the men's tent, suiting up for his own walk-on? What if he saw Jesse with Tim before she had time to explain?

Becky Perdue's daughter snorted. "Some tryouts," she said. "All they did was ask how old you were and what size you wore. Daddy said he'd get a *real* part for me."

"Honey, your daddy's not running the show, he's only letting them shoot out here." Becky rolled her eyes at Mary Faith—*you* know how kids are—and leaned over to whisper: "Let's just sneak on in. This is kind of exciting."

Sissy shrugged and disappeared into the tent. Mary Faith looked around wildly, for Tim or Jesse or Stephen, and felt a bony hand pressing against the small of her back. She followed Becky Perdue in through the wide opening: there was nowhere else to turn now.

They moved through the gauzy space, white light seeping in from all sides, and Mary Faith waited for someone to stop her. She was in an all-female world now: in the back of the tent, another New Morning woman stood atop a folding lunchroom table. In front of her more tables, piled high with costumes and handwritten signs, were laid out end to end. Mary Faith saw Lily Lightsey off to the side, fingering a checkered gown as if she were a customer in a dry-goods store.

"Move on up," someone said behind her, and they all pressed forward, gathering under the woman who stood up high and beckoned them closer.

The woman waited patiently—self-possessed, bored almost—and then held her right hand up into the air for silence. "IF I CAN JUST HAVE YOUR ATTENTION FOR ONE SHORT MOMENT."

Mary Faith slipped in closer to Becky, who was grinning like a fool with happy disbelief. "Isn't this something?" she whispered. Mary Faith nodded, mute: what if Marygail were in the midst of this crowd somewhere? She darted her eyes around the tent, but she could see only forty other Due East women, most of them old like Lily Lightsey, most of them giggling ferociously at their good luck to be here this very minute. They could have been spectators at an execution.

"IF I COULD JUST HAVE YOUR ATTENTION, LADIES." The woman atop the folding table looked like a TV character herself in her black

☾

jumpsuit, a leopard skin headband pushing back her thick red hair. "THANK YOU."

Finally she lowered her voice and tried on a conversational tone: "Thank you, ladies, for showing up at this short notice. Our schedule's been all turned around by the weather, and we're getting in this shot much sooner than we anticipated. I'm the assistant director. I want to fill you in a little further about the costumes and what we need you to do out on the beach."

Mary Faith thought it was safe now to take a closer look for Marygail, and she twisted around slowly. Not a sight of her—the crowd scene's look was going to be old and frumpy. She should have known that Stephen's wife wouldn't be caught dead lumped together with the old ladies and the blond teenager: she'd probably get *her* costume and makeup on out in one of those trailers.

"We want you to bear with us in this makeshift dressing room. The wardrobe mistress has been out here since five o'clock this morning, and she intends to transform you all in half an hour." The forty women whooped and applauded. "We have your name pinned to your costume, so when I finish you can head on over to find it. Now, there were some special faces we needed up front—have you got that list?" An assistant handed up a clipboard. "Right. Lily Lightsey? Did she get here? Good. Good. Nice to see you. And Cecelia Perdue—" Sissy swallowed a whoop of joy and raised her hand in front of Mary Faith.

"Now. We gave you an idea of the story in town, but let me repeat it so you know what you're doing out there. Ladies? May I please have your attention? We are running BEHIND SCHEDULE HERE. Thank you. Thanks."

Mary Faith tried to picture the moment when they all left the tent: Becky Perdue would probably have succumbed to movie fever and tried on her own costume by then. The mood in the tent had reached a pitch of near hysteria, and she could imagine a symphony of shrieks and cackles swelling up like the sea itself when the extras moved down to the beach.

"This scene takes place after two boatloads of women have sailed out to the fort to confront the soldiers. Everybody here has come out in the second boat —you'll see two big rowboats in the water when we get down there. That's our starting point. Don't worry, you don't have to get your feet wet. We'll be shooting the principals coming in and disembarking, but we need a wide shot

☾

of you folks—we're going to see the whole crowd of you coming from a distance, pulling your skirts up and marching along the sand. We're going to need you to look VERY DETERMINED and VERY RIGHTEOUS and VERY ANGRY: the director will tell you how he wants you to congregate down by the water. The main thing is to follow his directions TO THE LETTER. We didn't have time to set down the track we wanted, so this shot is going to take a while. No giggling out there, O.K.?" The tent exploded in giggles.

"Right. Just keep those three words in your minds. *Determined* and *righteous* and *angry*. I'm going to let you get the costumes now and then go over to the makeup tables in back—ONE MINUTE, LADIES. Thank you. I'm going to let you get the costumes on, but please slip into them as quickly as you can. Ask one of the wardrobe crew behind the tables if you need help. Please. I'm going to need those two—Lightsey and Perdue—up here and the rest of you scramble into those costumes just as quick as you can."

Sissy turned to her mother and breathed: "I *told* you he'd do it. Daddy got me a real part!"

"Gracious, Sissy. Run on up and see what they want you to do." Becky turned to Mary Faith and said: "Sure you don't want to try and get your face on camera?"

Mary Faith, miserable, shook her head no. Why had she let Tim take her this far? She couldn't pretend to just run across Stephen now; Jesse was surely in costume already, recruited to replace some missing soul and march with the women across the sand.

"I can't tell you what fun I'm having." Becky Perdue craned her neck up to see over Mary Faith. "I told my husband last night I want that divorce after all, and now look at me. In the middle of the costume tent. There's *some* justice in the world, isn't there?"

How could Becky Perdue just babble on that way, when they had to find a way to get out of this tent? Now she and Becky were the only women in the white light not busy with the rummaging for costumes and the pulling them on behind sheets hung up for screens, and somebody—that redheaded monster in the jumpsuit—was going to come on over and ask them to get out. "You going to see if they need anybody else?"

"Oh, I'm not interested in being part of this foolishness. I'm just going to watch the show and enjoy my freedom," Becky said, and now Mary Faith

☾

registered what the woman had told her. She was getting a *divorce*. Becky Perdue was getting a divorce, and she was drunk with the relief of it, turning herself into one of those steamrolling southern women who drive past road-blocks and let themselves into costume tents just because they feel like being there.

The assistant director had spied them, gossiping and useless, and now she was heading over to vent her fury: Mary Faith had *known* what was coming. Stephen would see them being escorted out by the assistant director herself. This was *not* the way to plan a wedding.

The woman was brisk and annoyed, and Mary Faith ducked her head down. "Can I help you ladies?"

Becky Perdue shook her hand and said gaily: "Why, it's such a pleasure to meet you. I'm Becky Perdue—I own the fort." And then, drawing her free arm around Mary Faith's shoulder, just as formal as she'd been introducing her daughter: "This is Stephen Dugan's friend, Mary Faith Rapple."

Mary Faith considered taking off at a run for the tent flaps, but the assistant director smiled distractedly and said she'd have someone get them coffee when they had a free moment. "And you can watch from behind the camera out there—did you get a pass?"

Becky winked at Mary Faith once she was gone and whispered that they'd better find Tim to warn him about passes. "This is just a holiday for me, I can't tell you."

Mary Faith looked at her with wonder: this was the same sad soul who'd looked so bereft on River Street, who had run her car into a tree the week before. How had she found out about her and Stephen? Introducing her that way: Stephen Dugan's friend. Did everybody on this movie set know? Maybe she could find Jesse and Tim and get home after all, before Stephen saw her out there to pressure him. He was going to let loose of Marygail for once and for all, and she shouldn't have shown up to make it harder for him. When they made Stephen's next screenplay, she was going to be introduced as his wife. Couldn't she just have *waited*?

Becky was saying: "I wouldn't so much as tiptoe near Sissy—look yonder, they're pulling her hair back. She'd die of shame if I came within three feet of her now. Come on, Mary Faith. Let's go get those passes."

There was nothing to do but follow her back through the tent and the flurry. Women were having their hair rolled and twisted into crowns atop their

☾

heads at the makeup tables, and they were sitting Lily Lightsey down to go to work on her face: she was unfastening her gold hoops when two women came up behind her and eased her down into a folding chair. Mary Faith hated the way they pressed down on her shoulders, as if she were a child.

"I hope to Christ they don't shove her around that way out on the beach," she said fiercely. She was *sure* she was muttering under her breath, muttering with dismay that she'd imagined this crowded day would be a good one to surprise Stephen with a wedding date, but as they passed behind Lily the old woman spoke up:

"Honey, I been taking care of *my*self for eighty-one years. You watch out for *you*."

Mary Faith swung back in confusion, but Lily was staring out at nothing as the makeup women, netting her hair and smiling knowingly, leaned over her.

Tim and Jesse were waiting for them behind the tent—at least her son hadn't been sucked into the maws of this production company—and Tim said they weren't shooting the men until after the lunch break, when they'd come running from the fort behind the actors. The men weren't even getting into costume yet.

"They're *soldiers*, Momma," Jesse said. "AND THEY DON'T SHOOT PEOPLE."

Mary Faith went down on one knee and hugged her son to her—she could have kneeled that way forever, squeezing him tight—but he wriggled free and jumped up and down as if the ground were a trampoline that would not let him settle.

"They're getting us passes," Becky told Tim.

Mary Faith squinted up at the fort and said: "Don't you think we're in the way?" Now that she could see what a bad idea it was to come out to Claire's Point, she wanted to vanish back to Due East. But Becky and Tim turned incredulous faces on her, and Jesse said: "Oh, Momma, they're just *starting*. I want to see some soldiers."

"I've got to drive back to town and get Nippie to the Stations at noon," Becky said, "but we could watch them set up. Come see Sissy, Mary Faith. Come see my daughter in a *movie*. I can't believe it's really happening."

Tim watched her closely—Tim was staring her down, daring her to say she didn't want to see Stephen—and Mary Faith turned away from his gaze in defeat.

☾

She stood still, breathing deeply so Jesse wouldn't see her flustered, and she knew even before she heard the three of them giggling and sidling away that Stephen had chosen this very moment of confusion to come.

He was just a white speck walking down from the fort—a flash of sandy hair and a glint of glasses—but he could have been a falling star ready to crash down on the spot where she stood. Tim must have seen him coming too: he was leading Becky and Jesse away, letting her concoct her own lies to explain what she was doing at the movie location when she'd promised to stay away.

She could flee, this very instant: she could follow Tim and Becky and lose herself in the crowd behind the camera, or she could run off and hide in the back seat of the little blue car. She stayed put, staring at the sandy dirt and running her foot through the dry tufts that tried to sprout there. She drew X's and crosses and circles with the toe of her sandal, calculating the time it would take Stephen to reach her.

He must have seen her from up high—he was heading straight toward the tent—and she braced herself as he drew closer. Tim Rooney had been trying to break them up since the day he'd laid eyes on her and now, now when she and Stephen were so close to breaking up his marriage instead, Tim had brought her out here to see if he couldn't set off more fireworks. Mary Faith ran through the lines she'd spat out at Stephen when she read that Marygail was going to be in the movie: she'd told him that he was a snake in the grass, a deceiver. She told him that he didn't have any intention of marrying her.

Now he was almost upon her and now—with the sun rising lazily through the high clouds—she could see that he wasn't coming in anger. The breeze whipped his hair back and he shoved his hand through the sparseness of it, then shoved his glasses back up his nose. There was something miserable and pathetic in his motions: Marygail must be here, in one of those trailers after all, and he was coming to warn her off.

He hitched his pants up and broke into a trot as he neared. Something was wrong. Something aside from her presence there: his mouth, his very beard, twitched with the wrongness.

"Mary Faith," he said. He stopped dead in front of her and watched her the way Tim had: waiting for her to explain herself.

"I came—" she started.

"Never mind," he said. "I know, her sister says she's been working her way through the Due East phone book. I knew she'd call you up. Damn it—"

((

Mary Faith couldn't guess what showed on her face: was it the wrongness showing, reflecting back under the sunny sky?

"Mary Faith, we have to talk." Stephen was already moving away from the tent, off toward the water.

"Don't they need you here?"

He threw up his hands, bewildered. "They don't need me. No, they don't need me! I wrote the godawful script, didn't I? They've *got* their script."

Now there was nothing to do but follow him the way she'd followed Tim and Becky. She could make out her son on the last patch of dry sand, moving in the shadow of a camera perched on a tripod. Reflectors of golden foil— modern offerings to some space god—were scattered about the beach, casting strange trapezoidal images. She could see Tim distracting Jesse, pointing out to the seagulls and the sailboats.

"Please, Mary Faith. Please. Just come."

She followed him as he took off away from the camera, away from the boats: they'd anchored two big sloops offshore, the same ones that had led the parade of fishing boats in the Water Festival, and Mary Faith watched the sails billow out on the water, sun-bleached and achingly white. Two long rowboats were pulled up on the sand. Stephen had done this: Stephen had imagined boatloads of women sailing themselves through a treacherous sound, rowing up to the shore, and now Stephen was walking away from her on the damp shoreline.

Mary Faith stumbled again in the muck: Stephen's feet were sucked up by the mud, but still he hurried her away from the film crew, releasing his feet from the black holes and plopping them down again relentlessly. Just past a jetty the beach curved—he was leading them that far away, and the fiddler crabs darted in terror as they approached. She could feel the soft crunch of old dark shells underfoot. There was something wrong in the very way he walked, in the strange set of his shoulders and the flapping of his hands at his side.

He passed the jetty and slowed for her to catch up. After another fifty yards of silence they came to the barnacled remains of a dock and Stephen said: "Here." He led her out to sit on the eaten-away planks, and they lowered themselves awkwardly. Now the movie set—the beach, the tents, the fort— was a distant city, and she and Stephen were alone in the blank bright light. The water licked in mud-black and indifferent on the shore beneath them, and Mary Faith felt a splinter digging into her hand.

☾

Their legs dangled together over the water. If only he would start, if only he would bless her out for showing up, or warn her that his wife was back there in a trailer. The waves slapped out the minutes passing.

"Marygail's real sick," he said finally. Mary Faith didn't know what the words meant: they danced away like the shimmers on the water. She only knew that they were all wrong. She had come out to Claire's Point because they were free of Marygail now.

She waited.

"We're trying to keep her out of the hospital. She's coherent one day and then—she won't see a doctor. Her sister's stayed a week now. She thinks she's going to come on down and be in this movie. They'll put her in a straitjacket before they put her in front of the camera."

She waited.

"She's in bad trouble, Mary Faith. I think she's cracking up."

Now she could define the wrongness of it—now she could see what the look on his face had been, coming down from the fort. It was pitying: that look, that sound. Stephen's voice was full of pity.

"I can wait, Stephen." She heard how sharp and bright her own words crystallized. SHE HAD COME OUT HERE BECAUSE THEY WERE FREE OF HIS WIFE. Cracking up? Crazy? The woman was as shallow as the water beneath their feet. Shallow women didn't crack up: you had to possess reason in the first place to lose it. She wanted to let her sentence sparkle on and on like the waves stupidly repeating themselves—I can wait, I can wait—but she held her tongue, and she held her head back rigid, refusing to turn it in his direction.

She imagined his shoulders hunched up beside her, his glasses slipping down his nose and his beard worming around his mouth. She could feel his breath choking itself out: that same choking that came once with the passion and the wrongness of her being a girl. Had he been choking with pity for her all along, then?

"I've got to see her through this," Stephen said, and she was so repulsed by the sound of his voice—the wavering, the shame—that she rose up, all at once, and balanced herself between two wooden planks. The dock swayed beneath her feet. The splinter was deep in her palm now: a sharp bright needle wedging itself into her hand.

"I can wait," she said again. Motionless on the dock, she waited for him to

☾

answer. She waited for him to say: Yes, wait, just a while longer. This is a new morning, he'd say. Now the sun is shining and they're making my movie and we'll get through this. I won't leave you. *Come on.*

He didn't answer. He wouldn't speak his own lines. He wouldn't speak the trite words he'd written for this ending: No, you can't wait. No, I can't do this to you anymore. You have to go on with your own life.

GO ON WITH YOUR OWN LIFE! A made-for-TV movie.

This was not happening: Stephen was so caught up in his melodrama that he thought she'd be willing to star in his new production too. Did he picture her walking back alone on the shoreline? Did he imagine her walking back alone to Jesse? What lines would he give her to speak: did he want her to ask Becky Perdue to bring them back to the Point? Did he want her to ask another madwoman to bring them home because *she had to drive Nippie to the Stations at noon?*

He could not possibly imagine her driving back to Due East with Becky Perdue. No one could go on for three more years, or five more years, or ten more years cutting recipes from the *Courier* and dragging a caterwauling child home from fights he'd picked in a waterfront park. Years couldn't just roll out that way, like film through a camera. There wasn't that much blank film in all of Due East. Did Stephen think she could wait three years for a father to call her sweetheart and kiss her on the cheek again? Didn't Stephen know that he couldn't let his characters get swallowed into nothingness that way—no, *come on,* people beat their wives and swallowed thirty Quaaludes and swam out into riptides instead. People pretended they were going mad.

Stephen had imagined her all wrong: hadn't he made his army of women sail a salvation boat onto a point where the land ended and the sea began? Hadn't he made them determined and righteous and angry?

But there was no determination, no anger in her—she was as innocent of feeling as those golden reflectors back in the sand. Stephen had taken off his glasses and pressed a palm to his eye: how old and red his eye would look, under that hand.

Come on. *Come on.* Say something.

"Jesse will be fretting if I don't get back soon." She could wrest this scene from him yet.

She waited: and he raised his face. She saw that his eye was not red at all, only welled up with that terrible pity. She thought maybe that he mouthed the

☾

words *I'm sorry*, but she was not watching him anymore. She was watching the endless space behind him, the space where a sickle moon dangled, as vague as the pale sky.

She walked off the dock and felt the shore slippery beneath her feet.

Everyone had read the script but her: hadn't Lily Lightsey told her to watch out for herself? Hadn't Becky tried to warn her? Suddenly she could see black lines on a white page, lines that had chilled her so that they'd seeped into her memory:

> And priest in black gowns, were walking their rounds,
> And binding with briars, my joys and desires.

She was walking back along the beach alone, just as Stephen must have imagined it, remembering lines from his dissertation. Becky had tried to warn her: that priest must have gotten to Stephen after all. *There* was the missing scene, the one she'd been no party to.

He'd known all along how he meant to end this: he'd meant her to blame a priest for his betrayal. He'd waited to make his movie, he'd waited for her to come to *him*—he'd waited for Good Friday, when she could blame a priest. When all Due East would shut down and mourn, the town's reason setting as its religious fervor lit up the sky.

Now she felt a tingling, some sensation between thought and emotion prickling up in her hands with the thorn. Determination? Anger? Righteousness? She was almost round the curve that would take her back to the crowds and away from Stephen for good. What if she wrote her own scene here, a scene when she let loose of her own reason?

She would stop dead in her tracks just before the curve, and she would let her voice float back to Stephen, on the swell of drippy violins. "I'm sorry too," she would say. "I'm so sorry."

But she had rounded the curve already, her feet dragging through the quagmire, and now she could see the real movie taking shape before her. An army of women was descending to the beach from the tents, their sagging costumed bosoms pressing on with their newfound determination and righteousness and anger. The old ladies of Due East had been transformed.

She could see from afar a child perched on a tall man's shoulders, watching the women come to drown him in their massing tide.

☾

That was her son clinging to the man's head. That was Jesse. Jesse needed to get out of the path of the onslaught.

Stephen must have imagined her cradling Jesse when she reached him, and fixing his lunch after Becky drove them back to town. He must have pictured her holding Jesse's foot when her son couldn't sleep, walking him out into the cool air when croup choked him in the dead of night.

Stephen had imagined the rest of her life for her: had imagined her buried in Due East, possessed of half a degree and a handful of Latin phrases. *Inter faeces et urinam nascimur.* She was coming closer to Stephen's movie with every step, and she walked right into the shallow water, wading her way back slowly to the crowd behind the camera. Her sandals soaked up, heavy on her bare feet, and she trudged toward her son: Jesse waved his hands in a frenzy, calling her to him.

Jesse would be getting hungry.

He would be wondering where she had disappeared.

And now Becky Perdue was coming toward her, her red kerchief fluttering in the breeze, her arms stretched out in greeting.

He hadn't come after her, to tell her to wait. There was nothing to do but follow them home.

(

☾

28

Your Own Free Will

"MARYGAIL, COME ON IN THE HOUSE THIS minute. You can't wander around by the water in your nightgown, now. Come on in and get you some decent clothes on."

"I'm practicing, Gracie. I'm a Hollywood star."

"You're not a star, and you're not in Hollywood. Stephen told you last night, they're not going to use that scene."

A white and frothy twirl around the big backyard: the nightgown swings out waist high. "I'm singing in the rain."

"It's not raining. Cut it out. Get on back in the house, now. You have to eat something. Stephen's taking you to the doctor the minute he gets back from the fort."

"Hello, Doctor. Are you an officer, or an enlisted man? May I have this dance?"

"Stop it, Marygail. Stop this play acting. This instant."

A slow collapse to the ground, white negligee floating out to muddy itself on the ground.

"I don't want to go see a doctor."

"There now. See? I knew you could make sense. You made sense all day yesterday, when you thought you were going to be in the movie. And the doctor says if you come of your own free will he can see about medicating you outside of the hospital, since that's what Stephen's so hellbent on doing."

"I'm singing in the rain."

"Marygail, you're singing in the sun. Come *on*. I heard you up all night. No wonder the crazies are coming back. Momma's going to be here tomorrow and slap you in the hospital soon as she sees you if you don't pull yourself together. You haven't eaten hardly anything in two days."

"I'm fasting for forty days and forty nights. I'm getting baptized!"

"You're not getting baptized any more than you're singing in the rain. That priest said he couldn't let you go through with it until you get your reason back."

"I couldn't *do* it with my reason."

"Exactly."

"Doctor, do I look crazy to you?"

"You look crazy to *me*. And I'm the one going out of my mind from taking care of you. Go on. Stay on the ground in your bare feet. I've got to get in there and cook for Maureen, anyway."

"Maureen! Maureen! Where's my darling precious daughter?"

"Your darling precious daughter is sick with worry. She's out at the fort with her father and they're coming back here in less than an hour to get you to the doctor."

"She's not out at the fort. I wouldn't let her out there, with those husband-stealing sluts. Betrayers!"

"Stephen had to get her out of *here*, didn't he?"

"She's stealing my scene!"

"Oh, don't be an idiot. Bad enough you're crazy. Stephen wouldn't let her be in that movie. He said himself it's trash."

"She took my scene and now she's taking him away from me. Stephen let that little *girl* do my scene!"

"What am I doing, talking to a lunatic?"

"Doctor, I am going to be baptized in the moonlight. Would you care to sponsor me?"

"Excuse me, Miss Out of Control. I have cooking to do. There's no *way* you're staying out of the hospital."

"I'm going to go down by the water and let it wash me clean."

☾

"MARYGAIL, PULL THAT NIGHTGOWN BACK DOWN OVER YOUR HEAD. Are you going to make me *drag* you back into the house?"

"Why Gracie, no. No, honey."

"All right then. Come on in before the neighbors see you. You might as well be naked."

"I'm so very sorry. I can't come in just now. I have to go down to the church to see the doctor."

"Marygail, get back here. Don't you walk off in that direction. Don't you do it."

A very sheer very white nightgown billows out and breezes through the yard.

"MARYGAIL, I AM GOING TO HAVE TO CALL THE POLICE TO GET YOU BACK. THEY ARE GOING TO HAVE TO PUT YOU IN THAT HOSPITAL AGAINST YOUR WILL."

A pause at the side of the house, under a magnolia tree in full bloom. White petals floating down, as Marygail listens intently.

"WE ARE GOING TO HAVE TO TAKE CARE OF YOU."

The nightgown floats off down Freedom Lane, a tall naked woman propelling it.

☾

☾

29

Blue Miniskirt, White Negligee

"MOMMA! DID YOU IRON MY BLUE MINI-skirt?"

Sissy was calling in from the deck, where she was sunbathing: it could have been summer in Due East that Saturday. I was in the kitchen, ironing Nippie's Easter dress—poor thing, she was up to a ladies size fourteen already—and trying to pretend that the steam rising up from the pores of the iron was what made me so misty-eyed. Since the day before, when I drove Mary Faith Rapple and her son back to the Point, I'd been tearing off on crying jags: the very ones I'd contained for twenty years of marriage.

Standing at the ironing board, I pretended I was weepy for Mary Faith being left that way, when it was as clear as the glass Sissy called through that I was weeping for myself. There was a pile of ironing on the floor that rose up as high as all I had to do, by myself. Find a job. Make Sissy love me. Send my boys off to college. Convince Jack that I didn't want him to ever share my bed again.

"No, I didn't iron your blue miniskirt."

"What?"

"Sissy, open the door instead of hollering through the glass that way."

"What."

She slid the glass door open and stood there in pink shorts and a pink tank top, an airy confection holding a *Playgirl* magazine in her hand.

"Sissy, whatever are you reading?"

"A magazine. Did you iron my blue miniskirt?"

"Sissy. Is that a *Playgirl* magazine?"

"Yeah."

"You mean yes, ma'am."

"Yes. Ma'am."

"Sissy, you throw that magazine in the trash this minute. You are thirteen years old." I had missed her big moment the day before: she and Lily Lightsey led the parade of women marching down the sand in Stephen Dugan's movie while I led Mary Faith, her lips clenched white, home with her son. No one in our family had seen Sissy, but she was sure the camera had lingered on her longer than on any woman there. Overnight she thought she was full grown, and she'd been dreaming in the sunlight that she was a movie star.

"Momma, I'm not done with the articles."

"Cecelia Perdue, don't tell me you were reading that magazine for the articles."

"There were a couple of good ones." I threw my head back with what I guess was laughter: Jack used to make jokes about men reading *Playboy* for the articles. Some pair of articles, he'd say.

"Don't laugh."

"I shouldn't be laughing at you, baby, looking at naked men."

"Well, I didn't know that was what was in there when I opened it. I was waiting around in that dumb trailer for hours for Daddy to come fetch me. So I read magazines." Now Sissy rolled her eyes off to the side. "How'd *you* know what was in *Playgirl* magazine?"

Where did she think I'd been living in the last twenty years? Outer space? Did I look that old to her, that cast out from society?

"All right, all right. Don't *look* at me that way. I'll throw it out when I'm done with the articles. Did you iron my blue miniskirt?"

"No, I didn't. I'm doing the Easter clothes."

"The blue miniskirt *is* my Easter clothes."

☾

"Oh, Sissy. You can't wear a micro-miniskirt to the vigil. Your daddy'll have a fit. He'll make you go right back into the house and change."

"Come on, Momma. I can't wear one of the old-lady dresses you wear."

"Sissy, I do not wear old-lady dresses. And I'm not wearing anything to the vigil tonight, your father's taking you. You have to pick out something decent."

"Aren't you coming with us?"

Now I saw how watchful she was. When her father drove her back home from the fort the night before, he'd come into the house to see if I hadn't changed my mind already. After one day! He'd given me three months to picture him lathering Judi up with baby oil, three months to imagine how she stuck her tongue in his ear and drew her red fingernails down his chest, and after one day he thought he could convince me that I didn't really want a divorce after all. So I'd repeated myself, right in front of the four children sitting around the kitchen island. I told Jack that I was going back to work, if I could find work, that I was going on by myself. I told him that I liked living on my own, and saw each of my children in turn flush with disbelief and shame for my lie.

"No, honey, I'm not coming with you. I've got a dinner party to go to tonight."

"You don't have a date!"

"No, Sissy, I don't have a date. I'm just going to have dinner with friends."

"What friends? Momma, we'll be *poor* if you don't let Daddy come back home!"

"What do you mean now, we'll be poor. I'm going to get a new teaching license—and your father's going to keep supporting you."

"He won't be able to. Those condos cost a fortune! And besides, Judi's suing him."

"Judi's *suing* him? Who told you that?"

"Daddy did. In the car coming home. She's getting Lamarr to start up a palimony case. She's going to stick him for every cent he's got."

"Oh, Sissy. Your father had no business telling you that. Getting you all upset. That woman can't get anything out of him."

"Oh yeah? Daddy says she stole half his records. She *knows* things about him. And he wants to come home and be a family again."

She waited for me to answer, but I had no answer to please her.

☾

"What's the big deal, Momma? I'm sick of living like this, everybody moping around all the time. You're depressed every day of the week. You were crying just now, weren't you? *Weren't you?* And you don't care if we don't have any money and you don't even let us wear the clothes we want to wear. I hate it here! God, I hate it here! There's no air to breathe in this stupid fucking house!"

"Sissy, don't you dare use that language in my house."

"Your house. Oh yeah, your house. Nobody else can have a life around here, you're so fucking self-righteous. You didn't even see me in the *movie*. Well, I'm wearing what I want to wear to the Easter Vigil." She slipped through the sliding glass door and slammed it shut.

I opened the glass behind her. How could Jack have told her such things? She was still a little girl. I moved outside to tell her how pretty she'd looked in that long flowing costume, but she was already stretched back out in the deck chair, her magazine open to a barrel-chested man-boy with the biggest *thing* I'd ever seen in my life. It left me as startled as a girl, but Sissy had already gone far beyond calling inflated phalluses *things*. She flipped the pages without looking up, every flip calculated to drive me crazy.

"You wear whatever you please, Miss. You can discuss it with your father, and you can iron it yourself."

She never did look up. I went back inside to Nippie's size fourteen dress, still stretched out helpless on the ironing board, still waiting to be flattened by my steaming iron. I'd finish its lacy collar, all the while thinking how wrong frills were for a plump girl like Nippie; and then I'd iron Sissy's blue miniskirt —I'd find it crumpled on the floor in her room; and then I'd press my own dress, the dress I'd wear for Tim Rooney's dinner party tonight.

I pressed harder on Nippie's collar, creasing more than I smoothed. How giddy I had felt just this morning, when Tim called me before breakfast to ask me over to the Point for a backyard barbecue. I heard my voice go fluttery and girlish at the invitation—see, Jack, see: I can find other men who do things in their boyhood bedrooms that you and Judi never *dreamed* of doing—but I calmed down directly when Tim told me that he and his friend thought Mary Faith Rapple could use the company. His friend: that would be the skinny woman whose breasts I'd seen at an open window. I'd show up in my long schoolteacher's dress to snatch sidelong glances at her and to console Mary Faith, who didn't want to be consoled.

☽

But I told Tim I'd go: it was better than sitting at the Easter Vigil three pews behind my own family. It was better than having Father Berkeley look down at me, and right through me, when he delivered the sermon. He'd be telling the parish that they had a new start, a new piece of land to build on. I'd rather meet the woman who let Tim Rooney tie her hands up.

Sissy opened the glass door slowly and made a big show of tossing her magazine into the garbage under the sink. She ran the tap until the water was flowing cold enough for her, and let the water slosh into a glass, and then drank it down one long gulp at a time, all without looking in my direction.

"Sissy," I said, and I concentrated hard on Nippie's frilly collar, "Sissy, I'm real sorry nobody got to see you acting in the movie. Let's throw a big party when they show it on television. You can invite everybody you know. You can invite all Due East."

She turned toward me and shrugged. "Can I invite Daddy?"

"Of course you can. I don't mean to keep you apart."

She set the glass down in the sink and stood still, looking out at the yard.

"Sissy, don't you know I love you?"

"Oh, Momma." When she turned around, her face twisted up in a grimace, I saw for the first time that afternoon that she was wearing garish blue eyeshadow, smeared on too thick. She couldn't bear to have me look at her that way, and she ran right past me and my pile of ironing. I heard her clunking up the steps to her room, choking down her own tears.

When I left for Tim's house at five that night, Sissy still hadn't come out of her room, and Nippie was mad at me too, for saying we could always rip the lacy collar off her dress. I drove down to the Point alone, my daughters' fury following me through the streets of Due East. I wondered how I would be able to look Tim's *friend* in the eye.

I was the first to arrive, and I stood in the kitchen helping Tim chop onions for the barbecue sauce, glad for an excuse to let the tears run crazy down my cheeks. We must have been standing just below Tim's bedroom, and every time I looked at his shoulders, bending over to hack away at garlic, I couldn't help but think of his rolling back in that window. Tonight, though the evening had turned cool, he was wearing a skimpy T-shirt like the firemen's shirts in New York. The shirt said *Resist: War Resisters League,* and I had a feeling he wore it to torment his father—Tim Rooney was his mother's son.

☾

At five-thirty, Mary Faith walked over from next door with her father and her little boy. She paled when she saw me sitting on a rickety kitchen chair in Tim's backyard: it was madness on Tim's part to think that she would want company on this spring night.

I paled, too. We hadn't exchanged more than two words in the car, going home from the fort the day before. Mary Faith had been rigid in the back seat, her arm around Jesse, her son sleeping restlessly against her. He knew what was wrong that afternoon. Even the movie crew knew: the gossip, from the assistant director on down, was that the screenwriter was having a terrible time. His wife was having a nervous breakdown. We all knew Stephen Dugan was leaving Mary Faith, finally.

I'd known better, of course, than to offer her any sympathy; and now, when she walked across the yard with her father, she knew better than to betray any need. She looked tired and listless, and she dragged a chair next to mine. The yard was unkempt—no one had done any gardening for years—but here and there patches of green struggled through, and Mary Faith and I ran our eyes over the brown flower beds rather than look at each other. The night was fragrant and clean, after the rains, and the pecan trees and azalea bushes stood out in stark outline.

Mary Faith's father went to light the coals, and we watched Tim heave the little boy up into the crotch of a mossy tree. Tim said his father had rushed to the liquor store to buy them out before they stopped selling at sundown. The rest of us, so quiet in the backyard, didn't look like much of a party. Tim had set out a jumble of kitchen chairs next to the old wrought-iron furniture, its white paint chipped almost clean away. The little boy was the only one making noise, and even his singing in the tree was soft and dim. Tim didn't try to get us talking: I caught him searching Mary Faith's face, but he put on a silly pretend grin when he spied me watching him.

Tim's friend—friend indeed—was the next to arrive: she let herself into the house and showed up on the back steps. She was so plain and diminutive that I couldn't imagine Tim stopping to pass the time of day with her, much less tying her up; but when he introduced her as Eileen Connelly, my memory stirred.

"Connelly," I said. "I went to school with Francis Connelly. And camp! Did you go to Camp OLPH?"

She laughed and said she remembered *me*. "Nobody in New York believes I went to a summer camp that gave six hours of catechism a day. Have you ever been out there, Mary Faith? By the Okatee?"

Mary Faith wasn't listening; she had risen and started off toward Jesse, halfway out on a long thick limb. I could picture a whole long night of unanswered questions put to Mary Faith.

It was difficult to look at Eileen Connelly without seeing her upstairs with her hands tied behind her back, but Tim stood with his arm around her shoulder, pleased as a bridegroom, waiting for me to make conversation. Finally I asked her about her brother Francis.

"I tried to get him to come tonight," she said. "But he wants to go to the vigil, and he thought we'd all be too pie-eyed to make it."

"We will be, time my father gets through pouring boilermakers down our throats," Tim said. "Why, speak of the devil!"

Now Bill Rooney stood at the top of the back steps, waving to the little crowd in his backyard like a lord mayor. Bill was still a good-looking man, but he had aged, his jowls and his belly both plumped out. He'd been Jack's biggest competitor for years, but Jack moved in on him when the resort companies came looking at Due East. I hadn't exchanged a word with him since Dolores's wake, when he'd been so stunned with her betrayal that his two sons had to propel him by the elbows up to the casket where Dolores lay, disapproving as ever.

"Hey, Becky," he called down. "Where you been keeping yourself? What do you think of Tim's girlfriend? Some artist, that little girl—but she'll be leaving us soon. My son has a way of making women disappear. Stop your blushing, Eileen. You'll never guess who I brought home with me. He's pouring us some good Irish whisky in the kitchen."

"I can't imagine who you've brought, Bill."

Bill Rooney beamed at his little surprise. "Come say hello, Father." *Father Berkeley.* Mary Faith was too far to hear Bill calling into the house, but she'd probably pack up her son and run off next door once she saw a priest at the party. I almost felt like packing up, myself, rather than face him. What had Tim been thinking of, throwing this sad bunch of souls together?

But Father Berkeley did not appear at the back door when Bill called him out: we all watched foolishly for his entrance, and Bill threw up his hands. "He'll be out. He's only going to stay a few minutes, anyway." Bill descended the steps. "I met him coming out of church. I *rescued* him. There was some war being waged over the Easter flowers—you know how those old hens can be. I told him we'd get him back in plenty of time to go over his sermon tonight."

"Christmas," Eileen whispered to me. "We're going to have to scrape the two of them off the grass." My face flushed up: I had no call to be so offended for Father Berkeley's sake, but I rose from my chair and slipped away from Tim's girlfriend.

By now Bill had worked his way back to the corner of the yard to pump his neighbor's hand by the barbecue—poor Jesse Rapple looked a shrimp next to the big old man—and to ride the little boy around on his shoulders for all of thirty seconds. He lost interest in the child quickly, the same way I imagined he'd lost interest in his own children.

Finally Father Berkeley made his appearance, pushing the screen door open with a tray full of beer bottles and shot glasses. He was wearing an old seersucker suit instead of the black he'd worn all winter, and his Roman collar looked out of place underneath the pale blue. He came directly up to me without a word and offered me a drink as if we'd never driven out to an empty field together.

"Here, Father, let me serve them. You sit down."

"I don't need to sit, Becky."

"Go on. Sit down and enjoy a drink while you're here."

"I'm not drinking tonight, Becky." It seemed to me that the tray wobbled in his hands. "I like to keep the fast from Good Friday to Easter Sunday. It's a good cleansing for an old profligate like me."

Bill Rooney must have seen me struggling to answer: he rushed over on the tail of Father's sentence to rescue me. "Boilermakers, Becky. Here, let me show you how to do this." He swallowed a shot gustily, and followed with the beer. "Hey, you must know about these. Your daddy used to throw them back at the K. of C. I *told* Tim we didn't need to bother with that white wine nonsense in the backyard."

The whisky stung my throat going down, and my eyes welled up again. I was doomed to be a weepy woman after all my years of resisting tears, doomed by irons and onions and drink and a divorce looming on the horizon. I pictured my father, maudlin and sweet, throwing back boilermakers with the men of the parish before he shipped off. The beer slipped down cool behind the whisky, and I knew I'd be drunk before Bill Rooney was.

I watched how slowly Father Berkeley moved among Tim's guests, and

☾

wondered how an old man made it through a forty-hour fast. His sermon at the vigil tonight would be something to see, full of his lightheaded cleansed spirit and his new land. He had reached Mary Faith by now—she hadn't packed up and gone home after all, but stared at him with a hard-eyed interest, and pulled a bottle and a glass off the tray. There'd be no need for him to speak to her about Stephen Dugan now.

"Fire's ready for the chicken!" her father called out.

"Ain't life grand. First barbecue of spring." Tim waltzed Eileen around the yard—she looked flustered, in front of Father—and then they walked off hand in hand to fetch the food from inside.

Already I could feel my head going light, the way Father's must be getting toward the end of his long fast: but that was physically impossible—I was only halfway through the beer. I chugged it down, and was finished by the time Father set the empty tray down on the table before me. We were all drinking fast, in our awkwardness.

Tim and Eileen trudged down the kitchen steps, their hands full of food and beer, and now the party settled into silence again. Now Jesse was back in the tree, humming to himself, and his mother was reaching into a scraggly flower bed to pull out old decayed stalks, and his grandfather was staring down at the hot coals. Father Berkeley and Bill Rooney sat on opposite sides of the round table, daydreaming. Or nightdreaming: it was almost twilight, and already narrow orange and pink streaks clashed at the edges of the sky. The sunset would be a spectacle.

Bill Rooney watched his son hand round the beers. "Where's the whisky, Timothy?" I could have done with another of those sharp stings down the throat myself.

When his son stretched out a beer bottle to him, he took it with a sigh. "Jesus, Mary, and Joseph, Timothy—excuse me, Father. Sometimes I have to call on the Holy Family for help—Tim, could you put on a regular shirt? Is this the way you dress for company?"

Now all the Rapples turned to the table with interest, the little boy hanging down from the tree to hear. Tim's father spoke to him as if he were a child Jesse's age.

"You tell him, Father. You tell him you don't have to wear your half-baked beliefs written on your shirt. It'd be different, Tim, if you'd ever served your country."

☾

I watched Tim wink at Father, flexing his muscles under the War Resisters T-shirt, and saw Bill's brow darken with rage. I could have been sitting in my childhood backyard: I could have been watching my father sitting out at the picnic table after he'd drunk a six-pack down by the dock. My mother was saying: "No unpleasant talk at the supper table," and Billy and my father were shaking their heads, disgusted at her dour reprimand, disgusted at each other.

"And why'd you leave the bottle inside?"

"Just waiting 'til we get some food in our stomachs, Dad." *Dad* sounded strange—pitiful, almost—coming from Tim's lips.

Now we were all slugging back the beer, all but Father Berkeley. Even Jesse Rapple set down an empty bottle: we were all waiting for Bill Rooney to heat up again, and set to work humiliating Tim. It would cover the silence, anyway. It would cover up that we had nothing to say to one another. Night was falling fast now, and there was a chill in the breeze. A slipper moon—a sliver, like the one my baby Jack smiled at—was rising high in the sky.

I went to stand under Jesse in the tree and tugged at his foot so he'd know I was there. "Look at that silver moon, Jesse."

The little boy shivered up on his limb, and when I put a hand to his leg and felt goose bumps there I saw that he'd turned his sad eyes on me.

"I want to go home. I'm cold."

Mary Faith slipped up beside me and promised her son a Coke. "With a cherry, Jess?" He stared out, willing to be bribed but not to give her a smile. She stood on tiptoe and reached up into the low branch to zip his jacket without a word: I saw how silent their time together must be.

Pulling her arms down, she brushed against me, and we both shrank away.

"I wanted to thank you," she said, embarrassed, "for the ride home yesterday."

I thought for one second that she was addressing someone else, not me. We didn't so much as look one another in the eye. "Oh, it was no bother. I had to get back."

"Well. Anyway. I'm grateful you didn't ask any questions."

"Oh . . ." I was drunk already. I was sure I would stumble across the yard, or giggle when Bill hollered out at Tim again. I was sure she would think once more, before the night was over, that I was an out-of-control fool.

"Momma, I'm *thirsty.*"

☾

"Run into the kitchen now, and fetch you a Coke." She lifted him down, and he wandered off, looking morose and resentful. Mary Faith turned to me.

"I'm sorry to hear about your divorce, Mrs. Perdue. I'm sorry I didn't react to that, yesterday." I saw what a terrible effort it cost her to speak to me at all. She struggled up another thought: "I have to think there's some good in what Stephen's decided," she said, and she wasn't speaking to me at all, only to herself, and all in a rush. "I used to think his wife was just some cartoon character. Just the outline of a person." I started: I remembered picturing Judi in a bubble bath, her nipples bobbing in the froth. "Now he's left me for her, and *I* feel like an outline. Like somebody who needs to be colored in." She was embarrassed at letting so much out at once, and turned away.

Once more I wanted to call her back. I wanted to tell her that she'd be all right, that *I'd* be all right. Father Berkeley's sober, I thought, and Tim is sane, and—no wonder I didn't call her back. I was too drunk, or not drunk enough.

I went to down another shot from the bottle Eileen had carried out. I would get drunk enough to tell Mary Faith—something. Anything. I'd tell her she was well rid of a married man. I'd tell her my own daughters were a puzzle to me, but she was clear as daylight: I saw in a flash, as if lightning had crackled in the sky, that she was full of the passions I'd spent twenty years hiding away. That's the kind of thing you see, on the way to letting go.

An hour and a half later, everyone in the backyard save Father Berkeley and the little boy was sated and dead drunk. Jesse was curled up in his grandfather's lap, threatening sleep but keeping one eye open on the crazy grownups; and Father looked asleep already, with both eyes open. Every fifteen minutes he said it was time for him to go, but Eileen Connelly fetched him more black coffee—how he'd be trembling by midnight—and brought out an angel cake she'd made for the occasion. I was so drunk that I had to bite my tongue before I said: "Isn't that *sweet*? An artist with domestic talents," but I didn't say it, I only thought it, and smiled all alone at the thought. I was as contented as I'd been the day I stole Ethan's bourbon and imagined myself in a hollowed-out log. Out of everyone's sight.

We were all out of sight at this backyard party: we all could have been invisible to each other, except for the lovebirds. Tim and Eileen had made a big show of serving every dish in tandem and sneaking in strokes and cuddles and kisses. Didn't they know they must be tormenting Mary Faith? They were

☾

tormenting me. The divorce laws should include a provision that no one is allowed to hold hands or coo in the presence of a betrayed wife or lover.

But Tim and Eileen finally sat themselves down on opposite sides of the table, and then the silence was crystalline. The cool sharp air felt more like fall than spring: I was falling, anyway. I was falling back into the pleasure of sitting drunk in a backyard of misfits while my family was home dressing for the Easter Vigil. I was enclosed with these people in the dark: the sky above us was a painted dome, not an infinite space: the stars were perfect white paint flecks, the new moon a flourish the artist couldn't resist.

It was getting on to nine o'clock, and finally Father rose and insisted that he really did have to get back to the rectory to look over his notes. He would be in his vestments, waiting in the sacristy, by ten-thirty.

"Oh, and you better have a look in at the flowers to see what havoc the Altar Guild has been wreaking," Bill said.

"Ah, Bill"—Father waved him away—"it's a small enough pleasure for them, those flowers."

"I like to tell you. I never did see women carry on so. It was like mud wrestling, tearing the flowers out of each other's arms."

Mary Faith spoke for the first time in an hour: "I can see that. Yes, I can picture a fight over flowers."

We didn't know whether to smile at her or pretend she hadn't spoken: her face was pinched and serious and she was very very drunk. I wondered if it was the first time in her life she'd ever gone over the edge. She was nodding her head, moving her eyes back and forth over an imaginary flower bed; and her father's eyes in turn narrowed with concern. He'd be putting her to bed tonight, pulling a quilt up over her, and maybe she'd tell him, finally, that she'd been planning to marry a man who was already married. Maybe she'd tell him she'd let her heart get the better of her reason. I nodded myself, before I knew I was making the motion: hadn't that been one of Father's favorite themes when he led the discussion groups through Pascal? Something about letting reason go. Something about the smallness, the finitude of human reason.

Father Berkeley was solemn, shaking everyone's hand good-night. "We'll see," he said. "We'll see if May Lukas triumphed. She picked a wildflower crown for the Blessed Mother."

"Is that what they were fussing over?" Bill Rooney's laugh trumpeted out —what a wonder that I had never seen Dolores cringe in his presence.

☾

"They're good souls, Bill." Father shook his hand. "I'll have to build them a bigger church for their flowers."

Somewhere far away, a buzzer sounded insistently. I couldn't place it, and I wondered if I was being summoned; I saw Mary Faith trying to fix on the sound, too.

"That's the door," Tim said. "Uh-oh. Your brother'll see us pie-eyed after all."

Father shook my hand with an extra tug, as if he meant to jar me from talking to myself—how did he know that I was berating myself for my jealousy of Eileen, running off to answer the door? How did he know that I berated myself for how far I'd let my jealousy of Jack go? So far that I'd never be able to forgive him. I watched Father Berkeley walk away from us through the dark yard: he was so small now, so stooped, so old. You'll have to forgive him too, I told myself.

Father hadn't even reached the bottom of the steps when Eileen led out a visitor who was certainly not her brother. It took me a minute to recognize May Lukas under the single glaring light bulb. May Lukas, from the church, whose name had passed Father's lips not a minute before: she looked a fright in a pantsuit the color of the setting sun, and she put a hand out to stop Father's progress. Had she come to have Father settle the Easter flowers war?

"Father," May said, up at the top of the steps. "Father, we've been looking for you all night." She was practically in tears. "We waited at the rectory—"

"It's all right, May," Father said, very gallant, and he took her by the hand to escort her to the table. "It's all right. I thought that was a fine idea for the crown. A very sweet gesture."

"Father, it's not the flowers. I can't sit down. She's out in the car, this very minute, and I'm afraid she'll run off down the street."

"Who's out in the car?"

"Why, Marygail Dugan. I told you, Father. I *told* you she'd pick Easter."

I reached a hand over to cover Mary Faith's, and she was too drunk to cast it off: couldn't Stephen's wife let her be? How had Marygail Dugan managed to show up here?

"What in God's name are you talking about?" That was Bill Rooney, still bellowing though he could hardly keep his head up. "Who the hell is Marygail Dugan?"

"I'll go get her," Eileen said.

☾

"No!" May said. "No. Don't bring her out here. She's not wearing but—" She looked round at them. "She's not wearing anything ap*pro*priate. She showed up just after you left the church, Father—and we've been calling Stephen Dugan all this time. But there's no one home. Oh, Father."

"Sit down, May. Sit down and tell us what happened. And you go see to Mrs. Dugan in the car, Eileen—I'll be out directly."

"Father, I can't sit. I'm shaking from tip to toe. I never saw anything like it."

Mary Faith's hand was damp now beneath mine: still she hadn't shaken me off. "Daddy," she said, slurring, "Daddy, you don't want to hear this." She tried to stand, but sank down into her chair again, and the chair teetered, back and forth, back and forth. Her father, helpless, caught my eyes over the top of her head: she was going to be sick. Thank God Jesse had drifted off in his grandfather's arms.

May had stopped to smooth out the shakes from her pot-pink pantsuit, but now she started up again. "Marygail Dugan drifted in from the sacristy door just when we were finishing up, Father, folding away the purple cloth. She was wearing a nightgown. A white nightie. I mean to say: my breath was taken away."

Now Father Berkeley sat, instead of May: he sat and looked up at her and shook his head.

"The others wanted to call an ambulance to get her out of the church. They still want to call an ambulance, back at the rectory. But Marygail Dugan just walked right past them, right over to the front pew, calm as you please in her bare feet. She sat looking up at the statue of Mary for—three minutes it must have been, at the very least—without saying a word. Then she called me over and told me to look. I didn't see anything peculiar, unless she was making fun of the wildflower crown. *No, look,* she says to me, very intense, and still I didn't see anything. Finally she told me the statue was crying."

May paused, for effect.

"Father, she said the statue of Mary was crying. She said it in the most *ordinary* voice."

Tim shifted in his chair: "She must have read about that weeping statue in Chicago," he said. "She just stored that image up in her subconscious."

Bill raised his head and affected disbelief. "Oh," he said. "Oh my, we're very offhand about other people's carryings-on. It seems to me, Timothy, that I recall you seeing a statue *moving* in Our Lady of Perpetual Help two Christ-mases ago."

"So I did." Tim leaned back, calm and cool. "Now, I wonder where I read about that?"

"Father, you have to do something!"

Father Berkeley stretched his palms out on the table and considered. "I don't know what we can do, May," he said slowly, "but keep trying to call her family. They must be looking for her this very minute."

Mary Faith swallowed a tremendous gulp of air and sat herself bolt upright, throwing my hand off. "He probably is," she said, in a voice as calm as Marygail Dugan's must have been, seeing the statue weep. "Stephen is probably looking for her this very minute."

"Sit right there, Mary Faith," her father said, and his voice was full of an authority I wouldn't have imagined he possessed. "You sit right there—watch her, will you, Tim? I'm going to put Jesse down next door. I'll be right back to walk her home. You stay put, Mary Faith."

Mary Faith put a hand to her face, and I knew that she was finally crying. Maybe the tears would save her from the terrible sickness that comes when you've drunk yourself right out of your mind. Her father shifted the little boy in his arms and stood; he carried the sleeping child around the side of the house, and we watched him go wordlessly.

Now Mary Faith and I were alone with silly May Lukas and the three men. I knew better than to touch her again, but I rose: I meant to fetch her a cool cloth from inside the house.

Father rose after me and drew me aside. "Becky," he said, low and conspira-torial, "let's get Marygail Dugan back to the rectory. If you can sit with her, I can locate the Dugans. They'll be off to the police, if she's disappeared."

I felt myself shrivel away from the very center of my being. I'd sat with my mother, hadn't I, until she was so far gone that we had to have a court commit her? Father knew I'd agonized over it, and now he wanted me to sit with another woman gone over the edge. A selfish self-satisfied woman who'd pulled this craziness trick to break Mary Faith's heart. It was Mary Faith I wanted to sit with: I wanted to see to her, to wipe her face with a cool damp cloth the way my father had wiped mine. I didn't want to sit with a mincing pretending madwoman. *I wouldn't do it.* Tim had it all wrong: Marygail hadn't stored up any news article about a weeping statue in Chicago in her subcon-

(

scious—she'd probably clipped the article, and read it over three times a day, planning for this sham.

"Father," May whimpered from the table, "do you want my help?"

Father Berkeley shook his head slowly and tightened his grip on my arm. "I don't want Tim to see her," he said. "I want to get her out of this house."

Father, I can't. I can't help you anymore. I broke away from his grasp and said: "Father, you have to get to the vigil. Let Eileen drive her over to the police station."

He shook his head again.

I saw myself standing before a judge, telling him in a child's voice that my mother was incompetent. Telling him my mother was a danger to herself. Hadn't Father been in the very courtroom? Hadn't I asked him to come be witness to my betrayal?

"All right," I said. "All right. I'll go out there and put her in my car. I'll drive her to the police station myself. Does that satisfy you?"

Now he shook his head in anger, but I pulled away before he could stop me. I made myself put one foot down after the other, though I felt as green as Mary Faith had looked, and I ran up the kitchen steps before he could call me back.

I don't know how long I stood in the kitchen, wavering. The sink was filled with greasy plates and cigarette butts and beer bottles: drunk as I was, I lifted someone's half-finished warm beer and swigged it down. Through the kitchen window I could see Mary Faith curling herself up into a ball on her folding chair, her knees drawn close to her chin.

My ears filled with fluid, and I shook my head loose to rid myself of the low droning buzz: how could Father ask this of me? He had no pity. He never had. Wasn't he sitting at the garden table himself, hiding away and leaving me to do his dirty work?

I knew I wouldn't drive Stephen Dugan's wife to the police station. What could I do with her? Drive her back to my house, until I could reach Stephen? Watch her sit at the island in my kitchen? Would she have imaginary friends, too? Would she wave knives to catch the light?

I had to do something. Father was right—Tim couldn't see Marygail Dugan: he'd only see his own reflection. At least I could spare him that. I swung open the dining room door, praying that the walk through the house would give me

☾

the sobriety I'd need to deal with that young 'woman when I reached her in May's car.

But the front room was ablaze with light, and as I passed through the dining room I saw that Marygail Dugan had been in the house the whole while I stood at the kitchen sink. I shook with fury.

She was wearing a diaphanous white negligee, dancing around the Rooney parlor to imaginary music, slow and sweeping. She paused at the big black piano, as if she'd heard my approach, and pressed a few low keys, lightly.

But she didn't look up at me. She went right on careening around the room, and as I stood in the doorway I saw Eileen in a dark corner, biting her lips and helpless to stop the waltz. That's what Marygail was doing: she was waltzing, lifting the hem of the gauzy white gown, and two-stepping around the bald spots in the rug. Having the time of her life. I saw my mother lifting the hem of her nightgown to give birth to an imaginary child, and I moved toward the vision in white. I could have throttled her, making me see my mother that way.

Eileen threw up her hands and said: "She wouldn't stay in the car. She wants to see Father."

I could have throttled Tim's girlfriend, too. "Father's in the backyard. They're all cowering back there. Go see to Tim, for God's sake—don't let him come in here."

Eileen hesitated, but I glowered at her, and she left without another word. Marygail stopped her dance—she tilted her head back, to listen to the music fading—and watched Eileen disappear through the house. Her gown was absolutely transparent, and the lamplight caught its sheen: dark brown nipples pressed against the bodice, and underneath her flat belly a luxuriant patch of dark hair sprouted. A perfect body. Perfect pulchritude. A perfect little scheme.

Now she looked at me curiously. "Don't I know you?" she said sweetly. She wasn't out of her mind at all.

"Yes you do."

"Momma?"

I felt the breath slammed out of me. "I'm not your mother, for God's sake. Look, cover up." I took an old plaid blanket off the couch and threw it around her shoulders: she let it slip onto the floor, where it lay crumpled beside her muddy feet. Her toenails were painted red: did crazy people paint their toenails? My mother's had curled and yellowed.

☾

"I know you're not my momma," she said. Perfectly rational. Making perfect sense. "My momma is coming tomorrow." She sat herself down on the old battered couch, as if we were having a tea party: she patted the seat next to hers. I'd be damned if I'd sit next to her and be party to this obscene performance.

"My momma hates my guts," she said conversationally. "She thinks I made a very bad mistake marrying Stephen."

I bit my tongue for the second time that night.

"Soooo," she said, and pressed her hands on her knees, just like a little girl, "tomorrow she's coming down to take care of me. You know what that means, don't you? When your momma comes to take care of you?"

I could have slapped her silly. Yes, I knew what that meant. Wasn't I a mother, whose daughters didn't want my care? Wasn't I a daughter, who'd locked my mother away?

"That means," she said, and she stretched up on the couch to look right into my eyes, "that means she'll find out about the black holes."

Now I considered leaning down to give her shoulders a shake; the shaking would hold me back from slapping her. "Stop that talk," I said. Black holes: that was how I spent my afternoons. This woman couldn't face black holes—what was she but a mannequin, a painted doll who wandered through beauty parlors and convert classes? What had Mary Faith called her?—a cartoon. An outline. I pictured her on the tennis court all afternoon, or gossiping on the phone: I could imagine a woman like this spending her whole life talking, not a thought behind the words. She was an empty shellacked shell. This woman couldn't see black holes: I couldn't picture her seeing anything but her own reflection in the mirror.

Her own reflection. I had to turn my head away, so I wouldn't see Sissy glopping on blue eyeshadow in the bathroom. So I wouldn't see myself, numbering the gray hairs on my head.

"Black whooshing holes," she said pleasantly.

It was the pleasantness that startled me: now I did go to shake her, and her shoulders went rigid under my touch.

She stared at me, puzzled and hurt and little-girlish. "You shook me!"

"I certainly did. I don't like what you're doing one little bit."

Still she tried to draw me into a smile—she could have been Sissy as a

☾

toddler, after one of my outbursts of rage, grinning up at me, playing peek-a-boo: pretending we could make the anger all go away.

"I don't like *you* one little bit," I said.

She let the smile die slowly. Then she gritted her teeth, and when I turned away from her, she began to gnash them: the sound, the scraping, went right through my body. I swung around to make her stop, and all of a sudden I saw what an ugly woman she was. There could have been a floodlight beaming down on her face, casting its yellow light on her ugly big teeth. Ugly open lips. Ugly long horsey face. Now her tongue came up like a lizard's or a snake's, and swooped round and round her mouth, as if she thought she could lick herself clean.

"Stop it."

She stopped. She stopped and began keening instead, starting off low. "Make them go away," she said.

"Stop it now."

Her cry pitched up higher instead, and she reached out her hands to entrap me. "Make them go away," she said again. "I don't want to go to their church. No. I don't want their god. No. What kind of god is that, making black holes to suck us all up? If they keep sucking, you know, *eventually they'll get to us.*" She gripped the arms of the couch, and for one second I thought I was being sucked away with her. "There's nothing there!" she said. "There's nothing there!"

Now I did slap her, on the side of her face, and she sank back into the couch, trying to press my palm onto her cheek, where its red imprint still glowed. I pulled my hand away. How she repelled me: now she had spread her legs wide as she lay back, the nightgown not as much cover as gauze on a wound. How I wanted to beat her senseless. How I wished I would stop seeing Sissy's narrow face in her long one. How I prayed I would stop seeing my mother. Don't lift your nightgown. Whatever you do, don't lift your nightgown. But she touched its dirty hem, and I closed my eyes: I couldn't stop myself. There was my mother, spreading her legs and gasping. Stop it, stop it, I said: but I was only speaking to myself. Not a word had passed my lips.

Now Marygail Dugan was whispering, but I couldn't hear the words: some lilting gibberish, high and frightened. I opened my eyes, and she sprang up.

"Shut those air conditioners off!" she whispered. "Find the switches and shut them off. The hissing. I can't bear it."

☾

She was whispering into my ear, and her very breath, warm and moist, repelled me. I pulled her around by the wrist, to face me, and saw in her dark-rimmed eyes that she hadn't slept for nights. She had been pacing the floors of her house, trying to shut the hissing off: and I had been sleeping the sleep of the dead.

"Please," she whispered to me. "Please stop them."

Again I closed my eyes—I couldn't bear her nakedness, I couldn't bear the way she pressed her breasts close, like a lover—and I listened for the sound of my mother asking my help. No sound sang out: my mother had never called on me: my daughters didn't call on me: this one—this skinny sexual repulsive woman—called on me. If I opened my eyes, I would see her hair sticking straight up on her head, like a child's after she's stuck her finger in an electric socket.

I opened my eyes. Her hair was sticking straight up. She *was* a child: a child in the throes of a nightmare.

"Hush now," I heard myself say, and I brought her, against my will, to the couch. I sat her down and then, still unwilling, I sat beside her. I drew my arm around her—no, I didn't want to touch this death-skin, as cold and lifeless as the moon outside—and pulled her close. No, I didn't want her wet face pressing itself against my own cold heart. But she was pressing it there, wasn't she, nestling in like an infant and shuddering through cries that would soon be finished. No, I didn't want to lean my chin down on top of her head: no, I didn't want to comfort her. But I was touching her, wasn't I? Wasn't I feeling the warmth rise up through her skin and mine?

"You hush now," I said, and saw from the back of the house Father and Bill and Tim coming to help us.

"You hush." I didn't know whether I was talking to myself, or to this child who lay in my arms, hanging on to me for dear life.

☾

(

30

The End

THERE'S NOTHING TO DO BUT RESIGN MYSELF
to the first person for this ending. I can hardly write a news story,
dateline Due East. I can hardly write a feature entitled "Wives and
Mistresses Get On with Their Lives."

Marygail is better, in the hospital, but the healing will take longer
than any of us expected. The staff has caught her with pot, coke,
Valium, and—this just slays me—even some other patient's Thorazine.
She was stashing drugs in her drawer and her handbag and her jeans
pockets, and now her psychiatrist has added drug kleptomania to his
list of her neuroses. She is not psychotic anymore, not so long as she
sticks to her own medication, and she is living in a group cottage—it's
so filled with enthusiasm and good will that it looks more like a
cheerleading camp—on the grounds of the state hospital. All around
her are the big brick buildings with the locked wards housing the
criminally insane, and I shudder to think where she got the pot and the
coke.

She asked me to transfer her from Due East Memorial up to Columbia after Father Berkeley visited her one day. She does not want to be a Catholic any longer, and she wants to be as far away from him as possible. She says he gives her the willies, and I can't blame her for the emotion: it only gives me a chill to hear her use the same phrase Mary Faith used about the old man.

My daughter can't forgive her mother, but I drive her up to Columbia every Friday afternoon to visit anyway: if I protected her from seeing her mother get well, she might never forgive *me*.

Becky Perdue, of all people, is there on Fridays too. I suppose she drew the chore from some charitable women's group at Our Lady of Perpetual Help—she looked uncomfortable, even frightened, the first few weeks—but she is absolutely faithful. I hear her divorce is going through; she brings one or the other of her children the whole hundred and twenty-five miles to Columbia, and I am always taken aback to see her: she looks like a forties movie star, in her big padded jackets, with her loose Lauren Bacall hair and her red lipstick. Marygail has absolutely no idea why the woman has latched on to her, but she approves because Becky is beautiful and the other patients flock around her, moths to a light. Physical attractiveness and popularity have always been high on the list of Marygail's favorite virtues.

As for Mary Faith—and this is why the ending has to be in the first person, because *I* did this to her—I got a note from her, mailed to the *Courier* office. "I know you did the right thing," it said, in a childish scrawl she was trying hard to contain on the lined paper. "I'm sorry your wife's still in the hospital. Jesse asks for you. If you want to see him sometime—just the two of you—it would be all right with me."

And I see her still, walking down River Street with Jesse, looking as young as my daughter. Looking absolutely blank and absolutely hopeless. I know that this will change: I know that someday I will see her walking hand in hand with another man; or I won't see her, and will know that she has finally won that scholarship and left town. I know that she will probably get over it sooner than I will—after all, she does not have a mental patient to compare me to—but still I can barely keep my foot on the gas pedal when I drive past her and see her shoulders slouched down that way. I want to jam on the brakes, heave open the door, run over to lift Jesse into the air, and protect them from that bleakness they walk along in.

☾

I will never stop. I have the remnants of a conscience about me, and she is not some dreamwoman in black waiting behind a confessional screen.

Me, I quit drinking cold. I sold another screenplay and made sure this producer buys weather insurance. I'm keeping my daughter good company, and aching for her nightmares: children shouldn't see their mothers the way she's seen hers. I'm having a hard time going to work every day, with the bank account so full. I'm having a hard time sleeping straight through the night. I'm lonely, once Maureen is asleep. I'm depressed, writing commercial crap. I'm tired all the time.

I'm worried to death about Mary Faith. I'm worried about Jesse. I'm worried that someday I'll stop the car.

And: here's the only worthwhile thing I can think to say in the first person: I'm sorry.

I'm so sorry.

☾

31

The Beginning

I T WAS A DRY SATURDAY AFTERNOON IN JANUARY. Only two members of the Altar Guild drove out to Father Berkeley's field:

"What excuse did May use for not coming *this* time?"

"Oh, she's way past excuses now. She says she's done her duty. I don't believe she has any intention of *ever* coming back to work on the altar."

"Maybe you're right. She's been trying to stand apart ever since that business with Marygail Dugan. She thinks she was the only one to *notice* something was wrong."

The two ladies circled the foundation of the new church, stepping over piles of construction rubble and drawing their sweaters tight against the stiff breeze. They didn't come during the week, when the workers were there: the workers were all young men in tight torn jeans and mirrored sunglasses. The way they let their cigarette butts hang out of their mouths made it clear that they didn't want old ladies stumbling about, checking on the slow progress of Our Lady Star of the Sea.

"Anyway, I've been hearing that Marygail looks good as new."

"She *does.* She looks fifteen again."

"I wouldn't be a bit surprised to hear she's back to her old tricks."

"You know, May actually thinks it's going to be a new beginning for her and Stephen Dugan."

"Isn't that just like May? A new beginning! People don't make new beginnings in the middle of their lives. Look at Becky Perdue, dragging out to work every morning. She should have forgiven Jack. He sees what a fool he made out of himself. She could be home every afternoon to meet the school bus instead of trying to start over in the middle of her life. Who knows what those teenage girls are doing all alone every afternoon?"

"Smoking pot."

"Smoking *crack.*"

"Oh, I don't think you can get crack in Due East."

"Don't be naive. You can get anything you want you know where to go."

"Where do I go? Where do I go to get me some crack?" They giggled together, as comfortable in each other's company as they were standing aimless in the cool bright light.

"You have to feel sorry for the other little girl, the one that got left out in the cold."

"You don't *have* to feel sorry for her."

"But you do. Don't tell me you don't. What would you have done if your husband left you?"

"It *wasn't* her husband. Stephen Dugan was a married man, and may God strike me down dead if he ever had any intention of marrying that little girl."

"My word. It's hard to trust anybody anymore. It's hard to have faith in anything. Why, the very altar we've been tending for twenty-five years will be gathering dust."

"Dust to dust. Remember, man, that—"

"Oh, now. We don't need to get gloomy. We've got a few more months to *Lent.*"

"We've got a few more months before we see this church actually going up. We'd best be heading back to town."

They ambled back to the car and stood stock still to watch another car, a silver one, turn down the dirt road toward them. It was only Father Berkeley,

☾

coming on his own to check the site, and the ladies waved cheerfully before they clambered into the safety of their own sedan.

"He got *his* way. Having us all drive out to the ends of the earth."

"Oh, men always clap their hands and have us snap to attention. That's the way of the world, honey." They giggled again, and swung their car doors shut so that Father could have the site to himself.

They waved again, passing him, and then they pictured him parking up close to the piles of cement block. They imagined him behind them, circling the foundation they had circled, aimless and content in the pure clear light.

☾